"What Were They Doing?"

The scream burst out of her. She screamed and screamed, curling inward into a tight ball. "They were—! Oh, Christ, they were cutting—!" The screams continued, the occasional words becoming moans. Now she was clawing her own skin, raking her nails down her neck, drawing blood.

"Chandal! You will wake up now. When I count to five, you will be totally awake, totally peaceful. . . . One—two—"

Screams as her nails dug deeper.

"—three—four—five! You are awake! You are awake!"

The two men now knelt in front of Chandal, attempting to prevent her from doing further damage to herself. Each had hold of one of her arms.

With a contemptuous gesture, she flung them both backward as though they were stuffed dolls, then stooped down suddenly and jerked the bloodstone pendant from Luther's fingers.

She shuddered as she pressed the stone to her bleeding throat and then to her lips where she seemed to drink greedily of her own blood.

Books by Ken Eulo

The Brownstone
The Bloodstone

Published by POCKET BOOKS

THE BLOODSTONE

KEN EULO

PUBLISHED BY POCKET BOOKS NEW YORK

Another *Original* publication of POCKET BOOKS

POCKET BOOKS, a Simon & Schuster division of
GULF & WESTERN CORPORATION
1230 Avenue of the Americas, New York, N.Y. 10020

ISBN: 0-671-43533-7

First Pocket Books printing October, 1981

10 9 8 7 6 5 4 3 2 1

POCKET and colophon are trademarks of Simon & Schuster.

Printed in the U.S.A.

*For my Father and Mother
and Bob and Claudine
for all they have given
and all they have inspired
with their love*

In this breathless pause at the threshold of a long passage we seemed to be measuring our fitness for . . . the appointed task of both our existences to be carried out. . . .

—Joseph Conrad
The Secret Sharer

PROLOGUE

THE INTENSE HEAT OF THAT FRIDAY MORNING BROKE AS A surprise on the young boy who lazily padded his way up 85th Street on his way to the park. Well before noon, the temperature was above ninety. Thick clouds hung oppressively just above the skyscrapers. The city seemed barely to move and vapor rose steamily from the pavement beneath the boy's feet.

He ambled along slowly and kept his face turned away from the sun. Occasionally, he mopped the sweat from his forehead with his arm. He toyed with the idea of playing hooky. He hated school. His greatest wish was for summer recess to finally come.

He stopped suddenly to stare at the burnt-out, gutted remains of the brownstone. Four months earlier the building had been engulfed in flames. Like a brief flicker of a firecracker, life within the building was there, then gone, the horror of the moment barely noticed.

The boy unslung his school bag from his shoulder and paused. Something buried beneath the rubble had caught his eye. He moved forward, squeezed between the rickety boards that blocked the front entranceway and began prowling the ruins. He probed and prodded piles of brick and burnt timber with a stick, glancing around at the marrow of the ancient structure that left him perpetually in the shade.

Pushing a few loose boards aside, he peered down. Below him were the dark shadows of the basement, a deep well of blackness surrounded by charred brick walls. He knelt down and put his face to the opening. The dusty morning air struck him with the smell of burnt ash. He studied the minute specks of broken glass scattered like a multitude of stars in patterns over the floor.

He crouched there a moment longer, half-dazed. Then he rose and twisted around to look up at the loose beams dangling precariously above him. A white lace curtain hung limply from one of the glassless windows high above and gleamed with light. Abruptly there flashed across it a black shadow and then it was gone. A frantic image, fast and convulsed. A bird, he imagined. It probably had made its nest up there.

Drawing a deep breath, he turned to go. And then he saw it. A sharp fervid glitter. He reached down and pushed bricks aside. The glow grew brighter. Working faster now, he shoveled with both hands, flinging the bricks to one side as fast as he could. Suddenly a face peered up at him.

He studied it for a moment. A long moment. The face pressed outward. Flashed. Flickered. Slowly he lifted the odd statue from the ashes. The curtain above him fluttered as he became lost in thought. Then at last the boy smiled and quickly stuffed the statue into his sack.

"Hey, you there!" a voice boomed.

The boy looked up, startled. "Yeah?"

"What are you doing in there?"

"Nothin'."

"Well, come out of there."

The man looked down at the boy with concern. "You could get hurt in there."

"I wasn't doing nothing."

"Three people died in there. You want to be the fourth?"

"They died?" The boy gulped.

"Burnt to death. All but one. And they took her away."

"Away?"

"You want that—for them to take you away? You want to die?"

"No, no . . ."

"Then stay out of there."

Moments later the boy quickly ducked into a grimy-looking shop on Amsterdam Avenue over which, in weather-worn lettering, the name "J. Frisk, Dealer in Antiquities," was inscribed. The shop's shabby interior was overcrowded with lamps made from elephant tusks, odd sets of chessmen, ancient weapons, a stuffed monkey holding a lamp, skulls, human and otherwise, and other fascinations that caught the boy's eye.

"Can I help you?" asked the old man with pale face and watery eyes.

The boy placed the statue on the counter. "I want to sell this."

The antique shop dealer smiled at the boy, showing his rotted teeth. "I'll give you ten dollars for it."

"Ain't the statue worth more?"

"Not to me it isn't." The man greedily eyed the statue, waiting for the boy to make up his mind.

"Okay. I'll take the money."

As the boy left the shop, the old man stared at the dusty image. Shadows shifted. The dog that lay at the old man's feet began to growl in a low guttural moan. Head thrust forward, body taut, it snarled through bared teeth, prepared to defend or attack. "Quiet!" snapped the old man.

Locking the front door, he drew the shade, then crossed to the counter and picked up the statue. Smiling, he hastened to the rear of the shop.

Under a strong light, he examined the hieroglyphics inscribed at the base of the statue. Sweat had gathered in the wrinkles of his brow and ran freely down his corpselike features, but he paid no attention. At last he nodded and, trembling, placed the statue on a small ornate pedestal.

Strange, how after all this time, he was still capable of experiencing the brittle remnants of awe. His knees creaked as he prostrated himself on the floor before the statue. His lips began to move. Like himself, the statue seemed to expand and glow with new energy and life. A mild wisp of air circulated the room and the old man knew that once again the circle had been completed.

PART ONE

Origins

CHAPTER ONE

THE ROOM WAS SMALL AND AIRLESS, SEALED AWAY INTO AN existence of its own. So complete was its barricade that even the windows were closed to the light, making it impossible to tell day from night. Candles blazed at the altar and in holders beside the four short pews directly facing the holy circle. This was the only light. In prayer was a single woman, a crone, eighty at least and yet strong as a lean man in his prime. Her breasts were bare, long and firm still with large pointed nipples. As the crone prayed, a murmur began to rise from within her chest, an echo of her own desire, faint at first and then fierce until she made her nails into claws and turned them against her own flesh, digging them deep into the skin of both breasts. The pain brought a scream from between her lips and still she clawed deeper, bringing the blood.

In a surge of power, the goat materialized at the altar fully formed.

"You shall be satisfied," he hissed. She was trained to hear his words and heard plainly what he had spoken.

She relaxed backward, almost fainting as by his power he touched her sex, rippling through her and bringing her abruptly to a shattering climax.

She collapsed moaning and he waited until she had composed herself before he said, "She will come tonight. Call the coven in my glory."

"It's been three years now," said the old woman softly, wiping her face with her sleeve.

"She will come. Prepare the coven."

He began to disappear but stopped for an instant as he read one further question in her mind.

"Why are there so few of us who are young? Why is it so seldom we have a really young body to enjoy?"

"Because the young have so few needs," Ahriman said. "Old age and suffering, these are the things that bring worshipers to Ahriman."

"You have shown us that these frailties of the flesh can be overcome," the old woman said craftily. "But some of our members doubt. I beg you, Ahriman, to prove to them once again your greatness. Show them. . . ." The old woman hesitated, licking cracked dry lips, and then lowered her eyes. "Show them through me," she finished and then felt the hot flush of shame on her withered cheeks as the goat began to laugh.

"For your proof," Ahriman said contemptuously, "look to the one who comes tonight. She is the one who has mastered much of my understanding. Protect her. Learn from her. To the extent you help her, so shall you be rewarded." He smiled then and went away knowing that already the old woman was thinking of her reward.

"Tonight," she whispered. "She will come tonight."

The harsh sounds of traffic made her head throb. Her mind swirled. She blinked, the kaleidoscope of light nearly blinding her eyes. And the smell. Lilac. Heavy and suffocating. It seemed to emerge from some distant memory of an experience long forgotten. The aroma of lilac, so removed from her present life and yet surrounding her.

The taxi fought its way up Eighth Avenue, around Columbus Circle, and swayed onto Amsterdam, as if it were propelled forward by the rain.

Her head lay against the window; her mind wandered. It couldn't be New York. How could she have gotten from California to New York without knowing it. Ridiculous. Yet reality challenged her in the form of crowded sidewalks, dirty streets and skyscrapers all cloaked in a constant fluorescent glitter.

She wiped the damp vapor from inside the window and peered out. She tried to read the street signs. It was raining.

Black silhouettes against the wetness. People. So many people. Her thoughts spun around. Turned in on themselves. Became little twisted gorges of confusion.

Then a new terror took hold. Where was the driver taking her? Had she given him an address? She didn't remember doing so. But then she wasn't remembering much of anything.

She banged on the plastic partition with her fist. What was wrong with him? Why didn't he hear her? She banged even harder.

"Stop the cab," she screamed.

"What?" The driver turned to stare at her uncomprehendingly.

"I want to get out. Please. Stop the cab."

She felt the heavy door slam shut behind her. She was left standing on a dark, narrow street. She was the only person there. A sharp downpouring of rain lashed her. She had no raincoat, no hat, no umbrella. Her throat felt swollen and sore.

She glanced around but couldn't recognize her surroundings. There was only this nameless street. She grew angry with herself for not having made a more determined effort to ask the driver where she was.

She began to walk. Something drew her forward. Something. Was this really happening? Or would she wake up at the sound of the alarm, squint at the flickering luminescent digits and realize that it was all an incredible dream. She felt like a blind person, at the mercy of others. She had never been so lost.

Forcing herself to keep moving, she watched for a sign, waited for a signal—anything. There was only the heavy downpouring of rain. She passed from street to street, walking along wet sidewalks which failed to reveal any new awareness. If only she could stop, at least momentarily, she might be able to discover where she was. But her legs seemed independent of her body and moved with a will all their own. Faster, she had to move faster. *Don't stop, whatever you do. Just keep walking.*

Then, in a quick instant, some tremendous force took hold of her. She shivered. An invisible hand reached out, gently, slipped itself into her palm with such ease, such softness, that she let the tension of the moment flood from her body with the same quickness as the rain that now raced past her in the gutter on its way to the sewer. She no longer found it necessary to fight for direction. She moved forward, gaining more and more permanent mastery over her isolation, her fear, until at last she smiled. A kind of frozen smile that affixed itself to her lips, yet her eyes remained blank.

Still smiling, Chandal Knight no longer saw or felt any sensation that one could call her own. All meaning drained from her actions. No longer was she disrupted by her own inward chatter. The restlessness of dislocation vanished, giving way to a deeper presence of inner peace. Absolute and secure.

They sat on wooden benches organized in rows. Old men and women gathered in the rear third-floor apartment of a totally abandoned brownstone.

Chandal sat in the center of the room and listened to the muted traffic sounds which filtered in from the three narrow windows at the back of the apartment. She grinned. All of them wore the same unearthly smile.

Abruptly the door slammed shut. A rod was passed through two steel hooks across the door frame. A figure in black, the keeper of the door, knelt and bowed her head.

The ceremony was about to begin.

Chandal could feel her heart start to flutter. She felt the blood thumping in her temples. A dazzling flash of light burst across her eyes as the old woman lit the first candle.

A shudder of ectasy stopped midway in Chandal's throat.

"Darkness is the strongest of all weapons," the young girl beside her whispered. "A goddess who opens doors and reveals mysteries. . . ."

Standing beside a table draped with thick velvet cloth, the old woman lit the second candle. A crucifix hung upside down above the flames. Christ's body, twisted in helpless agony, seemed to writhe in the motion of the light.

The young girl laughed, a high-pitched animal sound.

Solemnly, the old woman gave a signal to the musicians. The drummers began a strong, pulsating rhythm, the thin, mournful sound of a flute joined in, and then, almost inaudibly at first, the voices of the singers rose. Women to the left and right of Chandal began to moan. Others jumped to their feet and danced around the room with such speed and exotic patterns of movement that it became impossible to distinguish one dancer from another.

A haze floated above the candles.

In a quick swirl, the old woman turned to face the rest of the room. Her eyes were searing points of light. Her shadow swayed and expanded out across the table and up the wall, bobbing against the cracked plaster of the ceiling. She raised her fists and the dancing ceased. Now her eyes burnt icy-blue in hypnotic brilliance as she turned them upon her worshipers.

She began to speak in a sharp metallic voice, communicating her thoughts in a strange, disconnected language. The others joined in, chanting, wailing at the top of their voices. Phrases were repeated again and again, allowing the energy within the room to accumulate.

For a second the drummers stopped, only to begin a new rhythm. Faster . . . everything moving faster, louder, the energy building, coming together as if shaping itself into an entity, separate and distinct, with a will all its own.

Chandal was on her feet now. "Take me," she screamed. "Take me!"

The old woman smiled at her and, stepping closer, began to remove Chandal's clothing. The chanting continued. Flowers and herbs and oils were brought from the table to the floor. A circle was formed.

After stripping Chandal naked, the old woman led her to the center of the circle, knelt before her, and began rubbing Chandal's body with ointment. Others kissed her, fondled her breasts. She wailed with ecstasy as the energy of the room rushed into her body, twisting and turning, driving itself deep into her being, like a snake slithering easily under its favorite rock.

What entered her seemed to be familiar, to have such a welcoming seductive nature and sense of belonging that the thrill she felt stunned her with a pleasure she had never dreamed possible.

A low howl issued from her mouth. Her whole body shook violently. Again she heard her own long, howling wail.

Inexorably the ceremony continued. Herbs were eaten,

animals slaughtered for the drinking of the blood. Amid the moans and the heaving, Christ was mocked and tormented, the crucifix defecated upon.

Finally the sounds subsided into unchartered darkness. The energy within the room slipped away, its essence spent. The last faint echoes died. All was quiet. Chandal's glance rested finally on the table. She gazed at the two black candles whose flames flickered weakly. Flickered once again and then went out.

Amsterdam Avenue was deserted as Chandal stepped from the building. The rain had stopped. She paused to listen for a moment. The wind swept down from the overcast sky, pushing the March air through the darkened street, gently caressing her face, murmuring, sighing, still heavy with the scent of lilac. It picked up a discarded piece of newspaper and blew it against her foot. She looked down and smiled. *The New York Times*. How long had it been since she had seen *The New York Times?*

Her smile widened. It was good to be home.

CHAPTER TWO

CHANDAL TOSSED THE MAGAZINE ON THE BED AND WENT TO THE side table to call room service. She ordered a BLT on toast and a pot of coffee. While waiting for the food to arrive, she decided to call Ron.

She lifted the receiver and started to dial the switchboard. No, she whispered to herself, softly returning the receiver to its cradle. Why should I? It was Ron's turn to call her now. She had left word with his secretary, hadn't she? Besides, she hadn't much money. A second call to California was beyond her planned budget. She had to remember to continually economize, until she was able to reestablish herself in New York.

She went into the kitchenette, which was empty except for a bottle of Scotch, and mixed herself a drink. On the way back to the only chair in the room, she stopped before the mirror above the bed. The face that she saw was still quite young for its twenty-nine years. She had never been really beautiful but it was still an attractive face, provocative. Ron Talon, her theatrical agent and more on again than off again boyfriend, had told her so, many times.

She glanced at the phone again. Why was it that Ron was never far from her mind these days? That this was so, bothered her, confused her and perhaps . . . She paused, a half-smile tugging at her lip. Yes, it was possible that her feelings for Ron had something to do with her being in New

13

York. As though she needed this space for a while to think things over.

Unconsciously, her eyes had fastened once again on her slim mirror image. She turned to examine herself in profile. Her figure had never been better, thanks to hundreds of hours of dance classes, jogging, tennis and just good clean California living.

She laughed softly to herself.

She had beaten the odds. She had grown back to health; mentally, physically and emotionally. It would be ridiculous to try to explain it to anyone, but in a way she felt brand-new. From the new shine in her hair to the new confidence in herself as an actress. Not—and here was the hard thing to reconcile—that there weren't enormous problems yet to overcome. The blankness of memory about her husband's death. Her mother's death, as well. It had been incredibly hard to believe that they were both gone.

"But I can't remember. Are you sure?" "I'm sorry," the doctor had said. "I'm terribly sorry. But you must believe me, face it. Look, here are the death certificates." "I believe you," she had said hastily. "I don't need to see . . ." Then she had choked, her tears blinding her as she read against her will the names on those two certificates of death. Justin Knight. Helen Briar. Gone. Both of them gone. But the important thing, she thought now, squaring her shoulders, was that she had survived. Through the pain, the horror, the blankness, she had survived. Even through the fire at the brownstone—she was the one who had survived.

There was so much more of her life to live, and she was prepared now to get on with it. There was no longer any doubt in her mind that she was something akin to a star and that soon she would be shining from on top of the world.

She took a last glance at herself in the mirror, before sitting with her drink at the desk and opening her checkbook. Her balance, as usual, was incredibly low. Still, she thought, there was enough money, just barely enough for her to secure an apartment and see her through until she could get a job as an actress. If her money did run out, there were always her rings and watch to sell, or at least pawn, and her wonderful mink coat—inherited from her mother. She loved these things. She would hate to see them come to such a mercenary end. Still, it was a gamble she had to take.

She leaned back, lit a cigarette and sipped her drink. She smiled. She hadn't felt this sure of herself in ages. She kept on smiling, thinking. . . .

In her mind she was trying to construct her conversation with Ron. What could she possibly tell Ron? He'd want to know why she'd suddenly decided to return to New York. It's easy, Ron, I have to know that I can come and go as I please. Where I please. That New York can no longer hurt me. That I can look this big, ugly, intoxicating, wonderful city square in the face and laugh. Face my past. Face the mystery. It's the final challenge, Ron. And I'm ready for it. Then I shall know, really know, that there is nothing more to fear. How's that for progress?

"Lousy," Ron said.

And Chandal was startled. Her gaze, veiled by eyelashes that drooped heavy with sleep, wandered about the room, to her suitcase propped on the bed, lid open, and came back to rest on the telephone she now held in her hand. Words began to parade through her mind. Ron's words. He was talking to her. Had she fallen asleep? She must have. Of course, and the phone had rung, she had picked it up and it was Ron returning her call.

"Del, are you listening to me?" Ron asked.

Chandal smiled. "Of course I'm listening to you, silly."

"I've been trying to reach you all night. Where have you been?"

"Right here."

"I've been calling every hour on the hour since four. They told me you weren't in."

"I . . ." Her mind quickly reconstructed the day. She had gotten off the plane at Kennedy at 6:05 P.M. She had taken a cab into the city. It had been raining. The driver had been unable to find the hotel. She had gotten out of the cab. Walked a few blocks. Found the hotel. Registered. Came upstairs, took a hot bath, read a magazine and ordered room service. She hadn't been out of her room.

"They must not have known I was here," she said. "I just got in around six."

"Del, it's nine o'clock here. It's midnight there. You couldn't have just gotten in. Room 628. You are in room 628, aren't you?" he asked.

"Yes."

"That's the room they've been ringing."

She shrugged. "I must have dozed off, I guess."

Ron sighed. "Jesus, Del. New York. I still don't understand it. The whole thing is crazy." There was a tremor of confusion in his voice.

"Look who's talking. You're sitting in the middle of the fruitcake capital of the world, and I'm crazy?"

Chandal was chuckling. Now Ron kept a hard note in his voice, as he persisted.

"What I want to know is where you got the idea. I saw you last night, didn't I? And you didn't say a word about New York, did you?"

"I was afraid you'd say . . ." Chandal hesitated, suddenly no longer sure of herself. Exactly when had she gotten the idea? She wasn't sure, just that she had suddenly packed her bags and made her reservation.

"Del, all I want to know is why. Why? To prove something to yourself?"

"Right. Not to mention the fact that I hate California."

"You never gave it a chance."

"Enough to know that I don't belong there."

"You have a career here, or have you forgotten that? Doesn't that mean anything to you?"

Chandal thought about it for a moment. Dear sweet Ron. Always the businessman first. Never putting his emotions before her career as an actress. If she had thought about it, she would have had to admit that it was his business-comes-first attitude that first attracted her to him. And the challenge of watching that ever-so-cool attitude melt away at certain moments, leaving him to twist a bit uneasily at having exposed some vulnerable and loving part of his otherwise tough personality.

"Is that why you've been calling me every hour on the hour? Because of my career?"

"You know it's not." His voice was soft, yet still tinged with an edge of annoyance.

"I'm glad to know that," she said after a pause.

Ron was speaking of contracts now, and the new Francis Ford Coppola picture for which she was being heavily considered. Chandal tried hard to concentrate on what he was saying, and not on the strange scratching sound that was coming from the small closet next to the kitchenette.

For a few seconds the sound stopped, but then it began again. It was as if something inside the closet had paused to gather more energy, to relocate itself closer to the door.

"What should I tell Coppola when he calls me?" Ron asked. "That you're not interested? Jesus, it's a chance of a lifetime."

Despite Ron's persistent voice which grew louder as he spoke of screen tests and obligations, Chandal could still hear the unsettling noise that echoed from behind the closet door. A scraping sound, dry and brittle. The harder she tried to listen to what Ron had to say, the more the sound persisted, forcing itself to be heard.

"Please, Ron . . . I need time to think about it, that's all. In the meantime . . ."

"In the meantime what, Del?"

She paused for a moment, her gaze fixed upon the closet door. She felt a sudden dizziness. She had most likely mixed herself too strong a drink. She wasn't much of a drinker, especially on an empty stomach. But no, it was more than that. More than a simple case of too little food, too much booze. It was the sudden anger that she felt. Anger directed at Ron for not understanding. For not caring enough about her to realize that what she was doing was necessary.

Shouldn't he be a little more understanding? More aware of her needs and wants as a human being? Theirs was more than just a client/agent relationship. Wasn't it? Or had she been mistaken after all. She had been wrong before. Mrs. Justin Knight—now Ms. Chandal Knight. Before Justin had died that night in the fire, hadn't he been involved with another woman? Hadn't he?

Chandal rubbed her forehead with her free hand, tried to drive away the thought. She could not recall their lives together while living in the brownstone. Nor the days prior to their move. After months and months of analysis, why hadn't Dr. Luther been able to help her reconstruct a single moment of her life during that period of time?

The sound from the closet pressed in on her, sending her thoughts scattering. But her anger remained, clung to her, and she cherished it for its deeply felt, uncomplicated essence.

"Del? In the meantime what?"

"I'm going ahead and looking for an apartment tomor-

17

row," she said with a marked edge to her voice. "I'm also going to register with a few agencies."

The sound came once more. It carried with it a low rumbling aftermath that seemed to reverberate in the walls of her tiny room. It grew louder and louder.

"Is there nothing I can say to change your mind?" he asked.

"You might have tried 'I understand. I care about you.'"

Chandal could tell he was affected by her last remark, by the way in which he sighed. But that was the only sound she heard coming over the telephone.

"I have to hang up, Ron."

"It's Monday," he slipped in hurriedly. "I can stall Coppola till the end of the week. Will you call me on Thursday? Let me know when you can come in for a screen test?"

"Yes. If I can."

"The city can be pretty rough when it wants to be. Especially when you've been out of touch with it for three years. Kind of like making love to the jaws of an alligator." He attempted a hollow laugh, then added, "If you decide to stay, and you have any trouble finding an agent, let me know. I'll see what I can do."

"Thank you."

"Oh, Jesus, Del—I love you. You do know that, don't you?"

It was too late. She had already hung up.

She listened for a moment. The sound in the closet had stopped. She shifted her glance around the room. Dim light from the bed lamp fell pale across the room, casting odd shadows on the green bedspread and the picture that hung lopsided on the wall.

What the hell kind of sound was that, she wondered.

She moved closer to the closet, stopped.

Abruptly she glanced into the kitchenette. There was only the faint sound of the faucet dripping.

Damn it! I know I heard it.

She edged closer, reached for the small ornate door handle and was just about to open the closet door, when a loud knock turned her with a start toward the front door.

"Yes, who is it?" she breathed.

"Room service," came the raspy voice.

"Oh." She relaxed a bit.

The door swung open and a small man with a pock marked face and enormous bloodshot eyes entered with a tray. "Sorry it took so long. The kitchen was just about to close when you called. No room service after twelve o'clock."

"I'm sorry, I didn't know," she said pleasantly.

"There's a piece of paper on the desk. Gives you all the house rules." He glanced around the room. "Where do you want it?"

"What? Oh, on the desk."

"Five dollars and fifty cents," he stated, placing the tray down.

Chandal gulped. "That much?"

"You're in New York. Maybe in Iowa you could get it cheaper." He smirked. "You want me to charge it to your room?"

"No, here. I'll pay you now."

She rummaged in her purse for her wallet, the bloodshot eyes following her every gesture. Her hand pushed aside Kleenex, a comb, brush, cigarette case, pendant . . . pendant? Carefully she lifted the oddly shaped dark-green stone from her pocketbook and looped its silver chain around her forefinger. Tiny flickers of red glistened throughout the stone, throwing off sparks as from a disturbed fire.

That's strange, she thought. She hadn't remembered buying it. Or anyone giving it to her. Yet there it was. She let the stone fall into the palm of her hand where she examined it more closely, mesmerized.

The old man cleared his throat and moved to the door. "I'll charge it to your room," he muttered and turned to go. With the door nearly closed, he stopped and leaned his head back into the room. "The paper on the desk. It tells about tipping, too."

Chandal blinked and looked up. "What?"

The old man shook his head. "Forget it," he said and closed the door behind him.

Glancing about the empty room, Chandal began to hear the soft tapping of rain against her window. Her energy was suddenly gone, a wave of isolation sweeping over her as she sat still, once again gazing at the pendant. Trembling, she carefully held it up to the light. With a flickering of tiny specks, the stone dangled before her eyes. The chain was slightly tarnished and felt lighter than it looked.

Kneeling on the bed, she leaned forward toward the mirror and held the pendant up to her neck. She came face to face with her own eyes. Caught off guard, her vision blurred. It was as if suddenly her eyes were not her eyes at all, but someone else's. A stranger's eyes admiring the pendant. Violet eyes. A stranger's hands placing the chain around her neck and closing the rectangle catch, snapping the latch securely into place. A bony hand brushed against her cheek.

She shivered and glanced nervously at the pendant that now lay between her breasts. She felt guilty. She wanted to explain to the eyes that the pendant didn't belong to her. That although she thought the pendant lovely, she felt it only right that it be returned to its proper owner. The stranger's hands seemed to say by the caressing of the pendant, that it was all right. That the pendant belonged to her now. That she was its rightful owner.

Chandal let her body slip down onto the bed, bury itself deep into the soft folds of the bedspread. Lying on her back, she reached over and turned out the light. She listened to the harsh sound of a siren screech through the city streets below, until finally it faded away. Then all was quiet. Her mind hovered on the rim of space, her body weightless, formless, her consciousness the only consciousness in the universe, bathing in the cool red glow of the pendant.

Her only thought was whether she would be able to redeem that part of herself which was left buried away somewhere in this city. Yes. It would happen. Somewhere in the blackness of night a part of her roamed. It was inevitable that eventually the two halves of herself would meet. Perhaps it would happen now in the silence of this very room.

Perhaps.

Perhaps. . . .

She fell asleep, the pendant lying heavy upon her breast.

CHAPTER THREE

Several days had passed since Chandal had last spoken with Ron. Now she was having her lunch at a little place around the corner from her hotel. She was not enjoying the charming ambience of the cafe, nor her well-prepared meal, nor the marvelous day. It hadn't been as easy as she had anticipated, and she was filled with doubts.

Theatrical prospects had declined in New York in recent months and it was not at all easy to land a job. Modestly priced apartments were scarce, unless one was willing to live in dreary neighborhoods that only the bravest would dare to enter. Her ratty, miserable little hotel room was starting to depress her. She hated it; she loathed having to live there. The final blow was that she was beginning to lose her California tan. That, perhaps more than anything else, depressed her.

How could she tell Ron that she had made no progress whatsoever? Well, Chandal told herself, your concern is with your future, so get on with it.

She spread the realty section of *The New York Times* in front of her and started at the top. "Apartments Furn—Manhattan." A quick glance down the page told her that most of the listings were sublets, which was entirely out of the question. She would never feel a sense of permanency in a sublet. The remaining few listings bore a formidable price tag.

She was just about to call it quits, when she noticed a little ad tucked away in the lower left-hand corner of the page. It read:

RELOCATING FURNISHED SPECIALISTS
Luxury furnished apartments. Studios to four bedrooms.
$300 & up. Choose your own furniture. All apartments
located in modern highrise buildings. Minimum one year
leases. Call BU8-3448.

Chandal immediately cautioned herself not to become overly optimistic. The lower-priced apartments were probably no longer available. Or it could be one of those infamous "come-on" ads. Promise them anything, the moon, just as long as you get them there. After that, it's a matter of fast talk, persuasion and sales hype.

Still, Chandal found herself reaching mechanically for a dime. She was doing most things mechanically by now. Riding down in the elevator, picking up a newspaper at the local newsstand on the corner, walking across the street amidst a crowd of people with glazed eyes, sitting quietly in the corner of the little cafe, pressing the fingers of her right hand into the middle of her forehead to relieve the tension brought on by a sudden dizziness or to ward off the intermittent *click-click* sound located in the back of her skull, a sound not unlike that made by a sharp pair of steel knitting needles.

"Friendly Realty," the voice said.

And Chandal mechanically began speaking.

A jaunty, lopsided sign proclaimed the place to be Friendly Realty. Its wide-open door was painted a flaming orange, the welcome mat a screaming yellow, over which came the low roar of inflamed voices and the blare of electronic music. This had to be the most swinging realty company in New York.

Chandal hesitated for a moment. Then she shrugged, what the hell? She had tried everything else without much luck. Why not this?

She stepped inside the crowded office, slowly inching her way through the sea of faces, searching for someone in charge. She stood then, patiently, looking at the walls of the large room, blinking in amazement. Each wall had been decorated, apparently out of some mad desire, by many framed art posters ranging from the works of Goya to Warhol. The effect was chaotic and bizarre.

"You are?" the voice asked.

Chandal turned and saw that the voice was talking to her and that it belonged to a statuesque woman of indeterminate age, whose brunette hair hung freely about her face like Spanish moss. She was fashionably dressed and seemed quite harmless, not at all what Chandal had expected. But then again, Friendly Realty was not at all what she had expected.

"Oh," Chandal breathed. "I'm Chandal Knight. I just called a little while ago."

"Ah, yes. You spoke with me. Hi, I'm Miss Ramsey," stated the woman in a soft-spoken voice. "Let's step into my office, shall we?" She winked. "It's quieter."

"Right." replied Chandal as she entered the room.

Miss Ramsey wasted no time in making Chandal feel right at home. She immediately motioned to a comfortable chair and offered Chandal coffee.

Chandal found herself saying, "No, thank you. I'm a tea drinker." And this surprised Chandal, because for the life of her, she couldn't recall ever having liked the taste of tea before. She had always been an ardent coffee drinker, so much so, that it had taken three cups to get her started this morning.

"Tea it is." Miss Ramsey smiled.

"I don't want to be a bother."

"Nonsense. It's no bother at all."

Teacup now in her hand, Chandal listened as Miss Ramsey ran down the list of available furnished apartments. It was just as Chandal had expected. Underneath the glare of bright colors, wild decorations, rock music and cordial demeanor, beat the same old con-game heart.

Chandal placed her half-emptied teacup on Miss Ramsey's desk and tried to muster a polite smile. "I see," she said easily. "Well, thank you for your time."

The woman eyed Chandal intently. "Is something wrong?"

"The ad in *The New York Times* said three hundred dollars and up. All you've mentioned so far is the up."

"I see."

"Thanks again for your time."

Chandal rose and walked to the door, the woman following closely at her heels.

"I'm sorry that our ad was misleading," she said, holding the door open for Chandal. "But surely you understand that the cost of maintaining a highrise during this difficult time is expensive. Naturally the cost must be passed along to the tenant."

Chandal nodded indifferently.

"Perhaps what you're looking for is something along the lines of an apartment in a brownstone."

Chandal flinched, aware of a feeling of strain between her eyes. She felt something jerking within her—didn't feel it, really, but became conscious of it, became conscious, too, of a voice within her about to scream.

The fire flashed before her eyes. Thick lashing tongues of flames licked at her face, neck and hair. Just that fast the fire spread, engulfing her entire body. Hissing and crackling—a sudden flash, and then just as quickly the image vanished.

Still she stared, frightened eyes fixed on some distant spot in the past. People had died in that fire. Justin. He had died. Magdalene and Elizabeth Krispen, the old ladies who had owned the brownstone. They had died too. Now the image loomed again, burning deeper, claiming her. She could feel herself gasp for air as the fire began to consume her supply of oxygen. Screaming. Someone was screaming.

Chandal leaned unsteadily against the door frame.

"Miss Knight, are you all right?"

"I don't want to live in a brownstone," Chandal's voice was saying weakly.

"Here, you had better sit down."

The woman escorted her back to the chair. Chandal sat down, folding her hands in a matronly, spinsterish manner in her lap. Her posture was rigid. "I guess I should have eaten a little more for lunch," she said.

"Jesus, you gave me a real start there. I thought . . . well, it happens, I guess. Here, let me get you a glass of water." The woman chattered on, talked about dizzy spells and eating properly, the fast pace at which most people were living their lives these days.

Chandal listened, nodded. The room grew cool and dim. The thick brown carpet looked almost purple in the fading afternoon light and the garish pink walls appeared gray. Outside, dark clouds galloped across a slate-covered sky, and Chandal knew that she still had not won her battle. The fire—that night, the brownstone ablaze, sending incandescent sparks upward into the heavens, screams, Elizabeth's face in the flames, clutching at her shawl—it was all too familiar, and every horrible detail of that moment still lived within Chandal's mind.

"Don't you want the water?" Miss Ramsey asked, carefully studying Chandal's face.

"Oh, yes. Thank you."

Chandal sipped slowly, taking tiny swallows, allowing the cool water to moisten her dry lips, rather than actually drinking.

"Have you just arrived in New York?" the woman asked.

"Yes. On Monday."

Chandal forced her face into a reassuring smile as if to indicate to Miss Ramsey that she was all right. Still, the woman looked pale and distressed, like a mother whose child had just had a near brush with death, and who still waited for absolute proof that what she had feared most was not at all true.

Another strange face. Chandal blinked up at it.

"Lucy," the man said, "Marshall's on the phone. He needs a yes or no now." The face disappeared out the door.

"Will you excuse me," Miss Ramsey said, reaching for the telephone.

Chandal put her hand to her mouth and sighed. There was no doubt in her mind now as to the correctness of Dr. Luther's advice not to take up residence in New York. There were still too many destructive influences in the city that could trigger her illness all over again. Why risk it, he had said. You are totally well now. A few missing moments perhaps, time still unrecalled, but is the regathering of that time worth another possible breakdown?

Yes! Chandal thought in a sudden fit of determination. Justin and she had lived in that brownstone for the last remaining days of their lives together. She had doubts about those days, about her relationship with Justin. Could she go on with the rest of her life without knowing if those doubts were justified?

Often, under the careful supervision of Dr. Luther, she had come close, very close to remembering. So close, in fact, that images started to unravel themselves, and shadows though they may have been, they were images nonetheless. And with those smokelike, vaporous visages of the mind, sound. A baby crying. A cry? Perhaps only a bird in the night, its cry penetrating the thick walls of her room, causing her to dream a sudden image of desolation. Yet she was sure it was a baby crying. And the laughter and singing, voices that seemed to be celebrating a joyous occasion. It was all there, locked away in her memory. If only she could remember. She had to remember. Wanted so desperately to piece those sounds and images together, to piece her life back together and start anew. If only . . .

"Sorry," Miss Ramsey said, placing the receiver back into its cradle.

Chandal stared at her for a moment, then said, "I need to find an apartment soon. I haven't much money. I know I'm asking the impossible but isn't there anything you can do?"

The woman leaned forward and tapped tattoos on the desk with the tip of her pencil. "Are you married?" she asked.

"Widowed."

"I'm sorry."

For a moment the throbbing beat of Miss Ramsey's pencil was the only sound in the room. Chandal fumbled in her purse for a cigarette.

"Is it all right if I smoke?"

"By all means." She paused, allowing Chandal to light her cigarette, before asking, "Would you mind telling me what your occupation is?"

"I'm an actress," Chandal said, exhaling. She reached over and flicked out the match, dropping it into the ashtray in front of her.

"Actress," Miss Ramsey echoed.

If Chandal had had her wits about her, she probably would have lied, knowing that actors and actresses fall on the very bottom of the not-to-be-trusted list. Still, the woman's voice seemed unquestioning.

"Now, how come I knew that," the woman said with a smile. "The moment I saw you standing out there, I said to myself—she's an actress. I don't know how I knew, I just knew. Are you in the theater?"

"Films, mostly." She shrugged. "Things were slow in California, so here I am."

"I see," observed the woman.

"Can you help me?" Chandal asked, feeling the anxiety starting to build in the center of her chest.

Leaning forward, Miss Ramsey said, "I've got something that just came in today. There's this brownstone. . . ."

"I've already told you," Chandal interrupted, "that I really don't want to live in a brownstone." She crushed out her cigarette, her hand mechanically returning to the base of her neck, where it grasped the red speckled pendant like a worry bead, and began to rub the stone's smoothness.

"Oh, it's not the brownstone I'm talking about," the woman said with a knowing smile. "It's what is behind the brownstone that I'm talking about." She allowed a cryptic pause to hang in the air for effect, then added, "A carriage house."

"Carriage house?"

"Illegal, you know. Not supposed to be rented anymore. But, well—it's a friend of mine who owns the building. So if we're careful, if everyone shuts their eyes—nobody minds." She paused and smiled.

"Is it furnished?" asked Chandal.

"From top to bottom, with priceless antiques. Or so I've been told."

"Top to bottom?"

"Yes," Miss Ramsey said. "It's a duplex." She paused, then added gently, "Interested? Like I said, it's strictly illegal. That will bring down the price a bit."

Chandal could see the gears turning in the woman's head, a third eye observing her like a debit and credit sheet, ascertaining just how much she would be willing to pay for the rare privilege of living in an "illegal" dwelling.

"I can pay five hundred a month," Chandal said, biting her lip.

The woman smiled. "Let's go take a look at it."

Chandal stood up and followed the woman as she walked into the outer office, where she removed her black leather coat and fur hat from the closet. "Tony, if Marshall calls back, tell him I've gone out but the papers are on their way."

"Check," the unfamiliar face said without looking up.

"That's my nephew," Miss Ramsey whispered to Chandal. "He's a real shit."

Chandal chuckled.

Miss Ramsey kept muttering her way through varying subjects until they had reached the bottom landing. They stepped onto the street into a horde of scrambling people. "Let's walk, it'll be faster. Do you mind?"

"Not at all."

"Christ knows, it's cheaper."

Chandal nodded absently. Her attention had focused on the almost tangible pace of New York City that now hurried her forward. It was a phenomenon not to be found anywhere else in the world, this breathless feeling of being on one's way toward something. Something's coming, something's coming, she thought joyously, but suddenly in back of the exuberance a premonition ran through her like a chill. What? What was she racing so fast to catch up to?

CHAPTER FOUR

TWO AVENUES EAST AND SEVEN BLOCKS NORTH, THEY BEGAN looking for the house.

Chandal was immediately struck by the quiet tree-lined street that had escaped modernization. The buildings that lined the street were no taller than five stories and many of them had balconies with ancient, wrought-iron balustrades. There were a half dozen shops, several restaurants, two banks and a bar at the corner.

"It's a quiet block, isn't it?" Miss Ramsey declared.

"Yes, it is," Chandal said and glanced at the brownstone façades, the last remains of the American dream that seemed lost in the hazy sunset-colored brick. Worn-out buildings of yesterday, Chandal thought. These were weather-drab, pock-marked phalanxes, grim-faced and somber. Symbols of a more genteel era that had imperceptibly come to an architectural as well as a spiritual halt, to its last frontier.

Miss Ramsey stopped suddenly, bent her head forward to peer at the slip of paper she held in her hand, then squinted up at the building directly in front of her.

"It must be further east, toward the park," she said.

They walked a little further, passed the front of an amorphous blue-brick building, recently renovated, that seemed to intrude like an alien tower in an otherwise subdued neighborhood, and then on a little further, until Miss Ramsey stopped again, scanning the slip of paper which she had rolled up in the palm of her hand while walking.

"Here we are," she said cheerily.

Chandal stood there for a few uncertain moments looking up at the brownstone. It was very narrow, and peering into the walkway on the left, which separated it from the adjacent building, she saw just the edge of what she hoped would become her new home.

"Let's see if the gate is open." Miss Ramsey moved forward to the rusty iron gate and gave it a tug. Next she tried the latch. "Locked," she said. "Let's see if the super is in."

They climbed the slate-brown steps, passed through the glass lace-curtained exterior door and stopped in the hallway to press the super's button.

"It's still damn cold out, isn't it?" Miss Ramsey said, doing a little two-step to get her blood circulating. "What is it they say about March? In like a lion, out. . . ."

The interior door opened suddenly and Chandal found herself peering over Miss Ramsey's shoulder at a vivacious, cheery girl, whose red hair and blue eyes made her pale complexion sparkle. Dressed in a miniskirt, her hair pulled back into a pony tail, she resembled a relic from an earlier time.

"Hi, Doreen," Miss Ramsey said. "Is Mike in?"

"Oh, hi. No, he's down at the garage trying to get the car fixed."

"Do you have the keys for the courtyard gate?"

"Sure. Just a sec." The girl turned and headed down the hallway.

"You can also give me the keys to the carriage house, just in case I've brought the wrong ones," Miss Ramsey hollered after her.

"Right-o."

"Nice young couple. Her husband was wounded in Viet Nam. Nice fellow, though. If you should ever need anything, he's always willing to help." Miss Ramsey's expression changed to that of a protective mother. "You really should be wearing warmer clothing."

Chandal smiled. "It was eighty-six degrees the day I left California."

"Are you getting homesick?"

Chandal nodded. "A little."

"Well, let's see if we can help you get settled in all nice and cozy. The rest will take care of itself. A pretty girl like you should have no trouble finding new friends."

Chandal smiled. "Thanks."

"Here you go," Doreen said, handing Miss Ramsey the keys.

"Thanks. We shouldn't be long."

"Right. Just yell if you need me." Doreen was moving down the hallway again as if in hot pursuit of some fabulous orgiastic pleasure.

Chandal imagined her propped up on a sofa, her bare feet tucked under her body, watching "As The World Turns," while popping handfuls of jelly beans into her mouth.

"Where does she get such energy from?" Miss Ramsey sighed. "I never feel old until I'm around her."

Chandal laughed and followed Miss Ramsey down the steps, waiting with a heightened air of expectancy as she unlocked the gate. They passed easily along the walkway, which was a series of flagstones pressed solidly into the good, rich New York earth, until they rounded the corner and entered the courtyard.

Chandal could feel the color returning to her cheeks. The courtyard was not to be believed. It had two trees which hovered over the tiny carriage house, and a fountain, of all things, near center. Two rose bushes were planted on either side of the house's front door, their stems growing upward and forming an archway just above the doorway.

"Nice, isn't it?" Miss Ramsey said with a contented look in her eyes.

Chandal just laughed and shook her head. "I can't believe it."

Once inside, both women stopped at the edge of the living room to catch their breath. The room, although small, was crammed with chairs, sofas, coffee table, and floor and table lamps in haphazard profusion.

Large stones fashioned into a concrete framework formed the fireplace. The mantelpiece was a long, sleek piece of unpolished black marble, upon which sat antique clocks, candelabra and ornate picture frames. Chandal particularly liked the two overstuffed chairs that flanked the fireplace, and quickly imagined a modern fur throw rug spread between them. A touch of the modern here and there was just what the room needed. That, and a good cleaning.

"How's this for living?" Miss Ramsey asked.

Chandal shook her head in disbelief. "It's incredible. Just incredible."

They moved straight ahead into the small kitchen which was not much wider than the window occupying the east wall. To the right was an old-fashioned porcelain sink with soap-stained chrome-finished faucets carrying a ridge of dust along their tops, which Chandal blew away. She tested the faucets, first turning on the left tap, then the right.

"You can put a bigger sink in here if you like."

"I doubt that I'll be eating in much," Chandal said, shutting off the faucet.

"I don't blame you. Restaurants are the only way to go. Just as cheap eating out these days."

Chandal inspected the newly built, sturdy cabinets above the stove. "I see the previous tenant started to renovate."

"Oh, yes. He loved living here."

"Did you know him well?"

"Not really. Quiet sort of a man. Stayed pretty much to himself. A jeweler, I think."

"What made him leave?"

"I don't know really."

Pointing to a small door off the hallway, Chandal asked, "What's in there?"

"I think it's the den," the woman replied, making no effort to see if her guess was accurate. "Now the bedroom. . . ."

"May I see it?" Chandal asked.

"Oh. I believe it's locked. Doreen only gave me the one key." She turned away and began walking down the hall.

Chandal reached out and, with the slightest of shoves, opened the door. "No, it's not."

"What?" The woman turned.

"The door. It was just stuck."

Stepping into the room, Chandal saw at once the shabby interior was in great need of repair. There were water marks on the wallpaper indicating the roof leaked. Moldy magazines and books were left lying about. A great portion of the west wall had been stripped of wallpaper, leaving only the ugly remains of scarred and chipped plaster. Directly to the right of that there was evidence that the super or the local handyman had tried to repair the damage by nailing up paneling. For whatever the reason, the job had not been completed.

Something about the small, boxlike room struck Chandal as being unnatural. Perhaps it was the slight current of damp air that seemed to move through the room, carrying with it an odor. A thick, sickly, strange odor of age and decay. There were no windows. Still, Chandal was sure there was a thin veil of circulating air.

Half musing, she shook her head.

Miss Ramsey now stood quietly behind Chandal. "You're worried about this room, aren't you?" she said softly.

"It's . . ."

"Awful, I know. But the roof has been repaired and the owner assures me that he is willing to completely redo everything to your liking."

"Oh," Chandal said blankly.

Miss Ramsey raised her hand and placed it gently on Chandal's arm. "Believe me, we'll have this place straightened up in no time."

Whether it was because Chandal wanted so desperately for everything to be all right or because she believed wholeheartedly what Miss Ramsey had just told her, she found herself relaxing again and smiling.

"I can use it as a guest bedroom," Chandal said.

"Guests?"

"Well, you know . . . maybe a friend every now and again."

"You do understand, of course," Miss Ramsey said with a slight edge of tension in her voice, "that the house is to be used as a single occupancy only? The landlord wouldn't want a couple."

"I see. No, that's fine." Chandal shrugged. "I meant just in an emergency."

"Well, I'm sure in such cases that would be acceptable."

Just beyond the door to the den, there was a small foyer graced with an uneven but charming wooden arch. To the right of the foyer was the bathroom, which was large in comparison to the other rooms. The floor was tiled in pink and white, and there was an oddly shaped bathtub, which stood on four clawed feet.

"It's the kind of bathtub you see in movies," Chandal said

gleefully, already imagining herself sinking into a bubble bath.

"No shower," the woman said hesitantly.

"Suits me. I hate showers."

"If you change your mind, you could always put one up. That is, if you decide to take the house."

Chandal glanced up the narrow staircase to the left. "Is the bedroom up there?"

"Yes. Would you like to see it?"

"I'd love to."

"The light switch is right here near the banister." She hit the switch, but the room above remained dark. "Oh, dear. I'll have to get the electrician in," she said nervously.

"There's enough light," Chandal said, placing her hand on the railing. "I'd like to see it before making up my mind."

"All right, if you're sure we can see anything up there."

The stairs were narrow and steep; Chandal started to climb. At first she wasn't sure she heard the sound but after several more steps, she realized she had not been mistaken. Then it came, louder still. She had a flashing memory of a baby, on a rainy night, fearful in its crib.

She stopped to catch her breath, listened.

The sound was gone.

"Is everything all right?" the woman asked, also coming to a sudden and abrupt stop behind her.

"Oh, yes." Chandal tugged on the banister, as if to test it. "Just making sure the railing is sturdy."

"They built things to last in those days. Not like today. One touch and the damn thing falls apart."

Chandal was moving again, upward toward the darkness. The top of the stairs appeared to be getting further away with each step she took. Somewhere from above, the sound began again. The sound of crying. A baby. A low, mournful sound that hung in the air—echoing, rather than actually being there.

Chandal felt her hand grip tightly around the banister.

"Can you see anything?" Miss Ramsey asked.

Chandal squinted into the darkness, heard the baby cry again. And then everything was quiet.

"Miss Knight?"

"Yes. It's lighter up here."

At the very top of the stairs, a thin ray of light fanned out, making it a bit easier to see. Once Chandal stepped completely into the room, she could see that the light was coming from a large square-paned window facing the courtyard and a dirt-encrusted skylight sculpted into the architecture of the ceiling. Both the window and the skylight were nearly covered with the large outstretched limbs and branches of the two trees growing below in the courtyard, blocking out most of the late afternoon's natural light.

"Well, what do you think?" the woman asked, now standing beside Chandal.

Unlike the living room, the bedroom was plain and sparsely furnished. One huge bed, a dresser, a small table and chair. From the point where the skylight left off, the wide ceiling slab sloped down sharply to within a few inches of the bed's headboard. On either side of the bed, there were antique wall lamps that loomed out at Chandal like a pair of enchanting eyes in an otherwise plain face. Despite the cold bareness of the room, the lamps, sloped ceiling and skylight gave an unexpected charm to the entire place.

"You'll bump your head here," Miss Ramsey laughed as she stood under the sloped ceiling. "Especially if you wake up one night from a bad dream and forget it's there." She paused, then added, "Well, is it what you've been looking for?"

Chandal checked herself before her enthusiasm got the better of her. "Will five hundred dollars a month be acceptable?"

Miss Ramsey nodded her head. "Yes."

For a few silent moments, arms folded, Chandal surveyed the courtyard through the rain-stained window. Then she let her gaze run up the back of the brownstone opposite the courtyard, at the many windows that stared back at her, windows where sheets hung in place of curtains, others with plants and birdcages, still others with nothing at all. Vacant windows where the setting sun glistened, sending harsh reflected light back into the vaguely tired, vaguely confused eyes of their observer. Who lived in those windows, Chandal wondered. Why did they choose to live under such conditions? What drove people into small, musty dwellings, bodies stacked one upon the other, to live out their lives in quiet desperation? The thought of all those lives living in unspoken frustration and despair was a disquieting omen to Chandal, and yet it also awakened a curiosity.

"Are most of the people in that building poor?" she asked.

Miss Ramsey leaned forward and peered out the window. "Oh, God, no. Do you know the rents we get for those apartments?"

"I noticed that most of them look . . . well, undecorated."

"Don't let that fool you. We have writers living there. A schoolteacher. We even have a Wall Street broker. Of course, he uses it for nights when he doesn't feel like returning to his home in upstate New York, but that's most of the time."

"I wasn't aware you knew the building that well."

She shrugged. "I don't, actually. But I do get to see the leases when they come through the office."

"Oh." Slowly Chandal went through the room again, noting that she could see the top windows of the brownstone through the skylight. All the windows on the top floor were vacant. "Anyone live up there?" she asked.

"No. An old Polish woman used to live there. Thirty-seven years. But she died a few months ago. The owner has decided to leave the apartment vacant."

Chandal nodded, ran her hand over the back edge of the headboard. Much to her surprise it came away clean. She glanced around the rest of the room. Dim as the light was, she could see that it was also clean. "How long has this house been empty?" she asked.

"Oh, for some months now."

"That's odd."

"Oh? What is?"

"This room. It isn't dusty like the others."

"Mike probably started cleaning it."

"I see," Chandal said, letting out a pent-up gasp of air. What the hell was she waiting for? The house was ideal. It was conveniently located. She was within walking distance of the theater district. The living space was more than adequate and she would have to buy little or no furniture to make the place livable. So what was bothering her then? Was it the realization that if she took the house, she'd be forced to remain in New York? Or was it Ron? A feeling of guilt for letting him down?

Suddenly, at the corner of the room, Chandal stopped. She stood there firmly, determination oozing from her skin. She tightened her grasp of herself.

"I'll take it," she said quickly.

"Good," the woman said. And smiled.

Now they followed the flagstone path back to the brownstone. Along the way, Miss Ramsey reminded Chandal that the deal would have to be kept strictly confidential. That no formal lease could be signed under the circumstances, but that a letter of agreement would be drafted. That two months' advance rent was to be paid in cash to the super. And that under no conditions could Friendly Realty accept a finder's fee, but if Chandal wished, she could bring three hundred dollars in cash to the office in the morning, which Miss Ramsey would gratefully accept.

Doreen met them at the door.

"Here are the keys," Miss Ramsey said.

Doreen smiled. "Do you like it?" she asked Chandal.

"Yes, it's charming."

"Are you going to take it?"

Chandal nodded.

"Oh, thank God," the girl cried. "I was so afraid someone old was going to grab hold of it!"

"Doreen, tell Mike that Miss Knight will be moving in over the weekend. If he has the time, I would appreciate his taking a look at the bedroom light switch at the bottom of the stairs. It doesn't seem to work."

"He'll be glad to." She turned to Chandal. "Hey, see you soon." She smiled.

Chandal returned her smile.

At the bottom of the steps, Miss Ramsey said, "My office tomorrow. Around ten?"

"That'll be fine. And thanks."

"Hey, don't even mention it." The woman held out her hand. "I'm sure you'll be very happy here."

They shook hands and the deal was set.

"And remember, young lady. Until this weather changes, dress more warmly. I wouldn't want you to catch your death before you even have a chance to enjoy your new home." She turned the collar of her coat up, then said, *"Ciao."*

"See you in the morning," Chandal hollered after her.

The woman never looked back, merely threw her arm up over her head, sort of a "right-o" wave, and kept walking.

Chandal paused near the curb and wondered if she really should have committed herself to what seemed like such a permanent home. It was as if she had actually bought the damn thing. And the responsibility of caring for all those antiques. What if someone were to break in? It happened all the time in New York. Would she be responsible for replacing them? She found herself perturbed in a way she could not understand. She faltered, did not know what to think, where to look, what to do with her hands, until they reached out and opened the door of the cab. A cab? Without Chandal's realizing it, one had stopped in front of her. Jesus. She hadn't even seen him pull up.

"Where to, lady?"

"The Beverly Hotel, please."

"Right," the driver said and hit the flag on the meter.

Chandal took a last glance at the brownstone, at the dirty, lean structure, remembering that behind its more than disquieting façade was her new home.

Then, for a swift second, she saw, before she could quite believe it, a long-fingered hand that was nothing more than a tightly wrapped slither of bones, bulging with knotted red veins. The hand pushed aside a section of the lace curtain of the exterior door, and a basilisk mask of sorrow, with huge and blazing blue eyes, the dilated pupils swimming on a sea of milky whiteness, looked out at her through the glass. The old woman's face hovered for a moment, and then withdrew.

Seconds later, Chandal sat comfortably back in the seat of the cab, smiling. It had been a very profitable day. Her mind seemed to be fixed on that thought. Just over and over again—it had been a profitable day, until she felt herself dizzying from the monotony of thinking it.

A laugh bubbled from her lips as the old woman's face flashed before her eyes. *How wonderful it's going to be,* exulted an interior voice. *How wonderful to be back in the carriage house.* Her expression changed then. Her jaw was set in a wide grin.

Chandal's eyes focused suddenly, met the driver's stare in

his rear-view mirror. She wondered why on earth he was looking at her so strangely, almost as though he were afraid of her. For some reason the thought pleased her. She didn't know why, but it did.

She allowed herself to relax completely now. Yes, she mused, it had truly been a profitable day.

CHAPTER FIVE

THE VINTAGE MODEL JAGUAR, AN OLD X150, IMPECCABLY steel-gray and free of rust, rolled swiftly along the narrow canyon road three hundred feet above the water. Behind the tinted glass, deep in tufted black leather, Ron Talon tried to wipe away the lingering tension, the anxiety. With Chandal in New York, his life had changed. It was still hard for him to decide how he was supposed to react. He was not even sure in his own mind whether she had gone away to be in New York or merely to get away from Ron Talon.

He gripped the wheel, feeling the Jag hug the road as he took a sharp curve. His stomach churned slightly and he could feel the blood leaving his face. The sensation wasn't unfamiliar and he tried to overcome it, as he always tried. He had felt it throughout his career as a theatrical agent, during hectic negotiations with a producer, or when fighting for a better understanding with a client. It was fear but not—here and now—the fear of losing, but rather of dealing with something he couldn't understand.

He knew, as surely as Chandal must have known, that they had reached a new depth in their relationship that would soon call for new expression. Words as yet unsaid had seemed almost visible in the air between them. Words like marriage, for example. And, of course, that's what he feared she was running away from—saying words like marriage.

Gently he doubled his hand into a fist and struck the leather-covered steering wheel lightly. So now what? he

40

thought, seeing Chandal's clear blue eyes staring into his own. The Jag continued its climb upward.

Below, a maze of jagged rocks, bleached white by the sun's blaze, reflected light in violent intensity. Rocks that endured with fortitude the impact of the blue-green sea which roared with sudden explosion like echoes, its waves now broken, its tide rushing up onto the tiny patch of beach covered with seaweed. There was a stiff breeze blowing off the Pacific today and the breakers whipped up onto the beach in a steady crescendo.

Ron lost his thoughts in the roar and concentrated on driving until he found himself in Malibu, outside the high, arch-shaped entrance to what was once a private villa. In recent years the three-story mansion had been converted into twelve efficiency apartments, one of which belonged to Chandal.

His hand hit the turn signal and he slowed the car. He turned left onto the smaller paved road leading up to the main entrance. He slowed to a stop and shut off the ignition.

Good God, Ron thought, his eyes briefly sweeping the white Spanish-style house that stood utterly alone against the high cliff. Things had sure changed since the days of "Bulldog Drummond," "Hercule Poirot," and "The Thin Man." No longer was the world that simple.

Nor was it that rich.

Like all the other gilded palaces of Bel Air and Beverly Hills built by the Zukors, the Goldwyns, the Mayers and other movie moguls, the building loomed as a constant reminder of better days, when money flowed like milk from a healthy bitch that had just given birth to a litter of pups. When mansions sprang up everywhere, built with money made from hundreds of "B" movies of yesteryear.

Ron had always pictured Hollywood and its surrounding areas as the epitome of glamor, money and beautiful men and women. It was only after he began his career as a theatrical agent that he became aware of the rundown rooming houses filled with young people without a prayer; with no money to speak of; people lost in the quiet pursuit of broken dreams.

Perhaps Chandal was right to return to New York and the legitimate stage. Hollywood was a rough, tough life. The motion picture industry tended to strip emotions bare, leaving one with little sleep, lunches and dinners never eaten, cold cups of instant coffee, Miltown, No-Doz and four-thirty A.M. wake-up calls.

Ron sighed and stepped out onto the pavement.

"He won't bite!" boomed a voice off to the side at the sea-gate.

"That's, uh, good," Ron said, folding his arms across his chest and trying not to look the Doberman pinscher in the eye. Two things he knew about vicious dogs: Don't dangle your hands and don't look them in the eye.

The Doberman growled, saliva dripping from its jaws.

"Rusty, stop that!" The woman scowled, her voice shaded in fond annoyance. "Isn't he a riot?" She smiled, holding the dog lightly by its collar. "He thinks he scares people when he does that."

"A riot," mumbled Ron.

"Can I help you?"

"Yes, I'm here to pick up a few things from Chandal Knight's apartment."

"Oh, and you're . . ."

"Right. Ron Talon."

"Nice to meet you, Ron. Lucille Stoner here," said the woman, vigorous and quite attractive and no more than forty. Unconsciously she covered her wedding ring with her thumb. "If you don't mind, go on inside the back way. I'll come around to meet you."

"Right," Ron muttered neutrally and tried to take unhurried steps toward the indicated ground floor, which had its own private entrance by way of the garden path. Out of the corner of his eye he saw the woman's hand slip casually from the dog's collar as woman and dog disappeared inside the wire gate of the sea-wall.

His shaking hand found the screen door unlatched and he stepped into the deserted hallway. The inner door stood ajar. He strode forward, feeling as though he were an adventurer in a strange land following a blazed trail of open doors.

"Chandal mentioned you all the time," the woman said, appearing suddenly from a side entrance minus the dog. "Now why haven't I seen him, I used to say. That's odd, how I haven't seen him. Me, I see everybody. When you take care of a building, Lord, you're up and down stairs, here, there, everywhere, you see. So I said, why haven't I seen this man,

Chandal?" She paused, breathless, her eyes going over him inch by inch, taking in eye color, haircut, clothing.

"It is odd," Ron said, not mentioning that Chandal seldom suggested he visit her Malibu apartment. Instead she had preferred to go to his small home in the Hollywood Hills.

The woman continued to eye him calmly.

Ron shrugged. "Chandal asked me to send a few things to her in New York."

She held his gaze a moment longer. "I can let you in," she said briskly. Her trustworthy air indicated that she had a built-in radar for burglars and impostors and that he had passed her secret standards of integrity. She led the way, as her eyes now frankly appraised his rather unusual dress of black-tie dinner clothes.

"I'm going to an awards dinner," he found himself telling her, the information literally sucked out of him by the women's magnetic curiosity. He watched her digest the tidbit, her appetite more whetted, however, than satiated.

"One of my clients got nominated for an award," he went on, encouraged to see that the woman now held a key in her hand. "Sort of like an Emmy, only it's behind the scenes. Closed door sort of thing."

"Imagine that!" she beamed.

"It's not that big a deal. To be strictly truthful, the industry gives these awards to almost everybody who hasn't been winning Emmies lately. The ones it wants to keep happy, that is."

They stopped in front of Chandal's door and she fitted the key neatly into the lock.

"It sure would be interesting to know who wins," she said wistfully.

"The next time I see you, I'll let you know how it went," he promised.

Swinging open the door, she proceeded him into the apartment, hit the light switch in the foyer, then advanced over the deep white carpet to the large glass doors on the far wall where she pulled the curtains to reveal a breathtaking view of the sun setting over the ocean. Clearly she enjoyed showing off the apartment as though it were her own.

"She has exquisite taste, don't you think?" the woman said admiringly. Her eyes took in the antique seaman's chest in the corner, the polished driftwood coffee table, the circular couch and comfortable low chairs. It was a large room, made even more open by an arched serving counter that Chandal had had cut between the kitchen and that portion of the wall closest to the double window. Beside the doorway that led to her spacious bedroom was a glass shelf filled with cocktail glasses and liquor bottles.

Ron forgot the woman for a moment as a wave of emotion passed over him. Chandal had put such a stamp of her bright personality on this room that it was almost as though he could see her standing there beside him, gazing out over the ocean, holding his wrist instead of his hand as she always did. This habit had made him ask her once teasingly, "What are you doing—testing my pulse to see if I'm alive?"

Smiling slightly she had replied, "In a way, maybe. It's wonderful to feel the warmth of your skin, to feel your pulse beating away, so steady and real. It's wonderful," she repeated softly and he had said, "Not always so steady," taking her into his arms.

"How can she leave all this?" Mrs. Stoner now wondered out loud.

"Well, she's . . . Jesus, she's coming back."

"That's what she told me," said Mrs. Stoner. "But she won't be back. You'll see. She'll pay her rent for a couple of months and then one day a moving van will come and that'll be that. When you've had my job for a few years, you get to know these things. I knew just the way she said goodbye to me, that I was never going to see her again. And her plants." The woman took a step toward the window. "She gave them all away, see? She gave me a cactus collection and the rest to her neighbors. She'll never be back," she said regretfully and cocked her head suddenly.

"Oh, God," she squealed, "somebody's calling me. I never get a minute's peace. Listen, if I don't get back . . ."

"I know," Ron said. "Just close the door. It locks automatically."

"Right," she said, trotting off.

Ron stood silently for a moment, heard Mrs. Stoner's hurried footsteps retreating on the cement walkway outside and then down the stairs, until they became lost in the soft earth of the garden path below.

It wasn't until he had closed the door that he actually found himself acknowledging the acute loneliness he now felt. Feel it, he willed himself. Face whatever you came here to face—loneliness, whatever the hell it is—and get done with it.

Then he sighed, and saw himself for the coward he was. He had come to face nothing. He wanted only to be closer to Chandal. To be surrounded by the apartment she loved, by the ocean she claimed had healed her.

His heart beat in painful, dull thuds and he felt his eyes burning. Almost a week without her, the separation made more acute by the undeniable fact that she hadn't called on Thursday as she had promised, nor on Friday, nor today either and his pride had kept him from reaching for his own telephone.

Damn you, he told her fiercely, determined to be angry, to dispel the pain. Why didn't you call me? What are you trying to prove, Chandal? But he couldn't help thinking that perhaps she wasn't trying to prove anything. That maybe she'd just forgotten to call, was too busy to call, that really he was more agent than lover to her and for that matter, maybe she had a hot-shot New York agent by now.

Decisively, he pushed away this sort of negative thinking and stared around the room for clues to the missing Chandal. He noted that the heavy sterling silver lighter from the coffee table was gone. It bothered him that she had taken the trouble to pack the lighter, as well as the picture of her mother that used to sit on top of the stereo.

A quick glance into the hall closet revealed that she had probably worn her fur coat and that she had also taken her trench coat. Shoes and handbags were gone. She had packed thoroughly and yet, on the other hand, there was evidence of a split-second decision. Ashes still in an ashtray, two bottles of nail polish still sitting on the coffee table, records still stacked on the record player. Uncharacteristic of a chronically neat Chandal.

Ron nodded dumbly. He still could not shake the dull, persistent sensation that something was wrong. He couldn't get the thought out of his mind, nor could he free himself of his concern with Chandal's sudden departure. Something wasn't right, damn it.

Nervously he flipped on the record player. A record dropped into place, the arm swung into position and jazz began to fill the room at a very low volume. He stood in the dimmest part of the apartment now, himself merely a shadow. Only his eyes flashed visibly, restless, uncertain.

What the hell did he expect to find here? That he would come upon something that would prove him right? That Chandal was in trouble? Was he losing his senses? What, in fact, had he hoped to gain by coming here?

He needed more time to think. Everything seemed to be moving too fast. Chilled, he ran his hand over his arm and realized that it was wet. He had been sweating and he hadn't noticed.

He turned quickly and moved into Chandal's bedroom. It was cold, gray and still. The blinds on the windows were tightly drawn, blocking out the sunlight. He flicked on the bedside lamp and felt a slight pang. There under the lamp was his own picture in a small gold frame.

Gazing vacantly, he found his life story replaying itself in his mind like an MGM film. Ron Talon, who had had some pretty grandiose visions for a simple kid from Encino, who had majored in film at UCLA, who had gotten so far as to direct a few low-budget documentaries—which was more than the majority of his classmates had ever done.

The Ron Talon Story moved into the meaty part—starvation for the better part of five years, Heavy stuff, starvation. He smiled, remembering how he'd awakened one morning to see the world with fresh eyes. In the background of his mind a curtain went up and the MGM tap-dancers came out. This was a good old Hollywood movie. Where the hero finds that starving is out of character for him. He simply didn't want to wake up at fifty and be penniless. He had friends who were prepared to do that and he envied them in a way, but truth was truth. Being a theatrical agent—first an assistant in a large agency, then a full-fledged agent for the same organization, then manning his own agency—had been the white line down the middle of the road. But he was honest-to-God good at it and he found himself enjoying the work. Then boy met girl and the happy ending seemed sure to happen. Then . . .

"Then," he muttered out loud, "girl loses mind."

Now he began to open drawers, finding them completely empty, lined with white paper, still smelling faintly of lilac. As he closed the last drawer, he heard something bump against the wood. A small article, some piece of forgotten jewelry, probably, he thought, and reached into the far recesses of the empty drawer.

Even before he looked at it, he was surprised by the weight of the object. The thought came into his mind that perhaps it was an oddly shaped belt buckle, but then women didn't tend to own such things.

He whistled as speculation ceased, his eyes fixed on what was without a doubt a very valuable silver crucifix. It was no more than three inches long and odd in design. The tormented figure on the cross had been carved in agonizing detail, the artist seeming to suggest by the sharp downthrust of the head, the screaming lips and the twisted limbs, the degree of pain actually involved in crucifixion.

Ron stared at the object in distaste. He had sensed immediately that in some sadistic and medieval way the artist had enjoyed his work. And that no one, especially Chandal, could find the crucifix attractive.

Still, it was strange. Why would she leave such a valuable piece of . . . jewelry? He weighed the crucifix in the palm of his hand for a moment.

Worn around the neck? He examined it closer. No. The cross had a small silver ring through which a chain might be passed. But the ring was fixed at the wrong end of the cross—at the bottom. If the crucifix had been worn around Chandal's neck, it would have hung upside down.

In any case, Chandal had never mentioned coming from a Catholic background. There once had been a discussion about religion but she had quickly changed the subject.

Now, using the index finger of his left hand, he began to trace the outline of Christ's body, starting at the feet and working his way slowly up to the face, where the down thrust shadows of Christ's hair and nose cast long, dark streaks down his cheeks and chin so that it seemed as if his face assumed a grotesque mask.

Ron drew a deep breath, the atmosphere of the room suddenly assaulted by the heavy smell of old dust, the incense odor of cheap perfume. With his eyes still fixed on Christ's face, he began to feel a strange sensation. As if he had fallen away, back into another time, himself part of a divine allegory. This room could, with very little imagination, have been a crypt or a tomb, himself the unwilling spectator of a heinous act of brutality—a part of the darkness.

And he found himself thinking of old legends and stories he had read when a boy—floating in a fluid past.

In the next instant he let the crucifix slip casually into the pocket of his tuxedo.

Turning off the bedroom light, he retraced his steps into the living room where he sat down in a chrome-based rocking chair. He was exhausted. He could hardly bring himself to leave the apartment. It seemed as though to leave would be a kind of farewell to something.

Outside, the vast canopy of blue sky blended far off with the blazing sun in a shimmering horizon of fire. A motionless seagull sat on a stone, looking more like a statue cast in bronze than like a living creature.

For a moment the room fell hushed. The waves roared, mellowed, then lulled him in their persistence, as they washed his thoughts out to sea. Chandal became a shadow in his mind, weightless, formless, until he sighed, as if to release the last of her essence.

"Damn," he said, and realized just how much he was dreading this evening. In fact, he was ready to do almost anything to get out of it.

He glanced at his wristwatch, noted it was twenty minutes after six, and that while he could be late for drinks and hors d'oeuvres at seven, he could not be late for dinner at eight.

He reached for the telephone on a small table to his right and found it still connected. He took pleasure in the fact that Chandal still had a functioning phone in L.A. Why it pleased him, he wasn't sure. But it did. Later he could phone this number and have the cold comfort of hearing it ring.

By God, you've got it bad, he told himself grimly and heard his assistant, Mimi Halpern, say hello.

"Mimi?"

"Ron?" she moaned warily, her tone a reminder that he had absolutely promised her a free Saturday.

"Got a hot date tonight, you cute thing?" he asked.

"Yes, I have, you treacherous. . . ."

"Treacherous? Have I ever asked you to do anything I wouldn't do myself?"

"What is it you want me to do?"

"Something I can't do myself," he admitted, and held the phone from his ear as she screamed.

"Not tonight!" she said furiously. "I can't help you out. It's my first date with the guy. He looks like Dustin Hoffman. He's darling."

"You want to impress the shit out of the boy? Take him to the dinner tonight. The invitation's for two."

"The awards dinner? Ron, you can't be serious. It's six-thirty, for God's sake. I don't even know if he has a tuxedo."

"If he doesn't own a tuxedo," Ron said firmly, "he has nowhere near enough class for you. It's best you break the whole thing off right now."

"I'll kill you for this."

"Mimi," he said and dropped the façade, "I'm out of it. I just can't handle that dinner tonight. Do you understand what I'm saying?"

A pause and then he heard her sigh.

"Get some rest, Ron, baby," she said. "I want you to be in really good health when I shoot you on Monday."

"Thanks, Mimi."

He hung up, an invisible weight lifted from his shoulders. It was a luxury, he thought, to be able to suffer alone. And he reminded himself that Mimi had just earned herself another raise.

Silence. Ron let his body slide further down into the chair, let his arms rest comfortably against his chest. He was still unable to understand completely his motives for coming here today, to say nothing of Chandal's motives in going to New York. Carefully he said to himself: You're on thin ice here. To Chandal he would say . . . what? After a few moments, he allowed his eyes to close, relaxing completely, until his head dropped to his chest and he slept.

His face, inclined downward, seemed to contemplate the roar of the ocean as if he pondered the depth of it, as if he might wish to jump headfirst into it and find it absolutely bottomless. Images swam in his mind. Chandal drifted toward him, her face white against a dark background. Her eyes were on him now, her lips smiling. Suddenly he felt himself overcome by a desire so intense that he was able to control it only with difficulty. He whispered uncertainly, "I love you, Chandal." But he wasn't sure that was an answer to anything.

Abruptly, he sat up straight, his brief respite broken. For

an instant he was confused, groping. He'd heard something. He tried to think clearly. A sharp thud. Like the slam of a . . .

Still half asleep, he rose and stared at the bedroom door. It was now shut. Off to the side, the arm on the record player lifted back, a new record fell into place, and the needle returned to a playing position.

"Chandal?" he shouted and threw open the bedroom door. He listened to his voice echo through the apartment, while still another detached part of his mind listened to an alien sound, strange and distorted.

He turned back to stare at the record. Warped, he thought. Then as he listened further, he realized that the flat quality of the sound, deliberately nasal and off-key, was part of a chorus of human chants. The record must have been recorded at a high level of volume, because although he had not touched the audio control, the sound was three times louder than the previous recording.

He felt his face grow cold.

At that instant, the chanting stopped. In the silence he heard the mournful flat notes of a flute and then a woman's voice.

"Blood turn to stone. Stone to fire. Burn, burn, burn. . . ."

The voice faded away, replaced by a shrill, high-pitched sound of a whistle. Quickly Ron reached out and turned off the record player. "What in the hell is this?" he muttered. He lifted the record from its cradle. No label.

He shrugged. Probably a recording of some second-rate play that had closed in one night. He wondered if Chandal had been in the chorus of chanters. No jacket, he observed. Yet there was a design of sorts pressed into the center. He had difficulty trying to determine just what that symbol was. An animal? He squinted, and as he gazed uncertainly at the record, he suddenly had the uneasy feeling that he, too, was being gazed at. Something jolted him and he swung around. The room was empty and quiet. The silence was deafening.

Then a faint noise. At the sound he looked through the glass doors to the balcony, where he saw someone standing back in the corner, regarding him silently.

"Hello?"

The image vanished. He frowned and stepped forward. No, whoever it was had slipped down the back stairway that led to the beach. He squinted down, but could see nothing. "Damn," he breathed softly.

Moments later he closed the front door behind him, testing it to see that it had locked. Now he moved quickly down the single flight of steps, hoping to avoid contact with anyone.

"Mr. Talon?"

He turned with a start. "Yes?"

"Did you find what you were looking for?" asked Mrs. Stoner with a smile.

Her question pulled a grimace to his face. "Oh, yes. Yes, thank you."

"Please tell Chandal when you speak with her that we all were asking for her and miss her."

"Sure. She'll be glad to hear that."

"Really such a sweet girl. I hope she is happy in New York."

Ron let the back of his hand run across his mouth. Mrs. Stoner waited, still smiling. A kind of lopsided smile that made him extremely nervous. "Thanks," he said and pushed past her.

As he slid into his Jag, Ron could still see Mrs. Stoner watching him. What the hell was she waiting for, he wondered. Should he have tipped her, maybe? Or was she looking for a job as an actress? The woman remained motionless, looking after him.

In the rear-view mirror he watched the woman grow smaller, as the Jag kicked gravel up, dust swirling behind the car, until she was lost from view.

The tension he now felt carried him a few miles and then hunger took over to occupy his mind. He had dinner at his favorite pub—a steak, baked potato, French bread, salad and two vodka tonics, and then coffee at home in his den. It wasn't until then that he found himself restless again. He stared at the phone and willed it to ring, for it to be Chandal.

Slowly he formulated a thought. Dr. Luther. Chandal had talked about him often, fondly, as though Luther had guided her through impossible times. Only Dr. Luther, she had seemed to say a hundred times, could have saved her.

Ron took a swallow of black coffee. He shook his head wearily and tried to disengage himself from thought. The idea pestered him, grew into full flower before he could block it. Certainly Luther should be notified. He would want to know that Chandal had deliberately gone against his advice. Don't go to New York, he had warned.

Ron pictured a possible conversation. "Dr. Luther, I'm Ron Talon. A friend of Chandal Knight's." "Oh, how nice," the doctor would say, "and where is Chandal? Anyplace but New York, I hope."

Ron found himself reaching now for the phone. His lips were half-turned up at the corners in a guilty smile. "You tell her, doc," he muttered and dialed New York information. After a brief exchange, he received the number for Lakewood Sanitarium.

He paused for a moment before dialing through. He felt like a rat, a squealer. He knew what he wanted—a decision handed down from on high. From all-wise doctor to confused patient. Get some sense in your head. Go back to L.A. The squealer told me you disobeyed my orders.

Ron stared at Chandal's picture on his desk and dialed. It was for her own good, he told himself, and heard the voice say, "Lakewood, may I help you?"

"Yes. I'm trying to locate a Dr. Luther."

"I'm sorry, Dr. Luther is out of the country at the moment. Could someone else help you?"

"Oh. No, thank you. Ah, do you suppose I might get a number where he could be reached? It's very important."

"Is it an emergency?"

"Well, I . . . it concerns an ex-patient of his."

"If you wish, I'll take your number," the voice said briskly. "When the doctor calls in, I'll see to it that he gets your message."

"Thank you."

After that, Ron tried to watch T.V, tried to read, found he was biting his nails to the quick. The image in his head was that of the empty Malibu apartment where Chandal ought to be right this minute. At least she should be if she wasn't here in the Hollywood Hills with him.

He felt like a schoolboy with a crush but dialed the Malibu number anyway. Two rings and he knew that listening to a phone ring in an empty apartment wasn't going to solve anything. He had started to drop the phone into its cradle when there was a click as someone picked up the receiver. His heart leaped as a woman said hello, but immediately he knew it was an older woman's voice.

"Chandal?"

A pause. Some sort of strange music in the background.

"No. You've dialed wrong."

"Is this 724-4329?"

"4319."

"I'm sorry," Ron said. "I . . ."

In the next instant the connection was broken.

Ron frowned. He thought of the music in the background. That same flat quality. . . .

He hesitated and then redialed. This time there was no answer.

Slowly he replaced the receiver and saw himself standing in the shadows of the empty Malibu apartment. Around him the darkness seemed to have life and purpose. And he heard a familiar voice: "Did you find what you were looking for?" Ron saw Mrs. Stoner's smiling face again, her quick eyes examining him.

The Doberman's snarl echoed. Saliva dripped from its mouth.

Ron thought of distance. The sound of ringing like cathedral bells. It was the telephone.

"Hello?"

The line crackled, buzzed and then went dead.

In the silence he could feel exhaustion taking hold of him. He stood interminably by the phone without moving. He wished Chandal had talked with him before she had gone. He wished she had said something, anything, about her desire to go to New York. Just a word or two—something.

He stared out of his window at the empty street. How confused and alone he felt. There was something terrifying in the feeling. Moments later he dropped onto his bed. He flicked off the light. In the darkness the thought came to him: *"Let all dreams and phantoms of the night fade away, lest our bodies be polluted."*

And then he slept.

CHAPTER SIX

MARCH 22ND, SUNDAY, THE CITY SLOWED.

Doreen Hammer was sitting on the couch, the only place in the carriage house where a person could sit for more than five minutes without being disturbed. Her drink, not quite finished, tilted precariously on the armrest. With her feet propped gracefully on the corner of the coffee table, her hair thrust up in its usual ponytail, she leafed idly through a dogeared copy of *Vogue*.

"There, that should do it!" Chandal let the dust rag drop to her side and viewed the room, punched a pillow into submission on the stuffed chair near the fireplace, then frowned and stepped back to view the room's full effect from the door.

"Well, what do you think?" she asked.

Over the top of the magazine Doreen cast a perfunctory eye around the room and caught sight of Chandal staring at her. She looked around more attentively then and said, "I think it looks beautiful."

"You think?" Chandal asked rather doubtfully and sighed.

She had spent most of the day trying to put her stamp on her new home—chairs and sofas had been arranged to create new areas, the antique teacart had been turned into a bar, a few items had been discarded, others relegated to the brownstone's basement. She had, however, the uneasy feeling that nothing had actually been accomplished. That the personality of the carriage house was somehow independent of her, stronger than her, and that nothing could be done to alter it.

Absently Chandal brushed a few strands of loose hair away from her eyes. "You know, it's strange about the pictures, isn't it?"

Doreen reached for her drink. "What's wrong with the pictures?"

"They're cheap, to put it bluntly. I wouldn't have believed whoever lived here would fill his walls with bad pictures. He was an antique lover—a man of taste. I mean, can't you just picture a Degas over there?"

As Chandal spoke, she dumped an armload of debris into an empty box, then grabbed a jar of furniture polish from the small table in the foyer.

"Sure, I guess so. Who is he?"

"Are you kidding? He's a painter—a very famous painter!" She shook her head. "Doreen, from now on, don't admit to anyone that you don't know who Degas is."

"The secret will go to my grave with me."

"Damn! Look at the dust on this mantel. It's an inch thick."

"It's about the same depth as the dust on my mantel," grinned Doreen.

"Funny. Very funny."

Doreen said, "Mike doesn't think so."

Their eyes locked for a moment. Doreen stirred uneasily.

Chandal turned and finished polishing the mantel. "I just read where they had a great exhibition of Degas's works at the Metropolitan Museum."

"I've never been to a museum."

"Well, you should go. You'd love it."

"Okay. Next time you go—take me with you."

"What?"

"I'd love to go to the museum with you."

"Oh, sure," Chandal agreed. "Maybe some night we'll . . ." She broke off and pulled at the silver chain around her neck. The bloodstone jerked slightly. She thought she'd heard something. Her eyes quickly came to rest on the door to the den. She listened closely.

"What's the matter?" Doreen asked with unabashed curiosity. "You look a thousand miles away. Back in California with what's-his-name. . . ."

"Ron," Chandal muttered, still listening. There it was again—that sound. She could hear it faintly, a screeching of sorts. Like fingernails being scraped across a blackboard. She'd heard that sound before, hadn't she?

Doreen let her feet drop to the floor. "Chandal?"

"Just a minute." Chandal laid the dust rag on the mantel and moved quietly to the den. Hesitantly she opened the door and peered into the room, wondering what it was she had expected to see. The small light over the desk was on and swaying slightly, casting a moving beam of weird light back and forth over the desk's grimy surface and oblique shadows on the dampened walls. Yet the air in the room was perfectly still.

That's odd, Chandal thought. She hadn't been in this room today. Had she? No, she could say with confidence that she had not.

"Dreadful!" shrilled Doreen.

"What?" Chandal turned with a start.

"This room."

Chandal swallowed hard and then said, "Before, when I emptied the trash. Did you come in here?"

"No," Doreen said simply. "Why?"

"Well . . . the light is on . . . and it's moving."

They looked at each other for a moment, then Doreen shrugged. "You probably left it on."

"No. I haven't been in here."

"Sure you were. When I first came in. Don't you remember?"

Chandal hesitated, then shook her head.

"Sure. You even shut the door."

This left Chandal utterly perplexed. Once again she stared at the light.

"The first thing I'd do with this room is paint it," Doreen said, walking through the room like a contractor making a bid for a job. "Then I'd get a nice big furry rug, hang a few pictures. . . ."

Chandal saw Doreen more than heard her, saw her fumble around in the dimness, lifting old magazines from the table, picking up the candelabra, then spinning an old globe of the world until she came to study a group of islands in the Pacific. Suddenly the world seemed cupped in Doreen's tiny hands, and from nowhere—the faint tang of . . . salt?

Chandal sniffed. A more sinister odor took its place, a rottenness, yet at the same time bittersweet. She could feel herself drifting back in time. Back to the bare remnants of her existence, to the hard fact of human essence. She didn't feel well, something was wrong. She tried to tell herself it was the close airlessness of the tiny room, but she knew the lack of air, the vacuum she now felt, was in her. She felt stifled.

Doreen was talking again. Her chattering distracted Chandal, separated her from her own feelings. Something strange was occurring, Chandal thought. But what? Doreen's face became visible again as she stepped from the shadows. They moved out of the den, leaving the place to its own darkness, with Chandal still not sure just what had happened. Just what it was she had experienced. Doreen kicked off her shoes, sat on the couch with her legs tucked under her body and took an orange from the glass bowl of fruit on the side table. "This is a great place, really," she declared and dug her fingernails into the peel.

"Hey," Chandal blinked. "Do you know what you're doing?"

"Yeah, I'm eating your decoration."

Bemused, Chandal shook her head and turned to squint out the window into the courtyard, then glanced anxiously up at the fifth-floor window of the brownstone.

"I know it's part of the whole effect," Doreen chortled, "but look at it this way. The atmosphere you've created makes me feel comfortable, happy. Free to eat your oranges which, by the way, I can't help feeling are very bad for you. . . ."

"They're very healthy," Chandal said automatically, still staring vaguely out the window. "The Vitamin C, you know. . . ."

Outside, the huge expanse of blue sky was spotted here and there with slow-moving clouds. Dazzling sunlight streamed through the window onto Chandal's upturned face. It had begun as a wet, chilly day, a hard-to-get-out-of-bed day, but it had rapidly warmed and Chandal found herself unzipping her white cardigan sweater and throwing it lightly onto the couch, feeling comfortable in her thin flannel shirt and faded broken-in denims. The air in the carriage house was leaden and the partly opened window breathed a familiar perfumed magic. The exposed patches of earth which surrounded the trees smelled raw and fresh.

Still, Chandal was filled with a heaviness, a vague apprehension of sorts. A deep longing. What was she doing here? she wondered not for the first time.

Instinctively, she used the lilac-scented handkerchief which she had found lying beside her bed that morning and dabbed the side of her throat. The lilac sweetness assailed her nostrils. Quickly she shoved the handkerchief into her jeans' pocket. Then she threw herself onto a large pillow on the floor and folded her long arms above her knees.

"You know," Doreen went on without missing a beat, "I still have a feeling that a hundred years from now we'll all find out we shouldn't have been eating oranges. It's because of nature, you see. Nature's wonderful. If oranges were so good for you, nature wouldn't have made them so goddamn hard to peel! Like nuts. I'm convinced that nuts are deadly poison. Nobody can tell me different."

"That room," Chandal murmured.

Doreen blinked. "What?"

"The den, have you noticed? It has a strange odor."

"Mildew."

"But it's a sweet sort of—" She broke off.

Someone had knocked, no—pounded, on the front door. Emergency kind of pounding. Odd, uncivilized blows aimed at a door which had become, for the moment, an opponent.

"What in the name of God is going on?" asked Chandal.

Both girls stood at the same time.

"Oh, Jesus!" Doreen began backing away to the fireplace. "Oh, God—it's almost five o'clock!" she squealed. "I've been here two hours already."

"So what's two hours?" Chandal said lightly, but she had an uneasy glimmer of understanding.

The pounding grew louder.

So that's how it is, huh, Chandal thought and wrenched open the door to face Mike Hammer whose anger was disproportionately harsh for the offense.

He stared past Chandal to where Doreen stood, his lips pinched in rage. His wiry black hair dropped sharply over his forehead and stopped short of covering his deeply intense brown eyes. His lean body appeared unshaken, fitted loosely into corduroy trousers that were taken up sharply around his waist with a black belt. His plaid shirt hung open down the front, revealing a soiled T-shirt.

"Goddamn it, Doreen!" his voice boomed. "How the hell can you do something like this? Sit here all day!"

Chandal glared at him with contempt as he moved further into the room. Her eyes followed him closely. "Mike," she said steadily, "I'm afraid it's my fault. I . . ."

He turned to face her, his anger doubling. "I wasn't talking to you," he spat at her. "I was talking to my wife!"

Tight-lipped, Chandal glanced at Doreen.

"I'm sorry," Doreen said before Chandal could find the right words to cut Mike to ribbons. "I lost track of time. One minute it was three o'clock and then I turned around—"

"I want dinner!" he snapped. "And 4A has been trying to find you for an hour. The halls are filthy."

"Mike, please—" Doreen pleaded.

"What the hell do I care? You want people to say we keep the building like a pigsty, that's okay, I guess!"

Tears welled in Doreen's eyes. With a sudden desperate courage, she took the offensive. "You have no right to talk to me like this! To treat me like this!"

"Lower your voice," he scowled. "You're screaming."

"I'll scream if I feel like screaming!" Doreen burst into tears.

"Listen, never mind about dinner. I'll eat out."

Before Doreen could reply, he was gone, slamming the door behind him. The sudden and total silence, now devoid of Mike's energy, left the room with yet another sort of explosion. Something that had to do with despair.

Doreen stood motionless by the fireplace, tears coursing down her cheeks. Seeing Chandal staring at her, she turned away and stifled her sobbing against the back of her hand.

"I'm sorry," Chandal said softly.

Doreen didn't say anything for a moment, but when she turned back toward Chandal, she had stopped crying entirely. Her voice was low and even. "I'm fine now. Really. I'm all right." She paused to rub her temple with her thumb and middle finger. "I'd better go."

"Are you sure you feel okay?"

"A headache, that's all."

"Can I get you anything? Aspirin, water, another drink?"

"No, I'd better . . ."

"Not yet. Stay here for a minute. I'll fix coffee, okay? Please, sit here a moment. Don't try to talk."

Doreen looked at her and smiled. Then she began to laugh, the laugh of a girl who has just had a near miss with death and emerged suddenly from the shock, to find herself alive and well.

Disbelievingly, Chandal stared at her and forced a slight smile to her own lips. The smile felt dry and stiff, certainly nothing like the spontaneous mirth that now shook Doreen, who was laughing out loud until the tears rolled down her cheeks. After a few moments she fell silent, then opened her mouth to speak but nothing came out.

"Are you sure you're all right?" Chandal asked. There had been something so odd about her laughter.

"Hell," she giggled. "I'm used to it."

Over coffee, Doreen said shyly, "I hope you don't think too badly about Mike. He's really a nice guy. No, really. He just flies off like that and he can't help it."

"Why can't he help it?" Chandal asked shortly.

"He's full of feeling. It comes pouring out and there's so much of it, you know, that he can't stop it."

"You're very understanding."

"What sort of wife would I be if I wasn't?" Then she added, passionately, "You've noticed his hand, I guess? It happened in Viet Nam. He was so shot up, they left him lying on the riverbank. They thought he was dead. When he opened up his eyes he was the only living soul in the dead of dark with a hundred corpses. Well, you see, Mike started to scream. He screamed so loud, the medics heard him from almost a mile off where they had their hut and they came and got him. They found him all torn up and his three fingers ripped off. They fixed him up—as well as they could. But, well . . . he's torn up inside worst of all. He's so cut up he's in pain all the time. Sometimes I hear him crying in bed at night. He still has shrapnel in his skull." Doreen laughed now, choking a bit on her tears. "Isn't anything so bad, that there isn't something funny, Chandal. That metal up in his skull, sometimes it picks up radio stations. No kidding, sometimes I see him snapping his fingers and I know sure as anything he's picked up a rock station."

Chandal joined her in laughter. Yet despite her outward show of conviviality, she reserved a grain of her anger. Just a reminder that he had misused Doreen, and no matter what had happened, or what Doreen thought, he didn't have that right. The scene struck some distant memory in Chandal, one she could not quite grasp, of someone . . . her husband?

"I call him the man with the radio in his head," chortled the forgiving wife.

"You're too good, Doreen. No, really, you are."

"You'd be that way, too, if you were in my place."

"No. I don't think so. Not again."

"Again? Did your husband . . . you know?"

"No." Chandal stared at her. "Justin never mistreated me. We had a very happy marriage." Even as she spoke, she wondered if this was the truth.

"Oh. Just the way you said—"

"My mind was wandering."

"Chandal? Do you mind me asking . . . Ron. Are you in love with him?"

With a half grin Chandal replied, "Sometimes, yes, sometimes, no. If you know what I mean."

"I know what you mean." Doreen smiled back, then murmured shyly, "I was wondering something."

"What's that?"

"Do you think it's so important for a man's wife to—to have their child? Do you think Ron feels that way?"

"I don't know. Even if he did, I'm sure he'd understand if—" Chandal broke off, staring at Doreen.

"We just found out. I can't have children. Mike was terribly disappointed. I think that's one of the things that's been bothering him. It's been bothering me too. I've become obsessed with it lately."

"You can adopt," Chandal said firmly.

"Won't there be a difference?"

"No difference at all."

Doreen smiled suddenly. "Maybe you're right," she murmured, meeting Chandal's gaze. "Maybe it would be just like mine. I mean, if I were the one who took care of it—if I were the one who understood its needs—" Her face glowed and her smile widened.

She was still smiling when she left the carriage house.

For the next few hours Chandal kept busy, trying desperately to put the incident behind her. She washed wine glasses which were filled with years of dust, lined the kitchen shelves with bright yellow contact paper, cleaned the oven, scoured the sink and then began scrubbing the kitchen floor.

Fighting back a sudden drowsiness, she studied her face reflected in the white tiles through hot soapy water. Grime had loosened and begun to slide down her cheeks. She shuddered. It was like watching a face under a face. The first face evaporated to reveal the second face. She couldn't tell if she had begun to sweat or if steam merely settled on her, dampened her in a claustrophobic cloud.

Swiftly consciousness and subconsciousness became one. Memories appeared ready to pour forth. Chandal caught her breath. She tried to will herself to let it all out. It was there, so close, so damned close. It had happened before, but never so intensely, so tantalizingly, just out of reach.

Unaware of her actions, she reached for the knife that rested on the broad edge of the sink and ran her finger along the blade. So sharp. She pressed against it slightly and watched with fascination as a thin red line opened on her thumb.

A flash. A knife in someone's hand. Whose hand? Her hand. The image faded. Now she was in a museum. Vaguely, she could even see a room. Huge paintings. A phone rang in her memory. Your mother, the voice was saying. Suicide.

"Oh, no. Mama. Why?"

"Like mother, like daughter," breathed a disembodied voice.

She blinked and laid the knife aside.

Her mind kept wandering. She was a little edgy, jumpy, and could not fully understand the moment's reality. What the hell was bothering her? She was lonely, she knew that. She used the word unconsciously, then realized she had said it and even how ridiculous it sounded. The muscles in her cheeks twitched suddenly. She shook her head. *"Like mother. Like daughter."*

Involuntarily her eyes moved to the den. The door looked as though it had suddenly opened. It was too much—it was the final absurdity. She had to stop acting so goddamned silly.

She threw the sponge into the bucket, shrugged and dried her hands on the dishtowel. After a swift glance at the living room clock, she reached for the telephone. She gave herself no time to think, merely dialed the familiar number as rapidly as possible.

The voice in California did not sound pleased.

"Ron, it's Chandal," she said as matter-of-factly as possible.

"Oh," Ron said stiffly.

"Hey, don't sound all Greek and tragic. Or did I catch you at a bad time, because if . . ."

"No, I'm just surprised to hear from you, that's all."

"You don't have a date over there, do you? Some starlet who made you an offer you couldn't refuse?" She laughed shortly, and then discovered in the silence which followed that Ron was not amused. "Hey, you're not mad at me, are you?"

"Why? Just because you haven't called me in a week? Why should I be mad?"

"Ron. . . ."

She was surprised that she had forgotten how much this man mattered to her.

"Okay, I'm not mad," he acquiesced wearily. "If I was mad, I wouldn't pick up the phone on the first ring, would I? I'd play it cool. Maybe let it ring twice or something."

"Thanks for not playing it cool." She smiled into the phone.

"So, how's it going out there?" he asked. "Don't you miss all the sunshine? Your friends?"

"Yes, I do. And you. I miss you."

"Well, does that mean good news or something? Like maybe you're calling from the airport with your packed bags at your feet?"

"Ron, I'm sorry. I'm going to stay on here. For a while. I don't know how long."

An instant of chilled silence passed between them.

Chandal hurried on then with news: The address and phone number of the carriage house, the description of the carriage house, the agent she had made contact with last Friday who was already sending her to a reading on Monday. Finally she added that she had gotten into a good ballet class at Carnegie Hall.

"Well," he interjected, "it sounds like you're all set up, doesn't it? Like, say, permanently."

"I didn't say that." She hesitated.

"Jesus, Del. You're in New York. About as far from me as you can get, without leaving the country."

"Ron, have a little faith in me. There's no hope for us if you don't. . . ."

"What about the screen test?" Ron interrupted. "Can I at least tell Coppola you're willing to come back for that?"

"It's out of the question."

"Out of the question?" he repeated incredulously. "I'll pay for the flight, Del. I can't let you blow this opportunity."

She felt her temper explode. "Just tell him," she said sharply, "if he wants me for the picture, he can look at all the other screen tests I made for all the other pictures I didn't get."

"That's not fair, Del. It takes time. I did my best for you out here."

She heard the hurt in his voice, felt the space between them growing larger. "I don't know," she whispered past the lump in her throat, and then quietly said, "Ron, I can't talk anymore, okay? I'll call you." But she did want to talk to him. She did.

"When?"

"Soon," she replied vaguely. "Okay?"

"I guess it will have to be," he muttered.

"Yeah."

After a pause, she added, "Goodnight, Ron."

"Goodnight."

She clung to the receiver for a moment, then slowly, hesitantly, she let it drop into its cradle. She felt a dull ache inside. It carried her to the window as if to look for an escape. Pulling back the curtains at the side, she peered out into the dark shadows of the courtyard. She could see nothing in clear form, just outlines in a black landscape.

She folded her hands primly.

"I guess we showed him, didn't we?" she said in a low self-satisfied voice. *"We've never needed a man. Not in the past, not for the future."* The tone was prudish, self-satisfied. Underneath was a well of hatred. Always carefully hidden, of course. She'd hated now for such a long time. Most of all she hated the girl on whom she depended for life.

Blinking now, Chandal seemed to come up into a different level of reality. As if she'd lost a few seconds, maybe, of time. Yawning, she decided she felt terribly tired. She had to get some sleep if she was going to do a good reading tomorrow.

She washed carefully and dressed herself in a long-sleeved

flannel nightgown. It was a warm, comfortable gown. She had found it that morning tucked away in a bureau drawer and had washed it out. Perfect, she thought, then climbed into bed. Perfect for sleeping on a cool night.

Outside the rain began to fall quite heavily. It gave her an isolated feeling to lie there on her back and study the long shadows that cast themselves over the ceiling. Ron . . . why was she so confused about her feelings toward Ron?

Her eyes closed, then opened. She heard herself sweetly humming a familiar song. She felt anxiety slip away.

Sleep, dear. I'll sing you to sleep. You like this song, don't you?

Yes. Yes, I like this song. Her eyelids drooped again.

Abruptly Chandal sat straight up in bed. A tapping sound had roused her, some sort of a rhythmic series of taps, almost like a language.

Are you there? Tap-tap-tap.

Are you awake? Tap-tap-tap.

The taps changed to a different sort of sound now. Like fingernails being dragged across the side of the house.

Jesus. Tree branches. But, what a sound. Almost sensuous, personal in some way to her. She felt her heart pound.

There was silence. The pure heavy rain surrounded her.

"Tree branches," she murmured. Tree branches blowing against the house. She let out her breath in a long sigh that led her back toward peace. She never felt herself come to the borderline dividing wakefulness from sleep, but somehow she had passed over the boundary, because she was dreaming.

A real dream, terribly real. She heard a sound, loud, grating, like two pieces of metal being rubbed against each other. Trembling, she waited.

The door to her bedroom opened and footsteps came stealthily across the floor. She strained to see the man who stood in the shadows at the edge of the bed, staring at her. He stepped forward now, his tall, muscular body moving with a natural, animal litheness emphasized by his broad shoulders and narrow hips, until he towered over her.

Overhead there was the sound of movement again, a tapping sound. Persistent and rhythmic.

Her eyes took sharper focus. A stranger in some way, yet familiar—Mike. It was Mike. The muscles in his face strangely immobile, yet his eyes intense, hypnotic.

"Chandal, wake up," he whispered, bending over her. She stared up at him silently, noticed how his bare chest, covered with thick black hair and a light layer of sweat, moved in and out as he took deep shuddering breaths.

Repulsed, she longed to scream, to dig her fingernails into his flesh. To fight him in some way.

"Relax," he said, then sat down on the edge of the bed.

Transfixed, she watched him smile as he slid the covers from her unprotesting body. She felt his hand running up her leg, caressing her thigh. Then, very gently, his fingers moved higher.

"Aah," she sighed in greedy lust, working herself against his hand.

Then instantly a sharp thought pressed. Think, think! Chandal told herself. She was filled with frenzy. Mike mounted her. Her lungs ached for air as he began probing his erection between her legs.

Her frenzy turned to terror. She gagged and struggled against the terrible pressure against her spine. The blood rushed and pounded in her head and ears. Her limbs thrashed and jerked, wildly trying to stop Mike from entering her. A thick, syrupy liquid gushed between her thighs. She hit him. Saw that his cheek was bleeding where she had apparently clawed him. Her tongue pushed out between her teeth and then she screamed.

With a sudden wrenching of terror she came awake, streaming with perspiration that ran steadily down between her breasts and down the small of her back despite the chill of the room. Lying naked atop the sheets she felt tears begin to flood her eyes and she couldn't summon up the concentration to decide what to do next. She couldn't think or move. She could only lie there gasping for air. Her eyes were wide open and her lashes flickered out of control.

She let one hand come away from her side but so slowly it barely seemed to move. She managed to get two fingers on the light cord attached to one of the small lights beside the bed and pulled. The room suddenly jumped to life in the dim glow of a yellow forty-watt bulb. The room was empty.

Stunned, she tried to rise. She would never make it. She'd never be able to leave the bed. Small tremors ran through her body as seconds, minutes passed, while beneath her eyelids images hovered. Finally she managed to bring her feet to the floor. Then she lifted her hands, took hold of the headboard, and with a forceful lunge brought herself to her feet.

In the next instant she heard the front gate of the carriage house slam shut. The room fell into a perfect silence. Was she dreaming? Had such a vivid experience been nothing more than a dream? Then, with a rush of breath . . . Yes. It had all been a dream. She almost fainted from the sudden release of muscle tension in her legs and back.

Involuntarily she looked at the bed. The tightly bunched sheets were wet. Still she was motionless. She couldn't remember all of the dream now. Only the beginning. Mike's face. A face she despised.

Silently she began to move, until she found herself huddled on the couch in the living room. She had put on every light in the house. Poised with a cigarette dangling from between her fingers, riveted with anticipation, she glanced at her watch. It was a little past three. She waited.

Somewhere around four o'clock she finally managed to return to bed, where she lay sleepless, obsessed with images. And something else. With some feeling inside of herself she couldn't understand. Something that drew great pleasure in remembering Mike's face.

After a while she let all thought slip from her mind and dropped into a deep dreamless sleep. The last thing she saw was a bony bloodless hand covering her eyes against a circular flood of light that shone down on her from the fifth-floor window of the brownstone.

CHAPTER SEVEN

"DAMN!" SHE MUMBLED THROUGH DUST-DRY LIPS, BUT HIT THE alarm button cleanly, uncompromisingly, then sat up straight in bed. Her mouth tasted of stale cigarettes, and a general stiffness had worked its way through her body.

Chandal paused for a moment. Her sleep-befogged brain was trying to make some sort of sense, as she slouched forward. It was morning now, not night. "I'll never make it," she groaned, as her feet smacked the cold floor.

Face down, she let her fingers begin to work gently through her fine brown hair. Then she groped for her robe, drew it forward, sliding her arms into the sleeves. Somehow she managed to free her body from the hypnotism of the bed that pulled at her to lie down, just for another half hour, to curl up in a fetal position, to be warm . . . sleep.

"No," she mumbled, rose and shuffled in slow motion to the door. She rocked lightly back on her feet, reluctant to go down the stairs. The banister, a sleek hand-carved wooden affair, offered something to cling to. Years of hands brushing the wood had polished its surface to a high sheen, a sheen that bespoke numerous comings and goings. Of life on the move. Discipline, she reminded herself. You must have discipline.

Eyes barely open, she descended the stairs. Through heavy-lidded slits she groped her way into the bathroom. "Umph." Now she faced herself in the mirror, as she held onto the sink with both hands and prayed for the curtain to lift in her brain.

"Mi-mi-mi-mi-hummm!" she hummed loudly and noticed that she looked gritty from lack of sleep. The kind of grit that didn't scrub off even with the liberal punishment of a luffa sponge, but rather had to be slept off. Even the mere thought of sleep drew a sustained "ahh" from between her lips. She bent forward and turned on the taps over the tub.

"Oh, God, you beautiful thing, you're going to be marvelous in that reading today. 'Sister Susie shelled seashells by the seashore.' Listen to those sibilant esses. Always, Chandal, always you have sibilant esses after a sleepless night. Especially, you ass, when you fill the hours by chain-smoking. Well, you'll learn, you'll learn," she grumbled. She squirted toothpaste liberally onto her brush, then brushed, rinsed, brushed again, then closed the bathroom door to trap the steam.

Still fighting back her drowsiness, she studied her face through the mist that had started to form on the mirror. *"It will be okay. We will be okay,"* the voice whispered. Then, abruptly, she felt the incandescent flash of last night's dream cross her mind. She would never have believed that a dream could be so real. Images continued to form and for a moment she was almost in the dream again, but she forced the images away by concentrating on her own ghostly grimace glaring back at her from the mirror.

"You're changing," breathed the voice in her ear.

No. No, I'm not changing! Mike's face smiled at her and her breathing quickened. Anyway, what if I am changing? So what?

Slowly she let her robe fall to the floor and stepped into the tub. She soaked, took great pleasure in shaving her underarms and every inch of her legs, a job she usually hurried through.

Later, standing naked before the bedroom mirror, she wondered. Have I changed? Don't overanalyze, she warned herself and reached for her pendant. She held the chain at eye level and allowed the stone to dangle in the bright morning light that streamed through her bedroom window. Hesitantly she pressed the veined pendant to her lips. It was smooth and cool. People change, she told herself. So what?

She turned away and slipped into her panties. She enjoyed the sensation of the silken garment against her freshly scrubbed skin. Then she patted cologne on her throat, upper arms and thighs.

By the time she left the carriage house, she had achieved new vigor.

Locking the front door, she dropped the key into her shoulder bag, which was large enough to accommodate her folder of eight-by-ten glossies with résumés attached to the backs. She smiled and saw herself as she stood there in tight black pants tucked into high boots, an open-necked silk blouse, knotted green scarf and fur coat. God, she felt good. Somehow the grit and the exhaustion were all gone.

Chandal had taken only two steps when something stopped her abruptly. A primitive awareness that she was being watched. She turned quickly and glanced up at the brownstone's fifth-floor window.

The old woman's face appeared to hang suspended, framed by a rectangle of aging brick. Chandal stared at the woman plaintively. The woman smiled and beseeched Chandal with her eyes not to be sad and then—vanished. It was as though the woman had never been there.

Chandal drew back instinctively. She remembered that that particular apartment was supposed to be vacant. A Polish woman had lived there at one time but she had died. At least that's what Miss Ramsey had said.

Still wrapped in thought, Chandal nearly bumped into the mailman at the outer gate. The man looked at her inquiringly, started to speak, but Chandal merely raised her hand in a brief wave and moved rapidly away.

Wasn't that the same woman she had seen on Thursday? Staring at her from the front door of the brownstone? Then, in a quick return to a carefree attitude, she thought, who cares? Something propelled her forward until she was walking at a fast clip, her hair under a tan beret blowing in the crisp breeze. She didn't notice the admiring glances that were riveted on her, but instead concentrated on how great it was to be back in New York where the action was. So unlike indolent California where actors hustled themselves off to the beach or sat by their swimming pools waiting for their phones to ring.

She skipped lightly down the subway steps. New York was easier to get involved with. Actors could make rounds of the smaller theaters themselves. They could even make contact with a Broadway show if they knew how to go about it. New York was action!

She was more than a little excited as she emerged from the subway, crossed Broadway near Times Square, walked to Ninth Avenue and entered the dark recesses of a small pocket-size theater.

Hastily a nonentity handed her a fact sheet and told her to read it carefully. Chandal sighed, dumped her bag onto an empty chair and sat. Removing her beret, she shook out her hair, crossed her legs, and began perusing the fact sheet.

Jesus, seventy-two dollars a week—like it's a big deal—hey, don't do me any favors here, Chandal thought as the stage manager handed out sides. I can't afford this job. I'll starve. I'll have to take in three roommates in my single-occupancy illegal carriage house. Eagerly she studied the sides. God, it looks good, she thought, hungry to be on the stage again in a really good role. I hope I get it. And grinned at how badly she wanted this job that would land her in debtors' prison.

"I don't know why I bother to come to these calls," the lackluster female who sat next to her said, unfolding the *Post*. "It's cast, of course, at least our part is cast."

"Why our part?" Chandal asked, looking up from her sheet of dialogue.

"Because we're the young leading lady and the young leading lady is always sleeping with either the playwright or the director."

"Really? That's good to know," chuckled Chandal. "Maybe I can set something up for their next play."

"They're booked years in advance," the girl said, straight-faced, without looking up from her *Post*. "Now if you're thinking about the year 1990—oh, shit," she interrupted herself. "Well, that's it. The pits. Just what I needed." Moodily, she tossed aside the paper.

"What's the matter?"

"Billy Deats," the girl snapped. "It's not sour grapes or anything, but that kind of thing really makes me sick."

"I don't understand what you mean."

"What I mean is he's a rotten actor. Not even passable. Yet everything he touches turns to gold. Two Broadway hits in a row—rave reviews on bad performances—I mean, atrocious —everyone in the industry's talking about it—and now I'm reading he just signed to star in a new film. . . ."

Billy Deats, repeated Chandal in her mind and wondered why she wasn't feeling good for Billy. He had been a friend from a happy past. She remembered how Justin and Billy would play chess all night while she would fall asleep on the couch. Their Greenwich Village outings together, the parties, the crazy, unbelievable things they had done together. Good old funny charming Billy Deats. She was glad to hear that he'd made it. She was always glad to hear when a friend made it. She wasn't one of those jealous . . . Thoughtfully she reached for comb and makeup and went through the motions of fixing herself up a bit. Looking into her own eyes in the mirror, she seemed to see anger there, an anger way out of synch with anything she should be feeling. Why was she so furious at the mention of Billy Deats' name—of hearing of his success?

"Chandal Knight?" the voice bellowed.

"Yes, right here."

"We're starting on top of page sixty-two."

"Right. I have it."

"Good. You're reading for the director. Inside and turn left."

"Thanks," she breathed, then moved forward through the small door and turned left. So far she had done nothing wrong. A few more steps and she found herself standing on a tiny stage ominously lit by one bare bulb clamped to a stepladder.

She shielded her eyes from the glare and stared out into the audience.

A few seconds passed before the director caught sight of her. He smiled broadly and picked his way through a row of theater seats.

"Chandal Knight?" he asked.

"Yes."

"You have an interesting résumé. I see that you've done some film work in California."

"I prefer the stage."

"I'll see what I can do. You look right for the part."

There was something about the man that Chandal disliked. He was too sure of himself, his voice was too loud and he made even a simple remark sound like abuse.

"Just drop your things over there. I'd like to see you do the monologue on seventy-one."

"But the stage manager said sixty-two."

He smiled. "Seventy-one." His smile tightened. "Please."

Chandal moved away to the side. She was surprised to find herself trembling as she dropped her coat and shoulder bag on the chair. The authority which he exuded overwhelmed her, and a wave of nausea broke in the pit of her stomach.

"I'm waiting," he snapped from the back of the theater.

"Ah, there seems to be a mistake."

"Mistake?"

"I'm here to read for Sara. Seventy-one is . . ."

"Rachel. That's right. I would prefer that you read for Rachel," he said in a bored tone.

Chandal shook her head. Rachel?

"Would you prefer not to read, Miss Knight? It is Miss, isn't it?"

"Ah." She held up her hand again, the light causing her to flinch. "Yes—*Miss*."

"Well?"

"Well, what?" she challenged.

"Would you prefer not to read for the part?"

"I'll read for any goddamn part you've got!" she exclaimed.

"Good," he replied.

By the time Chandal had reached center stage, everything including her stomach had settled down. Having decided, she was prepared to act the hell out of the role. Control, she reminded herself, and began the speech. She felt a great rush of excitement as the words poured from her mouth. Her eyes sharpened with contempt as she screamed.

"People! A bunch of animals who know nothing. Pig-grunts for talk, pig-squeals for laughter. Crude-faced men. Plump women showing off their fat and calling it cleavage. They know nothing, I tell you!" she cried bitterly, the speech rolling from her lips like poisoned honey. She was on fire now. As if by remote control, she turned the page, punched forward in a rush of foul language, and concluded the speech midway down the page with an ironic smile.

She paused, breathless, her heart pounding, the script glued to her sweating palm. She stared out at the director. She could sense that he had not been disappointed. Yet his face remained like a steel mask.

73

"Thank you," he said shortly. "You'll be hearing from me."

"Thanks," Chandal said and pushed her way off the stage. Jesus, she felt great. Really great!

"And now, recapping today's headlines," the news broadcaster's voice continued, but Ron Talon was not listening.

Eight thousand Btu's of conditioned air cooled the bedroom, drying the moisture on Ron's naked body. He wiped the last of the sleep from his eyes and reached for the towel.

Two cups of coffee and a shower had put him back into reality, just where he wasn't altogether sure he wanted to be. He knew his conversation with Chandal last night had been a bummer. She had sounded so obviously happy about her new carriage house, so innocently greedy for every small joy, that it was impossible to entertain a disturbed thought while she was speaking to him of her successes.

However, when he had mentioned love, the future, her career, she seemed uneasy. And so it went—the private grieving for a girl he knew was making a goddamn mistake!

For a single, angry moment he was tempted to forget the whole damn thing. Ron Talon was too sharp a guy to be snubbed without good reason. Better to forget her and be done with it.

"Shit!" he scowled and knew that to forget Chandal would be impossible. He wrapped the towel around his body and moved to the dresser. He had propped the crucifix against the mirror. He studied it for a moment, then looked up at his own image in the glass. What the hell was bothering him?

Something about the face on the Christ figure. Was he imagining it, or had the face changed in some way?

The crucifix felt warm to the touch as he took it up and held it in the palm of his hand. Now a feeling of nausea pushed up into the base of his throat.

With a small forced laugh, he tossed the crucifix face down on top of the dresser and strode into the living room. Nervously he dropped on the couch and drew a cigarette from the glass case on the table. He stayed still for a minute, puffing away, and then he glanced out the window. Usually he would take time to pause over two poached eggs with bacon and get things aligned, but not this morning. This morning he'd lost his appetite. He puffed again. His mind wandered. Now he shivered, somebody stepping on his grave, no doubt.

The announcer paused. "Cloudy today with possible rain late afternoon, temperatures in the mid-eighties. . . ."

Ron reached out and flicked off the radio. Puffing on his cigarette, he hurried to dress. His mind was still racing, his thoughts focused dead center on the crucifix. "Damn," he muttered.

He was drawn once again to the dresser. He stood in silence for a minute or two, staring at the crucifix. He began to feel a weakening of thought. It might be better, no matter what happened, to accept everything, to acquiesce where Chandal's demands were concerned.

He leaned against the dresser, waiting for some savage rebuttal, some power within him to scream: No! Make her see reason! But the power, if it had been there, had been extinguished.

Seconds later he emerged from the bedroom with his blue blazer over his arm and a twenty-dollar bill in his hand. The money was for the cleaning lady, a cheery woman who appeared Monday and Thursday mornings and seemed, with a simple flick of her wrist, to turn chaos into order. He stuffed the bill under the vase on the hall table. Out of simple habit of living alone, he took a last look around.

The house stood hushed, a faint flicker of morning light streaming through the Venetian blinds, casting rows of harsh lines across the living room carpet.

Ron sighed, flipped his blazer over his shoulder, and started out. There was nothing he could do about Chandal now but wait. His thoughts shifted to business matters as he locked the front door and strode toward his Jag. But still, a faint image of Chandal lingered in the back of his mind.

Laughing softly to herself, Chandal swung out the theater door. Contented and carefree, she made her way halfway up the block, then ducked into a phone booth to call Thelma Rose, the agent who had set up the reading.

"Thelma, this is Chandal."

"Chandal who?" grumbled the hurried voice. "Dear, I'm busy. I'm very busy today."

"You sent me for the reading at the Pilot Theatre. Chandal Knight."

"Oh, did I? How did it go?" The voice relaxed slightly.

"I think I'm going to get the part."

"Did the director commit himself?" asked the voice, alive now with interest.

"Not exactly. But he's going to call me back and—"

"That's good. But that's hardly the same thing as getting the part."

"Thelma, I know I'm getting the part. Don't ask me how I know, but—"

"Dear, my phone's ringing off the hook. Call me tomorrow. What was your name?"

"Chandal Knight. K-N-I-G-H-T."

"Thanks for calling. Maybe I'll have something else for you tomorrow."

Lesson one on how to get thick with a New York agent, Chandal mused, as she took quick sidesteps among the walkers, covering the pavement in a series of swift, darting strides that brushed past drooping onrushing flanks of human animals. Make the agent think you're valuable. By the time she finds out you're probably not going to get the part, maybe she'll get you another part. A soap or a commercial or a Broadway play. Chandal could not contain her joy, her optimism.

With a sharp gesture, she threw up her arms and yelled, "Yay!" Her voice resounded up, down and across Broadway, rose in full-bodied vigor over the roar of traffic. The only person who turned to look at her was a young man who carried a trombone case in one hand and a lighted joint in the other.

"Hey," he whispered, winking, "you want to get stoned?"

Smiling broadly, she strode past him up Broadway. She felt better than she had in days. Weeks! The smell of success had aroused her in a way that she had not experienced since her college days, since even before that, when she was a little girl doing her dance for Aunt Mildred.

Success would take some time, she knew that. But she was willing to wait, and that made her feel good.

It wasn't until she stood in the Drama Book Shop, while glancing through monologues for women that, for the first time, it hit her. She drew in her breath sharply and the slim manuscript slid from between her fingers to the floor.

Incredible, she shuddered to herself. Or rather, impossible. How had she come to forget? The old fear that had kept her off the stage for at least eight years. The nauseating panic, so acute, that she had actually refused to make an entrance. Then, the word had gone out. Nobody would hire her. For that matter, she had been too frightened to take a chance on herself.

Someone tapped her on the shoulder. "Here. You dropped this."

"Thanks," she managed to reply without any clear focus and felt the play book shoved back into her hand.

It was the stage fright, she remembered, that had first made her want to leave New York. To go to California. She and Justin had intended to go to Hollywood.

"Yes!" she whispered and remembered that much clearly. What she couldn't remember was why they hadn't gone. Why had they stayed?

But as she automatically went through her day—lunch at Chock Full O'Nuts, ballet and modern dance at Carnegie Hall, a quick stop at the Equity lounge—the thought that stayed with her was that she had somehow forgotten what should have been impossible to forget. The stage fright. The damned stage fright. And not far behind this recurring phrase in her mind, teased another worry. What if she were to get a part? Could she take it? Would she dare take the chance again?

She wandered now into several agents' offices where she was received with hostility or not at all. Their rudeness made no impression on her. She was wrapped in her own thoughts. Christ. Stage fright.

At a small dance shop she bought black tights—Lord, $9.98—and ended up in front of the Booth Theatre where a poster-size picture of Billy Deats jumped out at her.

She glanced at her watch—6:45 P.M.

Why not, she shrugged, and purchased a ticket. Rear balcony, the cheapest seat available. It gave her a charge to be seeing a Broadway show again, the black-skirted, white-collared ushers who handed out playbills, the murmur of the growing crowd, the knowledge that, Jesus, this was Broadway. Broadway!

Chandal settled back in her seat as the lights dimmed and

thought—"Give 'em hell, Billy—" and knew sixty seconds into the play that it was going to be one of those deadly, embarrassing theater situations with the acting so bad as to make people slide down in their seats. Billy himself was the worst of the lot—so bad as to make empathic sweat pop out on the back of her neck—and she could only reflect that opening night must have been one of those magical transforming performances that occasionally occur in the theater.

Here and there giggles rippled through the audience at inappropriate times, more often sighs of boredom or disgusted grunts from patrons who had spent good money for tickets. From time to time, people walked out.

After the show had dragged to a conclusion of sorts, she dreaded the curtain call, but relaxed when Billy walked out to accept his lukewarm, but polite applause. He stood center stage with a beaming smile and no awareness whatsoever of how dreadful he had been.

Chandal pounded her hands together loudly and didn't care that people glanced at her with raised eyebrows. Here's to you, Billy. Here's to a guy who made it even without that much talent. And chuckled at her immediate relief in the thought that now Billy was moving on to films and would never need embarrass himself again. His acting would look a hell of a lot better on film.

She blended into the crowd that poured out in an orderly fashion from the four center theater doors. A few celebrities were in the audience; one she recognized as Joan something. Last name beginning with a T. Tanner, or Tessman or something. The crowd murmured as Joan T. swept through the door clad in a tight black, glittering-with-diamonds gown, on the arm of an anonymous bronzed god. A photographer appeared suddenly, cried, "Joan! Here, Joan!" as she signed her name into the book of a known autograph seeker, a man who knew everyone and had spent uncounted years adding to his vast collection of signatures.

Joan T. posed with the autograph book, smiled and then waved as laughingly, her escort pulled her into a waiting limo, the chauffeur dutifully closing the door behind them.

The parade of theatergoers continued uninterrupted, hats and coats donned in mid-stride, a burst of laughter, a pipe lighted, a cab hailed, until Chandal laughed and gestured to the doorman that she would wait at the corner for Billy Deats.

"He's always the last to leave," the man said good-naturedly.

"I don't mind. I have all night." She had a sudden thought. "Is anyone else waiting for him?"

"Not that I know of, Miss. He's a loner."

"A loner? Billy?"

"Excuse me." The doorman turned away apologetically to try to expedite a taxicab jam. Three different parties were fighting over two cabs.

"Who are you?" asked a voice suddenly. "Are you anybody?"

Chandal considered that as she smilingly studied the face of the professional autograph seeker.

"No," she decided finally. "I guess to you I'm not. I'm nobody."

She knew by the flash of surprise in his eyes that he was seldom wrong and took satisfaction in the fact that he had mistaken her for a celebrity. That had to mean that somewhere along the way she had picked up "Star Quality."

Giggling to herself, she stepped further back and imagined coming face-to-face with Billy. Thank God, she never felt obligated to tell actor friends the truth about bad performances. Her wide-sweeping rule was: If you go back stage, tell everyone you meet that they were marvelous. If you can't swallow that, don't go back stage.

Billy would, without a doubt, be delighted to see her and she . . . She bit her lip and remembered how it used to be when she and Justin were dating. Sometimes—God, so many times—Billy was there. Either as a threesome, with Billy as a single, or as a foursome, with Billy seldom taking out the same woman more than twice. Uneasily she focused on that mental picture of Billy, Justin and herself, and she wondered why she didn't think of Justin that often. And had never really experienced the kind of grief she should have since his death.

Almost wonderingly she watched Billy drop from the picture in her mind and now she concentrated on the tiny image of Justin and Chandal, looking at each other with so much love. And yet she couldn't feel that love anymore, not even now, when she tried to summon it. She could only look rather blankly as the two remembered lovers leaned toward each other, touched, kissed in a special private manner.

"Why can't I grieve?" she had asked Dr. Luther. "I should grieve, shouldn't I? I loved Justin. I know I loved him." Dr. Luther had shrugged and talked about "incomplete mourning" as though it were a usual thing, a defense mechanism used by many people, not just her.

But it would be good, yes, wonderful, to see Billy Deats again. Involved in her own thoughts, she had completely missed Billy as he came from the backstage door. She blinked, saw him climb into the back seat of a black limo, and began to call, wave her arms and run toward him.

There was an instant now that seemed to her later to have happened in slow motion. Herself in a long graceful stride that for a moment held her in midair, her long flowing hair gliding like smoke behind her. In front of her Billy turned, also held in a freeze position. Plainly he was caught off guard. In that moment his eyes locked into hers. Shock, even panic. Something passed between them, an undercurrent. Something, not exactly hostile, but almost a backlash of fear.

"Billy!" she screamed and the moment was broken.

Hurriedly he slid into the car, his face now composed, expressionless, and slammed the door behind him. Slowly the limo merged into traffic.

"Billy!" she screamed and leaped into the street. With her fists she pounded on the car window. Deliberately he turned his head in the opposite direction as the car inched forward, wedged in by other cars.

"Billy!" she yelled and found her arms being firmly held. She turned in shock to face a policeman who remonstrated gently with her.

"Miss, you can't do things like that. . . ."

"He's a goddamn friend of mine!" she gulped and couldn't believe the tears that began to run down her cheeks.

"Oh, I see," the cop said, turning her arms loose. "That's the way it is, I guess. When they get that big, well . . . Don't do that sort of thing again though, huh?"

"Okay, thanks," she murmured and forced herself forward, a strange certainty forming in her mind. In some way, at some time in the past, Billy had let her down. An image. Herself dialing. "Billy, I need help." The help had never come.

And with the image, a vague piece of her past dropped into place.

CHAPTER EIGHT

CITY BLOCKS DISAPPEARED, GROUND OUT UNDER HER BOOT heels. The tears were gone. Left behind somewhere in the neighborhood of the Booth Theatre, or the Majestic, or the Belasco.

It wasn't until Chandal stood at the outer gate to the courtyard that she had a sudden puzzling thought. Then she wondered why it had taken her so long to come to it. Billy had let her down in some way, she remembered that much. But the fear on his face—surely that didn't compute. No, the fear made no sense.

The gate latch felt cold against her fingers as she released it. Billy's face—not the face of an actor on a success trip, nor arrogance, nothing like that. But fear.

"A loner," the doorman had said. Billy had never been a loner in his life. He had been a hanger-outer. One of the crowd at the Sacred Cow or Joe Allen's. She closed the heavy steel gate carefully behind her.

Lost in thought, she walked slowly, her heels hollow against the flagstone. Breathing the wet air of the night, air that blew lightly over the dark city roofs and then dropped swiftly, turning the courtyard into a mild vortex, she felt the key slip easily into its lock and reached for the door.

"Chandal?"

"What?" She turned sharply and came face to face with Mike Hammer. "My God," she breathed. "You scared me to death."

82

"I'm sorry." His face, shadow-soft and relaxed, smiled over her.

"How did you . . . I didn't see you."

"The basement door. I noticed your light was out. I came over to put in a new bulb," he said and grinned with the air of a magician as he produced a lightbulb from his jacket pocket. "It'll only take a second."

Mike moved closer to her now as he reached up and unscrewed the defective bulb. In the almost complete darkness she felt like a small figure lost in the huge shadow of his body. His breathing grew louder as he reached up and screwed in the new bulb.

"It could have waited until the morning," she said in annoyance. "I'm sure . . ." She broke off, her breath caught in a short gasp. The sudden glare of the unshaded bulb shone directly onto Mike's face, and Chandal noticed at once the deep gash, raw and purple, on his right cheek.

He turned and their eyes welded.

"There, that should do it." He smiled.

"Thanks," she said coldly and turned to let herself into the carriage house.

She felt Mike's hand grope at her arm.

"I hope I didn't wake you up last night," he said.

"I . . . I don't understand," she stammered, and awkwardly removed her arm from his grasp.

There was a long silence. Chandal watched Mike's deformed hand run nervously up and down his trouser leg. The courtyard about them was silent, as if everyone in New York slept or were standing about quietly watching.

"The outside gate," he mumbled. "The damn thing kept blowing open. It's supposed to lock automatically." He shrugged. "I thought maybe you heard me hammering away out there."

"Is that what that was?" She let out a pent-up sigh. "I thought it was the tree branches."

"That too, I guess. It blew up pretty strong last night."

A glistening darkness swallowed them. Blackness lit by shimmers of water droplets illumined by moonglow. Even the trees shone like wet distorted skeletons and an old cobweb on the grillwork of the window looked like black gossamer.

"I guess I owe you an apology for yesterday," he said softly.

Chandal stared at him without answering.

"I was just tired," he explained. "That's all. Just tired."

"It happens, I guess."

Mike watched her for a moment. Then he said wryly, "I know what you're thinking. You're thinking that I . . ."

"How did you get that scratch?" Chandal interrupted.

"What, this?" His hand reached to his face. "A damned cat. A stray in the building."

"Oh. I—I just wondered. It looks like a nasty cut."

"It's not bad." He stepped aside under the dim bulb, the downthrust shadows of his hair and nose casting deep, penetrating patterns over his face, as if attempting to hide in the dark recesses of the wall. "Well, like I said, sorry about yesterday. Goodnight."

"Goodnight."

Mike hesitated, something curiously watchful in his intense eyes. She felt drawn to meet his gaze and then, as she did so, she had a falling-away sensation, a blurring of consciousness, as though she was on the verge of fainting. With a great effort she fought off the feeling, straightened her posture and returned Mike's stare. He nodded slightly, almost as though he had received a signal, and faded away into a vaguely blinding mist.

She watched his shadowy figure descend the basement stairs, pulling the outer door closed behind him. Only when he had gone could she see clearly again. Still, a feeling of nakedness and vulnerability remained in his wake.

Entering the carriage house, she flicked on the living room light. The room warmed a little under the glow of the Tiffany lamp, and she had the sudden sensation of being welcomed, as though the house reached out to pull her forward. It calmed her, separated her from the outside world.

Still wearing her coat, she wandered through the room, and propped herself against the door frame of the den. What was it she had happened to call this small damp room . . . just yesterday morning? The words had come idly into her mind—the room that wept. She smiled at this romanticism for mildew. And yet . . ."

She turned her back on the room. After hanging her coat in the closet, she made tea and toast, swept up a pail and rag which had been left in the middle of the kitchen floor, and deliberated whether or not to call Ron. She reached for the phone, dialed 1 and the area code, then angrily slammed the receiver down.

Lately, the moment she concentrated on Ron, she was filled with anger, but had no idea where it came from or what to do with it. Love, and longing in one breath, and in the next the feeling being transformed into near hatred. She couldn't understand it, she decided, as she sipped at her tea and nibbled at her toast, burnt just the way she liked it.

For an instant she could remember very clearly the tenderness and the passion Ron had been able to arouse in her so easily. There had been times when the last remaining barrier between them had seemed paper-thin and she had been on the verge of giving herself to him completely. Saying words that could not be easily taken back. Something had always stopped her. And now, perhaps, she would never be able to find her way back to him. What the hell is happening? she wondered, but she could not hang onto the urgency of the thought. She found her attention divided; other matters compelled her interest. She had no control of it. It was as though she were standing at a crossroads with arrows pointing in two different directions. She could not choose which way to go and obstinately decided to take both courses, running back and forth between the separate paths.

But then, she considered, her day-to-day life seemed to be like that lately. She found her emotions running along two main streams. She took great delight in acting again, in fixing up the carriage house. In little details of clothing that she had never considered before. She also took great joy in compliments, embracing praise and flattery.

The other stream was a feeling of bitterness that drove her into rages, until she could only feel a deadness in herself, a void from which it was almost impossible to emerge.

Absently, she ran her hand across her forehead, then massaged her temples. Finally, in a state of numbness, she took a hot bath and got into her nightgown. Her skin was slightly damp, now, with warm sweat. She felt herself slipping deeper into a dreamlike state and roused herself to get a book. Something to focus her attention on. Her eyelids felt heavy as she curled up on the living room couch and opened the cover. Such an old book. Something from the book shelf in the corner of the den. She read for a while without remembering what she read. The words wouldn't stick. She kept losing her place and having to backtrack. Then there were isolated unrelated thoughts: A fire in the fireplace would be so nice. One of those huge logs that burned for a long time. The way it used to be . . . no, she had never been here before. . . . Let's see, where was she? She couldn't remember a word she'd read.

After about half an hour, Chandal knew that somewhere within the carriage house was an odd sound. At first, when she heard it, her consciousness did not register it as sound. It was so faint, it might have been only a feeling, or an automatic functioning of her body, blinking, or her heart beating in her chest cavity. It was the absolute stillness that left her sensitive to every murmur. But as the sound persisted, she began to isolate it. She sat perfectly still as the sound grew louder. By degrees. Yes, it had grown louder.

What is that? she wondered. She could not identify the sound. And she realized now that it was not coming from any particular source. Not from the kitchen, nor the den, nor upstairs from the bedroom. Instead, it seemed to be coming from all directions at once.

After several minutes she clenched her fists and bit her lip with the effort of forcing herself to listen harder. The den. Yes, she was sure the sound was coming from the den. She turned resolutely to the small door, determined to discover what the sound was. Crying. . . . A baby crying.

She approached the door. Yet, at the last second, in spite of herself, she averted her hand. A sudden exhaustion overtook her, propelled her downward within as though she had stepped into an elevator and descended into the bowels of the earth. It was a dark place, a place where one forgot certain things such as identity, a place where one lost one's will. Where one ceased to be.

She sat back on the edge of the bed and watched the candlelight flicker against the sharp features of the old woman's face. The old woman's eyes were alive, deep blue and hypnotic, yet the rest of her body appeared dead.

Chandal wondered if she was dreaming. Who was the woman? It was as if she were experiencing double vision. Around the woman, two little faces appeared. Children.

"She's dead," one little girl said.

"No, she's just sleeping."

"No, Mother said she's dead. That's why Father is crying."

"He loves her?"

"I think."

Chandal sat riveted. She was in shock. She watched as the two girls played with the woman's body. Pulled at her. Played with her face and hands.

"Kiss her," the older of the two girls said.

"No."

"I said kiss her!" She forced the girl's face against the lips of the old woman.

"Please," the girl screamed and began to cry.

"Shut up, Elizabeth. Mother will hear us."

"I'm going to die now!"

"I said, shut up!" She slapped the little girl.

"I'm going to die," she moaned.

"No, no, you're not. You'll never die. You'll see. We'll live forever. I promise."

"Are you sure?"

The older girl smiled. "Yes, dear sister. I promise."

The younger girl was thinking of a song. Chandal heard the song in her mind, the refrain running silently with the words:

> *Sleep, little one, and be good,*
> *The birds are all in the wood;*
> *They fly in the wood*
> *From tree to tree*
> *And soon they will bring*
> *Sweet sleep to thee.*
> *Sleep, little one, and be good.*

Chandal let her eyes fall shut.

Deep in a trance, she removed the pendant from around her neck, and then she began to rock at the edge of the bed, as though rocking in a chair, softly thumping time to the rhythm of the words she now chanted.

"May your blood turn to stone. May your bones decay and crumble."

She knew, without seeing them, that her brothers and sisters had joined her in ceremony. As the chant continued, she pointed the bloodstone westward, and rubbed its surface. She laughed with delight, knowing no medicine on earth could save him now.

CHAPTER NINE

Ron Talon skipped the cocktail party at MGM in the annex building and had a little taste of his own before heading to the Las Palmas Country Club.

He called it the Bordello Palace.

There were eight tennis courts surrounded by streets with trees, and walls that concealed swimming pools, private sea worlds and houses that might have been built by Ali Baba and the Forty Thieves.

All the courts were occupied, mostly by the local pros, except for one court to the far right, in which some children were racing about, yelling. On the far left, closest to the clubhouse, was Ron himself.

"Deuce again," he grunted and wiped the sweat from his forehead. He placed his toe on the foul line and prepared to serve. The sun was beginning to set, yet the heat persisted and wrung large beads of moisture from his brow, shoulders and back. Sporting a full day's growth of beard, he looked like a construction worker.

It was Friday, the 27th of March.

Angrily, Ron flung the ball into the air, and smashed his racket down hard, knocking the ball five feet out of the court.

"Out!"

"Right," Ron grumbled.

He dug a second ball from his pocket and felt a slight, nagging flutter of heart. What the hell are you so nervous about, he asked himself. The guy has the best backhand in

California. It's only right that he should win. Still, Ron really hadn't been prepared to lose seven games in a row. He had never lost seven games in a row, and despite his gracefulness on the court, there did not seem to be much of a chance for his making a comeback.

"Just a minute," Ron said and stepped off the line. With one violent tug he removed his tennis shirt. The heat was really starting to get to him.

"Hey!" the big guy's voice roared. "No stripping!" Then the voice laughed.

Determinedly Ron strode forward, planted his foot solidly on the line. Up went the ball, down came his racket, out of the court went the ball.

"My ad," the voice said with a smile.

Ron shook his head and asked, "Can I take it again?"

"No!"

"So that's how the game is played, is it? Thanks a lot, Paul!" He reached for another ball.

He had just completed the second of two more bad serves when someone hollered, "Ron Talon—telephone!"

In the same instant Paul hollered, "Game!" His racket went whirling up in the air and he caught it neatly as Ron reached for his shirt.

"One more game?" Paul asked.

"Right!" Ron grunted and headed for the pro shop, leaving the big guy hunched on one elbow under a tree, chewing on his gum and smiling.

Ron walked quickly through a row of canopied tables, past a group of tourists sipping vodka gimlets, past the Hollywood studs with unbuttoned shirts and gold medallions hanging on their hairy chests, and two or three gorgeous women with Palm Springs suntans. The women in L.A., Ron mused, tended to make the women in other parts of the country look less . . . what was the word? Wholesome. That was it exactly.

"Fuck him!" one of the Palm Springs goddesses cried. "Let him wait."

Ron flinched, smiling at his last thought. Then he ducked inside through a huge sliding glass door, where he was immediately smacked in the face with a burst of conditioned air. He gasped, caught his breath and reached for the phone.

"Hello," he said as he wiped his face with a towel.

"Ronald, it's Mimi."

Something was wrong. Mimi never addressed him as Ronald unless something was wrong.

"What's wrong?" he asked.

"Paramount just called. They're refusing to sign McCracken's contract."

"Did they give you a reason?"

"No. They want to discuss it with you personally."

"Damn!" He dabbed his forehead again with the towel and then tossed it aside, thinking: That's what I get for handling a shit-kicker nightclub performer. Circles of black formed in front of his eyes. He blinked them away.

"Anything else?" he asked weakly.

"Wooder wanted to know why there were three hundred dollars' worth of telephone charges deducted from her last royalty check. She claimed it should have been no more than a hundred."

"What did you tell her?"

"That she was welcome to look at the slips."

"And?"

"She threw a fit, naturally."

"Naturally."

"And you had a call from a doctor—" she stopped herself, —"let's see. Oh, here it is. Dr. I. Luther. Returning your call."

"Oh, Jesus. I've been waiting for that call all week. Did you tell him I was here?"

"No. But I told him you could be reached at home around seven. I told him to call collect."

"Good." Ron glanced at his watch. 5:05 P.M. "Mimi, I've gotta run. And thanks."

Dr. Luther was the last person Ron had expected to hear from today. He could not hide his perplexity. What dominated his mind, as he returned to the courts, was total comprehension of the void he now felt and the difficulty in sustaining any semblance of his normal life style. His whole body, like his mind, seemed to have been suddenly set adrift.

The big guy's smile broadened when Ron announced that another game was out of the question. "Oh, well," he said. "There's always paddle ball."

"You know something, Paul?" Ron said. "Even though you're a prince on the court now, someday all your sneakers are going to have holes in them!"

The big guy didn't say anything. He merely smiled and sipped his freshly acquired gin and tonic.

Ron bent and scooped up his racket. In the next instant a dizziness assaulted him. He reached for the net post, his head spinning. His legs started to give way as if his limbs had suddenly been amputated.

"Say, buddy—you all right?"

"It's this fucking heat. I think I must be dehydrated or something."

"Get yourself some salt tablets."

"Right," Ron grunted and straightened up. Fighting back the dizziness, he turned.

"You really should sit down. You don't look good."

Ron's impulse was to move. "See you tomorrow," he said. Unsteadily he walked down the curving pathway, lost himself in the shadow of the tall trimmed hedges and came to his car. He tossed his racket into the passenger seat and stepped in. Without clear thought, he aimed the Jaguar toward home.

Scrawny flocks of pigeons scattered over the rooftop. Through the gray matter of her brain.

At some time or other in Chandal's early life, she had become acutely aware of time passing. Perhaps it was a sharp stirring of an autumn breeze at the end of what she had considered an endless hot summer. Time for school, time to buy winter clothes, no more grapes from the vine, they're gone for another year. "I don't want to grow up!" She had recognized the futility of her own plea and turned away before her mother had to deal with another unsolvable life issue.

Now today, it was a softer breeze with a stunning hint of balminess that warned her that once again the seasons were about to change, that time waited for no man's permission, but merely passed. Time passes, Chandal reflected wryly, as she stood by the open window, and I am obsessed.

Today, it was the Billy Deats issue again. On the one hand, forget him. Write him off as an old friend down the drain, who gives a damn anyway. On the other hand, Billy's good-natured face seemed to swim before her eyes as an old friend she had no right to forget. If she wrote off Billy, it was writing off Justin's best friend. It was almost like writing off

Justin in a way. She concentrated on the image of Billy in her mind. His eyes seemed to darken. His mouth hardened.

Suddenly she had a flash of memory. Someone had been talking about Billy Deats. *Billy has been ours for some time,* the voice had said. *He belongs to us now.* Puzzled, Chandal drew her eyebrows together. What sort of sense did that make? She shrugged and let the image go.

"Billy Deats," repeated Chandal into the telephone receiver. "That's his professional name, yes. Thank you, I'll hold." She paced the length of the room slowly, carrying the white princess phone with her. Her eyes kept returning to the courtyard, where delicious light mist lingered. An evanescent distillation, gentle. The rain had stopped sometime during the morning, and she thought, it's going to be another beautiful day.

"I'm sorry," the voice shrilled in her ear. "We don't have a Billy Deats listed."

"That's impossible. He's starring on Broadway. He has to belong to your union."

"How is the last name spelled?"

"Deats. D-E-A-T-S."

"Oh. E-A. I've been spelling it E-E. Just a minute."

Leaning her elbows against the window frame, Chandal let her gaze follow the branches of the tree upward. An image of herself in jeans, book in hand, climbing up to read out loud. To play all the different characters in the story. When had acting become something else? An ego trip, where one only wanted to be good to win compliments. Why now when she pictured herself acting, was the praise spun honey, not the excellence of the work?

Even now she shivered with delight to think of herself giving a brilliant performance and winning the admiration of her peers. More, she wanted more. Her eyes were as vague now as the tenuous wisps of fog that slipped by in gently writhing mutation against a sea of blue sky, dissipating slowly.

"Just—too—much," she said aloud in a slow, fierce voice. She pressed her finger to the receiver button several times. "Hello! Oh, shit!"

"Yes, I'm here."

"Billy Deats, is he listed?"

"Yes, but there isn't a phone number."

"You're membership, aren't you?"

"Yes."

"How would you reach him if you needed to?"

"We have an address, but I can't give it to you."

Chandal paused, feeling in some inner chamber the anger build up to the point of explosion. "Would you," she ground her teeth, "have given me the telephone number if you had found it?"

"No, I'm sorry. That would have been privileged information."

"Oh, Jesus!"

"Are you being sarcastic?" inquired the voice sharply.

"No, just amazed!" Just amazed as all hell, she repeated to herself, and slammed down the receiver. But then all human beings amazed her. Including herself. Most of all herself. Like those spurts of crazy energy that had led her around the city these last three days at desperate speed, even after almost sleepless nights. She knew this frenetic energy wasn't good. It was almost like being on uppers. And yet she couldn't hold herself down. Shopping sprees, interviews, voice lessons and dance classes.

She remembered one super-charged dance exercise where she was all over the place, jumping higher and further, extending wider, deeper and taller, spinning two for one faster than anyone else in the class. "What do you think?" she'd asked rather uncertainly, seeing the instructor's eyes on her. "Well," he'd replied with irony, "you'll never be in a chorus line." Meaning that she couldn't blend into a group, that she was attracting attention to herself by doing everything a little different from everyone else.

In back of all this outward energy was something else. A vague apprehension that somehow she was losing control of her life. There were moments when she was completely herself, and then, immediately afterward, she would discover she'd lost time. That an hour, sometimes more, would have disappeared and no way could she remember what had happened.

Yet there had been images. Images that had started to form a pattern, and then fled. Disquieting images. Images that conflicted, and confused her. As though parts from separate jigsaw puzzles had been scrambled together. One puzzle was hard enough, but two . . . The look on Billy's face. Her own indifference about Justin. The children in her dream, who were they? She had seemed to know them so well, as if their childhood were part of her own intimate memory.

Chandal leaned forward now and sat on the window ledge. Tiny puffs of breeze blew against her neck, against the folds at the open throat of her silk blouse, caressing the flesh delicately, stirring her to shiver with a sudden pleasure, and then, in the next instant, fear.

Sooner or later we all turn homeward. Chandal felt the impulse in her blood. As if she were possessed by an instinctive urge to return to the brownstone. To relive the night of the fire. The days and weeks prior to the fire.

Lately the urge had become so great that she seemed to be levitated by her own frenzy. It was as though she were expecting to find absolution among the ruins. A self-deliverance of sorts.

Yet in spite of this awareness and her reasonable efforts to return home, to remember those days, there was also within her an emotional stampede in the opposite direction. A cold, sinking sensation, like a stomach cramp, came over her. And a voice within her that whispered: *Stay away, you don't want to know. Stay away.*

Chandal had to remind herself that she had always been a somewhat sedentary person who responded slowly, perhaps belatedly, to change, to big upheavals. Yes, she reassured herself. She had only been in New York eleven days. She needed to give herself time to adjust, that was all. Perhaps in a week or so she would return to the brownstone. Face it. Accept what the confrontation had to offer, and then get on with her life.

Still, the gentle breeze that now caressed her cheeks, felt something akin to the lull before the storm.

"Hey, whatcha doing hanging in the window?" Doreen bobbed into sight from around the corner of the brownstone, her khaki culottes emphasizing legs a bit too thick at the knee, legs that tripped along on dainty narrow feet, as if the feet components had been stolen from a china doll and affixed to a knobby-kneed Raggedy Ann. A bright blouse further emphasized the rag doll quality, and red teased curls completed the image. Doreen's pale face was, however, intensely human and vulnerable. In it the only bright splash of color was made by her vividly painted, deeply bowed lips.

"It's a gorgeous day!" cried Chandal.

"It's the time of year for spring colds."

"Bitch, bitch, bitch," mocked Chandal lightly.

"Can I come in?"

"You'll be doing me a favor if you do, because believe me, there's something very frightening in here."

Doreen's eyes widened. "What do you mean?"

"Come in, come in," Chandal said uneasily and added, "One look is worth a thousand words!"

Doreen had disappeared from view and had begun to tap at the door before Chandal had finished speaking. Opening the door, Chandal dragged her forward by the crook of her elbow and left her standing in a mound of tissue paper, boxes, packages and a dozen shopping bags which were strewn haphazardly about the carriage house.

"The damn place is a mess, yes?" Chandal stated cheerfully. With a gesture of extravagance, she waved her arm about the room whose customary immaculate order had vanished in the maze of shopping debris.

Doreen continued to stare dumbly.

"I lost my mind," Chandal explained helplessly.

"No kidding. I hate to ask, but. . . ."

"About a million dollars. I think I bought everything. Cookware at Zabar's, copper pots and things to hang in the kitchen. Satin sheets at the Bath 'N Sleep Boutique. A beige silk skirt from Bloomingdale's."

"Bloomingdale's," echoed Doreen, white-faced.

"I know," nodded Chandal. "I mean, I can't even afford to walk through the *door* at Bloomingdale's. What do you think of that short red nightgown? It's right at your feet. For God's sake, don't step on it. It cost forty-five dollars."

"It's sexy," Doreen said, not looking at it very closely. "Who's it for?"

"And here—" Chandal went on, unaware that she had ignored Doreen's question, "silk panties. Fourteen pairs of them. One for every day of two weeks, or two pairs for every day of one week." She shrugged. "If I feel like changing a lot."

"Chandal," Doreen managed at last to say. "What did you do?"

"I don't know," she groaned. "But it was sure in hell a lot of fun!" She bowed her head sheepishly. "To tell you the truth, I really don't know how I'm going to pay for all of it. Look at this."

She began to uncover the largest of the wrapped packages. In the next instant she held up an exquisite oil painting, *Autumn in New York*. "Just like the song. What do you think?"

Doreen's eyes regarded the painting. "I think it's great," she said and flopped into the arm chair. "Also expensive."

Chandal deliberated over this, then reluctantly said, "Yes and no. I suppose so. I mean, you know, I thought how nice it would look over the fireplace. This room is so dreary. Hey," she said, putting the picture aside, "wait until you see the shoes I bought. And the new spring coat. They'll be here in the next shipment."

"Next shipment? How much stuff did you buy?"

"A lot. I've been at it now for three days." Chandal lit a cigarette and tossed back a few loose strands of hair. Then she knelt and plunged her hands into a shopping bag at Doreen's feet and brought forth rolls of wallpaper. As she spoke, she placed each roll into Doreen's lap. "This is for the room that leaks. This for the kitchen. This for the bedroom." The last she unrolled with a grimace of disgust. "Why I chose a dark blue for the bedroom I'll never know."

"Because you're nuts, that's why!"

"No . . . I'm not," Chandal said with a frown. Then smiled. "Just happy. Things are starting to happen! My agent called me for a commercial. I read for them on Wednesday. I've got a callback for the play at the Pilot Theatre, and . . ." She let a cryptic pause hang in the air. "I've been invited to a party tomorrow night."

"Oh. Who by?"

"My agent. She called and said there's a costume party. Theatrical type of affair. And I'm invited." Chandal winked. "She said there were people who were interested in meeting me. Isn't that great?" She blew cigarette smoke in Doreen's direction.

"I guess," Doreen mumbled.

"You guess? Is that all you can say?"

She shrugged. "I guess."

"That's what I like. Someone who has a tremendous vocabulary." Chandal grinned.

Doreen made no response. She leaned back against the couch, and after a moment forced a smile. It seemed a painful attempt.

"Where did you buy that statue?" she asked hastily, to change the subject. "What is it, some sort of God or something?" She carefully lifted the heavy statue from the box.

Chandal glanced at the Gothic creature now sitting in Doreen's lap—with twisted, folded legs. Cloven hooves. Part man, part beast, the creature seemed to wear a look of disdain on its goatlike face. An abrupt silence froze the room. Chandal caught her breath and stood motionless for a moment in an attitude of wistful supplication.

"Interesting, isn't it?" she murmured. "I found it in a little antique shop on Amsterdam Avenue. As to what it is, I haven't a clue."

"What does it say?" Doreen asked, and stared at the symbols at its base.

"Beats me. I only studied one semester of high school French," sighed Chandal, "two years of college German, and that was that. It would be great, wouldn't it, if I could step forth and say, ah, yes, that's from the lost civilization of Latep, I know it well. I am also the only human alive who still speaks the dead language of the Latepenese. At that point, I would modestly translate and—"

"And I would drop dead from admiration," finished Doreen.

"Right!" Chandal smiled. "But I loved that ugly thing the minute I saw it. Then when the salesman told me how lucky it was, I had to have it. Listen to this, Doreen, anything I want, I can have. All I have to do is ask the statue for it. That's what he said. So what do you think?"

Doreen absently held the half-shadowed face between the palms of her hands. "That's better than throwing coins in a wishing well," she laughed. "Can I use it sometimes?"

"Sure. I wonder where I should put it."

"How about the mantel?"

"I was thinking of a small table, or a stand. Something like a pedestal."

"What about the antique shop? Were they out of pedestals?"

"Doreen, what I'm leading up to is a favor."

"Hmmm."

"When Mike carried those antiques down to the basement for me, he said there was an airtight room down there. That it was sort of a vault where valuable furniture was stored. And I was wondering . . ."

"The only pedestal I know about," grinned Doreen, "is the one Mike claims he keeps me on."

"Can we look? If nothing else, I'd like to get that little inlaid table I had Mike take down, although it's too low."

"I'm not supposed to go down there."

"Why not?"

"Mike said not to."

"Doreen, you're a disgrace to modern woman. Do you have a key?"

"I don't think so," Doreen said, a note of finality to her voice.

Chandal paused, then shrugged. "Well, I guess that's that then."

"I'm sorry."

"No, it's all right." Chandal took the statue from Doreen's hands almost protectively, as if in some way the statue belonged to her more specifically than anything ever had in the course of her life. "I'll put it on the mantel for now," she decided, and cradled it for a moment before setting it carefully in place.

On the mantel the creature became at once the focus of the room, compelling the eye even as it had in the dusty antique shop. Chandal was unable to resist touching it once more and laid her hand almost reverently against its cheek. The creature seemed to meet her gaze.

"Chandal? Did you just make a wish?" queried Doreen.

Suddenly the desire rose in Chandal so strongly, that she could almost see it. Success. Not so much for the money. But to be someone. She straightened, trembling, and thought: *It's important. Success. This time, I'm going to have it. All for me.*

"What did you wish?" asked Doreen in a small voice.

Chandal turned. Felt taller, beautiful in a way. All of these things that were spread before her on the floor of the carriage house—she knew it was only right that she have them.

"I wished," she said in a cool remote voice, "for success. To be a star, Doreen. That's what I asked for. And that's what I'm going to get."

A sudden stir of breeze touched her cheek, causing her to turn with a start to stare once again at the statue. The eyes of its goat's head glinted like pieces of glass and stared evenly back at her. Its lips, snakelike and fat, appeared to vibrate with utterance. Its entire surface seemed to glow as if coated with a thin layer of fresh blood. Chandal felt an extraordinary thrill of desire as she watched the statue expand, grow enormously large, like a strange mystical inflating of stone and metal, until finally it loomed immense and throbbing with life. It was as if all reality, all thought, had been drawn into it.

"I'm here," the voice whispered. *"I'm in your blood."*

And Chandal smiled.

CHAPTER TEN

RIVULETS OF SWEAT DRENCHED HIS TENNIS SHIRT, STAINING THE couch pillow and mixing with cigarette ash from his almost defunct cigarette.

It was 7:25 P.M.—10:25 P.M. in New York.

Dr. Luther had been speaking for a full minute. Ron had never in his life heard such rich-toned, warm and yet neutral, noncommittal pleasantries in his life. He wondered if Dr. Luther was deliberately affecting it, or if his psychiatric training had been so encompassing as to make such conversation normal, even second nature.

"Uh, what I'm asking," Ron ventured during one of the clinical pauses, "is whether you believe I should insist that Chandal come back here. To L.A.!" he emphasized defiantly, fighting another of those deadly significant silences.

"I'm not sure you should do anything," the doctor said drily.

Stunned, Ron considered this information. "Do you mean I shouldn't try to get her away from New York?"

"Perhaps she doesn't like California. Have you thought of that? Or, forgive me for putting it bluntly, perhaps she is only in New York to run away from a relationship she's not ready to deal with. You should understand that when I knew her, Chandal had made only elementary progress in understanding her feelings toward her husband's death."

The words penetrated Ron like small daggers. It was impossible for him to conceive of Chandal's emotions where other men were concerned. He seemed to hear a replay of long conversations with Chandal. Conversations always about the present or the future. Somehow never the past. The past, he had reasoned, was gone. Didn't matter, didn't have to be dealt with, didn't even—secret gladness—have to be remembered. In that manner her psychic block had been his protection.

"We can't pretend that she doesn't have to face it," Luther went on with long-distance X-ray into Ron's mind. "She does."

The cigarette was burning Ron's finger. He crushed it out in the ashtray and sighed grimly. "So, what do I do? Nothing? Just stay away?"

"The most important thing," Luther remonstrated gently, "is for you not to force her hand. Don't lay down ultimatums. The best way to make her stay in New York is to order her to leave."

"Then you're not at all concerned?"

"I didn't say that," Luther murmured in even, noninflected words.

Before Ron could respond, the doctor had launched into another monologue about manifestations of anxiety, perception of reality and inner life. It wasn't until he mentioned neuroses that Ron actually allowed himself to acknowledge the truth. That Chandal had been ill. Mentally ill.

He found himself shaking with anxiety, the kind of anxiety that comes when simple and unspeakable things surface. Things that lie buried and known, but unconfessed.

He was suddenly uncomfortable, physically so. Slowly, with strained effort, he got off the couch and walked a little distance to the window, carrying the telephone.

"I understand," he muttered. "Yet I don't."

"In what area are we not communicating?"

"Well, you seem to be indicating that Chandal may be suffering a relapse of sorts."

"She could be. Yes."

Ron stood there for a moment staring out the window and not knowing what he should say next. The silence was thick, almost tangible, but he could tell there was a great deal of sympathy and concern being felt some three thousand miles away at the other end of the line. Ron groped for another cigarette.

"Dr. Luther?"

"Yes."

With the phone clamped between his chin and shoulder, Ron bent his head to the match. The tiny flame sent sulfur into his eyes. He withdrew, squinting, as he said, "So what should I do? Go to New York?"

"Well, has she issued an invitation?"

Ron found himself unexpectedly, inconceivably angry. "Goddammit, please stop playing the shrink with me. What can I say—what can I possibly do—to convince you to talk man-to-man with me, rather than as doctor to some sort of confused layman who might be needing the couch himself."

Ironically Dr. Luther hadn't proved to be the comforting influence that Ron had expected. Instead he was more of a catalyst. Ron was feeling the same dizzying confusion he'd suffered all afternoon. He started to apologize, when unexpectedly a chuckle released itself over the wire.

"I wonder," Luther said, still chuckling, "exactly what you want me to say. Did you call me for instructions, permission, forgiveness . . . ?"

"For openers, you could tell me exactly how sick you think she is. That's the part I haven't been able to get. Chandal isn't the screwball type, at least she doesn't behave that way with me. She isn't the sort who does something like this—"

"That's what the neighbors said," Luther offered, "when one of my latest patients killed his father and stepmother. He was such a normal kid, everyone agreed."

"I'm not the neighbors," Ron snapped. "I'm the man who's in love with her. And Chandal's not—" He paused. Something unspoken had warned him.

"No, of course she's not." Luther seemed to measure every word he said.

"Is there anything I should know?" Ron forced himself to slow down. His head had begun to ache slightly from the strain of the conversation. "Anything that might, for instance, give me a clue as to what's happening. I know about the amnesia. I know about her past before that point. Why do I feel like there's a lot more I could know, that I *should* know?"

"Do you know about how her husband died?"

"In the fire, yes."

"Do you know how her mother died?"

Ron felt a momentary impulse of fear. "No." He frowned. "Just that she died during that period of time Chandal can't remember."

"Doesn't want to remember," corrected Luther.

"You know that, I don't," protested Ron. "How did her mother die?"

The doctor gave a deep sigh and, with the release of breath, said, "She committed suicide by jumping from her hospital window."

Ron's mouth gaped open. After a rather long pause he found himself shivering from the conditioned air, even though he had wrapped a heavy woolen sweater around his shoulders. He knew only after some time had passed that he had made up his mind. "Here's what I'm going to do," he said bluntly, no longer caring what Luther might think the right course of action to be. "I'm going to New York to see her. I'm going to take her to dinner and see if she eats. I'm going to take her to bed and see if she can make love. I'm going to talk to her, listen to her, try to make some sort of sense out of what's happening. And I don't really give a damn what you think about all of that."

Unexpectedly Luther's voice descended a notch into confirmation. "It's what I'd do if I were you," he said. "By the way, please feel free to call me if you should need my help."

"I'll do that."

"I still have a very deep concern for Chandal's well-being."

"I appreciate that. And thanks. Goodnight."

"Goodnight."

Ron slowly lowered the receiver. After that he went to the refrigerator, took away a bottle of beer which he drank in the shower. He felt marginally better. He put on his bathrobe and slippers and lay down on the couch in the living room.

Without paying attention to what he was doing, his mind empty, he wasted time reading the warning on the Dristan bottle that he had had in his medicine chest for months. The night was heavy.

. . . He spent the rest of his time lying on the couch, thinking of nothing, a strange heaviness in his chest. He clipped his toenails. He counted the cracks in the ceiling, called Chandal, read—called Chandal, and finally shoved three Dristan tablets into his mouth and moved into the bedroom.

There was the pain. The splitting pain in his head that blotted out all else. It left him oblivious to his surroundings. To the passage of time as well. He stretched out on top of the bed for an hour, maybe two. He was glad to resign himself just to stay still.

His head buzzed slightly from the beer.

He didn't move. He waited. He knew he wasn't waiting for anything specific to happen, yet he had the odd feeling he was in the midst of a happening, not its conclusion, but its beginnings, a shifting of sorts, like standing solidly on ground that had been suddenly hit with an earthquake.

Yet he didn't fear the thought. He couldn't understand why he didn't. No fear, no apprehension. This reaction astounded him.

It was midnight when Ron finally crawled under the covers, and two in the morning when he dialed Chandal's number for the last time. No one had ever picked up on the other end. Ron was amazed. Despite how impossible the situation had become, he remained determined, even at this late hour. He was brutally fatigued. His eyes were strained and bloodshot, but he sat quietly, trying to reassure himself that he would make everything all right.

Finally, somewhere around four o'clock he fell asleep.

The dream came upon him swiftly, leaving no chance for escape. He was swept forth by a sudden supernatural power and passed like a spirit through a veil of thin mist that stretched out before him.

At first he was confused as to where he was. It wasn't until he glanced up that he realized he was standing in a forest of crucifixes. Huge, twisted treelike crucifixes that shimmered in the glow of a lustrous moon. He imagined it was raining. But when he looked closer he saw that each branch, each tree trunk, spewed blood. Wild, fountainlike spurts of blood.

Something pulled him forward—a compulsion, an obsession—one step at a time until he felt the earth crumbling under his feet, heard the dry clumps of clay falling away, down, far down, and still he moved forward.

Before him a mass of light flashed in a constant tremulous motion. Shapeless, it appeared to expand in every direction, and then vanished for a moment. In the next instant it appeared again. He moved closer so that he could examine it, keeping his eyes fixed on the light for fear it might disappear.

Instantly the light resolved itself into the shape of a girl.

"Chandal," Ron breathed. It was Chandal.

As he stood there, hushed and still, he could feel depression like fog souring and dampening the night. Clouds began to gather, moving in a cluster before the moon and hovering for an instant like a black mask before a face.

Then a cry from above.

His eyes darted upward as he sought to see beyond the ceiling of thick yellow clouds. And there it was.

The black hawk circled above the dusty droplets of crystal, its sleek presence a whisper on the wind. With hooked beak and curved taloned feet rolled into clawed fists, it seemed to fade in and out of focus, only to emerge again like black and soft smoke. Then it was gone, features faded except for its eyes. Eyes that searched the ground below for its next prey.

The hawk screamed.

Lights flashed and Chandal turned and started to run through the reddish glow of darkness.

"Chandal!" Ron cried. His body tensed. Became unfamiliar and awkward. He was caught in a strange unseen embrace that clung to him and rooted him to the spot. His heart beat wildly inside his chest. There was the sting of tears behind his eyes.

"Run, Chandal! Run!" he screamed.

She turned, slipped. Breathless, she regained her balance and began to run again, her eyes arched upward.

The wind shifted, and with it—the hawk.

He closed his wings and, with a sudden plunge, forced himself into a headlong dive.

"Help me!" Chandal screamed, but without hope.

The hawk ripped the back of her neck partially off with its powerful beak.

"CHANDAL!" Ron wailed helplessly and watched as she dropped to her knees.

Chandal reached out, started to crawl toward him, the blood seeping down onto her arms, luminous ripples that sparkled blue-black as they ran through the palms of her hands.

The hawk circled back, seemed to float above her for an instant, then dived again.

She screamed as his sharp beak tore the flesh from her throat. A long, mournful scream that transformed itself into a violet mist, a mist that hung before Ron's eyes for a moment, then crept away, slowly, until all that remained, far out on the horizon, were wisps of vapor which soon ebbed and eddied away into nothingness.

In the pitch-black of the night, Ron sat up suddenly in bed, listening.

Something had jarred him awake. He lay there, wondering. Gradually he realized—a cry of some sort.

He switched on the side lamp.

He stared at the clock. It was just past five. The house was very quiet, but outside the garbage truck was already making its harsh daytime noises. He felt exhausted and would willingly have gone back to sleep had his wondering not left him with an unmanageable confusion that made sleep impossible.

Wearied, he lay there and waited.

CHAPTER ELEVEN

THE DEVIL SPUN HER AROUND SUDDENLY AND LAUGHED IN HER face. Chandal drew back and tried to smile, but he grabbed her now and began to swirl her around in the vast mirrored room. Caught in the flashing green light, the reflected images, the heat of amassed bodies, Chandal felt dizzy, breathless. There was even a moment when she thought she would faint.

A kaleidoscope of characters rather than people dashed past her. White wigs, black masks, plastic faces. Captain Hook chased Daisy Mae. Chandal tried to reach out to them, but they brushed past her, decidedly bent on desecrating comic book folklore. Cartoon characters mingled in each other's cartoon strips, raced toward each other, collided and scattered.

The music blared and laughter rose everywhere. No one kept still. Chandal broke away, turned, and felt the devil turn her again, twice more, until she fell backward into his arms.

"Whala!" he exclaimed and the dance was over. With an eloquent flourish he returned Chandal to an upright position. "Wonderful! Wonderful!" he concluded in clipped sophisticated tones. "What is your costume, may I ask?"

"Eva Peron." Chandal reached up to straighten her blond wig, thinking: So, the devil is English, is he? and pictured him standing on a lush green lawn with a croquet mallet in his hand.

"Ah, yes. It's a good costume for a dancing girl like you. By the way, I hope you're not angry with me for sweeping you

108

away. The door opened, I turned, I looked, and there was this ravishing creature. Might I hover at your elbow for a while?"

"My elbow would love a drink."

"Champagne and wine on the table to your right. Or, if a mixed drink is preferred, there are two bars, one upstairs in the greenhouse, and the other one right through the archway."

The disco lighting had ceased for the moment. Softer music had begun and a gentle glow of chandelier light revealed what Chandal suddenly recognized to be an almost exotically lush townhouse. The entire west wall consisted of sliding glass doors opening onto a patio where, cool as the night was, a few party guests were still enjoying the lit view of Central Park as seen from Fifth Avenue. Traditionally dressed maids and bus boys wandered through the large, high-ceilinged rooms, serving hot and cold hors d'oeuvres and clearing empty plates and glasses.

On a sunken level was a heated swimming pool where a few guests seemed to be swimming—naked? Chandal wondered uneasily and then caught a glimpse of giggling nudity, as a flat-chested, long-haired model type rose from the water, more like a young male god than a woman. Beautiful though. Pure and sexless.

Embarrassed, Chandal glanced behind her into the less threatening atmosphere of a library. Her first impression was of a strictly male room—heavy leather-upholstered chairs, a silver tray of brandy and snifters on the desk.

"I think I'd rather have a mixed drink," Chandal said, still gazing at her surroundings.

The devil laughed. "It's right out of a fantasy, isn't it?"

"Not my fantasy," decided Chandal. "It's too—you know, much! Too much wealth, too many people, too many servants, oh, it's just . . ."

"I'm very sorry to hear that," murmured the Englishman.

"Are you? Why?"

"It's my house," he breathed in her ear and pulled her toward the bar. "What'll you have?"

Chandal was still red-faced, standing alone at the window looking out on the patio as she sipped her dry martini and told herself for at least the tenth time what an ass, what a damned idiot simpleton she was, when a hand touched her on the shoulder.

"I heard you were here and that you don't like my friend the devil's townhouse," announced a familiar sardonic voice. Chandal turned in confusion to stare at a man who was flamboyantly out of costume. At once she recognized him as the director she'd read for at the Pilot Theatre. His relaxed self-assurance, his well-tailored dark slacks and white open-necked shirt, even the small imported cigar between his fingers, plainly spoke of a man who enjoyed being the only man who hadn't dressed for the masquerade. Except for the guests at the swimming pool, naturally, but even their nudity was a costume of sorts.

He stood in a trapezoid of light thrown out through the open library door, feet planted solidly to the ground, his sharp-featured face open, smiling. "Remember me?" he asked.

"You're the director at the Pilot Theatre."

"Ah, yes. But do you remember my name?"

Chandal bit down on her lip. "I'm afraid . . ."

"It is always a good practice to secure the director's name. Especially if you're interested in the part." His smile broadened confidentially. "You are interested in the part, I take it?"

"Yes," Chandal said quietly, nodding, her eyes still focused on his face.

He laughed softly, his eyes twinkling under light, airy brows. "Rachel is an actress's dream. She is spirited, my God, is she spirited. Powerful. A bomb that is ready to explode."

"But she's not at all like me," she blurted out and then reflected that she had made another stupid remark. One that could very well cost her the part.

He didn't seem to be taken aback at her single-minded pursuit of the point, but was rather pleased with it. "Yes and no," he smiled.

"She's a—" Chandal stopped herself.

"A bitch," he filled in succinctly.

"Thanks. Thanks very much!"

"You're welcome." He grinned at her anger. "I enjoy that unexpected bitch quality in you. That Evita costume emphasizes it nicely."

She pinched her eyebrows together and frowned.

"Are you enjoying the party?" he asked.

She let her frown relax. "I think I'm getting ready to. My enthusiasm is just about here." She laughed and leveled her hand just above her bust.

"What an exciting place to be," he said politely.

She wondered if she was supposed to react to that, and if so, what sort of reaction was expected. Was his comment a prelude to a flirtation? But already she was shaking her head. He wouldn't be the sort of man to flirt. He'd be more the direct sort: *Do you want the part or not and how far will you go for it?* She gulped and wondered. How far would she go? It was a good part, a damned good part.

"Aren't you going to ask me if I am?" he asked and paused to draw cigar smoke up into his head.

"If you are what?" she replied blankly.

"Enjoying the party."

"Oh, sorry. Are you?"

"Not particularly. I don't care for parties. Never did, even as a kid. You've grown prettier since I last saw you. I wonder why that is?"

"Comes with practice, I guess," she said, trying for flippancy.

He didn't respond. Instead he simply gazed at her, his body erect and still, his blue-green eyes the only part of him in motion. He must be in his mid-thirties, she judged. Greek-hewn, something finely sculpted and polished. A person who exuded a sense of possessive pride, as if to claim whatever he wished to gaze upon.

Uncomfortable, Chandal said, "Is there another . . . ?"

She couldn't finish the sentence. It fluttered in the air for a moment like the broken wing of a bird, then dived.

"Yes?" he encouraged her.

"Oh. Nothing." Then suddenly that was all. She had made all the talk she could muster.

He had to fill the vacuum by stating the obvious. "You haven't been back in New York very long, have you?"

"No," she said and thought: *He's making fun of me. He knows very well I've just come from California.* But his face was devoid of sarcasm and his question was of an ingenuous nature. Yet there was something in his slightly darting eyes. A strangeness.

"Well," he said, and with a decisive swing of his body, he turned to face the room fully, "I'm getting myself another drink. Would you care to join me?"

"Thanks, no."

"That's what I'm going to do: go over and down a few." His eyes moved around the room slowly, then he took a step forward.

"Wait," Chandal said, putting up a slightly shaking hand. A curtain seemed to be sliding back and forth between two areas of her mind. "You still haven't . . ."

"Eric. Eric Savage." He turned back to stare at her.

"That's a nice name," she said awkwardly.

"It used to be David Stein."

"Oh, well—"

He dropped his eyes, contemplated the glass in his hand. "You really are Rachel, you know." He turned his gaze upward now, and their eyes locked. "If you don't believe me, see for yourself."

"What do you mean?" she said with a half chuckle of confusion.

"Sometime tonight, without giving yourself much chance to think about it—you just wander over to that mirror wall. Just stand there and look very deeply into your own eyes. If you can be as honest with yourself as I think you can be, you'll see it. Way back there in the back of your eyes, you'll see it."

"What?" she asked, and for no reason felt her heart begin to race. "What will I see?"

"Rachel," he smiled. "You'll see Rachel." Then he turned and walked away, adding over his shoulder, "You read for me again on Wednesday. Have a nice time tonight."

She felt herself shake and realized she was laughing. Tears blurred her eyes and then in the next moment she swallowed her martini in one swift gulp. It felt good—hot and cold all at once and it soothed her varying emotions as effectively as water on fire.

A plump, rhinestoned, bleached blond suddenly seized Chandal by both shoulders. "Chandal?" she wheezed.

"Thelma," blinked Chandal. "Thelma Rose."

"Dear, I thought I recognized you. I've been studying your picture. I still can't place meeting you, but you must have made a good impression or I wouldn't have been sending you out."

"Thelma, what am I doing here? Did Eric Savage . . . ?"

"A lot of money," said Thelma sagely, myopically viewing the room. "Have you been to the bathroom? Solid gold fixtures in the one I was in. Dear, I'm sure you're going to get this role. We have to arrange something about the commission, you know."

"What do you mean?"

"Well, you know, technically I can't ask for a commission. It's way under scale, a mini-contract. But I do these things for my people and—"

"Oh, sure, Thelma. I understand."

"Good, good. . . . Oh, there's . . . yoo-hoo! . . . Excuse me, dear. Yoo-hoo!"

Chandal smiled as she watched Thelma blunder her way through the crowd.

The band struck up again because the devil had given them the cue, and people began dancing. The colored lights revolved and confetti filtered down over the crowd, floated like colored snow through the air, then submitted weakly as awkward feet ground it into the floor.

The devil tossed a football into the air, and shouted: "Come on, God, let's play catch!"

A priest grabbed the ball and screamed: "Touchdown!" not to be outdone by his adversary.

A waiter struggled through the French doors, precariously balancing a tray of drinks. Chandal reached out. Moments later, she reached out again and then again.

Chandal could feel herself getting pleasantly tipsy. The party noise swirled and eddied around her. Her smile radiated uncontrolled until the grin was fixed on her face and she felt herself so goddamn friendly that she could barely contain herself.

"How's it going?" Thelma asked.

Chandal aimed a smile in her direction and nodded.

"A little tight, I see," laughed Thelma from the arm of a girl as they sauntered by on their way to the powder room.

Chandal tried to nod no, but somehow nodded in the affirmative. Thelma winked. Chandal tried to nod again, but Thelma had disappeared. This little mistake made her feel the need for dignity within herself. Enough of this drinking, she scowled. She set herself a dignified expression, something that would convey proper decorum.

Hell, she whispered to herself and took another drink. Now, as she tried desperately to look outward from herself, squinting to focus upon the other guests for relief, she suddenly stopped her gaze on a woman who had just removed her mask for a moment, then quickly placed it back on her face. Miss Ramsey! The woman from Friendly Realty.

Chandal rose and made her way through the kissing festival to the door, wearing a smile which she tried hard to keep from falling lopsided. In the press of bodies on the crowded dance floor she brushed against sharp thigh bones, elbows, and a hand that patted her rump gently and then withdrew. She heard the hand get slapped by another hand, but never looked back.

The smells hit her next, caught in her nostrils. The mingling of exotic perfumes, fragrant hair sprays, scent-dabbed shoulders, cigarette smoke and the sweat of hot dancing bodies.

"Miss Ramsey!" she shouted over the crowd.

"Where are you going?" queried Eric, faceless, bodiless. Only a familiar voice in an anonymous ocean of people.

"What? Oh, I'll be right back." She rushed forward now as the woman turned and began to leave the room. Chandal darted after her, blindly pushing through the crowd. A wild song bellowed forth from a group of men who blocked her way.

"Miss Ramsey! Wait. It's Chandal!"

The woman had disappeared into the hallway now, as if deliberately trying to avoid her. Chandal followed swiftly in her footsteps. However, when she reached the hallway seconds later, the woman had gone.

Chandal's eyes flicked around the huge expanse of empty space—at the front door, the harsh points of light that sprang from the modern wall fixture, the inlaid cabinets, the spots of light that fanned out across the ceiling—as though she was surprised to see that Miss Ramsey was actually no longer there.

Finally she lowered her head, pressed the toe of her shoe into the design of the floor and sighed. As she lifted her face and gazed once more at the front door, an odd look came into her eyes. A vagueness, as if somehow she had lost a small fraction of time and space.

Something made a clicking sound.

She heard it quite distinctly—a small sound like the clicking of a camera shutter.

She couldn't name its essence, but the source was clear—it was coming from inside the base of her skull. Her mouth and nostrils seemed to take in a sudden gush of cold air. Yet the palms of her hands were slick with sweat. She held them out in front of her. They were trembling. She realized that most of the physical sensation had gone from her fingertips. They were cold, numb, no longer a part of her.

Something tickled her nose, a faint odor of . . . lilac?

Click.

She cleared her throat, and as if by some built-in command, turned slowly and started back into the main room. She knew someone was with her. A familiar presence of. . . . She felt overcome by the sudden feeling of fatigue and age and a longing for—what? She could not tell. Within her mind, images fluttered: an old woman lying in a coffin. Her mother? No, someone else. Her brain groped. What was it? Something from the past?

The party seemed to go on forever. Time slipped away. The room hummed with conversation, punctuated with laughter. People came and went, leaving a residue of chatter and stale jokes ringing in her ears. She wasn't quite sure whether her eyes were open or shut. Whether she was actually present at a party or dreaming. She stood quietly with an inane smile on her glazed features, swinging her head from the flurry of one group to the next.

Her dazed brain groped to make some sort of connection. Images dovetailed, became grotesquely distorted, out of all proportion to reality. Her stomach tightened. She felt the color drain from her face, the strength ebb from her body.

Blood?

"What?" She turned with a start.

"That's what she said." Thelma smiled, having appeared unexpectedly at her side. Chandal stared at her nervously. "Listen, dear," Thelma went on, "we're going over to my place later. Just a few of us. Would you like to come?" She squeezed Chandal's hand gently.

"No, thank you."

"Now, dear—Eric Savage will be there. He—"

Chandal interrupted. "No, I don't feel well."

"I insist," Thelma demanded. "Just a few friends. Less crowded. You'll feel a thousand times better. Please, dear, it would mean a great deal to me."

"No!" Chandal cried and pulled her hand free from the woman's grasp, but it was as if she could not free herself.

"All right," smiled Thelma. "But you will come to my place soon, won't you? You'll love it. You must promise me you will."

"I will," she agreed reluctantly.

"Good. Good. Now I simply must have a taste of that delicious-looking food. My God, those rolled strips of Peking duck and the side dip of orange sauce look divine. Too bad, I never really liked caviar and this is supposed to be the best. I think I'll make up a lot of little crackers and spread it on thick. Then I thought I'd take them home in a napkin for my daughter. Do you think that would be all right?"

"I . . ." began Chandal doubtfully.

"Eat, dear. You can't pass up a spread like this. If you're dieting, then cold roast beef and melon wrapped in bacon strips. But do eat. It'll relax you," she said and then she was gone, having disappeared once more into the crowd.

Chandal was suddenly aware of how dull she felt, in comparison with all the lighthearted inventiveness around her. She was not usually this ungracious a guest. Usually she loved meeting new people, joining in conversation, seeing their homes, learning more about their lives.

But this evening she felt protective of herself, as if she had need to weigh every statement, consider each action. From the very moment she had stepped across the inlaid tiled foyer, she had felt her whole body bristle with warning, on the alert for faults and failings of any kind.

Perhaps Eric was right. Perhaps she should take a good look at herself. More out of a reprimand than curiosity, she turned and moved to the mirrored wall. She was determined to be objective about what she saw within the bluish art deco glass.

The world swam around her for a space of half a dozen thumping heartbeats. Much to her surprise she was smiling. She was also displaying a bit too much bust, but this only made her smile more. Her eyes fastened on the pendant that lay between her cleavage. Just right. Perfect.

She felt the nipples of her breasts begin to swell slightly

under her blouse. Impulsively she moved closer to the mirror, her eyes blazing with sensual pleasure. She brushed the thick blond hair back from her forehead, adjusting the wig's recalcitrant strands with her fingers. Her costume fitted her snugly and the high heels gave her legs elegant definition. Her eyes, enormous and blue, seemed to sparkle against the vibrant glow of her skin. She felt a thrilling sensation, that of being fully alive, as she ran her tongue over her lips. Slowly, she began a circular motion with her hips that promised what a pagan ritual possessing her would fulfill.

Then something shifted. As swiftly and unreally as in a dream, with as much detachment as though she were viewing herself through a stranger's eyes, she witnessed herself as another being. A face behind a face. It appeared for no more than a second or two, then vanished.

Chandal stood in front of the mirror in a state of bewilderment, unable at first even to realize what it was that she had just seen. Her image blurred. She wanted to look away, move away, but as she gazed at her image in the glass, she couldn't determine which part of her body was supposed to move first, or which way she was to go. Then she felt a touch of panic—fear. Even while she reassured herself that this couldn't be happening, she also saw herself riveted to the spot, utterly helpless—incapable of movement.

The party was too loud now. Too wild. Chandal had a difficult time controlling her urge to scream. She wanted to stop things from moving, but she was trapped within her own confusion.

Move. She had to move. In the next instant she felt herself turn. Felt it more than saw it. Her eyes darted around the room. Her one idea now was to get away from this party unnoticed. She groped her way anxiously through people, through the hall. As she reached for her coat, she felt quite sure she heard people calling after her. Calling her name.

But that was absurd, really. She couldn't have. There was far too much noise to be able to hear any individual voices. Nevertheless she carried the imagined voices with her. "Chandal, don't go. The party is just getting started. Relax. Chandal! The party is in your honor. Chandal!"

Chandal reached for the doorknob, yanked the door open violently, and disappeared into the night.

CHAPTER TWELVE

BEFORE THE TAXI HAD CLEARED CENTRAL PARK, THE CABBIE squirmed around and, with a speculative grin on his chubby face, said, "You just coming from a party?"

"Yes. A party."

"Did you have a good time?" he asked, much too intimately.

Chandal frowned. "Not really."

"Oh."

By the time they had reached Central Park West, the broken rhythm of the ride with its stop and go action began to churn Chandal's stomach. A steady pounding began in her chest and a fine perspiration broke out across her forehead.

Her mouth felt full of cotton, and when without warning the cab made a sharp turn which threw her heavily against the door, the nausea started to gather in her throat. The taxi leveled off again, continued on smoothly. She let herself relax, and leaned back in her seat. Grateful for a moment of hushed quiet, she closed her eyes and let her mind wander.

Then, very abruptly, the cab stopped.

The sound of the cabbie pushing up the meter's flag brought Chandal out of her stupor. It was a nasty sound. The sound of shock. Cataclysmic. It made Chandal feel that the familiar world was in some strange way meaningless, or rather, that it no longer had the meaning that she had always taken for granted.

"Three-eighty," the man announced after a brief silence.

118

Chandal fumbled in her pocketbook and handed him a five-dollar bill. "Thanks," she said wearily, and closed her purse without waiting for change.

"Right."

Even before she opened the car door she had realized that something was wrong. She closed her eyes and opened them again—squinted into the darkness.

"Where are we?" she asked.

"What?" the man barked, himself having been lost in thought.

"This is the wrong street."

The cabbie peered from his window. "Three West 85th Street. That's the address you gave me. Three West 85th Street."

"Are you sure?"

"Hey, lady—I don't make up addresses. Here, see." He held up his clipboard. "I write each call down on my sheet. Three West 85th Street."

Chandal stared out, caught by the sudden image of the brownstone that loomed out at her. She still didn't know where she was or what she was doing here, but she was drawn by the sight of the brownstone's somber façade. All reason, all foresight, all judgment were momentarily suspended in her mind.

"Hey, lady. You all right?"

"Yes," she breathed.

"Look, if you want—"

"Thank you. This is the correct address. Thank you."

"Suit yourself."

As if on cue, Chandal stepped out onto the pavement. She shut the car door behind her. What she felt was an overwhelming sense of guilt, a lust for punishment.

"That must have been one hell of a party!" boomed the voice behind her. The engine roared, human and mechanical sound blended, faded, and then the street fell hushed.

Incomprehensible—to her at least—and unbearable as well. Yet, here she stood, unwillingly, in front of the lost brownstone of her memory. Despite its recent renovation, its somewhat modernized alterations—it was, unmistakably, the same brownstone that she and Justin had lived in for more than a month before. . . .

She observed the building with eyes that recorded details

no camera could now know. As it had appeared that first day Justin had taken her to meet the two sisters. And now it all came back to her. The long narrow windows, vacant and eyelike, black with soot, that almost entirely sealed off the outside world. The zigzag crack, which extended from the roof of the building and made its scarlike way down the wall, vanishing just above the second-story windows. The faint glimmer of stained glass, whose distorted Gothic images seemed to dance in place above the front door. The bodiless faces, decomposed vines. The eyes that stared with sockets void of light, of life, above the thin line of blackened brick that formed the window ledges. A world, Chandal thought, condensed to a small plot of real estate. Detached, mysterious. A world which had no affinity with the neighborhood, but which reeked of the dull, sluggish reality of the two sisters who lived within.

Christ! Chandal now clutched her pocketbook close to her. Twice she had told herself to walk away, not to remain standing in front of the brownstone. But it was a request outside the limits of comprehension for her. Mistake or not, she was here now. This was her real reason for coming to New York. Wasn't it?

Leave now.

Quit it.

Turn away. Walk away.

No!

She stepped closer.

Blood turn to stone. Stone to fire. Burn. You will burn.

She stopped herself. It was a dangerous thought, mean to frighten and weaken her. To trick her out of her resolution to remember. She had to remember. Must remember. She had no right to fear for her safety . . . nothing. She mustn't fear. She moved closer.

"Open it remains," whispered the voice within her, *"and we can close it nevermore."*

Chandal stopped, her face peering upward, her white hands limp against her black pocketbook. She remained motionless for several minutes, as if fallen into a deep trance.

Then she heard it, the shrill cry, coming from the third floor. Distant voices shouted, came closer, pulled her back away from the flames that shot from the windows as though propelled from a blow-torch. A confused clamor of action around her. Frantic movement as the flames roared through the building; the fire jumped upward, a living, blazing tongue running along the pitched roof, licking and hissing its way across the entire front of the building.

All at once an old woman's face appeared at the window. Chandal remained motionless—their eyes locked. It all seemed to be happening now in the old woman's eyes. The violet orbs dilated swiftly as she gazed down at Chandal. They seemed to expand enormously as her voice whispered seductively: *"Let me enter you. You may enter me. We will become one."*

In the next instant, the glass rectangle of the single window was blackened over with smoke and grime. The old woman's face vanished, then emerged again from the darkness. Her face muscles twitched violently, her voice an incoherent wail carried by the wind from the burning building. She made this horrible sound without moving, with only her mouth working. Little tufts of her hair caught fire. Her eyes began to ooze from their sockets. Her blood beneath her skin began to boil.

"Birth is not a beginning," wailed the old woman. *"Death is not an end!"*

Chandal grinned.

And so did the old woman as she thrust her body forward against the glass. With a crash it burst open, and she almost fell headlong into the street. She straightened herself up, her eyes flamed red with passion, her nostrils opened wide and quivering. Like a beast gone wild she pulled back her lips to bare her small yellowish teeth. She hissed:

"When you see the blood, when you see the blood, I will pass, I will pass into you."

Chandal listened to the woman's calm, sleepy voice. Her words slipped into Chandal's ear like a drug, which after being injected, had the effect of engulfing Chandal's memory like a soft cloak, making it seem as though it had never happened.

And then it did happen.

The old woman jumped, her body falling through the air like a rag doll, until it smashed on the pavement before

Chandal's feet. The blood splattered onto Chandal's dress, hands and face.

Chandal had screamed.

Was screaming now.

In the next instant she was running into the night.

The pig squealed and coughed blood as the knife ripped open its stomach. It screamed until it was dead. Only then did the others in the room begin to scream, to howl with laughter.

Candles flickered, their flames dancing within the darkened room. Grotesque shadows festooned the floor, walls and ceiling, while a cacophony of distorted human forms danced and shrilled before a crucifix turned upside down. Overhead a figure formed, with the teeth of a shark and a goat's head and the tail of a serpent.

The old woman stood center, erect and robed, reading out the incantations. The veins in her neck swelled, saliva formed at the corners of her mouth, and still she ranted until exhausted.

"Overthrow the Almighty," she shrieked. "Bring all things to a low degree. Use toilet seats for your thrones. Use their thrones for your toilet seats! Turn above to below. The way to rise is to descend. Justice through sin . . . sin through justice. . . ."

The woman stopped. Gasped for a breath of the putrid air, laden with the odor of rotted wood, candle wax, incense and sweat. In the brief pause she clawed at the flesh between her breasts, taking away a pendant. Lifting it to her lips, she kissed it, and then spoke, "Every evil in the world has been gathered into the bloodstone. Let us worship it!"

Screams rose, while bodies shuddered.

"Overthrow the world!" the woman screamed. "Abolish it! Create an everlasting bonfire. A fiery consummation where the black truth will blaze, will be seen, will be felt, touched, heard—goodness, let it burn up and become clean, become one with Ahriman. Ahriman is all. Let the aged spirit of Hell become one with the young. Let the young bear children. Let all children become the sons and daughters of Ahriman. From this world to the next: from utility to creation . . . let Ahriman become King. Let Ahriman become King, and then cometh a new beginning, when he shall have put down all rule and all authority and all power.'' With her final breath, she gasped: "Let Ahriman become King!"

Chandal's head throbbed, her eyes burned, her heart ached. She opened the door to the carriage house, flicked on the main light. The breakfast dishes were still on the table, spattered with crumbs, jam and dried egg yolk. She took off her shoes, went upstairs to the bedroom, slipped out of her dress and got into bed.

She wondered why it had taken her so long to get home. Her emotions were diffused. She remembered going to the brownstone, remembered fleeing into the night. But what she could not remember was what she had done after that. She closed her eyes, but nervous exasperation forced them open again. Blinking, she peered intently into the thick darkness above the skylight. The stars were hidden by a thin mist and the moon floated lazily in the endless atmosphere. Panes of glass squeaked in their window frames, the wind moaned around the house, her body felt numbed as she explored an icy corner of the bed. I am going to sleep, she told herself, I am going to sleep. She buried her face in the pillow.

In the next instant, tears flooded her eyes. Suddenly she felt very young and alone. The night of the fire remained indelibly etched in her mind. Over and over she relived that one horrible moment, the confrontation with the old woman just prior to the woman's having lunged to her death. Again and again Chandal challenged her memory, listening, hoping, yet in the end she had to acknowledge she did not know what had happened, what the old woman had been trying to tell her. If she was trying to tell her anything at all. Perhaps Chandal only imagined the woman was talking to her prior to her jump. . . . If only she had someone to turn to. She was unable to banish from her thoughts painful reminders of Ron. Oh, God—help me. Please help me. Guilt weighed heavily on her conscience. For what, she wasn't sure. Sometimes it seemed as if the night would never end and sometimes it seemed as if it had always been night.

Sometimes . . .

She wiped the tears from her eyes.

Sometimes . . . the thought escaped her consciousness, and she found a kind of momentary mystical justification for everything.

From somewhere far off, the phone rang. She was too tired to answer it.

She turned over on her stomach, and then mindlessly passed into a deep sleep.

After a moment, a slight cool breeze moved through the room and, as soundlessly as a serpent slithering through grass, it whispered:

"Age, pain and deformity beget despair. Despair begets discontent. Discontent begets evil. The unification and fusion of this aged evil spirit with young and healthy bodies is our mission. Let the young dream dreams, while the old see visions. Let the sun turn into darkness and the moon into blood. Henceforth, let the kingdom of God be closed."

THE BLOODSTONE

PART TWO

Coming Apart

CHAPTER THIRTEEN

FOR THREE DAYS NOW SHE HAD SAT ON THE SAME PARK BENCH. Waiting. Her energy level had plummeted. Yet at her core she knew she was well-rested and vital. She had tried to call forth this vitality but something refused to budge. Something imponderable, as efficient as insulation, blocked her vitality from expressing itself. There was a heaviness within, a weighted insistence. It pulled, tugged, as if it were trying to turn her inside out.

Sometimes she seemed to listen for a sound too far off to be perceived as yet. But it came closer, that silent voice that would instruct her, perhaps lift the cloud of confusion and forgetfulness from her mind.

Occasionally she smoked, inhaling the poison like fragrant air. Although it made her heart beat rapidly, the smoke seemed to still her thoughts until she was full of interior silence. No questions for the moment. No answers.

It was Tuesday, the 31st of March.

Another unproductive day, Chandal thought, and realized she had forgotten to call her service for two days now. She knew she should care about that and the fact that she had stopped making rounds, but the truth was she didn't give a damn. She didn't even care about all the bills that she had accumulated and had no way to pay. She didn't care that the phone had been ringing incessantly every night—probably Ron—and that she had refused to answer it. Even the problem of Billy Deats seemed vague and inconsequential to her now. Strange how she had been so involved in that worry. Even to the point where she had finally written him a letter in care of Actors' Equity with instructions to forward.

Screw Billy Deats, she thought succinctly, and pulled her trench coat tighter around her, more out of conditioning than chill. Actually, she noticed, the day was warm. Springlike. Peaceful.

Tomorrow was her final audition at the Pilot Theatre. It was the one clear focal point of her week. If she got the role, she wouldn't have to feel she'd wasted the week. And somehow, smiling serenely, she knew the role of Rachel was hers.

In front of her, a nondescript man stooped over his shopping bags, took a tinfoil package from within, opened it and began to toss handfuls of breadcrumbs to pigeons.

Idly she watched the birds begin to flock around him. Something caught her ear, a clicking sound, and she glanced down at her hands. Stranger's hands holding small sticks. The sticks clicked together, down, up, down, then stopped, seemed to weld together in a familiar design. A cross. She studied it thoughtfully.

A child entered the park with a German shepherd puppy on a leash. The pup, full of bounding energy, pulled free of the child's hands, charged through the flock of feeding pigeons and ate their crumbs. Sounds of fluttering wings, the child's shriek, the rustling of the old man's shopping bags as he rapidly moved away, all penetrated the vacancy of Chandal's mind.

She blinked as though she had suddenly come to life. Her eyes teared in the bright sunlight and her body pulled free with a sudden convulsive jerk. There was something bothersome in the back of her mind. A feverish urgency. She had to remember. She had to remember before it was too late. Otherwise she was in danger. She was convinced of it. Fear mounted, vibrated to a high pitch, crawled along her tongue like bitter gall.

"I've got to remember," she said out loud and knew that in some way it had become vitally necessary. Otherwise she was about to lose something. One clear thought: There was more than one way to die.

"Don't worry," whispered the voice in her head.

"I've got to remember!" she insisted stubbornly. If only she could reclaim that forgotten time in her life, understand what had happened during that time, then perhaps she and Ron . . .

"Don't think about it," ordered the voice.

Chandal froze. It was the first time she was relating to the voice clearly. Whose voice was that? she was able to wonder for the first time. She could feel a tight knot of anger in her gut, but ignored it. She went on thinking: Whose voice? Mine? No, someone else's.

She felt her hand close around the pendant. She fought it, tried to unclench her hand, but her fingers curled tighter as though she embraced a part of herself. Her fingers convulsed around the stone and then, reluctantly, relaxed. The voice continued to whisper, but now she couldn't make out the words, couldn't concentrate.

Billy Deats, she thought dreamily. Somehow she was convinced that Billy knew what had happened at the brownstone the night of the fire. That he would be able to fill in those lost days and weeks. He had helped Justin and her move, hadn't he? Surely he had come to the brownstone often?

". . . no."

"Yes!"

"Don't think about it!"

"What?"

Silence.

Ron lay gasping for breath, bathed in sweat.

He awoke Saturday morning with a full-fledged case of flu. He decided through a swimming headache that he had all the symptoms—from head to stomach to throat. Not only that, he knew he had a soaring fever. Exactly what the illness was, he couldn't be sure. His thermometer was nowhere to be found, but he knew from the alternate chills and hot flashes that his body heat was on a rampage.

Fluids, he reasoned vaguely, and managed to down a glass of orange juice before his stomach rebelled and forcibly ejected it. After that he succumbed, with patience honed by misery, to bed rest and hours of holding his head over the toilet bowl.

Sunday he was worse. One sweat-soaked, nauseated and laryngitic bundle of human flesh, still with one obstinate train of thought. At all hours he called New York. He no longer looked at the clock, just obsessively dialed the memorized number, letting it ring until he could no longer hold the phone. Then he waited to gather the strength to dial again.

On Monday he called in sick.

"Sick?" Mimi's worried voice retorted. "You sound like you're calling in dead!"

"Funny," croaked Ron. "Very funny."

"Have you seen a doctor?"

"I'm too sick to go to a doctor. I can't get out the door. I'd rather die."

"My boyfriend is a doctor. Maybe I can get him to make a house call."

"Thanks." Ron hesitated. "Mimi, I have to hang right up."

"Why?"

"I haven't time to . . ." He slammed the phone on the hook and raced for the john. He barely made it, not that it mattered much. There was nothing solid on his stomach, just an intangible gall that seemed to have settled at some unreachable depth within him.

On Tuesday Mimi's boyfriend appeared, too young surely to be a practicing physician, but Ron decided he was in no position to be choosy.

"You have a fever of over 103 degrees," the young man smiled cheerfully. "Have you been taking aspirin?"

"I've taken them," Ron grunted, sinking lower into the bed. "Holding them down is something else. What have I got—flu?"

"It would seem so. Whatever brand it is, you've got it bad. Let me take a look at that throat. Yep, you've got streptococcus, on top of everything else. I can give you something for that and maybe something to bring your fever down, but you belong in the hospital."

"No hospital," Ron croaked firmly.

"Look at you. How long since you've held anything down?"

"Ah. . . ."

"I thought so. You're dehydrated, infected from your ears down, and the least we can do is get some glucose in you and run a few tests. I'll be honest—I've never seen anything quite like this."

"No hospital."

"You're as stubborn as Mimi said you'd be."

"And you—" Ron said with gloomy triumph, "don't look anything at all like Dustin Hoffman."

"What?"

"Just the feverish ravings of a sick man."

"I'm giving you a penicillin injection—any reaction to penicillin? Good. And I'll have the drugstore deliver two prescriptions. One for the infection and one for the nausea. If you're no better in a day or two. . . ." He frowned.

"Hospital," agreed Ron and managed to write a check and say a civil goodbye before the next dash for the toilet.

Dehydrated, he reminded himself ten agonized minutes later and walked swaying into the kitchen for ginger ale and ice. He stared at the drink for some moments and then held it against his throat. The ever-present nausea subsided somewhat.

Still holding the cold drink against his throat, he swayed back to bed, and automatically dialed the New York number. After three rings, he was prepared to hang up when a click told him that someone had picked up on the other end.

"Hello?" he mumbled, spilling ginger ale on the sheet. "Chandal?"

"No," said a masculine voice. "Chandal is out. Can I take a message?"

Ron paused, a wave of confusion all but covering him. "You are?" he asked too bluntly, though he didn't care.

"The super. Mike. I can take a message."

"Oh," Ron answered, as if the word had pages of meaning, such as: I sure in hell am relieved you're the super, or: Even if you are the super, get the hell out of there, or: Tell Chandal it's Ron. Tell her it's very important that she call me. Which was finally what he managed to say.

"Right," said Mike's young, energetic, healthy voice and the connection was severed.

He sounds like a good super, thought Ron bitterly. He took a sip of ginger ale and lay flat in bed as he closed his eyes. No fooling around with supers, Chandal. It's a very cheap thing to do, especially when the man who loves you is in Los Angeles, languishing on his death bed.

He could feel his eyes closing. He remembered that he was upset about something, but exactly what he wasn't sure. The last of the sunlight was blackened out as his heavy eyelids closed, and he fell into an unusually deep sleep as if he had descended a ladder into a very dark hole where he was a captive. Around his neck dangled a heavy object that swayed as he walked and beat against his naked chest. Without touching it, he knew what it was. An upside-down crucifix. And he knew that the anguished screaming face of Christ had once again changed.

At the foot of the steps leading to the Metropolitan Museum of Art, Chandal hesitated, then slowly, counting the steps, followed in the wake of brisker, more purposeful visitors.

"Most of us come near it at one time or another," Dr. Luther had said. "Sometimes only for a moment, sometimes for a day, a week—even a month."

He had been speaking of insanity. He had gone on to quote Herman Melville: "In all of us lodges the same fuel to light the same fire. And he who has never felt, momentarily, what madness is, has but a mouthful of brains."

Dr. Luther's words had not been a comfort to Chandal then, just as they were not a comfort to her now. Was she, Chandal wondered, mentally ill? Was the voice she had heard, actually there? Or was it just a fragment of her overworked imagination?

She shook her head. As quietly as she could, she tried to control the confusion she felt at this moment. Everything had been moving so fast. She had to slow down. Relax. Why was she pushing herself so hard? As if her very life depended on it.

Dr. Luther had explained it all very clearly. "Amnesia may obscure little or much or even the whole of memory. In your case," he had added with a smile, "it's little, and I'm sure that the missing segment of time you are experiencing will return to you spontaneously, when you least expect it, at a party, while walking down the street, in the shower, and that you will return to fully functioning consciousness."

Yet there was something about it that didn't make sense. If Dr. Luther was so sure she was going to be all right, why had he cautioned her not to return to New York? And why did she feel she needed to be forgiven? Why did words like *blameless* and *unjudgeable* keep recurring in her mind? Had the fire been her fault? Was that it?

Chandal frowned. A circus act, that's what it was. Like tightrope walking between the towers of the World Trade Center. The higher you go—the more they pay. The more they wait for you to fall.

Stuck now with her present hit-or-miss thinking—no time, really, to put the pieces together—she punched her way through the door. Inside, she stopped to make a contribution. She wasn't sure exactly what she'd given, but the man looked at her oddly before shoving across a patron button which she affixed to her collar with fingers that trembled slightly.

She let herself wander, stopped to stare searchingly at a vast urn, intricately molded into hundreds of faces and human figures, all entwined, some chipped, with heads missing, bodies incomplete. She shivered and moved on. Statues, vases, jewelry. She stared down at an exotically painted mummy and wondered who he was. What man was this who had lived and loved and had thoughts privately and distinctly his own?

She wandered on with no sense of direction or purpose. Through an English square, around an Egyptian temple, now silent, deserted, where once worshipers had assembled at the first Christian church in Egypt.

"Chandal?" shrilled a voice from behind her right shoulder. "Here you are. I've been looking all over for you."

Turning, Chandal was dragged from Egyptian history to American contemporary art. "Doreen," she murmured, glancing at the guard who stared in their direction, "what are you doing here?"

"We had an appointment to meet, remember?" Doreen's voice was still high and rather nervous, as though she were ill at ease in such a cultural setting.

"I . . . I must have forgotten," Chandal breathed, trying to indicate by her own example that a lower voice level was desirable.

"What's this place?" Doreen relaxed slightly and dropped onto a marble ledge to view the ruin. "It looks boring as hell, doesn't it?" She giggled and covered her mouth with both hands. "Look at that, there are stones missing, even. You'd think they'd make some copies, wouldn't you—fill it in a little."

Chandal smiled and continued to stare at Doreen. She could feel a bit of normality return, but still had no recollection that she had made an appointment to meet with Doreen that day. For that matter, she had no awareness of conscious decision to come to the museum. She had merely found herself in front of it as though by a wizard's magic. She shrugged. "Come on. Let's go look at the paintings."

"Okay. Sure."

"I meant right now," Chandal said as Doreen continued to stare in a bemused sort of way at the ancient temple.

"Okay. I was just trying to imagine why they have a guard in this room. What is there to steal?"

"Maybe they're afraid that people would chip off souvenirs. Or maybe paint it."

"You mean grafitti?" Doreen giggled.

"Or someone could hide in the temple," Chandal realized suddenly. "During museum hours, you know, and then later, after everyone had gone . . ."

"Geez, you'd make a terrific thief," Doreen decided. She briskly gathered up her purse, and proceeded swiftly and competently to the exit. "Now which way?"

"I'd like to see the American Wing."

"No." Doreen immediately spun in the opposite direction. "Let's go upstairs first. Up that big staircase. What's up there?"

"Paintings."

"Oh, good. I'm going to get cultured."

Side by side they hurried up the stairway, delivered from the scrutiny of one set of guards' eyes into the observation of another set. Scarcely had they entered the first of many rooms, when Doreen asked: "Who do you like the best?"

"Rembrandt. He's always been my favorite. Look, here are his wife and his mistress as he painted them. Hanging right next to each other. I wonder if either of them conform to that day's standard of beauty?"

"I don't know." Doreen turned abruptly away and darted into the next room.

Chandal followed more slowly, caught up in a great sense of history, of universal memory, where images had been frozen and framed by the mysterious minds of its artists. Uncharted time and space left for others to decipher.

She wandered through the doorway and came upon Doreen, who stood at the base of a large painting of a girl, gazing at it with rapt attention. The artist was unknown, Chandal noted, and she felt sorry that he had lost recognition for this work. She found it a compelling portrait and noted the youth of the girl and the broken window over her shoulder—indicative, the plaque explained, of an unhappy love affair.

"She lost something too," Doreen said suddenly. "Just like me."

"What did you lose?" asked Chandal, rather startled at the comparison between this pale dreamy girl of centuries ago and Doreen, who was bright, contemporary and, more than anything else, vibrantly alive.

"Mike. I lost—I think I've lost Mike."

"No. God, no. It couldn't be."

"He's in love with someone else."

"Who on earth is he in love with?" gasped Chandal.

Doreen continued to gaze in a fixed way at the portrait.

"Doreen? Who do you think . . . ?"

"I think he's in love with you," breathed Doreen, still refusing to look at Chandal.

"Mike? Doreen, no. You can't think that."

"Can't I?" she asked bitterly. "It's true. Do you know that sometimes Mike stares out of the window for hours, just trying to catch sight of you. Oh, I know," she added on a softer note, "that you don't have anything to do with it. Although . . ."

"Although what?" asked Chandal sharply.

"Although he is so handsome, don't you think? I always thought he was the most handsome man I ever looked at." Doreen's eyes were wistful.

Abruptly something flashed into Chandal's mind. A half-forgotten thought that Doreen and Mike were a very strange combination. Despite his deformity, Mike was dramatically handsome and without a doubt very appealing to women. And there was a strange power about him, sensuous and compelling, a power that any woman would find fascinating. Doreen, on the other hand, was the plump, jolly, not-very-pretty type.

Chandal hurriedly put such a disloyal comparison away and linked her arm through Doreen's. "Don't worry," she whispered, "because believe me, I would never . . ."

"I know." Doreen brightened. "I'm sorry I even mentioned it. Maybe I'm just paranoid on the subject of Mike. Forget I mentioned it, okay? Geez, I don't know how I could have said that to you."

They wandered on into various rooms, then down a hallway of glass cases containing ancient jewelry, urns, fans and other articles of a vanished age. Doreen continued to chatter as they made their way, still arm and arm, down the long stairway. Chandal's attention wandered. The old nagging syndrome. Her constant effort to remember, remember. She could not escape its power when it pulled as hard as it did at this moment. She could feel herself start to tremble as they came to the lower level and faced the exit door.

"Look," Doreen exclaimed, "there's a container for donor tags. We're supposed to drop them inside."

"Not yet. I want to see the American Wing." Chandal was surprised at her own insistence.

"Oh, let's go. I wanted to get a bite to eat. I thought—"

"I have to go in there. Don't ask me why, I can't explain. It's just that—"

Doreen tried to pull her toward the door. "You're shaking. Chandal, you're shaking all over. You need air or to sit down or something."

Chandal hurried on, unaware now of her surroundings. There was just an unexplainable obsessive pull toward the American Wing, where a sign proclaimed that there was a special exhibit this week.

A change of atmosphere hit her first. A different sort of smell, a mustiness not apparent in any other room of the well-ventilated museum. Slowly, the two girls advanced through the door into a room that had been assembled as a cathedral. Even the lighting seemed to filter through stained glass. On the walls were lights in holders under huge oil paintings. There were wooden pews on either side and down the center ran a red carpet like an aisle of blood up to the altar.

For a moment the room made her physically dizzy, as if an earth tremor had occurred beneath her. The floor seemed to quiver. She felt sick and shivered, as some dim and horrible memory rammed against the walls of her consciousness, then died away, leaving her numb, her head throbbing, as if from a brutal blow.

She reeled blindly from the cathedral into a smaller anteroom, where her mind recorded images of gleaming rose-wood tables, high-backed chairs, vases, gargoyles, side-boards, a hand-carved chess set of superb workmanship. She heard herself begin to moan, could not stop.

"Chandal? What's wrong?" Doreen's voice, high-pitched, scared.

Turning, Chandal once again faced the cathedral room. A sort of paralysis had come over her, held her immobile, as she gazed upon the icon art—crucifixion too realistically cap-tured, the agony of Christ intense, the blood thick. Corpses upon other crosses being robbed of their clothing by the poor. The Virgin Mary, her mouth sad, her eyes dull and compas-sionless. A human skeleton, lance in hand, riding on a white stallion.

She shivered and a pain developed in the center of her forehead. As though something inside of her concentrated very hard now, almost lusting after the blood that oozed from the wounds of Christ. Sweat began to gather on her neck under her turtleneck sweater, began to roll down from her hairline. Death. She could see it so plainly in the mummified body lying in its shallow grave, and in the face on the Virgin Mary who gazed up at her son on the cross. Now Chandal felt her knees buckle and sat down quickly on a low stool, swaying slightly from side to side.

"What's the matter?" Doreen's voice said as if from a far distance.

Chandal breathed in harsh desperate gasps. A pain shot across her chest and seemed to plunge inward like a knife.

"Doreen," whispered Chandal, "I'm sick."

"Sick? What kind of sick? Are you going to faint?"

"What's wrong here?" inquired a masculine voice and Chandal felt hands come up to support her on the left side. Doreen's clammy fingers still clutched her right arm so hard as to bring bruises.

"She just needs a little air," mumbled Doreen.

"Should I call a doctor?"

Chandal began to protest, imagined that the doctor they would call would be a psychiatrist. And, of course, a psychia-trist would soon decide she needed to go back to that place. That was why she must never let anyone see how confused she was. Some unexpected inner strength lifted her head, relaxed her hands which had been clenched into fists.

"Thank you," she said in a refined, almost prudish voice. "I can't imagine what came over me. I'm all right now. Quite all right." Head held high, she rose and walked steadily toward the exit ahead of Doreen who followed somewhat breathlessly, heels scraping loudly against the polished floor. Chandal looked briefly over her shoulder and something in her icy blue eyes hastened Doreen's gait.

Side by side now, the two girls made their way across the lobby. Chandal took tiny ladylike steps that carried her forward at a deceptively rapid pace. She was in control now and clucked gently as though she remonstrated with some inner self. She would remember in the future never to attract such attention to herself. It wasn't proper. It wasn't. . . .

She neatly extracted her donor button from her collar and dropped it into the bin. It wasn't the ladylike thing to do, she reminded herself. No. She would have to be more on her guard after this.

CHAPTER FOURTEEN

. . . DISTURBED.

What does "disturbed" mean?

Dr. I. Luther peered over the tops of his half-glasses at Chandal Knight's folder. Case history number 33236. It was late Friday afternoon. Outside the narrow lead-paned window of his office, which faced the huge expanse of lawn that encompassed most of the front grounds of Lakewood Sanitarium, it was raining. Soft rain. Steady rain. A rain filled with many thoughts. The word "disturbed" passed through his mind once again.

Over the years he had hoped that the word would take on new meaning for him, that it would change or that some other word would appear to clarify its meaning so that the word could be transmuted into an absolute.

He thought—of that frightened young girl. A February night. She had cried herself sick. Fainted. Found herself surrounded by windows laced with steel net. Lakewood. He had gone to her. Had helped her relax. She had screamed suddenly: Fire! . . . A quick series of injections. Then sleep.

Commotion became stillness.

And soon a year had passed with Chandal progressing from "mental illness" to "health." It had been a startling recovery which began in September of that same year. Her confusion had suddenly vanished. Overnight, it seemed, she had everything under control. She was no longer "disturbed." It had happened too suddenly to please Dr. Luther. Not, unfortunately, too suddenly to please the Board of Examiners.

He glanced again at the folder before him and remembered how the empty pages began to fill. Notes doubled. Full chords filled the binder. Notes written below the allotted space. Hurried notes. Sudden thoughts that had seemed important to him at the time.

His fist curled tight now as he tried to extricate himself from thought. It was one of his concentration tricks. Tense a part of your body to get the brain's attention, to get it off whatever particular treadmill it had begun to pace at a given moment. This afternoon it wasn't working.

Beyond his window clouds shifted, causing yet more shadows that changed the day. An overhang supported by four round pillars that extended to the edge of the walkway continued to shield people as they waited for cars to pick them up. Others decided in sudden fits of frenzy to make a mad dash for it.

The door to his office opened abruptly and he looked up, momentarily squinting.

"Dr. Luther! I didn't know you were still here."

It was Nurse Sharp, one of the hospital's part-time medical secretaries, a registered nurse with more of a penchant for clerical work than for patients. Nurse Sharp was assigned to Luther whenever he found himself with an excessive work load. She was wearing a dark blue suit, suede and expensive.

"I'm afraid so," he sighed.

"I just finished a few letters for Dr. Hess. I thought I'd check your file. To see if you needed something done."

"I'm all caught up at the moment. Thank you."

She shook her head and frowned. "You look tired."

"Just restless. I'll be all right."

"Well, have a nice weekend."

"You too."

"Bye."

Without looking back, she departed quickly.

Luther sat for a while with quiet thoughts. Then he stood up and removed his lab coat. He looked taller without it. Broad shoulders. Narrow waist. He pushed his arms through the sleeves of his sports jacket. Now he stood behind his desk, with an apprehensive sense of things disassembling. He was uncertain how to react to Chandal's sudden return to New York.

He had had many strange cases, but out of all his many patients, he had always felt there was something unexplainable about her recovery. She had appeared totally healthy upon her release from Lakewood. Yet . . . something didn't fit.

Over the many months that followed her release, he had tried to put all doubt out of his mind. But somehow he had never freed himself from her bewitchment, or had freed himself only temporarily, then had found himself once again drawn to her file. Drawn again to listen to the tape recording of her voice that he had listened to so many times.

On sudden impulse he withdrew a small tape machine from his desk drawer, dropped quickly into his chair and pressed the start button. There was no need to check the label to ascertain the tape's contents. It was the voice recording of Patient 33236, C. Knight, a 26-year-old Caucasian female.

The click of the machine echoed abrasively against the walls of his almost airtight office. A brief silence followed before her words filled the room.

"Because I have seen what I have seen,
Because I have been where I have been,
Because I have communed with those who
know . . .
I am who I am."

Chandal spoke dully, without emphasis, her voice deeply unhappy. There was desolation in what she was saying, a darkness, as if laced with eons of medieval superstitions.

He punched the button. There was no impulse to rewind the tape and listen again. He knew the words by heart. He knew, too, that Chandal had never remembered saying those words. And that she could not explain their meaning.

Were they part of a dream she had once had? A hallucination? A fantasy of sorts? Or did they have meaning? Were they part of and the cause of her amnesia?

He dug into her folder. Turned pages until he found what

he was looking for. He took the note away and read it silently.

Chandal's expression, appearance, and the impression she makes are all fairly normal now. She is about seven-eighths of the time young-looking, facial features relaxed. She has almost completely lost the disoriented quality which plagued her throughout most of her sessions. Yet there are fleeting moments when she slips into a much more prudish posture. Restricted and somber. In these moments she refers to herself as WE, fluctuates from poor to fair contact, and speaks very little and shyly. During these unusual brief periods, her eyes change from wide-eyed and normal to a more dreamy and introverted expression. Eyes become narrow slits.

Seven-eighths of the time, Luther mused. It had always been the remaining one-eighth that had left him feeling vaguely uneasy.

Luther now took a breath deeper than usual as he wished that he had gotten more information from Ron Talon. He hoped that he had left Ron with the right sense of urgency. He found himself thinking it imperative that Ron call him once he'd reached New York City.

Carefully he placed the note back into Chandal's folder and closed its cover. He had closed the cover once, thinking it was over. This time he wasn't quite that sure.

CHAPTER FIFTEEN

WHEN CHANDAL CAME BOUNDING DOWN THE BEDROOM STAIRS, her living room smelled of air that was three days old. The apartment was musty-smelling, yet at the same time a little too warm. She looked tired, like a person who had just put in two long eight-hour shifts back-to-back. Without pausing in the living room she ran toward the kitchen, her feet making no sound on the new green shag carpet.

"What are the big pills for?" Doreen asked from her usual slouched position on the couch.

"Headaches. They're for the headaches."

"And these?" She held up smaller pills in a green bottle.

"What? Oh. Blood pressure."

"That's it? Blood pressure?"

"That's what the doctor said. All I have is a slight case of elevated blood pressure. All the other tests were negative."

It was due to Doreen's insistence that Chandal had finally spent three excruciating hours in St. Luke's Hospital, where she had undergone a series of tests after the incident at the Metropolitan Museum of Art. They assured her that she was in perfect health, that she need only relax and take life a bit more easily. If, however, the fainting spells continued, she had been advised to see a neurologist. Prescriptions in hand, more annoyed than cured, she was released.

Chandal now paced the kitchen miserably, her hands thrust deep into the pockets of her skirt. She looked up once and saw Doreen staring sadly at her. Her deep blue eyes gushed over with sympathy and compassion.

"Doreen, stop looking at me like that!"

"Like what?"

"Like I'm about to die or something. I'm fine. Fine!"

"I know, but . . ."

"But what?"

She shrugged. "I don't know, I thought maybe . . . well, I thought maybe you were pregnant."

"Pregnant!" Chandal stood there and stared her in the eyes. Doreen stared back.

Chandal suddenly felt a fear at being joined to such an ongoing chain of life. It was as if Doreen had struck a nerve that Chandal had thought was well protected, blocked off. Her fear surged forward. Strange kicks in her womb. Milk sucked from nipples. Constipation, stomach cramps, and sleepless nights. Maternity. But she had wanted this at one time, hadn't she? If so, why so intense a reaction on her part now? Through a confused haze she heard Doreen's voice.

"Is there any reason why you couldn't be?" Doreen asked.

Chandal struggled to regain control, felt herself drawn to reply against her will. "I haven't been with a man. Not since Ron. And besides—"

"What?"

"I . . . I have a prescription for birth control pills."

Doreen nodded. "I see."

Chandal's fear ebbed. Something new took its place. Not really new, merely new in its intensity. Success. Stardom. There weren't any words. How bright her future seemed. Startlingly she regained focus, felt her vigor return.

"This is ridiculous!" she exclaimed, throwing her hands into the air. "Me standing here talking about being pregnant. I gotta get the hell out of here or I'll be late for rehearsal."

Chandal began flying around the room, pushing aside magazines, rifling drawers, peering behind pillows and under chairs. She stopped abruptly and turned to Doreen.

"Damn it!" her voice boomed.

"What's the matter?"

"My script. You haven't seen a blue script lying around here, have you?"

Doreen's forehead rippled with distress as she reached beneath her crumpled body. "You mean this?"

"Yes! I mean that!" She snatched the script from Doreen's hand.

Doreen looked away sheepishly. "How does it feel to be a working actress?"

"Great."

"It sure didn't take you long," she mumbled. "I mean, you got the part just like that."

Chandal smiled cynically and snapped her fingers. "Just like that!"

Chandal had to admit she'd been pleased with the way she had handled herself at the audition on Wednesday, not to mention having entirely charmed Eric Savage. If she had been out of practice as an actress, she still had more nerve and courage than she had imagined.

Her pleasure, however, hadn't been destined to last very long. When she had telephoned her service on Thursday from a pay phone to see if there were any messages, they had informed her that Eric Savage had been trying to reach her all day. That she had been cast in the role of Rachel. In mid-sentence Chandal shrieked:

"You're kidding!"

"No, you go into rehearsal tomorrow."

"Tomorrow," she gulped. "Are you sure?"

"That's what the message says. Rehearsals begin Friday, April 3rd. 10:00 A.M. Pilot Theatre."

Chandal stood, receiver in hand, and stared blankly at the pedestrians and traffic going by. She thought of the hours spent in acting classes, dance classes, voice lessons, even the hours of reading hundreds of plays. And the dreams, the courage to risk all to go against impossible odds, the knowledge that if you failed, it would be too late to do anything else. That the definition of your life would be failure. All this so that she could finally, finally, win a role like Rachel in an authentic New York play. And all for seventy-odd dollars a week.

"Thank you," she said in a rather dazed manner and found that she had slammed the receiver on the hook almost viciously. Of all the reactions imaginable, she would never have expected to feel as she did. This frightened, depressed, ironic realization that she had spent a good many years and an enormous expenditure of energy and money for an ultimately meager end.

Eight-thirty. Friday morning. Toast, a small glass of orange juice and two cups of tea.

Chandal sat perched percariously on the edge of her chair, the remote thought still numbing her mind: Stage fright. God! It gave her the jitters as if she were opening in front of Clive Barnes, Walter Kerr and John Simon today, instead of just attending her first day of rehearsal. *What if I freeze? What will I do then?*

Preoccupied, she made the bed, emptied an overflowing ashtray, and washed two days of dirty dishes which had piled up in the sink. It was so hard lately to keep the place clean. She just didn't have her mind on it. New York apartments got dirty too quickly anyhow. Dust was like a second skin to furniture, window ledges and floors. Hurriedly she ran a vacuum and then dusted with a feather duster, not the most thorough of methods, but to hell with it. She knew she was stalling anyway. Knew that it was getting late, and that soon, very soon, she had to face what she hadn't wanted to face in years. Could she cut it as a professional stage actress? Anxiety ripped her apart like a knife.

But the first day of rehearsal turned out to be a soothing interlude. Chandal surprised herself with the ease with which she went about doing her job, despite the harrowing week she had had prior to getting the part.

From the first moment of the first read-through of the play, Chandal found that she habitually drew a deep breath and upon releasing it, had somehow given up a part of herself, sacrificed herself for the sake of the play. She could feel herself tremble as she waited for the transformation to take place. Waited for the soft core of her personality to become rigid. Where once there was love, let there be hate. Where once there was magnanimity, let there be self-absorption. In a way, she thought with a great deal of Rachel's satisfaction, it was like selling a part of one's soul.

The empty hours of the next two days began to fill. Her energy doubled. Also her demands. Fits of anger quickened the tempo. Pages of dialogue were deleted from the script.

Actors complained that Chandal was being unreasonable. A few threatened to quit.

On Monday, Chandal was impossible to handle. There was no stopping her. No talk could calm her. She hadn't slept well the night before. Twice she had gotten up, both times because she had thought she'd heard a baby crying in the downstairs den.

Standing frozen in the doorway, Chandal realized that the baby's mournful wail had suddenly ceased. She had peered into the darkness . . . her eyes dissolving, disappearing into the now soaked walls. "Like tears," she mumbled and felt a rush of nausea. Why did she think that there was a connection between this room and the brownstone on 85th Street? Was it only because of her recent visit there—the shock of reliving the final moments of the old woman's death? Still . . . she could not go on. Her head was splitting. All she wanted to do was close her eyes, just for a moment.

Yes, close your eyes.

Yes.

Close them now. We need our rest.

Yes.

She shut her eyes and gave herself over to the voice that calmed her. Whose voice?

Mine.

Yes.

Near dawn, she had finally fallen into a deep sleep.

Now she was up, battling with fatigue—exhaustion. Best not to think about it, she scolded herself. Just concentrate on the play.

She had put on a simple cotton dress. Her hair was combed back severely and her face scrubbed. No makeup. The eyes that had been tearful for so many days were clear now. More than clear. Bright. Too bright. Her smile broadened. So did her voice, also too bright. Too loud.

"May we begin?" Eric Savage's voice dripped sarcasm. "If it's not too much to ask, Ms. Knight. We have read up to your entrance twice and I don't feel disposed to do it again. I know it's Monday, but—"

Chandal barely flicked her eyes up from her script. "I'm really not responsible," she murmured in a disinterested way, "if the rest of your actors read their roles with no more preparation than they take to read the *Daily News*."

Stunned silence reigned only a moment before Brad Sorel, the male lead, flung his script to the floor and said furiously, "I personally will be expecting an apology from Sarah Bernhardt before I read another fucking word!" He glared at Eric Savage. "And if you think I'm kidding, get ready for a surprise."

Eric looked at him sharply. "You're welcome to quit if you like," he said levelly. He spoke with the exaggerated patience that teachers use when addressing a naughty child. "What I choose to say is one thing. But I run my rehearsals in my own way. My actors don't lay down ultimatums. Now either pick up your script and get off your fucking high horse, or . . ." he smiled, "walk out the door."

Redness crawled up Sorel's neck as he glanced around for support. Unfortunately, his former confederates had buried their eyes in their scripts, leaving no doubt as to where their allegiance had fallen.

"Shit," he muttered in strained bravado and, after an indecisive instant, gathered his script from the floor.

Chandal turned cold satisfied eyes on Sorel and thought only, I'm doing it. I'm breaking his will. She had known from the beginning that this was necessary. Sorel was playing Rachel's husband. In the play, Rachel had fashioned this man into a weakling. An emotional cripple. Chandal intended to do the same thing to Brad Sorel.

For this reason she had begun to slap Sorel viciously during key scenes, even though neither was off script. The slap had been initiated in an improvisation and Eric had murmured in satisfaction, "That's good. Don't lose it."

It was permission enough, although Sorel constantly complained that she slapped too hard and was not using a stage slap.

Chandal knew that Sorel had degraded himself for the first time today. She would see to it that it would not be his last.

"Doreen! I'm late. Late, late, late. . . ."

"It's only nine o'clock. You have plenty of time."

"Now where the hell is my bag?"

"Hanging on the banister."

"Goddamn it! This place is a mess again. I keep cleaning it, and it keeps getting so goddamn filthy!"

"You want a pill?"

"For what?" Chandal scowled.

"Blood pressure."

"There is nothing wrong with my goddamn blood pressure! Now put those pills down."

"All right, all right. How about a headache? You have a headache?"

"No, Doreen. I do not have a headache. What I have is a real pain in my ass. You. You're that pain, Doreen. And get your feet off my couch!"

"Okay. Okay. Sorry."

"Shit. Come on, I want you out of here."

"You go. I'll lock up."

"No!" Chandal gave her a sharp stare. "I don't want you prowling around while I'm not here."

"Prowling around?"

"That's right. Someone was playing around with that statue. I found it turned nearly facing the wall yesterday. Somebody was fooling with it."

"Well," Doreen insisted, "it wasn't me!"

"Oh, shit. Just leave now, okay?"

"Okay!"

Doreen turned back at the door and eyed Chandal warily. "You're nuts, you know that? You're crazy nuts!" With that she stormed from the carriage house.

Chandal stood motionless for a moment. She looked around, feverishly examining every detail of the apartment. She stared uneasily, trying to concentrate on just how she had left things.

An instant sharp thought pressed.

She scanned the room again. Her only concern, oddly, was that no one touch her statue. She picked it up now. And as her mind drifted for a moment, her hand touching the creature's face seemed to respond and began to tremble slightly.

Chandal held the statue up to the light and heard again the soft-spoken man's voice at the antique shop and how he had praised the statue she was now holding. Her hands began to steady. There was something about his voice that settled her nerves. He had appeared to be in his seventies, yet there was something youthful and solid about him, a feeling that he had cheated death and would continue to do so.

Carefully she set the statue down. Yes. The man had been

right. "Just ask the statue," he had said, "and he will grant your wish." Silly—yes! But the old man had said it so simply, yet so seriously, that Chandal had found herself drawn by his persuasion.

Only when she glanced at her watch now, did the enchantment of the statue cease. Viciously she slammed the front door of the carriage house closed. She fumbled for her keys, damning all locks because her fingers were stiff and she could not find the right key, much less get it quickly into its slender niche.

"Goddamn it!" she grumbled and finally slid the key into the lock. A quick flick of her wrist and she turned and walked through the hazy courtyard.

Chandal was unaware of the old woman, her face bloated, full, yet drained of blood, watching her from the fifth-floor window of the brownstone. The woman's vacant eyes followed her, clung to her psyche, lusted after the youth that had once been hers. Yet she knew Chandal belonged to another, and that after all—she was fortunate enough to have gained what little had been offered her. An outpost on the edge of darkness. A pitiful post to be sure. Yet she was lucky to have this much.

Thousands of eyes looked greedily back at her.

Rats' eyes. They had become her pets.

She withdrew from the window as soon as Chandal had vanished from view. Yes, she mused, everything slips away as if it were merely a matter of a day. And then night comes. Night without dawn.

Slamming the outer gate shut, Chandal began walking toward Central Park West, her footsteps falling with heavy blows, steps that traveled through the cement-encrusted landscape as though caught up in a race.

CHAPTER SIXTEEN

THE MAN PASSED HIS HAND OVER CHANDAL'S THIGH. THE lights flickered. The tiny loveseat rotated slowly on its axis. Chandal moved her tongue against the roof of her mouth. Her gaze was fierce and strong. She felt that she had lost her sense of time and space, that she had been out of her body in some new place. But now she knew her body better than ever before.

"Stop!" she said and laughed. She moved her leg an inch or so—closer. "My husband is watching us."

"Let him watch. It will do him good to experience a bit of jealousy."

Smiling, Chandal cupped her hand over his and ran it further up her leg. She shivered with joy, even pride. Her eyes shone with a new light.

"Do you think my husband is capable of jealousy?" she asked.

Hesitantly, almost timidly, the man moved his hand in a circular motion between her legs. Never before had he been allowed to do such a thing. And yet he knew that Chandal's whims often ran to the bizarre. As his hand slid to her pubis, she spoke.

"You haven't answered my question." Chandal's smile broadened.

Covertly he inspected a portion of Chandal's upper leg, and, at the same time, fumbled for his lines. What on earth was she trying to prove, he wondered. Against Chandal's milk-white skin his hand appeared like a tan leather glove as he dug his fingers deeper into her flesh.

Chandal laughed with pleasure. "Oh, poor Anthony. I seem to be less and less married every time I see you. In fact, I think that by now I'm not married at all."

The man cleared his throat discreetly. "I . . . I only wish it were so."

Chandal pressed closer. Clasped her legs together into a sailor's knot, and trapped his hand in place. She began to rotate her pelvis slowly. At the same time, she pressed hard against his hand and used it as an instrument of masturbation.

"Say the word, just one word," she groaned, "and I'll divorce him. But I know you are not capable. . . ." She pressed harder, moved more quickly, her voice coming in short gasps. ". . . You won't say it. You're too afraid. All men—afraid of me."

Torn between fright and a wild impulse to laugh, Chandal watched as he slid his knee closer to her leg. He clutched desperately at her and loosed a steady flood of words as though afraid that, if interrupted, his very life would be in jeopardy.

Chandal tried to withdraw from his embrace, but he held on with frenzied strength. With his face buried between her breasts, he caressed her center.

At that precise moment, Eric Savage stepped silently onto the stage. Seeing him, the man pulled away from Chandal. At the sight of Eric he flushed, as if he had forgotten that anyone else was in the room. In the theater.

Chandal, meanwhile, focused her attention on herself. Adjusted her dress. Smiled.

It was Tuesday, the fifth day of rehearsal. April 8th.

At lunch, the actors left in a closely knit group, exclusive of Chandal. She sat on the stage and watched them go, observing the significant glances they exchanged, the care that was taken not to look in her direction.

"Aren't you going to lunch?" Eric asked from the door, somehow not fitting the time-hallowed image of a director. His clothing was always so neat—today a white shirt collar was revealed from the neck of his black cashmere sweater. He wore loafers and a well-tailored pair of silk trousers. Too neat, too conservative—even his hair was cropped a bit too close to his bony face.

Yet despite his non-theatrical appearance, Chandal knew that the actors all worshiped him for, as everyone knew, he bestowed his praise and his insults fairly. Still no one in the company knew, from day to day, where one stood with Eric Savage.

"You really should eat something, you know," he said and took a step forward.

"Maybe later," Chandal replied faintly. "I need to be by myself for a while."

"Okay. By the way, you're doing fine. Better than fine. You're even better than I thought you'd be."

"Yeah. I'm real popular too, don't you think?" Chandal commented wearily.

"We're not running an election here." He smiled suddenly. "People should learn how to lose as well as how to win. You are winning. They are losing. They'll get over it." He paused. "In the meantime, try to grab a bite. You're thin enough."

"Okay," she muttered and watched him disappear into the lobby.

Chandal waited for the outside door to close, and almost collapsed with relief when it finally did slam shut. The silence which followed told her that she was totally alone in the theater.

She closed her eyes and willed her mind to go out of focus for a moment. To let go of the shattering realization that always hit her the instant rehearsals ceased and she was no longer in the play, but instead back in the real world.

Awkwardly, she covered her face with her hands and let the tears come. That she was in trouble was undeniable. Her emotions were no longer controllable. She knew it. She was not altogether certain what the other people thought. It was just that in rehearsal she actually seemed to become Rachel and she hadn't the will to pull back, to be a nice person. To be herself. The tears rolled down her cheeks as she rose from the edge of the stage and began to pace the set.

It was strange how divided she seemed to be about the play. On the one hand, she was totally absorbed in a way she had never before experienced. She had been rehearsing only a week, and already she knew most of the lines. But it went a lot deeper than that. The passion of Rachel seemed to find a deep root within herself. And she could not shut it off. That was the point. She could not shut it off!

In only two and a half weeks the play would open to previews, a week later to critics, but by that time, what kind of claim would Rachel have on her?

Almost mechanically Chandal dried the tears from her cheeks and climbed from the stage. She knew she should eat something. Her usual toast for breakfast just wasn't enough.

She hesitated in the lobby for a moment. There was a strange silence in the darkened place. It felt cold. She found herself breathing carefully. Her eyes were shiny and tired.

Off in the distance, a phone began to ring.

She listened.

Her mind clicked suddenly onto a small, quiet, private, dim room: the brownstone. The room was located to the rear of the brownstone. Inside that room, Chandal watched herself huddle in the corner, frozen with fear.

The phone continued to ring.

What do you want from me? What!

More clicks—a camera. Justin's camera. They had gone to the park. Chandal had been worried about her mother's health. Her hypochondria. Click. Justin kept clicking the damn camera! *Please, Justin—don't take any more pictures!*

. . . Around and around . . . this way and that way and around behind. . . . She suddenly yanked the receiver off its hook. "Hello!" she cried, and then turned and realized she was standing in the lobby of the theater, that she had just answered the pay phone hidden away in the corner.

"Chandal Knight, please," requested a low, somehow familiar male voice.

Her mind came back into sharp focus. "This is Chandal."

Harsh breathing came from the other end. Nothing more.

"Who is this?" Chandal demanded.

The voice uttered something she couldn't understand.

"I can't hear you."

"The play," said the voice hurriedly. "You've got to get out of the play."

"Get out?"

"It's only the beginning," the voice warned. "The next time it's a bigger play, a better part. And it keeps getting harder and harder to say no." The voice broke.

"Billy?" Chandal said suddenly. "Billy, is that you?"

"I tried not to look at you that night. But when I heard about the play . . . I owe you this much, Chandal."

"Billy, please—don't hang up. I have to see you. Please. I know something"s going on. Something to do with the brownstone. Maybe you can—"

"Don't tell anyone, whatever you do."

"No. No, I won't." She paused, then added: "Billy, I have to see you. Talk with you."

"Tomorrow," Billy said unwillingly. "I'm staying at The Boulevard. 83rd and Central Park West."

"I'm writing it down. I'm off tomorrow."

"No! In the evening. 11:00 o'clock. Not before, not after. 11:00 o'clock."

"Billy, I'll be there."

"My apartment is not listed. Check with the desk."

"All right."

A sharp click told her that Billy had hung up.

Somehow, over a lunch of chef salad and a glass of white wine, Chandal thought that now it would all be different. Billy would be able to help her. Billy had always been so helpful in the past. She knew that he had the answers she'd been looking for.

She was getting closer to the truth. Images were starting to flood her memory. Something had gone wrong in the brownstone. She was sure of it now. Her mother's death, the fire, her feeling that Justin had been unfaithful to her, it all was more than fantasy it was a truth.

Or why else would Billy have run from her that night? Why had he called her now, warning her to get out of the play? Yes, she thought determinedly—everything would be different now.

Rehearsals would also be different. This time she would refuse to give way to the bitchiness, the hatefulness. She just had to be stronger. Jesus, she had to be. Because she had a sinking feeling that maybe it might boil down to that or giving up the role. Just as quickly she pushed the thought away. Giving up Rachel was impossible. Rachel was a part of her now.

If Chandal could have seen herself at that moment, she

would have seen too deep a crease work its way across her smooth young forehead.

In rehearsal that afternoon the anger within her surfaced from a deep spring in her subconsciousness. Everything bothered her, especially the child actress who was to play her daughter and who worked for only a few hours every afternoon. Not only was the child too ugly to be on a stage, but she had little training and even less talent.

"Come again?" Eric asked.

"You heard me. The girl is an amateur."

"Oh, really? I think she's quite good."

"You should replace her," Chandal said, a note of finality in her voice.

"I'll be the judge of that," he grinned, more amused than anything else. "Now, why don't you do your scene and I'll take a look for myself at what you mean."

"I think I can do it off script."

"Good enough."

Chandal could feel the silence out front as she began the scene. As much as the other actors despised her, she could tell they were driven to watch her act. "She's giving a brilliant performance," she had heard one of them whisper once, and in the next breath had come the sarcastic reply: "Performance? She's not acting, if you ask me."

Now she faced Brad Sorel, who could not meet her eyes, but instead stared down past her chin. Behind her the child fidgeted on the couch.

"I can't concentrate if she moves," Chandal shrilled out and Eric said, "Mandy, please sit very still until you're actually in the scene."

Chandal smiled hatefully at the ugly child and then began the scene with a good deal of charm and control. Fairly much on cue, the child tried to get her attention. Chandal shushed her gently and continued her dialogue with Sorel and the other actor who played Sorel's older brother. The child began to whimper in an especially irritating way.

"Please stop that," Chandal said as Rachel and could feel her nails dig into her palms. "I'm trying to have a conversation."

Inside her head, the knitting needles began clicking again. But the sound was different this time. It was linked with a wail, an animal noise that seemed to come down through the ages, a nexus of horror, vibrating and buzzing at the base of her skull.

The scene continued. The child's whining became intolerable. Chandal felt the spiral within, but never felt the actual explosion, never knew when the lid blew off her anger, letting it spill over like boiling lava. She only heard herself begin to yell, felt her hand over the child's mouth, squeezing, and her only wish was that she could squeeze harder, dig holes into the child's fat jaws. The tears on the freckled cheeks were repulsive to her and she had seized the child now, was shaking her as hard as she could. Voices yelled at her, arms held her, hands forced her fingers open.

"My God, Chandal, what the fuck were you doing?"

Chandal was crying now, hysterical, worried that she had hurt the child. People mobbed around her. Eyes. She couldn't stand the way their eyes stared at her. Those hateful eyes. And then from out of nowhere, the child's mother reached out and slapped Chandal hard across the face.

At first there was absolute silence. The actors were stunned. Not even Savage would look Chandal in the eye. Then, frantically, each actor found someone to whisper to. Finally there was an avalanche of chatter.

"You bitch!" scowled the child's mother.

Chandal froze. A strangely quiet look came over her face as she stared at the woman. Then she rose from her chair and left the theater. Voices called after her. She paid no attention. She was thinking only of the woman's face. Memorizing it in a minute way, feature by feature.

"Let her burn," she murmured. "Let her burn."

CHAPTER SEVENTEEN

HER BODY SEEMED FROZEN IN ITS HOOKED-OVER POSITION. HER back ached from its roundedness; even her neck strained from her head's tightly tucked downward position. And still she curled closer inward upon herself, protecting her anguish, her crushing embarrassment from the eyes of the outside world.

Her life was going around on a circular inside track as if a needle had slipped into a record groove, and the circles were reducing in scope, growing smaller and smaller like a whirlpool, sucking her deeper and deeper inside herself, and she couldn't seem to break free, to stop the cycle. And she wanted desperately to break away. . . .

Distracted, Chandal became aware of two different sounds inside her head. Nothing imagined. No, she was sure she actually heard them. A jeering laugh that echoed and then stopped suddenly, and began to spit out vulgar words. And the other voice, a muted wail of protest which eventually died away in the reverberation of the heinous laugh.

She thought of the child's mother, just as ugly as the child. Like mother, like daughter. People like that ought not to breed, to duplicate themselves on the earth. *"Fuck her, let her burn,"* sneered the voice.

Chandal straightened up to glance around the small restaurant. She had no idea how long she had been sitting in the cramped two-person booth. It could have been ten minutes, or an hour. Tears stung her eyes as she thought that what was

158

more to the point was the fact that she'd been swearing, making grotesque statements like a real loony. She'd seen them, people like herself. Some of them resembled normal citizens of the earth. And yet they talked to themselves, lived in private worlds, often violent, obscene worlds like the reality that tugged so often at her.

Startled, Chandal met bland gazes, or pleasant gazes, or even belligerent gazes from people in the coffee shop. After a moment of deep consideration she came to the conclusion that she had not spoken aloud. That her thoughts, the insane voices in her head, had remained private. This time.

Moisture splattered from her eyes like a short burst of rain that cleared quickly. She wiped the tears away with the back of her hand, smearing makeup across her cheeks.

What could be more awkward, more terrible, than the way she was acting? she wondered. Out of control. Completely out of control. First, two different horrible scenes at the theater in one day. One merely embarrassing, the other . . . Oh, God, she thought, and closed her eyes as another outburst of tears threatened. Bitterly she thought it wasn't bad enough to be crazy in the theater where everything, even the worst, might be overlooked as an overwrought, over-temperamental actress, but now here she was humiliating herself in public.

She straightened up with a sigh. "Oh, shit!" she mumbled and rubbed away the last of her tears. She pulled a crumpled Kleenex from her purse, dabbed her eyes, after which she reached for a cigarette, lighted it, inhaled deeply, and then allowed the smoke to filter slowly out of her mouth and nostrils.

She tried for a brief moment to put all the pieces together. All the associated thoughts rattled through her mind in a flash. Once more she felt a rush of embarrassment at what had occurred during rehearsal. She opened her free hand and stared at it. Then she thrust it down her blouse to grab hold of the pendant. She stayed in that position for a moment, wondering—wondering what she should do next.

She continued to take in deep lungfuls of smoke.

For a moment, she toyed with the idea of calling Eric Savage and laying it all on the line. Everything. Her amnesia. The voices inside her head. That she had once been confined in Lakewood. And yet . . . it was too ridiculous even to be considered. Somehow she had to find the courage to present a false front, to act as if it all made sense. For as long as she could. Because the moment anyone knew, it was all over for her, as she was well aware. They would make sure they confined her again. When all she needed was a little more time. She was so close. Billy would . . .

The small stub of her cigarette suddenly burned her finger, her elbow jerked backward instinctively, and she flinched as cup and saucer crashed to the floor of the restaurant. Like someone abruptly awakened from a deep sleep, Chandal peered in a daze at the trace of tea and the broken china.

"Are you all right?" asked the young waiter, frowning, but trying hard to conceal his annoyance.

"I'm sorry—I . . ."

"I'll get you another cup."

"No, thanks. I can't imagine how it—"

"It's all right. It happens all the time. Nothing to worry about."

Helpless as a child, Chandal watched him clean up the mess she had created. She concentrated on feeling less awkward, wondered how a guru would act if he had just shattered a cup and splattered tea over everyone, but then gurus probably didn't break cups or drink Lipton tea.

By this time, she had become not only paranoid, but hypersensitive. The conversation around her became the buzzing of a hundred angry bees. The smell of hamburgers and onions was suffocating. Through it all, her mind grappled with odds and ends of thought like showers of sparks from the end of a firecracker.

"There." The waiter smiled rather pointedly, thinking about his tip, no doubt. "Are you sure I can't—"

Chandal mustered a brief smile. "Thank you. No."

She thought that she was coming apart, and that this was the precise instant that her senses would probably leave her. She trembled in cold sweat and the next instant she was fever-hot. She closed her eyes, set her lips tightly, and an indefinable expression flickered across her face. She had to hold on to the one thing that mattered above all else. Her role in the play.

For some unfathomable reason she had come to feel she did not exist without the play. It was her only proof that she was part of the functioning world. Where would she be without it? Nowhere. She'd be a nonentity. Gone!

She reached for her purse. She would use another approach with Eric. She would appeal to him as an artist. Eric would understand, she thought desperately, and fumbled in her purse for the play's contact sheet.

Her fingers trembled as she went down the list and paused at Eric Savage's name. All she had to do was call him. No, better still—go to his apartment. Explain to him. She would find the right words. Surely she would find the right words.

But it took hours of walking, of agonizing before she was able to do it. To overcome a raging sense of pride that came bubbling up out of nowhere, a pride that threatened to strangle her when she imagined herself saying words like, "I'm sorry, Eric. I was an undisciplined fool for acting the way I did. I'll never do it again."

I'll choke, she thought fiercely, if I have to say that little inane speech.

Then, just as quickly, a tremendous sense of guilt swallowed her. And fresh tears, virginal tears sprang from her eyes. By the time she had dried them, she was vulnerable, innocent and pressing Eric Savage's doorbell.

"What the hell are you doing here?" he said, propped in the doorway of his East Eighties apartment, drink in hand.

"Hi," she said, in a tiny voice. She stared weakly over his shoulder at his lavish sunken living room. The lights were dim, and there were lighted candles on the coffee table.

"Could I come in?" she said, then added flatly, "I've come to apologize." She glanced sideways and caught a glimpse of herself in a vast mirror. Her face was drawn, haggard, the color of chalk. Her whole appearance was stark and lifeless. It was all in her mind, she assured herself. But she couldn't help thinking she looked so much worse than she had appeared yesterday, or the day before, or a week ago. She couldn't have become so run-down in such a short time. Frozen from the blustering April night, she ducked her head and focused on her gloved fingers laced tightly together.

Abruptly Eric pulled her inside and across the dining area, then down into the living room. "Sit!" he said, winking, and poured her a glass of sherry from a tray on a side table.

Chandal watched dazedly as he screwed the top back on the

sherry, handed her the glass, and then pulled a chrome leather-upholstered chair up close beside her and seated himself. She sensed some quality about Eric that she could not understand. But she saw the amused quirk at the corner of his mouth as though he was possessed of a quiet, secret glee.

"Drink," he said and fastened his eyes upon her in an interested sort of a way.

Obligingly she sipped and gagged slightly. "I'm sorry, I—"

"Touch your tongue to it and then run your tongue over the roof of your mouth. And then drink."

Surprisingly the method worked somewhat, and Chandal managed to swallow almost half a glass before setting it down on a seashell coaster.

"I don't know how I could have done—" she hesitated, "—what I did in rehearsal today."

Somberly he nodded, staring into his drink for a moment, and then back at her with a flushed, strangely expectant gaze.

She said uneasily, "I have no idea how it got—how I got so far out of hand."

Eric settled back in his chair and thought for a moment before saying, "The truth is it's usually that way with the truly brilliant. It's strange, isn't it, but I personally have always found it to be so." He spoke as quietly and as matter-of-factly as he could, making Chandal lean forward on the couch to hear his words.

"What do you mean?" she asked.

"You're all a little unhinged," he said, smiling somewhat to take the sting out of the words. "Sanity ceases, creative madness begins. You, however, have the honor of being the maddest artist I have ever encountered. Also—" he added almost absently, "—the most brilliant. Drink your sherry."

Chandal drew in her breath sharply. "Brilliant? Do you think I'm . . ."

"Most people won't stand for the madness," he said as if to himself. "They'd rather have predictable, interpretive acting. Good, standard, no fireworks—they understand this. They prefer it. Rather than putting up with that kind of pretty scene you treated us to today."

He continued to talk about genius as he rose from his chair, his body moving in slow rhythmic patterns. He adjusted the dials on his stereo system. The music filled out, became mellower, richer. She was watching the way his hands controlled the sound, as if he were conducting a private symphony beneath his words, each vibrant chord punctuating, emphasizing the mood he wished to convey. He turned to her.

Trembling, she met his eyes. "You . . ."

"I worship genius," he said simply.

"So then my part in the play is . . ."

"No." He smiled mirthlessly, watching her closely. "I can't save you. You're out of the play."

Vast emptiness settled inside of her. *You lost it!* snarled the voice she had come to know. *You stupid bitch.*

"Please," she stammered. "Help me. You must help me. I—I can't lose. . . ."

"There's nothing I can do," he said, and took a small sip of his drink. He was waiting, she realized and rose, took a deep breath and began backing slowly toward the bedroom.

His eyes followed her movement not with affection or distaste or amusement or any other emotion familiar to her—but rather with what she would describe later as ultimate professional curiosity.

She detached herself from his gaze, and turned toward the door.

The bedroom was lush and silent, hidden away in the rear of the apartment, cell-like—a womb of sorts.

He stared eagerly at the arrogant thrust of her full breasts under the sheer fabric of her blouse. He felt his eyes narrow as he studied her face. There was an expression of excited horror on her lips. And a scornful look in her eyes that troubled him faintly.

Yet he knew he had to have her.

He watched as she undressed silently. He almost moaned when she stepped from her skirt. She wore only her panties now. Black. Made of material that resembled a spider's web. With his gaze fixed on her, he had to admit that he wanted her more than he'd ever wanted anyone. Had he fallen for her? Was that it? No, it was something else. Something that shot from her body like heat streaming from the mouth of a volcano.

Slowly she rolled her panties down over the pink expanse of her upper legs. There was a kind of hypnotic beauty about watching her expose her body completely. She stood naked before him now, looking askew, frail, as if some change had come over her. Her face was immobile, only her eyes darted about the room.

For an instant neither of them moved.

Her breasts were full and firm, the nipples ruby red. A small tuft of brown hair seemed to bristle between her legs. Every part of her body brimmed with perfection—the flatness of her stomach, the narrowness of her waist, the sudden excellent curve of her hips, the well-sculpted legs, smooth and trim.

Without looking at him, she stepped awkwardly to the bed and sat. She laid her head back, letting her soft fine hair spill across her slender shoulders.

Her breasts appeared fuller now, swollen. He found himself suddenly drawn by a desire to squeeze them with his hand and watch them swell even larger, watch the thin blue veins that ran upward toward her neck explode with a fresh burst of blood.

He moved closer, stood before her, as naked as she was. She did not touch him, although he made it known that that was what he most desired. Instead she reached out and hit the light switch.

Darkness.

And in the darkness he felt an odd tension in the air, as if a new entity had entered the room, a pleasurable, yet vindictive force of energy set on injuring him in a sort of retaliation for his past transgressions. He moved forward blindly, ignoring the sensation.

With as little disturbance as possible, he climbed into bed. In the next instant he dropped his leg over her body and kissed her lips, then dropped his head to her neck where he sucked her flesh, pulling it away from the side of her throat in playful love bites. Then he ran his hand over her breasts. Squeezed. Harder. His fingers pinched the nipple between his thumb and forefinger.

"You're hurting me," she whimpered.

"Don't you like it? The pain?"

He closed his fingers harder on her nipple.

She moaned.

His hand dropped quickly between her legs as he rolled over on top of her. "Oh, Rachel," he moaned and felt her breasts surging against his chest. His face was pressed tautly against her cheek and he could feel the heat radiating from her skin. Hot. She was so hot.

He felt her shudder, felt her nails begin to dig into the flesh of his back, felt her fingers run wild through his hair, over his hips, between his legs. She groped for his erection, caught hold of it and guided it into her.

He began to lose track of time and space as she kissed him. Unpleasant kisses, too violent, too demanding. Control. He was losing control. Felt her fingers probing him, felt something hot and gushing flow over his belly. She was taking him, seducing him in a way he had never known before. Sex had never been so repulsive or so overwhelming. He saw a side of himself that was pure evil, pure lust.

A violent pull began to tear at his stomach, causing an intensified longing and loathing at one and the same time. It was as if his emotions sprang from the deepest part of his soul and could not be controlled, their essence being felt for the first time.

He felt possessed by a power so grotesque, yet so intoxicating, that he was unable to deny its force. He groped with his body, penetrating her inner mystery. He heard her whisper: "Fuck her . . . fuck her good. And me!" The voice faded into a heavy, gasplike breathing that rose and fell in little shudders from a spittle-filled throat.

"Eric . . . Eric. . . ." Her distorted voice seemed to emanate through a megaphone, obscenely seductive and ugly. Her breath burned his neck. Her teeth tore at his flesh.

In quick succession he thrust himself forward, deeper, harder, his longing and loathing existing side by side, each struggling to dominate the final moment of climax.

The persistence of disgust finally gave way to sheer joy. The joy increased, became burning shafts of fire. He cried out, lunged against her and sank down, deep within her. He tightened his grasp on her waist and pressed her further into the mattress.

Overpowering lust consumed him. Everything roiled inside him, a terrible driving need to spend himself completely. Obsessed with fulfilling his desire, he closed his fingers around the flesh of her buttocks, driving her to him. He heard her scream: "Fuck me!"

She screamed, and screamed again.

He pumped harder, faster; the blood throbbing through his body, pulsating through his brain. He gasped, pulled her up in his arms and then suddenly exploded—a long, shuddering orgasm that seemed to go on forever.

And then he felt his body sag, breathless and exhausted, to a limp position beside her. His first reaction, his only reaction now, was one of disgust. Her grossness repelled him. He found it impossible to look at her, to touch her, to lie beside her any longer. Could she sense his revulsion, he wondered. She must have, because she said:

"Don't you see how perfect it is—how perfect for the play?" Her voice was odd, not at all her own.

Sickened, he did see. "Somehow," he said, "I'll make sure you do Rachel."

"Good," she whispered. "Good."

He tried to rise from the bed. She reached out and grasped his arm.

"Don't go," she whispered. "Tell me how much you liked it."

He did not speak, and in a perverse way, he felt a sadistic pleasure in not answering her. He knew he had her now. He knew that the situation was now under control. His control. And this, more than anything else, was important to him. Lying beside her, he reached out and held her hand.

The room was silent for a moment.

What was she thinking, he wondered. What would he tell her if she confronted him? If she accused him of being sickened by the whole experience. He would not protest. Nor apologize. He would simply be honest with her. There was nothing strange in what he had felt. Many men had experienced similar feelings when they lost control of themselves. Surely she would be able to understand that.

Now he glanced at her from the corners of his eyes.

A pale light filtered in through the window and stopped just short of her face. He could not make out her features. Yet he could feel she was smiling. Experiencing a quiet amusement. He could also feel the strangeness of her grasp. Her fingers felt cold and thin. Bone thin. The flesh seemed to hang loose between her fingers.

"Chandal?" he whispered.

There was no answer.

He peered beyond the soft shaft of yellowish light. Yet her face was still hidden by shadows.

"Chandal, are you all right?"

And then she moved her face into the light.

For a swift second, before he could believe or react to what he saw, a long fingered hand that was nothing more than a loosely tied bundle of blue veins, placed itself tenderly on his cheek.

The old woman smiled at him, her raw, crinkled skin that stretched over the many folds of her eyes and mouth, wrinkled even more, and her fabled skull face of death glimmered white beneath a heavily applied rouge that covered most of her corpselike cheeks. She hissed at him like a snake through cracked and bloated lips: "I love your passion, Eric."

And then he screamed and realized that in the middle of his bedroom, surrounded by darkness, he was not alone, there wasn't any doubt, and he wasn't going crazy, the old woman was still propped in his bed, breathing, and Eric screamed, and the cry echoed down the long hallway and he was about to explode because—the old woman would not go away and she would not let go either, her fingers gripped his arm and Eric struck out with his free hand but it was no use, the old woman clung tighter and now they were facing each other and the old woman's violet eyes smiled at him, laughed, she laughed and he screamed, his breath coming in short gasps until it stuck in his throat and he gagged, while the room turned and spun and the old woman grabbed tighter and Eric tried snapping her fingers loose, but they would not loosen, they held on to him for dear life, dragging him under as she hissed and laughed and he fought—wide-eyed—but it was too late, she had him, held him, pulled at him, and she would not stop until she had finally dragged him under, and that's where he was going, under, under, it was no use—he was going under . . . the gaping O of surprise smeared across his horror-stricken face.

Chandal stood naked before the mirror. The bloodstone pendant hung between her swollen and bruised breasts. With the eyes of a stranger she viewed Eric Savage's limp and exhausted body sprawled out on the bed, asleep.

"See?" said the voice. *"He has learned to accept it."*

The stranger within her smiled and then the sound of her voice was gone. But its effect lingered. Chandal stood, scared and trembling. Her image appeared clear in the glass. Her consciousness returned. She stared helplessly at the bruises on her breasts, at her sweat-coated skin, disheveled hair, and smeared makeup. "Oh, God. . . ." she groaned and threw her hands up over her face. "What have I done?" She stood isolated, paralyzed, knowing she could never forgive herself.

Eric moaned and rolled over on his side. Chandal caught sight of his naked body in the mirror, as a sudden spasm jerked at his leg.

Hastily, she dressed. Slammed out of the apartment and down the stairs. She pounded down the pavement, breaking into a run but slowing again, shattered by a violent pain in her chest, propelled mercilessly by the image of Eric Savage, his naked body spread wide to accommodate the passion of his obscene dreams.

At the corner a group of men, all drunk and out on the town for a night of fun, blocked her way.

"Where are you going, baby?" barked the tallest of them.

They all laughed.

In their faces Chandal saw her own confusion and shame reflected. Completely disoriented, weak and shaken, she stumbled headlong, passed their howls of laughter, into the night. Deeper into the ever present abyss that awaited her.

CHAPTER EIGHTEEN

CLOUDS THICKENED OVER THE CARRIAGE HOUSE AS THE FIRST brush-strokes of night began to darken its crude brick-stone face. Like a hideously painted mask, its reddish brick front grimaced secrets of those who had lived within for so many years. Images sprang into miniature jet-black view between the cracks and crevices of its malevolent, yet comic makeup: tiny pirouetting figures, dancers from another time, another stage, hellbent to express the intensity of their own pent-up emotions, while willing themselves to escape from their own stone skin.

Chandal stopped for a moment, listened to the whispers of the tree branches blowing in the slight breeze.

Secrets . . . the will-o'-the-wisp sound echoed in her mind. She went from room to room, drawing curtains and turning on a few lamps. In the den the light was especially dim and gloomy, and she made a mental note to get a package of higher-watt lightbulbs.

She sighed and turned her eyes to the yellowed parchment which she now held stretched tight between her hands.

"All human clay is subject to decay. But in Hell, we shall still be alive in this body—and this is better than annihilation."

Standing completely still, her face pale, her eyes squinting from the room's poor light source, she considered this. Considered the carefully scribed saying written in a fine

Victorian penmanship across the deteriorating, perishable parchment paper.

After a moment she laid the scroll aside. It was old, possibly worth something. In any event, it was a curiosity worth saving. Strange words to be written in such dainty penmanship. Nothing else in the desk drawer seemed of interest. She tilted the drawer over the trash basket and let an assortment of debris and dust empty out. Then, using a damp cloth, she cleaned the grimy interior of the drawer.

Her thoughts threatened to wander toward last night and Eric Savage, who hadn't called all day. What was she expected to do tomorrow—simply show up for rehearsal as though nothing had happened? Or sit and wait until Eric called? She shoved her chin forward and decided to go to rehearsal. The most he could do was to send her home. And she didn't believe he would do that.

Unwillingly she let her confidence lapse a notch. Most people seemed to have dark, unpredictable sides to their personalities. shadow-selves so diverse as to completely alter, and sometimes dominate, the original creation. God knew she had her opposing slants. Last night, she had met Eric Savage's divergent personality.

A hectic flush of heat worked into her throat. Her thoughts raced around, unable to fall into any one line of reasoning.

It was really just a few instants that she had retained, nothing else. A fleeting memory of Eric's hands on her breasts, squeezing too hard. Something brutal about his eyes, as though they were punishing her for having digusted him. A leg flipped over her body, pinning her. The word "Rachel" spoken in an odious, shrill tone.

The question—the thing that eluded her—was how she had gotten into Eric's bedroom. She had gone over it time after time and always her memory stopped at a certain point. She had gotten up from the couch almost ill. She had lost the part, Eric had said, but something in his voice, some teasing element told her he didn't mean it, that there was still something she could do about it.

Hesitantly, almost timidly, she had moved. Eric's eyes had followed her. Had she been seductive in any way? That hadn't been her intention. She had merely crossed the room to stare at an unusual pen-and-ink sketch in a small chromium frame.

Then in the next instant, she had raised her eyes. It was all but impossible, yet there she had stood, naked before Eric Savage's bedroom mirror, and she had known that in some horrible way she had degraded herself.

It made no difference to her why it had happened. It had happened. She knew she should never have gone to bed with him. Not then, not that way. She knew only too well. But the knowing hadn't been enough, had it? She had allowed herself the experience anyway. But had she allowed it? It was hard to say. She had never even known the urge was there. If so, she would have guarded herself. Especially since it hadn't helped anything. Her part in the play, apparently, was as much in jeopardy as ever.

How could she really be sure, she thought now with sharp loathing, exactly what Eric Savage would do? What any man would do, for that matter?

"Why don't you pitch out that shelf of old magazines?" Mike Hammer snapped from the corner of the den.

Chandal turned with a start. She stood facing him as though suddenly stricken with amazement that she was really there, facing him in this small, shabby room. More to the point, she was amazed that *he* was there! She had completely forgotten his presence, despite the fact that he had been at work for most of the afternoon plastering the walls.

She waited, twisting her hands together.

"I . . . I think you could sell some of them to an antique shop," she began slowly, "if you wanted to bother. . . ."

"Not me," he sneered as if she had accused him of being a ragman.

She looked at him with sorrowful eyes.

"I didn't mean anything by it," she said.

"I didn't say you did. I'm just not interested, that's all."

"Okay!" Chandal suddenly laughed. "Then we'll pitch them." She gathered the magazines up in two armloads and dropped them into the large wicker basket she was using for trash. When she turned around to see what Mike's reaction had been to her sudden and swift obedience, she discovered that he had gone back to work, slapping plaster into place.

Motionless, she watched the wide expanse of his back, watched the muscles in his arms twitch heavily once or twice. She studied him in silence for a long time. Studied his broad shoulders and immense body that seemed to fill the entire surface of the wall he was now working on. With each new dip of his body, as he leaned down for fresh plaster, came a short gasp of air.

During the past week, Chandal had found that Mike all but inspired a feeling of visceral terror in her, an emotion so intense and so confusing that it required all her energies to avoid experiencing it, or at least to deny its existence. She had the strange sensation that Mike had been coming to her in her sleep. Dreams, she had told herself. Yet each experience had been distressingly vivid. There had been no sense of struggle, only a soft, effortless seduction of sorts. And there, in the shadows, Doreen was watching with glee. A terrible, pitiless exaltation.

"It has been ordered," she would whisper. She would say it over and over again as though Chandal should understand and sometimes Chandal thought she did understand on some deep somnambulistic level. Each dream brought with it a source of constant irritation and frustration. A blend of revulsion and longing.

Suddenly Mike stopped his work to glance over his shoulder. He saw Chandal standing directly behind him. He brought his hand up to his forehead and flicked salty beads of sweat from his finger to the floor. Awkwardly, Chandal reached for the clean towel that hung over the desk chair. She stepped closer.

"Here," she said.

"Thanks."

Nervously she turned away, her eyes scanning the room.

"This is really a terrible room, isn't it?" she said, not for the first time, and wondered why the only window in the den, the tiny arched window in the north wall that faced the courtyard, had been sealed off.

"Whose bright idea was that anyhow?" she asked, her head cocked at the window.

"Beats me. . . ."

"Can we do something about it?"

"Oh, sure. I really have nothing better to do than plastering your walls and knocking out your windows."

Chandal pointedly ignored his sarcasm. "Would you like a cup of tea?"

"Old ladies drink tea."

"Coffee?"

"I'll take a cold beer if you have one."

"I don't have one."

Their eyes locked for what seemed like a lifetime, but was in reality no more than a second or two. It was sufficient for Chandal to feel that she knew everything there was to know about him, past, present and future, and that there was a current which crackled between them.

Chandal wasted no time in averting her gaze, glancing at the wallpaper she had selected for the room. "Do you think this paper will lighten the atmosphere in here?"

Mike looked at the paper briefly. "I guess," he muttered and returned to work.

"I could add a few lights," she said slowly, "but there is only just the one wall outlet." She hesitated and waited for him to answer. He continued to work. "Electricians are so expensive. I guess I'll just have to wait," she said and moved closer. She found her eyes riveted to the back of his neck where his thick dark hair lay in longish curls. "Why in heaven's name do you suppose that window was sealed up?" she said hastily for something to say and flushed when she realized she was retreading old ground.

"Drafty," Mike said in a curiously gentle voice and flipped fresh plaster on the wall.

"Yes. You're probably right. The heater in this room isn't very big."

"That's what I mean."

Irresistibly drawn to take a step closer, she peered over his shoulder. "Anything I can do to help?"

"No, I'm about done." He smoothed out the last of the plaster and then laid down his trowel and turned to face her.

They were too close for convention's sake and yet he moved closer until she could feel the warmth of his breath on her face. Chandal's heart skipped strangely. An awareness that she was on treacherous ground flooded her being, but she was unable to turn away, was completely helpless to take her eyes from Mike's handsome face.

He smiled. "I'll let that dry. Finish it in the morning."

"I won't be here," she said.

"I have the key."

"Oh, yes—that's right."

For no reason Chandal could put her finger on, she felt her cheeks burn when Mike grinned and walked out the front door without saying another word. As if she . . . hell! Forget it.

She went back to cleaning drawers. She still had an evening to kill before meeting Billy Deats at The Boulevard at eleven. Dust was thick in the desk's interior, great old rolled top desk that it was. It filtered down in little puffs every time she removed another item from the drawer. It caught in her throat like sticky fiber and even coughing did not completely expel it.

Digging through the pigeonholes she found old stamps, a stack of yellowing envelopes, a broken pocket watch, pens and pencils and several cigars which crumbled almost immediately upon her touch. Something about the way the cigars disintegrated in her hand left her with a vague unsettled feeling. She had always feared death. She had always been afraid to even permit herself to consider it.

Experiencing a certain disquiet, she opened her hand and allowed the loose tobacco to fall like dirty snow into the wicker basket. The action itself became a baptism of sorts.

Turning once more, she unbuttoned the cuffs of her blouse, pushed her sleeves to her elbows and faced the desk. In the next instant her hand moved over an oddly shaped bronze handle just above the writing surface of the desk. The seams of the little drawer were so clogged with dirt and grime that she had thought the handle a decoration. The drawer was small, with dimensions roughly those of a pocket-sized cigar box. Hesitantly she opened it and reached in. Her hand closed on a small stack of business cards. She made an involuntary move to toss them out and then hesitated. Arthur M. Showalter, the card read. Jeweler. A business on Broadway.

Once again she reached into the drawer and withdrew a passport. A thirty-odd-year-old man, according to Showalter's photo. Distinguished as opposed to handsome.

The crying began then, though at first Chandal did not think anything of it. God, the baby probably needs changing again and feeding again and walking again—whatever made me get myself into a fool mess like this . . . all for what? Nothing. He loves her—he's always loved her. . . .

Chandal looked up sharply, the passport still in her hand.

Now the crying was deafening.

Where?

What baby?

She felt a coil of terror unwrap itself in a single shooting spurt until she heard herself begin to scream too, her cries blending with those of the baby's. She tried to suppress the sob which rose in her throat, desperately restricting the muscles in her larynx. It was useless.

On her feet now, she began to search for what could not be there and yet must be there. So close—just across the desk, it seemed.

Nothing, nothing.

"His crib used to be there," explained the voice coldly. *"Arthur wanted him downstairs so he didn't have to listen to the crying."*

Chandal still screamed, still groped with trembling hands through vacant space.

"He was a bad baby. He would have grown up to be like his father. I couldn't have that."

In a final paralyzing scream, Chandal found her hand clenched tight. She could not open it. Fear had turned to anger. To hate. She walked forward. She remembered now where his crib was. Just there, not three steps from the desk. Violently now, her hand curled tighter. She could feel the handle in her palm. She couldn't wait to see Arthur's face when . . .

Hand raised in a sudden sharp sweep, she paused, looking down into the crib. The hateful little face was screwed up tight. Tiny hands were fists beating the air. With a growl of animal rage, she began to plunge her hand downward. . . .

Chandal paused, trembling.

Silence.

She fell backward, hitting the desk sharply. Tears continued to roll down her cheeks, but she was past being able to relate to that. She could not even relate to her right hand that even now refused to relax.

Only one thing was clear as she donned trench coat and hastily changed from house slippers to flat walking shoes. She had to get out of there. She had to breathe some fresh air. She had to get outside her own madness.

She ran to get her purse, found the keys on the mantel and flung herself through the door as though pursued. What is happening to me? she thought hopelessly. What kind of madness? And felt her hand close around a crumpled bit of paper in her coat pocket. It was Showalter's business card, held all through the emotional explosion, and then shoved into her pocket almost in ribbons, but still an avenue to explore.

She stopped to hold the card up to the light. A sudden memory of a very old man. "Heavens," he had said, "but she was such a pretty thing at nineteen, charming and well informed—ah!" Chandal had watched the old man's faded blue eyes light up. "I have never seen anyone quite like her—never!"

She walked faster. She already knew the place. She had been there several times. She wasn't sure just when, but she had definitely been there.

She recognized the shop immediately, even from outside, peering in through the glass. Yes, she had been here before. She also recognized the jeweler who sat in the rear of the shop, jeweler's glass over one eye. Not the older man—this man couldn't be over forty-five.

"Yes, can I help you?" he asked in antisocial tones.

"Is—is Mr. Showalter here?" Her hand closed nervously around the crumpled card in her pocket.

"I'm afraid not."

"Oh, well, it's late. I'm surprised you're open at this hour."

"Nine to nine. That's the only way I can make any money these days."

"I see." She paused, then added, "Does Mr. Showalter come in earlier?"

"Not earlier or later. He's dead."

"Oh," gasped Chandal softly and felt a small shudder go through her body. "Thank you. Thanks very much. . . ."

"Can I help you with anything?" he frowned, disliking to lose business.

"No, thanks. Ah, Mr. Showalter—he was the same Showalter who lived in the old carriage house on West 71st Street?"

"All his life."

"Oh, I thought somehow he was only there for a short—"

"All his life," repeated the man laconically.

"I'm sorry to ask this, but did he die recently?"

"No, about three years ago."

"Was he married?"

"No." The man eyed her suspiciously. "Are you a relative or something?"

"Nothing like that. I just wondered. Ah, one more thing. Was he living with children? Niece, nephew . . . ?"

"What?"

"Children. Were there any children living there with him?"

"No. Whatever you're thinking, you've got the wrong man."

"I see. Well. . . ." The man had dismissed her now, had headed back to his work bench. Chandal still hesitated, now glancing at the blue velvet jewelry pad. An image of a ring appeared. Suddenly she realized she was staring at her ring. Justin had given it to her. She frowned. One of the two sisters—not Elizabeth, but Magdalen, the older, frailer sister—had had such a ring.

Chandal's head spun sickeningly. Remembering was not pleasant, not pleasant at all. Magdalen's picture hanging in the basement of the brownstone. Justin had taken her picture, hung it there. The basement had been Justin's darkroom. Now she wanted to stop the flow of memory, but could not. Justin lying in Magdalen's lap. How disgusting. Magdalen's white hair, catching a rosy glint from the rose-colored light shade. Her skin seemed for a moment young, soft and satiny.

"It was all her fault. You can see that, can't you?"

Blindly, Chandal turned and stumbled from the shop. She could see herself descending the basement stairs of the brownstone. The manikins. There had been manikins and the little door in the corner, the one that led up the side stairs to the attic. It was up in the attic. That thing . . . what was it—hidden away up in the attic. . . .

She stopped suddenly. Brakes had screeched—a car had missed her by inches. She tried desperately to retrieve her thought. What was she just thinking? Reality pressed in on her. The brownstone faded. She was standing in the middle of the street. Traffic had come to a standstill. People stood staring.

Somehow she started to function. Rapidly she picked her way through traffic and put distance between herself and curious pedestrians. It was only eight-thirty, she noted, still a long time before she was supposed to meet Billy. Her stomach seemed to churn and she realized she had hardly eaten a bite all day. Suddenly ravenous, she ducked into a coffee shop and absorbed herself in a club sandwich deluxe. The food was a vast relief and for a few hungry minutes she felt very calm.

Then she sat, quietly, satiated, and was able to see quite simply and with great clarity that she was in such trouble that escape was no longer an easy matter. That perhaps it was even possible that escape was no longer feasible. Grimly she laid her hands together and closed her eyes. It was funny how her one hope kept boiling down to Billy Deats. That perhaps Billy could help her when no one else could. It was more than a thought, more than a vague hope; it was a consuming passion that drove her headlong down Central Park West, although she knew she was too early, that Billy wouldn't even have returned from the theater. But she had no self-control, nor reason, nor common sense. Then, blinking, dazed, she came to an abrupt halt in the midst of a large crowd, some thirty or so people gathered in a cluster at the front entrance of The Boulevard. Three police cars waited, their roof lights sending red flickers of spinning light across the confused expressions on most faces.

The high-pitched, sharp wail of a siren stabbed upward from the west. A police emergency truck scurried around the corner and came to a screeching stop between jammed traffic. Somebody is dead, Chandal thought. They never send out those emergency trucks unless someone is dead. The siren was like the distressed cry of a woman moaning at a wake. Its blast quieted as two attendants sprang from the truck. Now, who could be dead? Chandal wondered. Had a woman been mugged? Had a child accidentally swallowed pills, thinking them candy? Had a man suffered a heart attack?

"Stand back, please," barked the policeman.

Another policeman turned and said, "He's dead."

Chandal pushed closer, watched as the attendants lifted a coat away from the body. Whose body? "Oh, my God," Chandal gasped, and stared down at Billy Deats, who lay crumpled in a heap, his hair streaked and caked with blood, his face swollen, his black bathrobe open from his waist down.

"Move back. Move back!"

People were being shoved now and excited voices were

heard everywhere. Still, Chandal could not move, could not take her eyes from Billy's face, the flesh of his arms and legs that hung flaccid, utterly without form, without life.

Quickly the attendants lifted his body and dropped it into a plastic bag. The image seared Chandal's mind like a hot branding iron. She knew she would see that broken body, that bloated face for the rest of her life.

With the quick flick of a zipper, the image was gone.

"He jumped from the 10th floor," shrilled a voice front-right of her.

"What was that wooden thing he was holding?"

"It was a cross."

Another voice—masculine: "He was holding it in his hands. Some kind of a religious nut."

"It seemed to me he was actually nailed to it," a woman explained. "Didn't you see the palms of his hands? They were both bleeding. And his feet. . . ."

"Don't be ridiculous. His whole body was bleeding. . . ."

Chandal stepped swiftly away and lost her dinner. It did not, however, erase the image from her mind. The image of Billy Deats lying limp upon a large wooden cross. Broken by a skyscraper leap into death. And yet Chandal, like the woman, had seen Billy's bloody palms, his bloody feet.

She turned back at last and saw Billy's body being loaded into the white emergency truck. But to her, Billy would always be as she had just seen him. In a shattered cruciform position, lying on the sidewalk outlined in chalk, bathed in a pool of his own blood.

CHAPTER NINETEEN

HE HAD KNOWN IT WAS GOING TO BE A BAD DAY AS SOON AS HE headed for the L.A. International Airport. It started, as always, with a series of minor annoyances. The cars on the freeway had been backed up for miles. He had literally come to a standstill in traffic.

Somewhere above the smog-choked city he was sure the sun was shining, but at street level everything was cloaked in a veiled yellowish mist. Cars and pavement shimmered like mirages in the heat.

From his car window there was nothing to be seen but a mass of metal motionless in a pool of choked air that clung to the city like ether. Spring was the season that the natives of Los Angeles were supposed to love best. It had always brought the two months of rain that would wash away the smog. On this particular April morning there was no rain, no clear air, only a veil of poison.

Ron Talon took out a pack of cigarettes, shook one into his hand and tapped it lightly on the dashboard. His eyes moved in slow sweeping arcs, still watching the freeway, checking out the long line of cars that preceded him. "Goddamn it," he mumbled and checked his watch. If the traffic didn't let up soon, he'd miss his plane. Everything around him was fairly quiet. There was only the low rumble of distant traffic that was Los Angeles.

Thirty minutes later, Ron hastened down the long airport terminal corridor searching for the right gate. Sweat beaded his forehead because of the oppressive heat and because the traffic had detained him just long enough so that there were only minutes before his flight left for New York.

Just after he entered the boarding gate, and as he was having his ticket validated, he was handed a message by the young woman attendant behind the desk.

Call before you fly. Mimi.

Ron growled, staring down at the slip of paper as though he had never seen a message before. Confused, almost unable to connect with the proper response, he could feel his heart begin to thump. Jesus.

"Is there a phone nearby?" he asked.

"Down the corridor and to the right."

"Thanks. Do I have time?"

"If you hurry."

He moved swiftly to the nearest telephone, which was not near at all, and dialed his office.

"Ron Talon Agency. Good morning," Mimi's voice shrilled.

"Mimi? This is Ron. What's up?" he asked warily.

"Hate to bother you, Ron. But Walsh doesn't want to pay fifteen thousand for 'Dan and the California Fever.'"

"Did you tell him that. . . ."

"It's the lowest group we handle. Yes."

"What about Antiqua?"

"He said he has never heard of her."

"What the hell does he mean, never heard of her. Tell him she's heading for big things."

"I did. He said no dice. He wants to talk with you personally."

Totally exasperated, Ron said, "Mimi, I have no intention of calling him now. So just . . ."

The public address system punched through Ron's ear and announced last call for his flight.

"Mimi, I've got to run."

"What should I tell Walsh?"

"Tell him—tell him you haven't been able to reach me."

"That's it?"

"That's it. Until I reach New York. I'll call you from there."

"Happy wings!"

"Right."

181

He hung up and, feeling his stomach rumble in a vaguely unsettling way, hurried toward his plane.

Wearing a brown blazer, chino pants and loafers, and carrying his Dunlap bag, he boarded the 11:00 A.M. flight, scheduled to arrive in New York at 7:00 P.M.

It was a smooth flight but his stomach continued to churn. He had forgotten to take Dramamine. He ate the small steak, left the eggs, drank the tomato juice and coffee, and was proud that somehow it all stayed down. It showed a certain amount of willpower.

For no special reason he thought of the crucifix packed away in the corner of his suitcase. He had sealed it in an envelope to take to Chandal, almost steadfastly refusing to look at it. Something worried him about the crucifix. He was also worried about his own health. He knew he was far from well, even after the week he had just spent flat on his back. He had lost a considerable amount of weight and his clothes were all too loose. A narcotic veil seemed to hang over his vision, even though for two days he had discontinued medication. More than anything else, it was an inner vibration that worried him, a certain conviction that he wasn't going to get well. No matter how hard he tried, he could not shake the thought that there was something dreadfully wrong with him.

There was traffic stacked for an hour over Kennedy and his plane was forced to keep circling until ground control finally gave the go-ahead to land. The boarding terminal was out of working order and he had to deplane by the steps. His legs buckled and he saved himself from falling only by clutching the railing, thereby painfully wrenching his shoulder.

At his hotel he found his reservation had been booked for the following night. When a new, more expensive, room was secured, he thought how strange it was that he should need a room at all. Shouldn't he be staying at the carriage house? Then, staring at the pale green hotel telephone, he realized that perhaps it was strange that he had come to New York at all. It was even possible that Chandal would refuse to see him. It took him a long time to pick up the phone.

Chandal lay face down on her bed, her face pale, strained with hours of tears. She had gone to rehearsal that morning, but had not been allowed to go any further than the box office. At that point she had come face-to-face with an adamant stage manager.

"I'm sorry, but there's been a complaint brought against you with the Board at Actors' Equity."

She had met his timid, but determined young eyes with an icy blue stare. "I don't give a damn about that and neither does Eric Savage."

"You can't rehearse until it's settled."

"The hell I can't!" she cried.

"I'm sorry, but it's my job to—"

"Your job? You don't have a damn thing to say about it. It's Eric's place to say whether I stay or go."

With high spots of color burning on his cheeks, the young man took a sealed envelope from his pocket. "Eric has asked me to give you this."

She gasped, completely stunned, and saw his pitying gaze.

Now, as she twisted uncomfortably on her bed, she could still see the three lines that Eric Savage had written:

"We'll try to get this ironed out. If not—Rachel is not the only part in the world. Hang in there until you hear from me. Eric."

It seemed to her that it was merely the final note in her despair. The despair that was wrapped around her own crumbling sanity, Billy Deats' death, and a sense that everything she did or said was part of someone else's master scheme and had nothing at all to do with her own life, her own decisions. Some kind of separation was growing complete within her. Who would she be without Rachel? At the end of all this? Who would she be? A ghostly image of Billy lying on the sidewalk, his body blood-soaked and broken, flashed before her mind's eye. God help me, she thought, now lying flat on her back. She lifted her eyes up to stare through the skylight. She had been trying to pray, but even this fleeting effort was diverted. Her gaze had fastened on the old woman sitting at her window on the fifth floor of the brownstone.

The woman acknowledged Chandal's gaze with a little nod and then, as the woman allowed herself to be scrutinized, she also let her eyes frankly study Chandal.

Chandal felt her tension relax. She had become very tired, almost to the point where she could not stay awake. Her eyelids drooped and then after a timeless interval flew open. For a moment she was confused and then heard plainly the knock on the front door which must have aroused her.

Hurriedly she reached for her robe and noticed without surprise that she was completely nude. "Just a minute," she mumbled, and walked barefoot down the stairs and opened the door, her robe haphazardly tied.

When she drew open the front door, the shaking figure of Doreen was revealed, her face lost in shadow, and there was something almost other-worldly about her. As she stepped forward, Chandal saw that she had been crying.

"Oh," Doreen said, her eyes widened.

Crossly, Chandal pulled her robe tighter. "I was in bed."

"I'm sorry," Doreen said constrainedly. "It's so early, I never thought . . ."

"Never mind. Come in."

Doreen stepped cautiously across the threshold. Chandal shut the door behind her and watched as Doreen's eyes darted around the apartment looking for something. Her gaze came to rest on the bedroom stairs.

"Is something wrong?" asked Chandal and reached for a cigarette from the small ebony box on the side table. Cigarette lit, she listened with half a mind and heard Doreen say she was looking for Mike, that he was nowhere to be found.

"He sure isn't here," Chandal said coldly and immediately switched the conversation to the old woman on the fifth floor of the brownstone.

"You mean she's up there now?" Doreen asked, pointing to the window.

"Yes."

"That's impossible. The apartment is empty."

"Doreen, I just saw her looking at me through the skylight. She's there!"

"It's not that I don't believe you saw something, Chandal— a shadow or something. But, believe me, no one lives in that apartment."

Chandal stared at her with a certain amount of determination. "I want to go up there."

"But—"

"If you don't want to go with me, then stay here. Do whatever you want. But if you won't let me have the key, I'll find some way to get in there—even if I have to take a hatchet to the door." Chandal ground out her cigarette in the ashtray and went to the hall closet for trench coat and shoes.

"I'll go with you," Doreen decided, white-faced. "But couldn't we at least try to find Mike first?"

"Forget Mike. I'm going now."

Shaking, Doreen led the way back to the brownstone, entered the hallway and unlatched the inner door. It wasn't until Chandal stood in the ancient corridor, dim, paint-chipped and shabby, that she realized this was actually the first time she had been in the brownstone. She had never even seen the inside of Doreen's apartment. Doreen intercepted Chandal's glance.

"I know the building's run-down, but the owner won't spend any money," she said defensively. "I expect one of these days he's going to renovate. When that happens, we all go. All of us. That's probably the real reason he's let so many vacancies pile up in the building. Less people to move out."

Chandal's attention wandered as Doreen nervously rambled on. The staircase was narrow, the treads of the steps rickety and old. On the second landing the hall light was out, making it almost impossible for them to find their way. Soot had formed a thick shield on the window at the far end of the hall, blocking out all light.

"Watch your step," Doreen cautioned.

As they started up the second winding incline, Chandal could feel the adrenalin pumping swiftly through her veins, sending the blood crashing to her temples. The pain in her forehead was like a dozen needles stuck into a pin cushion and pressed inward. Ignoring the sharp pain, she clung to the banister and climbed higher.

On the third floor, Chandal stopped and steadied herself against the grimy wall. Her palm came away wet and cold. Most of the hallway was completely dark except for a dim light that shone from the top floor.

Chandal hadn't realized the brownstone was such a tall building. Her breath came in deep gasps. She couldn't be that much out of shape, she told herself. Still, she was finding it difficult to breathe. Dance classes. When was the last time she had been to a dance class? She glanced at Doreen, who hesitated at the landing.

"Are you all right?" Doreen asked.

"Yes. Why do you ask?" Chandal demanded.

"I don't know. You're breathing funny."

Chandal resisted the impulse to snap at her.

Doreen stared at her for a moment. Then, uncertainly, she started upward. In the dimness, she reached her hands in front of her. She tripped, fell forward and recovered herself by grabbing onto the banister.

"Why doesn't Mike fix the damn lights?" questioned Chandal.

"He does. The tenants keep taking them."

Tenants? The word rattled around in Chandal's mind. She had never met any of them. Not coming, not going. Why was that? The stairs squeaked under her foot. What tenants? Chandal fought to control her breathing. She could see Doreen's shadow against the wall caused by the thin veil of light from above. But that was all she could see. A shadow moving upward. She followed.

"There's no one up there," the voice said.

Doreen's voice?

Was Doreen speaking?

Chandal spun around with a start. At first she could not remember where she was or why she was standing there, on the staircase, rather than in her own bedroom. Then she remembered and looked around fearfully. She rubbed her arms unthinkingly, trembling in the chilled air.

Doreen's silhouette loomed above her, blocking out most of the available light. She appeared to be standing on a mountain top. Chandal hesitated a moment longer, then stepped awkwardly to the top, where she murmured, "Maybe the woman came back. Did you change the lock on her door?"

Doreen looked at her nervously. "Come back? The woman is . . . she died, months ago. You'll see—it's just a musty old empty apartment. It's the one at the very end of the hall." Doreen hung back, key ring in hand.

"I know where it is!" Chandal had already marched down the hallway and now lifted her hand and began to knock in a spirited way.

A peephole from across the hall clicked open as an unseen eye investigated the racket in front of 5B.

"Open the door," Chandal demanded, trembling in her eagerness. "Here, show me the key and I'll do it."

At last the door swung open and Chandal sprang forward

into utter darkness. In the middle of the silent room she paused and knew on some deep level that there was no one in this room. And still she called: "Where are you?" Her voice faded away into almost a whisper as she acknowledged there was no one to answer. In quiet despair, she continued to edge her way through the room, fumbling along the wall for light switches that no longer worked, despite the fact that she had seen the old woman standing in a clear circular illumination.

"Well, what do you think?" Doreen asked in a scared voice, hovering uncertainly in the hallway.

Chandal stood now at the darkened window, her forehead pressed against the cold glass. "I don't know what I think," she said after a long blank pause.

From where she stood, she could see clearly into her own bedroom through the skylight. What a strange sensation to see oneself, one's own existence from another's point of view. She could see clearly the crumpled sheets of her bed, her pillow thrust against the large wooden headboard, the small table that contained nothing of importance, but somehow looked secretive and foreboding. She could even make out the two pill bottles that sat on the top of the table. For a moment, almost as if she had left her own body, she could see herself begin to undress. Slowly she removed her robe and stood before the mirror as she had done so often in the past days. She was standing there now. Naked. Her body was surprisingly healthy, frail yet full, her breasts large and firm.

Yet, at this moment, Chandal felt run-down and exhausted. Every bone in her body felt dry and brittle, and she knew that with the slightest touch, her limbs would snap like twigs. She lowered her head and rubbed the bridge of her nose with her fingers. When she looked up, the young girl in her bedroom was gone. Her room was deserted. Only her own image stared back at her in the wavy glass.

Slowly, at first, she studied herself. No, she was not looking at her own reflection in the glass, but at the reflection of an old woman. "No," she moaned. "No! Please, I don't want to get old! Please!"

"Chandal?"

"No!" she cried.

"Chandal, what's wrong? What is it?" Doreen stood at her side now and helped steady Chandal with her arms.

"What?" Chandal turned to meet her gaze.

"What's the matter?" Doreen's eyes were wide with fear.

". . . Nothing." Chandal gulped and felt her head and eyes jerk. She had a difficult time keeping anything in focus. There was something familiar about the apartment she now stood in. And frightening. A sense of despair and violence. A thin line between chaos and order. The gentle and the rough. The dark and the light. Gentle things, tender things, sometimes funny things. Chandal longed for this side of herself. And not the other.

"Well, what do you think?" Doreen asked.

"I'm sorry I doubted you."

Doreen smiled. "That's all right. Are you ready to go?"

"Yes, yes," Chandal breathed.

A short time later, she stood outside Doreen's apartment and politely said goodnight. She still didn't know what to think.

"Chandal, don't—don't look like that," Doreen said suddenly and flung her arms around Chandal's shoulders. "It'll all be okay," she said with smothered voice.

Chandal returned the pressure of Doreen's embrace and then gently freed herself. "I'll see you tomorrow, okay?"

"Okay."

There was something challenging about being alone again. When she was alone—that's when it tended to happen on the clearest level. She listened very closely. Only silence and in the distance, traffic sounds.

Back at the carriage house she found the telephone ringing and hurried to jerk the receiver off the hook. "Hello?"

"Del, it's Ron."

Unexpectedly, tears welled in her eyes. "Oh, God. It's so good to hear your voice."

"What's wrong?"

"Ron, I don't know. I'm confused. I'm . . . alone. I'm screwing up my life and I don't know what to—" She paused, choked.

"I'll be right over."

"What? What do you mean?"

"I'm in New York. I'll be right over."

"New York. Oh, my God, that's wonderful."

"I'm glad you think so." His voice was undeniably relieved. "I'm coming over."

"Ron—wait. Don't hang up."

"Why? I'll be right there."

"I just don't want you to hang up yet."

"It's okay, baby." In that marvelously warm familiar voice he continued to talk, to comfort her, until she was able to tell him to hang up and to hurry to her as fast as possible.

With a burst of joy, almost of rebirth, she rushed to straighten up the carriage house, to comb her hair and apply makeup. After thinking about it, she decided not to get dressed. She felt very light and sensual in her filmy gown of sheer, almost transparent, material. Underneath, her skin felt warm and expectant.

Wandering through the living room, she lit the corner Tiffany lamp and then turned on the overhead wrought-iron chandelier light, turning the dimmer switch to create a lovely half-glow.

Suddenly she froze. A scraping noise, dry and brittle. It was coming from the den. Her brief-lived happiness emptied out of her, left her with something akin to rage. Not a trace of fear. No, she was past fear at this moment despite the interior voice which seemed to be trying to whisper, to warn her about something. Unhesitatingly she marched into the den. The noise ceased immediately.

"Goddamn it!" she said clearly. Waited. Silence. Angrily she turned to leave the room and then hesitated unbelievingly. Fresh plaster dripped from the west wall. She touched the liquid that seeped from between fresh cracks. A little too oily to be water.

What then? What was it?

From behind her, hands squeezed her shoulders and turned her around.

"Oh, good God!" she cried. "Mike! You almost scared me to death."

"Sorry, I didn't know you were home." Mike was dressed in tight jeans, his chest visible through his partially open shirt. His hands felt hot through the silky material of Chandal's robe. The heat seemed to seep into her body.

She tried to force herself to break away. She could not. Could not keep her eyes from melting into his as he pulled her closer, then suddenly pressed his lips against hers. For a helpless instant she clung to him, returned his kiss fervently, and then found the strength to struggle. Violently she pushed at him, only to find that he had forced his lips harder to her mouth.

It was the knock on the door that helped her break away. For an instant they faced each other, their faces flushed, traces of Chandal's lipstick on Mike's lips.

Then, with a stifled cry, Chandal ran to the door, jerked it open and, weeping, threw herself into Ron's arms. An instant later she felt the coolness of Ron's embrace and turned to see his gaze fastened on Mike.

Gently, but purposefully, Ron put her aside and stood facing Mike, his eyes unmistakably fixed on the traces of rose-colored lipstick on Mike's lips, even as he rubbed it away with the back of his hand.

Chandal's face burned. "Ron, this is Mike Hammer. He—he's the building super. . . ." She broke off in embarrassment.

"The super," repeated Ron. He smiled briefly. "How do you do. I'm . . . well, God knows who. I'm not sure what my title is in New York. In Los Angeles I was—" he glanced at Chandal, "—I was Chandal's agent."

"Interesting," Mike said politely and slipped through the half-opened door. "Well, goodnight."

Chandal closed the door hesitantly. "Ron, I'm really so happy to see you. You believe that, don't you?"

"If you say so, I believe it."

"Would you like some wine? There's some wine in the refrigerator or I can make you a drink." She could not bear to look at Ron's face. Instead, she found herself thinking of the image of her lipstick on Mike's lips.

"I'll have just plain soda, if you have it. Coke or whatever. My stomach's a little upset."

She went for the Coke, still chattering, saying too much too fast about too little. She wondered if underneath her nonstop flow of words Ron felt the deeper silence between them the same as she did.

God, she wished she didn't have to talk to him, that they could just be together, just stay quiet. They could start with that. She was sure it would catch on from there.

"This Mike," Ron said.

"No Coke! Pepsi. Will Pepsi be all right?"

"Sure. Fine."

Chandal bit her lip and yanked the bottle from the refrigerator. "What a surprise. I mean it. Life is filled with little surprises, isn't it?" She could see that her hand was trembling. Some of the Pepsi spilled over the side of the glass. "Damn!"

"Anything wrong?"

"No. No, you stay there. It'll just take a second to clean it up. Surprises, right. Life is just filled with them. Some good. Some bad. I never expected you to be in New York. New York, of all places. Jesus, talk about a nice surprise. . . ." Chandal felt a hand place itself across her arm and looked up with a start.

"Relax, Del," Ron smiled.

She jerked her arm free and threw the towel against the counter. "I can't relax. I mean," she glanced around wildly, "how can I relax? One minute you're in California—then you're here. I didn't have time to get ready! Nothing's right. I'm a mess!"

"You look fine."

"No, I don't! You should have told me you were coming. People usually do give people some notice, don't they?"

In a remote part of her mind she was able to observe herself doing all the wrong things, saying things she hadn't chosen to say.

Ron looked at her sharply. "I'm sorry if I interrupted anything."

"Oh, shit!" She pushed past him and dumped herself onto the couch. "You didn't interrupt anything. Mike is the super—that's all. He's married, for Christ's sakes! His wife is my best friend."

"Then I don't see why you're getting so upset."

"Time. I needed more time!"

"Is that why you told me to come right over? Because you needed more time?"

"I don't know what you're talking about. What you're doing in New York . . . I . . ."

"I came to New York for one reason, and one reason only. To take you back to California with me. Where you belong. Where there's a part in a film waiting for you if you want it. California, Del—you remember. Where we met, where we fell in love. California. That's why I'm here."

"No!" she screamed. "I won't let them film me. They're

trying to see inside of me. Those goddamn cameras are not cameras at all. X-rays, that's what they are."

Ron was caught by surprise. Unguarded, a sigh escaped his lips, followed by a pause. "Del, what's happened to you? You're deliberately destroying your life. Why?"

She smiled and threw her head back defiantly. "I've begun to live according to my own beliefs. What is wrong with that?" Her voice was odd and forced. She was unaware that her face muscles had slackened, that she looked years older.

"Del, if you continue on like this, you may never be able to find your way back."

"When one burns one's bridges," she said cynically, "what a very nice fire it makes."

Ron dropped onto the sofa, confused. "Please, we haven't been together for five minutes, and all we've done is argue. I don't want to argue with you, Del."

"Why? Because we're liable to say the truth? That we—"

"No, damn it! Because I care for you, that's why!"

"Care for? Or do you mean—want to take care of? I don't need anyone taking care of me."

Ron swallowed. "Okay. What do you want then?"

There was a moment's hesitation.

"Del, let me help you."

"Help me? You want to help me?"

"Please, Del. . . ."

"No, stop, Ron, please. Don't say any more." Chandal's anger at having become the center of pity in this idiotic situation was mingled with a feeling of pride. A deep, desperate pride that told her she had to go it alone.

"I'm not going to pretend I'm not in trouble," she began slowly. "I am. But it's my trouble, not yours. You can't help me—believe me. No one can. Not in any way. I know you think we should talk about it. That talking about it will solve everything. But that's a lie. Ron, please. . . ." She broke off, her voice dissolving into a half-whisper. "If I dwell on it anymore tonight I'll come apart."

Now she was not sure of anything. She looked around the room, observing the small light that gleamed on the table next to the sofa. The light was not bright, but it spread a faint, rose-colored glow across Ron's face. She stared uneasily as she listened to Ron's heavy, irregular breathing. Why should the rose-colored light be so disturbing?

So many things confused her, frightened her. What she felt, and did not understand, was why her vision of Ron was now filtered by a gauze of distance. Everything in the room appeared larger, distorted. God, help me. She dug her fingernails into the palms of her hands and waited. For what, she didn't know.

Ron took a long time to rise from the sofa. He said nothing, merely shook his head in despair. Then he began to chuckle, the faint laugh of a person deeply wounded and helpless. Still laughing in an almost breathless confusion, he reached into his jacket pocket and brought forth an envelope.

"Here," he said and threw the envelope on the table in disgust. "You left this in California. I thought you'd want it."

Chandal, instead of thanking him, glared at him suspiciously. Her gaze was brief, Ron having now moved quickly to the door.

"If you want to reach me, Del, I'm staying at the Hilton. Room 912." Ron allowed the moment to hang in the air while he lighted his cigarette. After yet another moment he shook his head in disbelief and turned for the door.

When Ron had gone, Chandal spun around and reached for the envelope. Tearing it open, she removed the crucifix. Something was wrong, but Chandal could not quite put her finger on it. She stared at the crucifix closely. It was all there, if she could only get a grasp on it. Slowly, very slowly, she turned the crucifix upside down.

Chandal stood motionless near the table for a long time, the crucifix dangling upside down from her fingers, the tears coursing down her cheeks. Then she let her body sink helplessly onto the floor, sobbing soundlessly.

CHAPTER TWENTY

HE WOULD SEEK OUT THOSE WHO HAD BEAUTIFUL FACES. OR those with strength-packed limbs. Once procured, he would split their bodies in two so that he might examine with delight their internal organs. Age mattered little to him. He preyed upon the young as well as the old. When a child lay dying, he would sit upon its chest and take pleasure in helping it to die just a little more quickly. He would suck the breath from its body and laugh . . . after which he would will the child's body to burn in order to convert its spirit to smoke. His father was a monk. His mother a prostitute.

His name was Ahriman.

The old woman smiled. She remembered the *Book of Ahriman* well. She had read it often in the dim light of the attic, using the dust of old things to powder her fading complexion. Or during quieter times in the basement, where the air was cool and memories ran deep, where past loves were buried, where the watchful eye of her sister could not reach her.

Dear, sweet . . . sister. Where was sister now, she wondered and, upon wondering, found that an image from the past had jumped forward in her mind. "Magdalen," she whispered. "Magdalen, is that you?"

"Yes."

Wrapped in an old woolen sweater, Magdalen wore no makeup and allowed her gray hair to go wild upon her head. Her spectacles, thin and gold-framed, sat low on the bridge of her nose. Elizabeth watched as Magdalen lifted her hand to the neck of her cotton blouse, pulling the opening more tightly closed.

"Are you chilled?" Elizabeth asked.

Her sister made no reply, but merely stared vacantly from the brownstone window.

"Are we going to the attic again tonight?" Elizabeth moved slowly toward her, her tiny red corkscrew curls bobbing against her pale-complexioned forehead.

Magdalen sighed. "No. Not tonight."

"Would you like a cup of tea? And biscuits? That would be nice."

"I've asked you not to bother me when I'm like this. Why do you do it?"

Elizabeth lowered her head. "I don't mean to. Really I don't."

Magdalen turned to face her. Smiled. "No, of course, you don't. Forgive me." She placed her hand tenderly on her sister's cheek. "Why don't you go to bed now? You look tired."

Elizabeth pressed her cheek against her sister's hand. "Must I?"

Magdalen sighed. "Then if you'll excuse me, I . . ." Magdalen tried to withdraw her hand, but Elizabeth held fast.

"Please, Magdalen, let's leave the brownstone. Go away together."

Her sister laughed shortly. "Where would we go?"

"Oh, Magdalen," she said excitedly, "there's a little town called Elm right outside of London. It's lovely. Little country bungalows with miles of fields between them. There's one I've had my eye on. Just a tiny house with a garden and a flowering hedge . . . and jasmine blooming. I saw a picture of it in a book. Braided rugs, a piano. There's a verandah opening out onto the garden. On Sundays we'll go into town, what little of it there is—eat raspberries on the verandah, listen to music . . . oh, and there are awnings that roll down from the windows, and . . . birds—all the time. Winter and summer, all kinds, all colors." Elizabeth paused to stare into her sister's eyes. "Something we need, Magdalen—peace and quiet . . . just for a little while anyway."

Magdalen stared at her without expression for a long time,

then broke into a heinous laugh. Embarrassed, Elizabeth let go of her hand.

"Well, you can make fun if you like, but it's lovely!"

"I'm going to bed now," Magdalen said calmly.

"You can't stand me anymore, can you? Can't stand to be in the same room with me—isn't that right?" She lowered her eyes. "Magdalen, what has happened to us?"

Magdalen stiffened. "If I came over there and kissed you, would that make things right?" She paused, then added, "Would it?"

"You've hurt me—can't you see that?"

"Self-pity is my vice—not yours. It paralyzes the face muscles. Go on—look at yourself in the mirror."

"You're very cruel at times, Magdalen. It makes you unattractive."

"Then invent another me—one to suit your needs."

"I love you, Magdalen."

Magdalen shook her head sadly. "No, sweet sister . . . you don't love me. You tolerate me."

"That's not true."

"It is true! It has always been true. You still blame me for the past. Yet it was you who ruined our lives."

"Arthur. . . ." Elizabeth broke off.

"Yes?"

"You came between us. I loved Arthur and you took him away from me. And Steven—it was always you."

"And now you lust to be me! To be that phantom woman in your mind."

"NO!"

"Yes. You have always longed to be someone else. Well, Elizabeth—there she is." Magdalen took her sister by the shoulders and spun her around to face the mirror. "Can't you see her? Look closely—at your reflection. She's there, Elizabeth, lurking—waiting to be let in so she can stroll about the house in her nightgown—out onto the terrace where she will greet her lovers. Fan held daintily in her hand—bejeweled neck—velvet slippers. You'll speak of widowhood and deny them the pleasure of a white gown. You look at yourself in the mirror—you've become more beautiful. You'll give yourself airs—make fancy gestures—you're more beautiful still—you're almost there, Elizabeth. A green satin gown—more jewels perhaps. The hair! Something must be done about the hair. A different style—color. Longer, it needs to be much longer. Yes . . . yes, you can feel it now, floating softly down around your face—kissing parts of your body never felt before—gently gliding over your breasts. . . . You stand there shaking. You cannot believe your own loveliness. You are ready, Elizabeth. The altar is yours. GO ON, ELIZA-BETH—let her in!"

"NO-O-O-O-O!"

"Yes, you see—you don't know what you know anymore. Truth, illusion—it's all the same to you."

"No," Elizabeth whimpered, "it's not true. Please. . . ."

Magdalen smiled. "Goodnight, sweet sister. I'm glad we've had our talk." She turned and started for the door.

"Please, Magdalen, I need you. Don't leave me like this."

"Goodnight."

Elizabeth straightened suddenly, her violet eyes blazing. "Well, go on! Go to bed. But I'll survive. You'll see. I'll survive!"

The past dissolved. Now the old woman sat back and smiled cynically. She had survived. Magdalen was scattered ashes but she had survived. She felt young tonight and knew it to be so. This was her new body. Mistake, or magic, or madness, or child's play. It made no difference. This was her house—her temple now.

A whistle sounded. The ceremony was about to begin.

"The ultimate sense of powerlessness comes not from any confrontation between men," the *Book of Ahriman* had said, "but from the confrontation with Ahriman. The search for one's self finally leads, therefore, to an effort to acquire Ahriman's love, either as his servant or as his antagonist."

The old woman shivered and watched as the crone turned quickly from the altar and screamed:

"Ahriman is omnipotent!"

The crone stepped closer to the small gathering of men and women who knelt on the floor before her. "So man's insanity is Ahriman's sense. . . ." she hissed.

Somewhere in the room there was the harsh sound of a clock striking, quick and loud. The time was 11:00 P.M., the third hour of Ahriman on the day of Ahriman, the hour most suitable.

"Ahriman, strong and powerful one, chief of our covenant,

197

hear us!" As the crone called out, the old woman swept beads of sweat from her brow with her left hand, taking care not to drop the bloodstone she held in her right.

The room was smaller tonight and the air stank from demons and the skins of dead animals. Other smells emanated: mint, sage, rosemary, basil, candle wax and ash—all powerful and extraordinarily malign.

The old woman began to rub her bloodstone feverishly, the voice within her head moving as rapidly as her fingers. "Ahriman, by virtue of all that thou holdest dear, I clothe myself. O, Ahriman, give me strength so that fulfillment will be mine, even unto thy terms. Bring forth in me yet another child, a child for thy kingdom where the child will live forever and ever. Let all things return to me. Let me repent and become one with thee."

Outside the building, clouds continued to dissipate, while inside the room, the noise rose higher, and a red mist began to form near the center of the room, until the goat sprang forth full-blown, like a sudden flash from a smoke pot. Steam oozed from the goat's body, part human, part animal, while saliva dripped from the corners of his mouth.

The old woman shuddered. Others writhed around her, screamed and howled, as the red fumes drifted upward toward the ceiling, making them cough and gag, even the old woman.

The goat smiled, bared his teeth and emitted a belch of all-encompassing steam. Then he stuck out his tongue, a slithering mass of green flesh that resembled a tentacle.

He looked down at the old woman who cowered at his feet. "I cannot give thee," he hissed, "what thou requirest. Thy life itself is incomplete. Deliver to me the girl—wholly. She is still of them."

Then there was silence.

The old woman drew up and squinted at him. With terror and dawning self-knowledge of her failure, she whined, "When she is consumed with goodness, I cannot control her."

For the moment the goat said nothing, merely withdrew slightly, as whispers began to circulate around the room. He stepped closer and peered down sharply. Yet he spoke in an even, tolerant voice.

"The circle must be regularly attended. Communicants

must be totally devout. Stone, fire, and blood must be fervently worshiped. The words of Ahriman are the only safeguard against them and must be used, at all times, to drive them away. Ahriman commands you."

Having thus spoken, he thrust his arms violently downward and demanded:

> "Let all stone burn!
> Let all forests burn!
> Let all animals burn!
> Let all water burn!
> Let all air, wind and sky—burn!
> Let everything catch fire and burn!"

Then the goat, who stood so magnificent within the small circle, began to vanish. Like the sudden center of a vortex, his body turned inward and he dived downward into the floor, which opened and closed, revealing no sign of rupture once he had disappeared completely.

Silence. And then loud howls issued forth and the ceremony continued uninterrupted throughout the night. Some allowed their shadows to dance upon the walls of the room, while others howled and shrieked and swore; they drank blood and spat upon the floor, while still others turned everything topsy-turvy. Cigarettes were smoked, wine was drunk and spirits of evil were enclosed in vessels of glass and the corks rammed home.

"Finished!" croaked the crone in a hoarse whisper. She now looked exhausted and spent. Taking up a candle, she snuffed out its flame. Shadows shifted, the room grew one flame dimmer. Another candle was snuffed. Another and another. "Now we will be of ourselves for three weeks. Then we will meet again."

At the door, with the last remaining candle in her hand, she turned to face the almost lifeless human forms that were strewn about the floor, amidst blood and carnage.

"The circle is open," she breathed. "You may depart."

The breath of her last word extinguished the final, omnipotent flame.

The others dispersed almost at once.

But one old woman lingered a moment longer. A sense of

dusty desolation fell in upon her. She felt tired and satiated. She heard within her the raging of a hundred storms and she wondered if she was up to her appointed task.

Long ago, when she was young, she had lain naked in her room, dreaming of this very moment. In those days, when the brownstone had first become her sister's and her property— her mother and father having died suddenly—she often did not dress at all and wandered naked up and down the creaking staircase, around the mahogany newel posts and past the fretted balustrades, pretending she was a queen. And that she would live forever. A beautiful face and strength-packed limbs would always be hers. She would indulge in long daydreams in which she would imagine herself in other shapes, other forms, even more magnificent than her own. During these moments she could actually feel the vague embraces that would be hers for all time. The sinister caresses.

The thought of everlasting life was still with her as she closed the door on the death-infested room and scurried weakly into the arms of night.

CHAPTER TWENTY-ONE

OBSERVING A LIFELONG HABIT, HE WAITED UNTIL THE PRECISE moment to leave for his appointment. This moment was Monday noon, April 13th, New York time, making it nine A.M. in California. He thought in terms of time like that now. In distinct three-hour differences.

He took advantage of comparative calm to release his hold over the hotel room he now called home, before closing its door and heading for the elevator. He did not allow himself to acknowledge his anxiety until he had actually reached the street. He shook his head wearily. In the past twenty-four hours he had been attacked first by a fit of jealousy, then fear, then concern, finally depression.

With his head lowered, Ron Talon shoved his hands deep into his pockets and began to walk. The restaurant was located on Seventh Avenue, not far from his hotel. The rain had eased up around eleven, leaving a fresh mist through which occasional thin drops fell. By the time he had reached the restaurant, the sun had complete command of the day.

The brass plate next to the impressive cut-glass doors read: "The Shamrock." Ron was barely inside when he was met by a small pixie-type man dressed in a loud blue suit. The man smiled.

"Ron Talon. Right?"

"Yes."

"Welcome, sir! And right this way."

Ron found himself strolling effortlessly through a small

room which reeked with an effusive air of Ye Olde English Pub, catering to serious drinkers, hangers-out and others who, for reasons of their own required privacy and intimacy, hid away in the back booths—mainly in twosomes. It had been this way since 1921, and the little gúy had seen no reason to break with age-old tradition. The pub had first been his great-grandfather's brainchild, and then inherited and nurtured right on down the line.

The little guy finished his quick briefing with, "We also serve cold beer by the tap at a fair price."

Dr. Luther rose to the occasion with a footnote. "And the food borders on great!" He extended his hand with energy. "Hello. Ian Luther."

"How are you?"

"Hungry!" Luther grinned.

After a chat with the owner of the place, the waiter and the bartender, Luther ushered Ron up to a line of chromium hot tanks that contained what was without a doubt gastronomic delight. All eyes were on Luther as he ordered unself-consciously, but graciously: salad, corned beef and cabbage, boiled potato and some sort of cobbler with cream.

. "The desserts are primed to annihilate any diet, but, nevertheless, they shouldn't be passed up," he said pleasantly, but did not push the point. Together they made their way through the line. Ron's mind really wasn't on the chocolate eclair that was gingerly tossed in his direction.

What troubled Ron as they came back to their table was exactly why Luther had taken such immediate and personal interest in Chandal's problems. Although Ron had suggested financial remuneration, Luther had seemingly taken no notice. He was available, he wanted to help, he could drive into the city this afternoon, and he had suggested the pub as a convenient meeting place.

Why? Ron thought silently and watched as Luther delicately and precisely cut into the corned beef. He studied Luther's face for a moment. The penetrating blue eyes Chandal had spoken of, the furrowed brow, the sharp nose, the heavily lined face that seemed as if it had been carved from a piece of rough wood—they were all there.

But Ron's impression of hardness and cool reserve that he had gleaned during phone conversations didn't seem to match the man who now smiled at him from across the table while salting his potato. Everything about him was open and warm: the pleasant voice, the impish glint in his eyes, the cordial but rather envious air he conveyed.

"Your roast beef looks superb. I usually have that myself." He kept his gaze fixed on Ron's plate for a moment, then looked up and said, "Did you have any problem finding the place?"

"No. It seems it's famous."

"Infamous would be more like it."

Both men laughed. Luther waited a moment, hoping Ron would continue the conversation, but Ron was too distracted to be responsive.

"I wondered if I'd ever hear from you again," Luther went on. "When you're in my particular line of work, you get a lot of phone calls, you know. But I'm delighted you felt free to ask me to meet with you—delighted. I care about my patients. Past or present."

Amenities over, Luther settled back to eat until finally Ron turned the conversation to Chandal, and Luther regained his voice. Both men stepped carefully into the subject. Luther jabbed, Ron hooked. After what might be considered "round four," Luther leaned back in his chair, dabbed his lips with his napkin and commented effortlessly, "I was never really convinced Chandal was ready to leave Lakewood."

Ron blinked. "Then why was she released?"

Luther forked another piece of corned beef and chewed thoughtfully. At length he replied with a certain amount of irony, "Mental health, Mr. Talon, is largely a nebulous opinion held by each examining psychiatrist. In order to be released from a state institution, the patient has to satisfy an entire Board of Examiners. Chandal passed this test with flying colors."

"Are you on this Board?"

"I'm a staff psychiatrist. I make recommendations to the Board. Generally they give serious consideration to what I have to say. In this particular case I should have stated my point a bit more clearly but I was never really certain there was any reason to hold her. It was just an intuition. That wasn't enough for the Board."

The automatic quality of Luther's response set Ron back for another lengthy moment before he said, "What about her amnesia? Surely that should have swayed them."

"Very few psychiatrists believe in amnesia. At least, as far as you perceive the definition of the word."

"You mean they thought she was lying?" Ron asked bluntly.

"Not exactly. But they did feel that she knew precisely what had happened during her stay at the brownstone and chose not to remember. They labeled her amnesia functional, rather than organic, and attributed her condition to an emotional block and the inability to withstand the rigors of reality. Nothing more."

"It sounds to me like the Board of Examiners is full of crap," Ron said confidentially. He tried to surround the remark with a smile, but his lips refused to cooperate.

Luther laughed, his chest falling in and out in deep lunges. "I have told them so in other words many times," he said, then added on a more serious note, "still, she did display the usual signs of functional amnesia and all its classical phases. Complete dissociation, closely resembling somnambulism. Then a period of lightened oblivion, and then a return to full-functioning consciousness. At this point they saw no need to detain her." He smiled. "Believe me, you have no idea how normal, clean and wholesomely bright Chandal can appear when in the comparable company of the truly mentally ill. I think you can see that Chandal was a prime candidate to be returned to the world. Especially as she had maintained a job in the library for some months, effortlessly and in good spirits."

"I guess," Ron grudgingly acquiesced and turned to gaze about the pub more out of confusion than anything else. Bright green plastic mats failed to conceal the streaks of grease on the wooden table tops, nor the sawdust and cigarette butts strewn about the floor. Sunlight poured in through begrimed stained glass, migrating in long flashes across the room to a small cluster of sports pictures above the row of liquor bottles behind the bar. It seemed a perfect setting for a Eugene O'Neill play. Ron could almost see the illusive Hickey from *The Iceman Cometh* propped on the bar, involved in one of his many pipe dreams, relentlessly driving each man to test his illusions in action.

Still, the pub had its charm, Ron concluded, doggedly keeping his mind on Luther's smooth-flowing voice which seemed to be covering an abnormally wide field of topics, ranging from the fire at the brownstone, to the fact that shock and/or guilt complexes might have arisen from Chandal's being the only survivor of the fire.

"Good God," Ron cried. "She can't blame herself—"

"On a conscious level, no. But there is no telling what a person may think when pressed by the divisions in themselves. Divisions mean choice. There are alternatives and Chandal, like all people, had to select one or the other. Stay in California and build a future, or return to New York and relive her past. I'm afraid she has made the more dangerous choice of the two."

"But why? What would make her come back here?"

Luther paused. "Perhaps a desire to seek self-punishment. An absolution of sorts."

"Punishment for what?"

"For surviving. Three people died in the fire that night. Her husband and the two sisters who owned the building. Only Chandal escaped with her life. It's altogether possible she now blames herself for causing the fire. For killing her husband. The very quality of thinking the same thing over and over again makes us doubt that this thing was ever not so, whether real or imagined, or that there was any time in which it could not have been so. The past is a construction of our imaginations. Our memories change with us. Whether we are to blame or not makes no difference; we assume the guilt. It becomes our responsibility, brought on by our living too much in the past."

"Jesus," Ron breathed faintly. The idea staggered him.

An old memory cell exploded and spilled its thought into his consciousness. A memory still painful after twenty years. Ron had felt decidedly guilty—guilty?—yes, it was true . . . when his parents had separated, then divorced. As though he had caused the split-up.

The vague pain that had throbbed subtly beneath Ron's skull now became sharp and knifelike. Wearily he massaged his right temple, wondering if there would ever again be a moment when he did not have a goddamn splitting headache.

Luther took a long pull on his mug of dark ale and then offered: "The question is . . . what does Chandal believe now? Why has she returned to New York? Not that that's unusual under normal circumstances. Did Chandal like California?"

"I guess." Ron hesitated. "No, not really."

"Could someone have inspired her to return to New York?"

"I don't think so. There wasn't anyone to inspire her. She lived a pretty quiet life out there."

Luther folded his arms. "How about here in New York?"

"What?"

"Maybe she'd been in contact with a friend in New York."

"Not that I know of. At least she never mentioned anyone specifically."

"Before she left, did she seem upset?"

"Not in the least."

"But you said she didn't like California. How did you mean that?"

"It's always that way with actors. When they're in New York, they wish they were in California. And vice versa."

"I see." Luther leaned back in his chair. "Why does it bother *you* that she lives in New York?"

Ron abruptly felt the current shift between them. Friendly conversation, he realized, had suddenly become a hard-core interrogation. "Dr. Luther, when a girl I care for very much suddenly packs her bags and leaves in the middle of the afternoon without a word—it bothers me!"

"Is that the only reason?"

Ron reached for a cigarette. "I don't understand."

"The question is fairly obvious, isn't it?" Luther leaned forward and offered Ron a light.

"Thanks," Ron breathed, exhaling a mouth full of smoke with the word. He sat back and thought about Luther's questions for a moment. "No, I . . . I've thought about it. I mean, since I spoke with you that night. I really never allowed myself to consider Chandal's past life before that time. She had mentioned Lakewood, of course. What she'd been through. But I guess I just didn't want to think about it. About her previous illness."

"And you're afraid she is ill now?"

"Jesus, I don't know. You should have seen her the other

night. She just didn't seem to be the same person. I don't mean in looks, but in the way she acted. The way she spoke. I just mentioned California and it set her off like a torch. She kept screaming about how cameras were X-ray machines and how she wasn't going to let them look inside of her, and . . ."

Ron stopped suddenly and could see the look that crept into Dr. Luther's eyes. It was a worried look, a look that told Ron the man had abruptly shifted gears again and now possessed the time-honored look of concern. It was as if his entire expression indicated "what-you-just-said-doesn't-sound-too-good."

"Dr. Luther, what do I do? I tried calling her. She doesn't pick up the phone. I went back to the carriage house on Saturday. Again yesterday. I know she's in there, yet she won't answer the door. I have to do something. I just can't sit around and watch her go to pieces like this."

"Of course, of course. . . ."

Moodily, Ron dropped his napkin on the table.

"By the way," Luther offered, "you never actually asked me but I think you should know that I do believe in Chandal's amnesia. I believe in it absolutely. Only I don't believe that it's entirely a functional debility. I believe—and, of course, this is only my personal view—that her amnesia could be of an organic origin as well."

Before Ron could respond, Luther moved ahead.

"When Chandal first came to Lakewood, she underwant various tests. We checked for an acute infection, an epileptic seizure, a metabolic convulsion. We even thought that perhaps she might have suffered a severe blow on the head. After weeks of testing these were all ruled out. Yet I can't help feeling that her problem stems from something just as valid as an organic source. Something that is causing her loss of memory."

"Something?" Ron's eyes narrowed.

"Causing a blockage. Yes."

"But what? You said that she'd been tested."

Luther shook his head. "To be perfectly candid, I don't know. But if we could bring her back. In time. Perhaps then we would be able—"

He compressed his mouth over the rest of the sentence.

Ron waited, but he didn't finish it. He leaned forward suddenly. "Was I mistaken?"

"What?"

"Your roast beef. You've hardly touched it."

Ron sighed. "Don't mind me. I've had a hell of a case of the flu. Everything went out the window, my appetite at the head of the list." Ron saw Luther's sharp professional glance and hoped the topic of his health would not develop into a full-fledged subject.

"Well, if you're finished, then perhaps we might take a walk. It's really an extraordinary day."

"That'll be fine."

They paid the check and left the restaurant, walking down Seventh Avenue. The street was filled with the heady air of exhaust fumes, hot dogs, and bespoke of a slum in the making. Tenements were stacked like lopsided boxes atop every business imaginable. One thing good about the neighborhood, you didn't have to leave it. Whatever your needs, it was there, including *Beyond Your Wildest Dreams*, an X-rated movie playing at the corner movie house.

They walked up 46th Street and through the theater district, heading for Broadway. Neither man spoke very much. There was a traffic jam—an accident or something up ahead—and it took a few sidesteps to get through the gathering crowd.

"I suspect," Luther said once they reached a clearing, "that you love Chandal very much." Casually he flicked the next sentence at him. "Do you intend marrying her?"

Ron was caught off guard. "I'd like to," he managed to stammer, and he could feel himself tense.

Luther nodded. Wearing a blue jersey and tan gabardine trousers, with a rumpled English tweed jacket slung over his shoulder, he sauntered along like a poet of sorts. Without warning, he turned to Ron and said:

"I'd like to try hypnosis."

"Hypnosis?"

"I know what you're thinking. Well, you're mistaken. Hypnosis is not something magical or mysterious. Hypnosis is nothing more than a heightened suggestibility induced by another person. A therapeutic tool. Psychiatrists use it all the time to alleviate the pain and suffering of certain mental disorders."

"Then why wasn't it used with Chandal before?"

"It is not an approved method of therapy at Lakewood," Luther shrugged. "But I've had some remarkable results in private practice. Some excellent results. I would like to use a technique called 'Hypnotic Time Regression.' Through this process I will be able to bring Chandal back to an earlier time in her life. The period during the brownstone, naturally. One hopes she will experience feelings, images, thoughts, behavior from that period. She will behave just as though she were literally still living in the brownstone. And then perhaps we may be able to discover the cause of her amnesia."

Ron hesitated for a moment in the roaring bustle of the well-fanned Broadway crowd. Blinking away the hot spot of light that refracted from a store window, his eyes picked up the sudden seriousness in Luther's face.

"But won't that be dangerous?" he asked. "Making her relive all that?"

"I will try to avoid prolonged painful memories." He paused. "The question is, will Chandal allow herself to be hypnotized?"

"I don't see why not. She must want to remember, or why else would she have returned to New York?"

Both men were walking again. Luther took a moment to glance at his watch, then slipped easily into his jacket. "Consciously telling yourself you want something does not necessarily mean you're being totally honest with yourself. After all, it's her own brain that shields her from that information. That is, if her amnesia is functional as the Board insisted."

"Then you believe there is a chance that she *is* blocking her own way?"

"Where memory has been lost, it can reappear, with a vengeance, or as a gift. Chandal knows this from our many sessions together. The greatest mental block to hypnosis is the fear of revealing something that the subject does not consciously wish to divulge." Luther stopped suddenly. "I'm afraid," he said, "a great deal depends on you. On how strong a relationship you share. If you can persuade her to submit to hypnosis," he murmured, his face taking on the blankness of a seasoned psychiatrist, "I'm willing to give it a try."

Ron had no idea why he was suddenly afraid, why he had just almost changed his mind about acquiring Luther's help. It took a great deal of concentration before he could finally bring himself to say:

"I'll see what I can do."

CHAPTER TWENTY-TWO

TIME NOW STOOD STILL AND THE ONLY MOVEMENT THAT TOOK place was within her own body. Her appetite had diminished in the last four days. She had eaten less frequently, until finally she had skipped food altogether. Now she spoke with no one. She simply waited.

At first it was as though a little merry-go-round had suddenly sprung loose in her head and whipped itself into a frenzy, whirling around, faster and faster, its tiny horses moving up and down, punching against the soft tissue of her brain.

Then the racket in Chandal's head had softened and, like a propeller blade at optimum speed, her thought patterns gave the illusion of standing still. Nothing seemed hurried. Nothing important was emphasized. Just a buzzing sound which created a vacuum of isolation, until at last she had lost all awareness of who she was—where she was.

Each day brought with it a new activity. Endless hours had been spent before the mirror, or just standing or sitting perfectly still, or pacing from the den to the living room to the upstairs bedroom, as if she had been looking for something. The statue had been moved and studied in its new light countless times. Only to be moved again and re-studied. Baths had been taken, sometimes six or seven a day. Legs and armpits had been shaved until her skin bled. And the bloodstone pendant had been worshiped until she had fainted from complete and inescapable exhaustion. Only then had she been allowed to sleep.

Today, writing was her passion. Her obsession. The moment she had stepped from her bed, she had gone to the den, where she had begun to write, page after page, which she had immediately torn up and discarded into the trash. No concentration could have been greater, longer, and more complete.

The pen in her hand had scrawled ancient symbols, twisted and contorted, the same symbols that were lodged at the base of the statue which she had moved to the center of the dining table. She had only stopped writing long enough to peer at the statue, whose evil face appeared to be smiling at her. She had smiled back and reached for her bloodstone pendant.

Dawn passed into midafternoon, the sun rose, hung in the sky over the carriage house, and was now starting to dissipate in the west. The heat in the den was suffocating and drew large beads of sweat from Chandal's brow, yet she clung to her teacup, taking small sips of the hot liquid as if to cool her innards.

Only for a moment had there been an echo of resistance in her. Her own voice had risen from within and protested in choked tones. With her voice had come tension. Then her voice had faded and the tension had fled. A new sensation now caressed her body.

She dropped into a deep lunacy of illusion not of her own choosing. Her eyes flickered and scanned eons of surrealist landscapes of fire, where goat heads were suspended from tree branches, while below—demons with snakes for feet danced themselves into erotic frenzy. Animals appeared like gods with fangs for teeth and devoured the dead as they rose from their graves to walk the earth. Images merged. Heaven collided with Hell. Christ's face appeared in a setting of battle, torture and execution. From within the flames, the goat's head lunged forward, its lips drooling foam. The two faces collided, forming an atavistic mask, pre-human—half man and half animal.

Chandal dug her nails into the arms of the desk chair. She felt her body pulsate, felt it thrust forward violently, as though every fiber in her body was trying to change itself and form itself into another shape. She held fast to the chair, feeling a sucking sensation emptying her of her own life—

every image, every thought, passion, longing, fear, all being slowly, but expertly drawn from her body. The phone rang in the living room. She did not answer it. She hadn't answered it in four days—she would not answer it now. The phone continued to ring.

"I'm still here. You'll never get rid of me," the voice hissed.

Then startlingly, Chandal had a broken thought. It pushed up hard into her brain and she took hold of it like a drowning person does a life preserver. Her mind raced. Had she, was she supposed to answer it? Like a warning bell, the harsh ring persisted.

With a flash of white brilliance, Chandal's mind exploded and reality came rushing in. She was suddenly back in the den, sitting motionless, staring at the Hebrew symbols she had been scrawling all day.

She rose. Her eyebrows formed a quizzical expression. Her mouth remained a thin line. All color was gone from her face. She glanced at her watch. It was six-thirty. She had been writing for more than nine hours. It was incredible.

Quickly she glanced into the living room.

Don't answer it.

"Why?"

Don't.

"I must!"

No!

Chandal raced for the phone in panic. Would it stop ringing? Would she be too late? She wrenched the receiver from the hook.

"Hello?" she shrilled.

"Chandal?"

"Yes, Ron. Ron, is that you?"

"Chandal, let me be among the first to congratulate you. How does it feel to sit in the seat of power, on the right hand of God, as it were."

"Eric?"

"Yes. You sound surprised to hear from me."

Chandal was silent for a moment. Her palms were sweating. She rubbed her free hand up and down her skirt. Her embarrassment was overwhelming and painful. She could not bring herself to speak.

"Chandal, are you still there?"

"Yes," she breathed.

"Good. Now, are you sitting down? Because I have some wonderful news for you," he said softly and meaningfully. "Can you guess?"

Chandal tried to focus her thoughts. She could hear Eric chuckling, then laughing.

"Listen," he went on, "they want you back."

He continued to relate the various discussions that had taken place during the past week. How the producers were desperate to have her back; that the show was not the same without her; that the new actress who had replaced her just wasn't cutting it. She listened, not saying a word.

"Now, I guess, the question is whether *you* want *us*," he concluded.

"I'm not sure," Chandal admitted and moved her hand onto her face, stroking her warm cheek.

"I know what you've been through. The things that have been said. The accusations. But I can reassure you that's all behind us now. On a personal note—I really do miss your talent in the role. And I feel as they do—the show just doesn't have the sparkle when you're not there."

"It's nice to hear you say that," she murmured.

"I'm only sorry that all this had to happen."

"So am I."

"Perhaps a talk could prevent it from happening again."

"Talk?"

"Well, yes. Naturally we'll have to talk first. Get together. I've promised the producers that I would. It really won't take long. Just a little chat."

"When?"

"Tonight, if you're free. Just you and me. My place." His voice sounded flat—strange.

"Is it really necessary?"

"I'm . . . well, if you prefer not to. But we should get together again, you know, before rehearsal. Reach some sort of understanding. I'd feel better about it if we did." He paused, then added, "But then, you haven't said absolutely that you want the part back. Have you?"

"I'm not sure what I should do," she said. "What do you think? I mean, really think?"

"I think . . ." he began slowly, "that you are one of the

loveliest creatures I have ever seen. And I have no doubt at all that you are going to be a big, big star. And that Rachel is the role that will make you that star. Because I will see to it personally."

Chandal turned with a start as the door to the den swiftly slammed shut behind her. Standing perfectly still, she listened as a low moan emanated from within the room. Then, with a brief sense of purpose, Chandal turned back and spoke.

"Eric?"

"Yes."

"I'll be there."

"Good. Around eight?"

"That'll be fine."

"I'll be waiting," he said.

Slowly she let the receiver fall into its cradle.

At the hotel, Ron thought again of phoning Chandal. But she would refuse to answer—he was sure of that. No, he would shave and then lie down for a while. Physically he felt much the same. And his headache had gotten worse. He also found himself experiencing extraordinarily short attention spans; he just went through the motions.

He picked up the phone and dialed his office in California. Before the call was completed, he hung up. He wasn't prepared to deal with anything else at the moment. He drifted, sleepwalking, through his small room.

Finally he let his body drop on the bed and closed his eyes. Awkwardly he reached out for a cigarette, thought better of it, and let his arm come to rest at his side. How was he supposed to deal with all this? he wondered.

He sympathized with himself.

Moments later he was on his way out the door.

"Yes," Chandal said to the voice that would not take no for an answer. Perhaps it was because the park loomed all encompassing around her. Or perhaps she just hadn't the strength anymore to disobey.

The sun had almost disappeared from the sky, and from where she sat on the park bench, the only daylight left seemed to be captured on the smooth glaze of the lake's surface. Her face showed strain, but at the moment her entire being had been placed on hold. People who happened by would be unable to see her tension. The silk scarf she wore covered her hair and most of her face, causing deep shadows across her features. Her trench coat hid most of her body.

Far out on the lake dense, cloudy mist hung over the water's surface, and the little island that emerged from the center seemed completely surrounded by whiteness, divorced from the world. Chandal sat near the rocky edges and waited, the diaphanous puffs of vapor slipping gracefully past her feet.

In the shadows, not far behind Chandal, a lank skeleton of a woman in a faded, cotton coat stood to one side and observed her. The coat hung like an empty sack to her ankles. The woman's raw, red-splotched skin was tightly stretched over her face and hands, hands that were left dangling by her sides.

Like the mist that surrounded them, the woman drifted silently toward Chandal and then sat down.

Chandal appeared not to notice her presence.

The woman spoke—a sibilant hissing like escaped steam. "Don't make love anymore. Be one with yourself."

Chandal nodded. Softly, slowly, the woman continued her lesson.

"Everything is symbolic, everything is evil. God is wicked, evil and unjust. It was with this evil in mind that he created the world. It is because of this evil that Ahriman rules as King. It is for this evil that we must perpetuate it . . . and protect it."

The old woman paused and drew closer.

"The labyrinth of evil is a spreading tree. Beneath the tree—stone. Within the stone—fire. The enemy is approaching. We must protect ourselves. Let all sensations but evil fade. Love nothing but evil. The soul lives within the blood. Shed not your own, but that of others. Isolate yourself. Do not mingle with them, but only with the brethren. Worship only the anti-Christ. Worship only Ahriman, for in the end, He will save you."

The old woman gently placed her long bony fingers across Chandal's hand. "Make love only with the brethren. And only when Ahriman commands. Else be one with yourself. Go home. I shall take care of everything."

The old woman rose, pulled her coat collar up tight around her neck and disappeared into the night.

He tried to move. He ached. Struggling up slowly from sleep, he arrived first at an awareness of being hot, burning. The lids of his eyes, on fire, were barely able to open, scorched by a fierce light; he dared not lift them for fear of being blinded.

Eric Savage now began to remember. He had called Chandal. He had invited her to his apartment this evening. That was . . . around six-thirty, wasn't it? He had showered, shaved, slipped into his robe and dropped onto the bed for a moment. Just a moment's rest, that's all he had wanted.

Groaning, he sat up now and squinted at the clock. Eight-forty. God. How soundly he must have slept and he was only going to be taking a brief nap.

Still drowsy, still burning with fever, he let his body sink back into the soft folds of the mattress. Where was Chandal? he wondered. Had he been in such a deep sleep that he hadn't heard the doorbell? Impossible. Yet something wasn't right. Just what that something was, he hadn't the foggiest notion. His body ached. He was stiff. He had probably slept in the wrong position, that was all. Yet his skin tingled. He was hot to the very core of his being.

Moaning, he tried to sit up again, but something seemed to lie heavy upon his chest. Upon his very soul. There was a smell of coffee burning, wasn't there?

And then he heard it. The soft crackling of a fire. Outwardly, inwardly—fire. He began to panic now. Lightheadedly he forced his eyes open completely and saw smoke starting to rise from beneath his bed.

Oh my God! Raising his head with excruciating pain, he realized there were tiny sparks shooting upward around the drapes, beneath the bedroom door, from the closet, ceiling, walls. . . . Sparks! The goddamn room was on fire! He was on fire!

Flames now, everywhere.

Tears sprang to his eyes at the sight of the flames that licked at the bedspread, working their way toward his face. He tried to lift himself from the bed, but something pinned him solidly against the mattress.

His face bathed in sweat, his eyes blurred from the smoke that billowed upward, Eric Savage could only stare in dumb amazement at his own cremation, at his own death that flickered close. It was impossible, he thought. He was asleep. He had to be asleep. At any moment now he would awaken to find that he had been dreaming.

Suddenly his face froze. His eyes, open wide, grew even wider as the smell and pain of his own flesh burning finally reached him.

"O God!" he screamed. "Help me!" The muscles in his face drew up into a knot, his body jerked from side to side, fighting to lift itself, fighting to shake off the flames that danced over his legs, arms and chest. His fingers reached out, clawed at the silk fabric of the bedspread.

"Please, please—God! Help meeeeeeee!"

His scream rose in a single sustained note as his body, writhing violently in the flames, began to melt away. From within the flames his eyes bulged outward—the only thing left of him that wasn't on fire. His eyes—they seemed to be able to see themselves as they hung there, bodiless, faceless, until the flames . . .

. . . shot upward from the window. The entire brownstone on West 85th Street crackled with heat, ablaze in the night air like a bonfire set to ward off evil demons.

Chandal could see nothing clearly for a moment. She had left the park, had decided to return to the brownstone that haunted her memory. But now she was unable to think clearly. The moment she had set foot in front of the building, the image had appeared before her. The same image. The image that remained etched in her mind. Elizabeth appeared almost at once at the window, and in the next instant, the building was alive with flames, the same flames that had burned in Chandal's mind for the past three years.

Her mind snapped back—three years ago. She had been standing on the sidewalk watching people scurry about. Justin. Someone—help Justin! It was too late. She watched now as the flames ripped through the building. Elizabeth moaned, smiled, broke the window by thrusting her body through its glass.

It was as if Elizabeth was out of the fire now, her spirit swirling with the thick black smoke, twisting and writhing, until she went completely berserk and dived suddenly, seeking refuge within Chandal . . . and the thing that was now within Chandal was not Chandal at all—but Elizabeth, and Chandal knew that no power on earth but a straitjacket could restrain her.

Chandal stood trembling before the building. The street was quiet now. In the distance a dog began to bark, encouraging others. The melody of howls lasted for only a moment, giving way to a sudden hushed silence.

Chandal's memory of that evening suddenly fled. But there was something left in its place. She knew now that she had something within her, more than a memory, but something actually alive, something foreign to her, but familiar—a cohabitant. Elizabeth.

She tried to move, but could not. She couldn't think clearly. What should she do next? Eyes darting up and down the street, she began to notice everything. People, cats, cars, lights—too much, too fast. There were too many distractions. They slowed her down. Time was slowing down. She grew flushed now. Hot.

There you go. You're moving.

Drifting. Where was she? Why was she so sleepy all of a sudden? Exhaustion reduced her to slow motion. What time was it? What was happening? Something sharp jabbed at her. Her throat and ears were burning and sore. She had no strength. She had to move faster. She had to get away from the brownstone. From Elizabeth. She became annoyed with herself for being so goddamn slow!

Wait.

No!

You need to rest.

Liar!

She pushed on. There was no turning back. She was on her way now, down to the corner of 85th Street and Columbus Avenue, where she turned south and broke into a run. What was the strange pain in her back? A burning of sorts. A low flame. Yet sharp. Searing. Forget it, ignore it, just keep moving. That's it. You're doing wonderfully. Don't let her trick you. Just keep moving. You'll get there. Where?

Chandal slipped her key into the front door of the carriage house. A hand placed itself on her shoulder. Startled, she turned.

"Del, can I talk with you?"

Chandal could not move or speak, could only stare into the shadows at Ron Talon. With sudden grief-stricken abandon, she threw herself into Ron's arms and began to cry.

"Del. It's all right. Everything is going to be all right. Give me the key." Awkwardly he opened the door and guided Chandal inside. Before Ron could close the front door, her arms were around his neck again and he felt the dampness and heat of her tears pressed against his cheek. He eased the door closed behind him and pressed her head to his shoulder.

"Del, it's going to be all right," he repeated over and over again.

"I feel so ashamed!" she cried.

"Why?"

"I feel like I'm going crazy. That it's all my fault and I can't stop it."

"That's foolish."

"I can't help it. I can't do anything right anymore. I can't eat, I can't sleep, I can't even explain what's wrong with me. I can't even pray!"

"You will. Everything is going to be all right now."

"Hate. There's so much hate in me."

Chandal drew away and wiped her cheeks with her hands, and then brushed loose strands of hair back away from her forehead. "I'm sorry for acting like this. Really, I am." Her eyes appeared vague and bottomless. "I've been alone too long. Much too long."

She crossed the living room and dropped onto the sofa without removing her coat. The curtains in the room were drawn, the dim glow of the Tiffany lamp sprinkling gold and green and red splotches here and there, and the yellowish tint that fell across Chandal gave her face an unprotected look, lips dark and parted, eyes set too deep, too sad.

He went over to the sofa and sat beside her, holding her hand. "We'll talk about it later," he said. "You have to rest." He shrugged. "I could use rest, too. What do you say?"

"Will you stay here with me? Please?" She gripped his hand tightly.

"Of course." He smiled.

"Please, Ron. No matter what I say. No matter what I do. Don't leave me, please. Don't leave me."

"I won't. I promise."

Moments later, Ron sat beside Chandal's bed and watched her sleep. Maybe because he was exhausted, maybe because he had been expecting a different reception upon reaching New York, maybe because he hadn't expected to find Mike in Chandal's house, maybe because he hadn't expected to feel so goddamn jealous and hurt and helpless, maybe that's why he had missed the point the last time he had been with Chandal. The one point that was so painfully clear now. That Chandal was in desperate trouble.

CHAPTER TWENTY-THREE

"PERHAPS THERE COMES A TIME IN EVERYONE'S LIFE," CHANDAL said tremulously, her eyes bright, not with tears, but almost with ice that would later melt and run free, "when nothing of the past has any validity anymore. It's a sort of a boundary, I think, Ron, and once you've stepped over it, you can never be the same again, or feel the same way again, or . . ." Her voice dissolved and she took a sip of tea. Though it had no taste, the action of lifting the cup to her lips was a valuable fill-in, a way to keep functioning.

Ron faced her across the oval table in the L of the living room, that area next to the kitchen that had been set apart for eating. He stared at the layer of dust on the dining table that glistened in the morning light, at the soot on the kitchen window that faced him, at the dinginess of cabinet tops and unpolished mirrors and ornaments. He breathed in the dank odor of dust mixed with moisture and knew that all this was a symbol of how deep Chandal's problems lay. He hadn't told Chandal about Dr. Luther's offer to help. He had decided to wait for a more opportune moment.

He took his time, stirring his coffee, then placing the spoon on the saucer. "Do you mean you can never feel the same way about me again?" he asked. "I guess maybe that's a low starting point, Chandal. But for you and me, it is at least a starting point."

"I don't know," she said immediately, the words strangled in her throat. "You see, I'm not sure I'll be able to feel anything in the old way. Or even remember. I could see you, Ron, next month or even next week, and I'm not sure—" Her voice cracked. "I'm not sure I'd recognize you. I'm not even sure I'll know myself. Nothing is sure right now. Maybe I'll speak a different language or maybe I won't talk at all. I won't be myself, you see. That's what I've come to understand. I'll be her."

"Who is that?" Ron asked gently, folding his hand on top of her wrist. He could feel her pulse hammering. She shook her head. "Who?" he demanded and saw shame flit across her pale face.

"Elizabeth," Chandal replied hopelessly. "She's inside of me and she's swallowing me alive, almost like she's feeding on me. The more of me she consumes, the more of her there is. I can feel her opening up like an inflated balloon, crowding me out. And what I think, Ron, is pretty soon there won't be room for both of us inside me. She's suffocating me, killing me." Her voice had diminished into a thin whisper. "And I can't tell anyone. I shouldn't even have told you," she choked, "because it's unbelievable. It's fucking unbelievable, Ron, and I don't expect you to take me seriously." She lifted her chin and met his eyes squarely as the cold hard shine of her eyes now evaporated into a silent flow of tears that coursed down her cheeks.

Ron, looking at her with a mixture of bewilderment and pity, thought how little resemblance there was in this haunted, anxious face to the old Chandal in California who had laughed so easily and been so full of hope for the future. Yet his love for her was complete, wide enough to encompass both images.

"Tell me," he said, settling back in his chair, "exactly how this whole goddamn thing got started."

She tried to protest but had no further strength for it. The story came out in confusing bits and pieces, long rapid strung-together sentences interrupted by suddenly blocked segments of memory. There were several facts that emerged.

Chandal had no idea at all where she had gotten the impulse to return to New York City. She started packing her suitcases and an hour later she was at the L.A. airport. Secondly, since arriving in New York, she had acted in strange behavior patterns that had jeopardized her career and wrecked her finances. Finally, she was terrified to mention her confusion, both because she was afraid "Elizabeth" was eavesdropping and might retaliate and also because she feared being returned to solitary confinement in the hospital.

Ron spoke slowly, being careful to keep his expression nonjudgmental. "Do you think the whole thing is caused by this Elizabeth, or is there something more to it than that?"

"It's a whole group of people, I think. One of them is the old woman I've seen on the fifth floor of the brownstone. They're watching me. She's the only one I've actually seen, but I know there's more of them. I can feel it. When she's not there, I know that someone, somewhere, has taken over the watch." Her eyes raked his face, challenging him to mock her. "Do you believe me?"

He didn't even pause to think. "Yes, I do."

She stared at him, puzzled. "Why?"

"Because," he said steadily, "it's the one thing I can do for you. And anything you need, Del, that's what I want to give you. What I'll try to give you." He went on swiftly, aware that tears again brimmed in her eyes. "Now the question is why they should be watching you."

"I can't understand that either," she said eagerly.

"Oh, I know generally why," Ron replied, "although not specifically."

She paused, her eyes opening wide. "You do?"

"Yes. There's obviously something they want from you," Ron said. "Now we have to find out what that something is." He got up so suddenly, his chair tilted backward and he had to catch it with one hand to prevent its falling to the floor. "Come on."

"Where are we going?"

"I would like to see that fifth-floor apartment for myself. If the old biddy is there, we're off to some sort of a beginning, wouldn't you say?"

"She won't be there," muttered Chandal, but she followed him obediently through the front door into dazzling morning sunshine.

"This is better than California," Ron grinned and tucked her hand into the curve of his arm as they slowly paced down the flagstone path. She had been looking up into his face and now stopped suddenly, pulling him to a halt beside her.

"My God, you're thin," she said with new discovery.

"What have you been doing with yourself?" Then she cupped his chin in both her palms and kissed him with lips slightly salty from her dried tears.

The kiss left them both dizzy.

Ron murmured shakily, "That's the best kiss I ever had since that night when we parked in Laurel Canyon."

"Shut up," she said, laughing, the sun in her eyes, and added, "No kidding, why are you so thin?"

"I've been pining away for you," he said and found that he believed it. For the first time in two weeks he had a settled feeling in the pit of his stomach, as if he could deal with anything. "Let's go find that sneaky old woman," he said jovially, "and beat her wrinkled old ass."

"Ron!" shrieked Chandal as he playfully swooped down on her, securing her body in the crook of his arm.

In front of the brownstone they paused.

"We should get the key from Doreen," Chandal said, suddenly somewhat constrained.

"Who's that?"

"Mike's wife."

"Hmm," Ron said, tightening his grasp on her.

"Ron, about the other night . . . you see, that's part of this whole strangeness. That might be the hardest thing for you to believe—"

"While I'm believing," Ron said, "let's go ring her doorbell and get the key."

"Right."

Cutting across the sidewalk, Chandal led the way up the stairs, dingy and laced with decaying vines, and entered the inner hallway. Ron noted her hand hovering between knocker and doorbell. When she finally reached for the tarnished twirled handle, she found it immovable, stuck against the face of the door.

"Visit here often, do you?" he quipped and she broke into giggles as he punched the bell marked "Super."

Moments later her newfound gaiety was shattered cleanly in one blow with no more effort than one might take to shatter an acorn with an anvil. Ron's gaze went from Chandal to Mike and Doreen Hammer, who stood together in the doorway like immovable sentinels.

"I told you there's no one living in that apartment,"

Doreen declared adamantly with folded arms, feet widely and firmly stanced like a pioneer settler in a field, proclaiming her territory.

"But she was there, Doreen," Chandal pleaded. "Just let us have the key. Ron wants to look around."

"Sounds like the old Polish woman who used to live there," Mike shrugged. "But she's dead."

"Maybe there's another woman in the building," suggested Ron with the air of a compromise.

"No," Mike said pleasantly, not taking his eyes from Chandal's face.

"We don't have any old women living in this building," Doreen added. "The building's almost deserted. Besides, 5B is locked. You know that, Chandal. And even if an old woman could get in, what would she be doing up there?"

"Sleeping!" snapped Chandal. "Spying on me. Any number of things. I've seen her, Doreen! Do you understand that?"

Doreen's round red smile collapsed unhappily. She glanced over her shoulder at Mike.

Mike shook his head.

"All right," Chandal said, her hand on Ron's arm. "I'll ask Miss Ramsey about it then."

"Who?" Doreen asked blankly.

"Miss Ramsey," repeated Chandal in icy tones. "The woman who rented me the house."

Mike and Doreen exchanged a long puzzled glance and then Mike snapped, "She's crazy. She's really crazy."

Doreen said slowly, anxiously, "I rented you the carriage house, don't you remember? You saw the sign. Wait a minute."

She disappeared down the old linoleum hallway as Chandal hung limply on Ron's arm, her fingers the only alive part of her body, tearing into his skin like pointed claws.

"What are they trying to do to me?" she mumbled between chattering teeth. "It's a trick, Ron. I didn't see any sign. Don't believe what they tell you."

"I'm on your side, kid," he said lightly and bent forward to peer into the hallway. A putrid odor seemed to emanate from within the apartment, floating toward them in an unhurried cloud of tainted air. What was that odor? Ron wondered, fighting the urge to draw back into a clearer atmosphere.

Something chemical or even worse was the subliminal smell. Like rotted flesh.

"Here it is," Doreen said breathlessly, coming briskly down the hallway. She held out a large "For Rent" sign, green letters on a white background. "You rang the bell and I told you about the carriage house and took you over. Don't you remember, Chandal?" Her rouged cheeks stood out like round dots of surprise across her chalky skin. "You loved it," she went on. "You came back and gave me two months rent—"

"In cash?" Chandal asked tartly.

"Yes. Because, you know, the carriage house. . . ."

"I know," Chandal replied. "It's illegal," she explained to Ron and then her legs did give way.

"Look, do you mind?" Ron murmured politely, catching her about the shoulders. "If she could just sit down for a minute. . . ."

He wondered if they realized what a subterfuge it was. That the last place he would have thought to take Chandal was to the source of that foul odor. But there was that sudden drive of curiosity, something he couldn't explain. He simply had to see the inside of that large, dim, cavelike apartment. Swiftly he moved forward, supporting Chandal's weight. Doreen followed, wringing her hands, the sign propped forgotten in the dark hallway. Mike closed the door behind them and brought up the rear of their short processional.

Ron released his hold on Chandal and she dropped weakly onto the couch. Adopting an easy posture next to her, he waited until his eyes adjusted to the dim lighting before he began recording details.

There was a single shaded lamp burning in the living room. The furniture was covered with dark rose chintz. A few wine bottles supporting melted candles sat on coffee table and mantel. Embers of a fire sputtered in the fireplace, over which a slowly revolving spit was suspended. On this was skewered some meat being barbecued. The odor of the meat was apparently the source of the putrid aroma, Ron decided, feeling a tightening at the base of his tongue. His head swam giddily as he glanced away, noticing that the primary decoration of the room was animal skins and heads. An entire bearskin lay on the floor, a stuffed wolf stood in a corner. Deerheads looked gently down from their nailed-on plaques.

Smaller specimens from birds to snakes, even a skunk, were on shelves about the room.

"Taxidermy," Mike explained shortly. "I've been doing it for years."

"Where do you hunt?" Ron asked, his eyes back on the barbecuing meat.

"Upper New York. Canada. What I'd really love is to go on a safari one of these days."

"It's his dream," Doreen explained.

"Ah." Ron looked around, groping for words. "Are there any other apartments on the fifth floor?"

"Yes, one other," Mike said.

"Well, maybe whoever lives there is using—"

"No one lives there. The top floor is completely empty."

"That's not true," Chandal exclaimed. "Doreen, when we went up there the other night, someone opened the safety cylinder and looked out at us. Don't you remember? When I was banging on the door."

"I'm sorry, I don't. I told you before we went up there, that no one lives on the top floor."

"Then why was there a light burning in the hallway? All the rest of the hallway lights were dark."

"Not dark—gone. I told you that, too," Doreen said in a level voice. "The tenants on the other floors take the lights out of their sockets whenever they need one. That's why the top floor still has one. Nobody bothers to go up there."

"Doreen, why are you doing this? Why?"

"I don't know what you mean."

"Oh, shit! SHIT!" Chandal rose without warning and began to pace, staring first at Doreen and then at Mike.

Ron jumped in. "The other tenants. Can we speak with them?"

Mike shrugged. "It's a free country. You'll have to try and catch them when they're here."

"I don't understand."

"We only have a few tenants living here. A broker who only uses the apartment occasionally. A student, but he's very rarely here."

"And Sue Ann," Doreen added. "But she's in Europe. Italy, I think."

Ron shook his head. "I see."

Mike moved slowly to the fireplace. "I don't see what all the big fuss is about, anyhow."

Ron looked at Chandal, who refused to comment. "Well, you see . . ." Ron hesitated. "The woman upstairs keeps watching Chandal, and—"

"So?" Mike asked. "No harm in that."

"It could be very annoying." Ron tensed.

"Well, like I've said—there's no old lady living in this building." Turning, arms folded on the mantel, Mike looked Chandal full in the face for a moment.

Ron could sense a strange undercurrent between them, almost as if they were communicating on another level, or in another dimension. From the corner of his eye he watched Doreen take a step between them.

"God!" she cried. "Sometimes I wonder what we're doing here ourselves." She eyed Mike nervously.

Mike snorted faintly. He moved over to the front window and peered out of it, hunched over. "Well," he said, "it isn't so bad here once you get used to it." His voice was lower, a little blurred in the stifling air. "I was brought up on big dreams, you know. Where did it get me? Take the two of us here—ever since we moved in we've been going around and around, trying to figure a way to get out. There isn't any way. So what? There's a million variations on poor slobs like us." He rubbed the stubble on his face with his fist. "There's nothing to be ashamed of." He turned to face Chandal, smirking. "We all get a little crazy from time to time, so you might as well learn to enjoy it."

Chandal stood shivering, her eyes glazed over. Suddenly she said, "Ron, I want to get out of here. Right now!"

"All right," he said easily, and went to her side. "I guess she'll be better off walking," he explained and looked up to see that Mike and Doreen stood together blocking access to the small hallway.

Something hastened him, told him to get Chandal out quickly before they would have a chance to think about it. Grasping her arm, he pulled her after him as Doreen and Mike parted instinctively, clearing the way for them.

At the front door Chandal turned back to stare at Doreen. "I know why you're doing this, Doreen," she said piercingly. "You're trying to make Ron think I'm going crazy. But it's not going to work! Do you understand me? It's not going to work!"

Pityingly, Doreen smiled back at her.

Back at the carriage house, Chandal raged. "She's a dirty liar!"

"Is there some way we can prove—"

Chandal cut Ron off. "Almost deserted! Ron, when I moved into the carriage house, almost every window of the brownstone had signs of occupancy. You know, drapes, plants, shutters. I even remember thinking most of the drapes looked shabby so it probably was a low-income building. But the worst thing is to blatantly stand there and tell me I imagined Miss Ramsey and the Friendly Realty. That, at least, I can prove. I have a signed letter of agreement."

"From Friendly Realty?" Ron took a quick step toward the den. "If you've got proof—"

"Not in there!" she said, a feverish note of paranoia in her voice. "I wouldn't keep anything of mine in there!" She had disappeared up the stairs, leaving Ron to wait somewhat helplessly and confused. If she was really going to come down that staircase with a signed letter of agreement from Miss Ramsey of Friendly Realty! He shook his head as though to clear it. He had promised to believe her. He was a man of his word. He had never violated a promise to a client or to a studio, record company, casting director or commercial advertising agency. Certainly now, in the case of Chandal, he intended to live up to the highest letter of his unstated law. He was going to believe in Chandal, possibly even more than she believed in herself.

She stood before him now, ashen-faced, a muscle in her cheek twitching uncontrollably.

"They've taken it," she said, frowning as though to consider who the shadowy "they" might be. "They've rooted through all my personal things, Ron. And they took the letter of agreement, because it was my proof against them. And so now, of course, it's just my word against theirs." She pursed her lips as if in sudden thought. "Friendly Realty," she murmured. "It's on West 64th Street. 400—no, 300 West 64th."

The new hope buoyed her, sending her almost running down the flagstone path on Ron's arm. He could do nothing to calm her. In the back seat of the taxi she sat wringing her hands, silently willing the cabby to go faster.

"It's that narrow building with grating on the downstairs windows," she said suddenly and reached for the door handle.

"Easy, lady!" barked the driver, glaring at her through his rear view mirror. "For God's sake, you'll end up like a tube of toothpaste, you keep acting like that. Just a tube of skin around soft squished insides."

"We got the picture," muttered Ron.

"You see that truck in back of me?" the driver continued undaunted. "Truck drivers don't stop for nothing. They're the biggest bullies on the road. How'd you like to be under that truck, huh? For Christ's sakes, one of his wheels weighs more than you do."

"There's nothing in the world like a New York cabby," grinned Ron, as Chandal dragged him after her across the street. "The one I had out from Kennedy sang opera to me in Yiddish." His smile evaporated, as she offered no response. He had tried for lightness, what the hell, but she wasn't having any of it.

She was racing up narrow stairs. "It's upstairs, but I don't understand why there weren't any signs in the lobby. I'm sure—I remember there were signs." She came to such an abrupt halt at the top of the stairs that he almost ran into her. "Oh, Jesus," she moaned. "Oh, my God. Ron, Jesus, Ron. Just look. Oh, my God, look!"

"What? What in the name of—"

She stood, ghastly pale and washed clean of resistance, staring at a door.

THE NEW YORK SCHOOL OF KARATE, proclaimed a sign and an arrow pointed the way through the door, as though the average person who would have come to study the art of Karate wouldn't be able to maneuver through a doorway without proper instruction.

"This was Friendly Realty," she said dully. "It was painted all bright—orange, I think—and disco music was playing. . . . How were they able to do this?"

"Are you sure this is the right building?" Ron squeezed her hand and found it limp and cool.

"Oh, it's the right building, all right." As though mildly

curious to see the worst, she pushed open the door and a slender young mulatto rose from behind his desk to greet them with a smile and a swift glance downward to see that his pens and forms were handy for quick access. Ron almost hated to give the news that the potential double sale was not to be.

"Friendly Realty?" the man sighed with crushing disappointment. He had never heard of it. He had also never heard of a Miss Ramsey, the place had never been painted in psychedelic colors, and the New York School of Karate had been in business for six years. Open fifty weeks a year, he said hopefully. Their students had gone on to win brown belts, black belts and were the only really safe residents of New York City.

"We don't live in New York," Ron stated. "We live in California. Los Angeles."

"Oh. Too bad it's not San Francisco. We have a branch in San Francisco."

"I was here in March. March 19th. This whole place was a realty firm. Friendly Realty," Chandal said, her voice more curious than hopeful.

"You must be off a block. There was nobody here on March 19th. We were in Colorado. A Karate exhibition. Then up in Toronto for a week after that. Unless somebody was doing a number on you, you're mistaken." His eyes narrowed. "Hey, you weren't caught in a scam or anything?"

"No. No, nothing like that. Thank you." She turned away and then shrieked, "Ron—on the door! Do you see that?"

"What?" Ron and the Karate salesman asked at once.

"On the door! Don't you see?" She pointed, her fingers tense and trembling. "It's orange paint. That round spot."

"That's rust," said the man disgustedly. "And we just paid big money for a paint job too. Nobody takes time to do the job right anymore."

"It's not rust! It's orange paint. Ron, can't you see that's orange paint?"

Ron hated the doubt that stabbed through his faith. He turned to stare at Chandal. So soon, he thought self-accusingly. He had come to doubt her. So soon.

Later, back at the carriage house, as Chandal sat motionless on the couch, Ron broached the subject of Dr. Luther.

The idea of hypnosis frightened her, and yet at the same time Ron could see that she was interested. The primary attraction seemed to lie in the concept of herself safely asleep, and, through this peaceful trance, obtaining the ability to bring forth psychological data that had thus far emerged in sporadic rushes. Now, if Ron was right, the information might be obtained in a cohesive non-traumatic manner, while she would lie protected by Dr. Luther and Ron as well. Her fear was composed of the conviction that "Elizabeth" and perhaps others would know what was happening.

"So what?" Ron responded, stroking her arm affectionately. "What can they do, Del? I'll be here. Dr. Luther will be here. There's nothing they can do about that."

Chandal closed her eyes convulsively. "I'm not sure," she said, her voice thin, hardly vocal. "It's hard to say what they can do. I . . ."

"Go on," he coaxed.

"Billy Deats . . . he used to be an old friend. An actor. I thought maybe he could help me. That he knew something. Something that would help me remember. I called him. He was hesitant at first, but then he agreed to see me. We set up an appointment. When I arrived at his hotel, he . . . Oh, Jesus!"

"What happened?"

"When I got there—he had . . ." She shook her head. "He had committed suicide. He'd jumped . . . I . . ."

"Del, come on! Things happen. You can't go around blaming yourself. *Things happen.*"

"I guess."

"Don't guess. Know. Dr. Luther wants to help you. He feels you'll remember under hypnosis. Why not let him try?"

Chandal sat straighter on the couch. "What if I want to wake up? What then?"

"Then you tell him you want to wake up."

"And I can? I can just open my eyes?"

"We'll tell him to make sure you can."

She considered that, shaking her head in some inner indecisiveness.

"What we don't want," Ron said gently, "is to run away from this thing."

She raised her eyes to stare at him. He thought he had never seen her so childlike. There was that heartbreaking vulnerability spilling over from her intensely blue dilated pupils. Perhaps it was this dilation that made her seem so vulnerable, so dependent on what he would do or say, as if something within those eyes was a high-powered magnet, sucking at every impulse, every thought wave, within a radius of a hundred feet.

Reluctantly Ron let his gaze leave those inquisitive wells and travel on over the satiny clear skin of her small, delicate face; the sheen of soft fine brown hair pulled back with a wide cloth headband; the momentary peace that had settled over her usual anxiety.

"And Dr. Luther thinks I should be hypnotized?" she asked, keeping her eyes fastened on him.

"Yes. It's his recommendation, Del."

"Well, then—" She let her shoulders rise and fall in a slight gesture of acquiescence.

It was the only yes she was to give him, but it was enough.

Moments later she was curled up into a knot, sound asleep on the couch. Ron found himself drawn to stare through the window at the brownstone. He knew what he was looking for—for signs of life, as Chandal had said she'd noticed. Lights, draperies at windows, something. The brownstone stood dark, silent and deserted, its eyes dark and lifeless, as though it were a demolished giant who stood blinded and defeated by age and lack of care.

Ron sighed, turned off the lamp, and dropped uneasily into the chair facing the couch. His only thought was that somewhere—somewhere—there had to be an answer to all this. He stared at Chandal for a long time, then turned away. Logic—there had to be a logical explanation, or else. . . . No, he wouldn't allow himself the thought.

His eyes came to rest on the statue, whose Gothic features remained hidden in the shadows. A small shaft of light fell just short of its center, creating highlights over its folded legs and cloven hooves.

Ron's eyes blinked several times and began to close. What had he been thinking? Something about the statue. Rites and rituals. Priests and demons. Incantations on both sides. Not the statue—the crucifix. He had been thinking of the crucifix. It appeared before his eyes, rightside up. With a sudden thrust, as if a Las Vegas dealer were using it for a wheel-of-fortune, the crucifix began to spin. Around and around it went until finally it stopped. Upside down.

"Upside down," Ron mumbled and fell into a deep sleep.

CHAPTER TWENTY-FOUR

Now it was Friday, April the seventeenth.

The city had grown colder that night and there was no moon. The sky was clouded, without stars. It was the kind of night when no one should be alone.

Perhaps that was why Chandal had cried when Ron and Dr. Luther entered the house, causing Ron to experience a stab of jealousy. Probably a little in love with him, he thought, the way patients were with their doctors. In a paranoid way, he wondered if this was why she had agreed to the hypnosis. To see Dr. Luther again. He wished that the doctor had worn more clinical garments—a lab jacket or something less imposing, less distinguished than the simple open-necked black sports shirt that complemented his dark complexion and grey-blue eyes which always seemed to be calm, yet at the same time flashed with energy and purpose.

"I'm going to use this round piece of crystal," Luther was saying now, holding the sparkling ball between his thumb and first finger. "Do you have any idea what it's for?"

Chandal eyed the crystal ball, which measured approximately one inch in diameter. "It's supposed to put me to sleep," she said rather distrustfully and followed it with her eyes as Luther moved forward and sat in a chair facing her. The living room lights had been lowered to a very dim glow and the sparkle of the ball was an appealing focal point. Luther held it now about twelve inches from Chandal's eyes and slightly above eye level.

"I would imagine you must feel very tired about this time," he said pleasantly and moved the ball very slightly to the left. "You've been tense for such a long time now and it's so good to relax."

Chandal stared wide-eyed at the ball without exhibiting any signs of relaxing.

"You want to say something," Luther encouraged. "It's perfectly all right to speak, Chandal. We haven't begun. We're only talking."

"The shine of that crystal," she said sharply. "It isn't at all relaxing. I hate that—that whiteness. I can't stand to look at it."

Immediately Luther's hand closed around the small object and he dropped it into his coat pocket. "We don't have to use it. Is there something else you'd like to use? Something that gives you pleasure to look at?"

Her lips formed a tight little smile. "My pendant," she said, reaching up to remove it from her neck. "I love to look at it. It's called a bloodstone."

Luther stepped forward and took it from her suddenly hesitant fingers. "It's lovely," he murmured, returning to his chair.

Ron, sitting off to the side in the shadows, knew that Luther had not missed Chandal's reluctance to part with the pendant. He had merely chosen to ignore it. Luther now inclined his head in Ron's direction and Ron obediently followed the signal by pushing a button in a small mechanism that sat before him on the table. The slow steady beating of a metronome filled the room.

Luther continued to talk in a sleep-inducing voice. He suggested that all tension was leaving Chandal's body, that her eyelids were becoming heavy, that she wanted more than anything else to sleep. At the same time, he had begun to swing the bloodstone pendant very slowly from left to right. Chandal was to let herself sleep, nothing was going to happen except that she would feel very peaceful, very happy and confident. Her memory would be sharp despite the fact that her body would be completely relaxed, completely free of tension.

Chandal's eyes seemed distressed as though she struggled against an inevitable surrender. They fought to remain open, to stay focused on the bloodstone.

"It's perfectly all right to let go," Luther murmured. "You're perfectly safe, and so peaceful."

With a sudden sigh Chandal let her eyes close, swayed slightly until she seemed to find a new center of gravity in her chair, something that held her securely and would not let her fall.

Ron blinked and sat up straighter. It would have become very easy to fall asleep, lulled by Luther's voice and the low rhythmic sound of the metronome. Luther was administering tests to Chandal now, satisfying himself that she was in a hypnotic sleep. She was unable to open her eyes when challenged. Unable to raise her arm when told she could not. He continued to make suggestions as to her well-being. Later he would wish to awaken her, he said in a voice that inspired confidence. At that time he would command her to awaken and then count to five. She would follow his instructions and awaken at once to feel refreshed and filled with new vitality and relaxation.

"Do you understand, Chandal?"

She nodded slightly.

"Are you relaxed?"

"Yes."

"I'm going to ask you to go back to a time in the past. There's absolutely nothing that can harm you back there. You're perfectly free to remember and you're so peaceful that the memory can no longer hurt you. It can only help you. It can only heal you. Do you agree?"

"Yes," she said in a louder, mildly pleased voice.

"Well, then, do you remember when we first met? The first night you came to Lakewood—"

"That was her," Chandal said distinctly. "I wasn't there at all that night."

"Where were you?" Luther asked without surprise.

Instinctively Ron reached out and clicked off the metronome as Luther had indicated he might, once the session was underway. He had a faint twinge of misgiving. As though the slight frown that hovered around Chandal's lips had warned him he was going to hear things that perhaps he would be afraid to hear.

Slowly Chandal brought a clenched fist upward and buried it in her stomach just above the navel.

"Is that where you were?" Luther questioned.

No answer as her frown deepened.

"You can open your eyes without breaking your sleep," Luther directed calmly. "Go ahead now and open your eyes."

Ron was amazed to note that Chandal's eyes flew open with no hesitation. She looked perfectly awake now and completely normal. It's not working, he thought. She isn't hypnotized.

"The night when you first arrived at Lakewood," Luther began.

"I was too tired to fight anymore." Chandal's voice was low and slightly slurred as though under heavy sedation. "She was so much stronger than me and, anyhow, I didn't care anymore."

"What didn't you care about?"

She mumbled something. The words seemed deliberately muffled.

"What didn't you care about?"

"Oh," she sighed.

"What?"

"—the body. I didn't care about the body."

"Your body?"

"She wanted it. She took it. It didn't matter."

"Who took it?"

Chandal compressed her lips tightly.

"All right, then." Luther smiled. "We'll come back to that. Now I'd like you to go back a little further. You're packing. Getting ready to move into the brownstone on—what street was it again?"

"On 85th Street. The same block we already lived on. I want to go to California, but Justin—Justin wants to stay. I don't know why. He just changed his mind. And so . . ."

"Do you love Justin very much?"

"Oh, yes!" she exclaimed softly, a light coming into her eyes. "More than anyone in the world."

Ron was unprepared for the question and the answer, although Luther had warned him that this line of questioning would be explored. He had simply not anticipated the strong acid sting of pain in his gut at seeing that look of love on Chandal's face for another man.

"How do you feel about moving into the brownstone?" Luther prompted.

"It's spacious. It could be nice. But it's dark. And the building's so run-down. So gloomy."

"So you don't want to live there?"

She stirred restively. "I don't know."

"What about the owners of the brownstone?"

"They're nice. Two nice old women. Of course, they have terrible taste, but we can fix it up. Paint, paper. . . ."

"You're moved in now. You're unpacked and settled. Tell me how you like it now."

She seemed to strain for a memory just out of reach. A fleeting note of puzzlement touched her face and then she shook her head. "I don't believe I can remember. She doesn't want me to remember."

"Who is she?"

No answer.

Luther let a restful moment go by before continuing. "I'm going to make it very easy for you to remember, Chandal. In your right hand you will find a large ring of keys. A simple metal ring filled with all sorts of different shaped keys. Can you feel the ring? Do you see the keys?"

Chandal glanced down at her right hand which had closed around a seemingly real object. "Yes, I have it."

"You hold in your hand the keys to your memory. Do you understand?"

"Yes, I understand."

"Each one of those keys will unlock a room inside the brownstone," Luther continued. "Chandal, pick out any one of those keys and lead me into one of the rooms in the brownstone. Any one at all. The easiest one."

She sat puzzling over the keys.

"Something simple," Luther said. "The kitchen. That should be easy."

"The kitchen." She had picked out a key and seemed to stroke it.

"What do you remember the most about the kitchen?"

"The light. There was a light over the door leading to the basement." Chandal smiled somewhat sadly. "When the light was on, I wasn't supposed to go into the cellar. Justin had a darkroom down there and when he turned on the light, it meant he was developing negatives." She added in a depressed voice: "The light was on so often. He wanted to be alone with her picture."

"Whose picture?"

"Magdalen's picture. It doesn't make sense, does it? She was so old." She seemed to have concluded the thought and sat waiting for guidance.

"Can you take me into another room? The bedroom."

Sudden sharp disgust filled her eyes. "Justin! No—" She began to flail outward with her arms. "Justin—not that way! Oh, God. What are you—" A scream rose. "You're hurting me! You're hurting—!"

"Another room," Luther said swiftly. "The basement."

She sat breathing harshly. "That's where the mannequins are," she said after a shaken moment.

"What are the mannequins for?"

"I'm not sure."

"What do you imagine?"

She glanced up with sudden glee. "We needed them for the ceremony," she said.

"Ceremony? What kind of—"

"We were a coven of two," Chandal said in precise, almost primly inflected words. "It was ordered that the mannequins be used."

Luther hesitated and then murmured, "Coven? Did you say—"

Chandal's expression altered, her eyes changed with puzzlement. "What do you mean? I don't understand what you mean by coven."

Ron felt his hands clench into fists. He had had the sudden dizzying image of a separate personality. A refined personality, but underneath. . . .

"We were talking about the mannequins," Luther said.

"Oh. I don't know what they were used for. I believe the two sisters used to be dressmakers." Her face was totally guileless and straightforward. "Of course, we don't really know that much about them. They seem so open, but in a way they keep to themselves. You see, we live downstairs and they live up on the second level."

"Chandal, can you take me upstairs?"

"Oh, no!" she said swiftly. "We're not allowed to go up there."

"And you never broke that rule?"

"No," she muttered nervously.

"You have the keys to the upstairs rooms. Surely, at least once. . . ."

Her eyes widened. "You mustn't tell. Because, you see, if—they knew I saw them. . . ."

"What were they doing?"

The scream burst out of her. She screamed and screamed, curling inward into a tight ball. "They were—! Oh, Christ, they were cutting—!" The screams continued, the occasional words becoming moans. Now she was clawing her own skin, raking her nails down her neck, drawing blood.

"Chandal! You will wake up now. When I count to five, you will be totally awake, totally peaceful. . . . One—two—"

Screams as her nails dug deeper.

"—three—four—five! You are awake! You are awake!"

The two men now knelt in front of Chandal, attempting to prevent her from doing further damage to herself. Each had hold of one of her arms.

With a contemptuous gesture, she flung them both backward as though they were stuffed dolls, then stooped down suddenly and jerked the bloodstone pendant from Luther's fingers.

She shuddered as she pressed the stone to her bleeding throat and then to her lips, where she seemed to be drinking greedily of her own blood.

"Chandal—hear me!" ordered Luther. "You are awake! You are awake!"

Ron made a swift move to seize her which Luther intercepted by pulling him aside. "Not now—watch her eyes."

Chandal tottered, the pendant dangling loosely in her fingers. Her eyes had rolled upward in her head as her lashes flickered quickly. She mumbled a few unintelligible words and with a tremor let her pupils roll down until they seemed to focus on Ron's face without recognition. Then there was a thoughtful remembrance touched by something of hate. The hate grew, became intense. She seemed to sneer at him, taunting him. Then her features were possessed by a sense of bewilderment and terror.

In the next instant, she fell unconscious to the floor.

"Are you satisfied she's out of the damned trance?" Ron asked as he came from the kitchen bearing two cups of steaming hot coffee.

Luther glanced up from the dining table where he sat making notes. "She's normal again. Just afraid and exhausted. The exhaustion is partly a defense mechanism, allowing her to retreat into sleep."

"What would you call what happened to her?"

"Possibly retreating from a truth she was suddenly too close to. Even to the point of retreating into the other personality. You did recognize the other personality?"

"Jesus, yes. I would have sworn it wasn't even Chandal sitting there. And then when she jumped up and grabbed that damned necklace out of your hand. . . ."

"The interesting thing is her attachment to the stone. I had hoped she could separate herself from it, but as exhausted as she was, she absolutely wouldn't sleep until it was safely fastened around her neck."

"Maybe you shouldn't have let her have it," Ron said, absently stirring two teaspoons of sugar into his coffee.

"I couldn't take that chance. She's on unsteady footing emotionally as it is. Anything could make her snap at this point. That's how close she is to . . ." Luther seemed to interrupt himself. He reached for his coffee and grimaced when after his first sip he discovered he had omitted sugar. "I'm hopeful," he went on with a good deal of professional cheer, "that in the next session—"

"Next session, for God's sake," Ron interrupted, ashen-faced. "After what happened tonight—"

"She let us get very close, Mr. Talon. At great pain and risk to herself. She wants this—can't you feel how badly?"

Ron's face seemed terribly confused and young to the older man. Also unwell. Luther knew that Ron was suffering the aftermath of a severe flu, but he couldn't help wondering if it wasn't something more serious. He was also convinced that Ron would not tend to his own needs until he was satisfied that Chandal was well on the way to recovery. Ah, these young knights in their shining armor, he thought, shaking his head. He was, more than anything else, pleased that it could still be so in this world where sexual conquests seemed to be all. So love is not quite dead yet, he thought, and was glad that Chandal had found this young man with his rather remarkable dedication to her.

It occurred to him on his way downtown in a cab, that perhaps he was a bit of a romantic himself. For example, he hadn't bothered to mention to Ron that he had taken a hotel room in Manhattan for the following week. It was a simple thing to do at this time. He still had almost two weeks vacation coming before he had to return to Lakewood and his private practice. That he had planned to spend this time fishing up in the mountains was rather beside the point.

He was unaware of exactly at what instant he realized he was in danger. It was before the horn started blowing, before his cabby had slammed on the brake and swerved the steering wheel. Awareness came instead in a rush of subliminal energy, the bitter taste of fear on his tongue, the strangled cry that rose unbidden to his lips.

In the next instant metal had demolished metal as a gray Cadillac tore through a red light and slammed into the driver's side of the taxicab. Luther instinctively fell to the right, grabbing hold of the armrest to pull himself forward, snatching his legs out of the way an instant before they would have been severed from his body by the monster lips of the Cadillac's disembodied fender that even now had closed around the screaming cabby, crushing him and molding him into the contents of an impossibly small metal container. With a last terrified scream, the cabby watched his body explode with blood and begin to come apart in human strips that looked like ground meat coming out of a butcher's grinder.

Luther closed his eyes, held fast, and refused to give way to screaming. It was his finest triumph.

CHAPTER TWENTY-FIVE

HE WAS AWAKENED FROM SLEEP BY HIS HEAD SLAMMING AGAINST the windshield. The car was going into a tailspin and his body cleared the back seat when the car rammed headlong into the lightpost after the collision. Ron pulled himself up, glimpsed his reflection in the grimy blood-splattered glass, and the sight of himself, pale and unconnected to where he was, sucked the breath from his lungs, causing him to gasp for air. He woke completely then, covered in sweat, his clothes all rumpled, and wandered around the living room of the carriage house for a moment. Then he lit a cigarette and sat down, his mind blank, looking at the creases in his crumpled shirt. His mouth was full of the bitter taste of sleep and tobacco. He pulled out a handkerchief and wiped his forehead, trying to hold his mind steady against the shock of the car's collision and the horrible death of the cab driver.

What car? What cab driver?

A nightmare, he told himself. One of those terrible dreams so intense as to confuse itself with reality. Even the knowledge that there had been no accident was insufficient to remove the shock. His head was throbbing in a deeply impenetrable spot in the back of his skull. Suddenly, his cigarette was making him violently ill. He snubbed it out immediately in the ashtray and made his way hurriedly to the front door.

The night air offered a pittance of relief as he paced up and down the flagstone path. He was so weak that his legs threatened to collapse.

He seemed to hear the chorus of chanters. Some faint voice laughed. Laughed as Ron Talon stepped off the path and began to vomit. *Believe me,* a woman's voice seemed to cry, *there's nothing that can save you. Believe me!*

Ron straightened up. He had emptied the bitterness out of his stomach for the moment. Even the pounding in his head lessened as he stared up at the sky. He could feel something in him struggling to express itself and flushed slightly as he realized he was trying to pray. Then, humbled, he closed his eyes and felt the prayer pouring out of him on a wordless intimate level of one-to-one communication with the ruling power of the universe. And he could feel, he knew, he was being listened to. He was deeply peaceful, trusting, on a level he had never experienced. Expectant, as though an avenue was going to present itself to him.

His eyes flew open suddenly. Without surprise he saw what he knew he was supposed to see: The light that shone steadily from the fifth-floor window. Jubilant, he laughed. I see it! he felt like shouting. Felt like running inside and waking Chandal so that she would know he had seen it too. Just a little thing, perhaps, but on this slight level he had managed to enter into her reality.

Glancing at his watch, he noticed it was close to 1:00 A.M. Quickly he made his way to the interior entrance to the brownstone. He turned the handle and found it locked. Swearing, he tugged harder, hoping it was merely stuck. Suddenly the door gave way and came flying open toward him so quickly that he fell backward.

Doreen Hammer stepped forward, her red hair in curlers, her eyes narrow and accusing.

"I heard someone prowling outside," she said nervously. "My God, it's a good thing I didn't call the police."

"There's a light on in the fifth-floor apartment," Ron said eagerly. "I'm terribly sorry for disturbing you, but I need to go up there right away. . . ."

Doreen's face froze into remote lines. "Don't tell me she's gotten you involved in playing her little game. Haven't you caught on yet? She's hallucinating. She's out of her mind. I hate to say it. I mean, she's a good friend of mine, but the best way you can help her is to get a few tranquilizers into her. No kidding. That's what Mike says."

"She's getting professional help," Ron said slowly.

"I wouldn't give you a dime for a shrink," Doreen offered confidentially, sticking her small fists into the pockets of her long navy robe. "A friend of mine went to a shrink once, but it never did any good."

"Doreen, I don't mean to cut you off, but could you possibly give me the key to that apartment on five?"

"Mike was right!" Doreen gasped incredulously. "You're just as crazy as Chandal is!"

"Well, you could convince me there's no one up there very simply. Either go up there with me or lend me the key."

Deliberately, Doreen stepped full-frame into the doorway, blocking his way. "Mike wouldn't like it—"

"Doreen, I'm going up to that apartment."

"I don't have the right to let you in. You don't understand. Mike—"

"I don't give a damn about Mike!"

"Well," Doreen said stubbornly, a flush suffusing her cheeks, "I do. I can't let you in."

Slowly Ron stepped forward until Doreen's face was only inches from his own. Something in the depths of her china blue eyes startled him. Something out of place, incongruous to her gentle, rather shy, countenance. A hint that in back of her gentle façade a ruthless woman stood lurking, a woman whose wishes were not to be denied. Cautiously Ron put a hand on either shoulder. Something drew a shudder from between his lips as she glanced at him. He tore his eyes from hers and pushed her to one side. Quickly she dug her fingers into his back and desperately tried to keep him from proceeding.

He pushed forward, freeing himself from her grasping fingers.

She screamed.

Ron glanced backward, as both her arms came around his neck, dragging him back. He had no idea why he was suddenly so afraid of a woman whose strength was certainly far inferior to his own, even in his weakened condition. Perhaps it was the wild look on her face, something akin to that of an untamed beast confronting an enemy.

He grabbed her arms and managed to extricate himself. Unexpectedly he felt the tension slide from her body; she actually smiled. Something warned him. He glanced around just in time to see Mike leap nimbly down several steps and close in on his other side.

"I just saw someone in the fifth-floor apartment," mumbled Ron, suddenly aware of the awkwardness of his position.

Mike, however, was seemingly oblivious to whatever had been occurring between his wife and Ron. "You saw me," he said almost pleasantly.

"What?" Ron exclaimed, taken unawares.

"I was painting."

"Painting?" Ron snapped, wondering if the man could think him an utter fool. "At this time of night?"

Mike smiled bitterly. "In case you're interested, I have a head full of shrapnel from the war. Sometimes I can't sleep. So I work. Anything to get my mind off the pain."

"I thought you said no one lives up there?"

"They don't."

"Then why paint?"

"The landlord called. He's decided to start renting a few of the empty apartments."

"Quite a coincidence."

"Why? Most landlords like to rent their apartments, don't they?" He sneered as if daring Ron to make a reply. "By the way, how is Chandal this evening?" he drawled.

For a long moment the two men stood staring at each other and then Ron said distinctly: "From now on, how Chandal is is none of your business. I want you to stay away from her. You hear me? Leave her alone!"

"We'll let her be the judge of that, why don't we?" replied Mike evenly.

A strangled sound burst from between Doreen's lips and she wheeled around and slammed through the door of her apartment. Ron felt a sudden jolting return to reality. Good God, what had he been saying? Confused, he tried to get hold of himself, to put thoughts together cohesively.

"Now, if you don't mind . . ."

Pointedly, Mike indicated the door of the brownstone. Haltingly Ron retraced his steps and found himself quickly on the outside of the building, a locked door between himself and Mike. Back in front of the carriage house, he stared upward. The fifth-floor light had been extinguished. The window lay empty and deserted of life. But he had seen it. That was the important thing.

So what? jeered a sarcastic observer. *What does that prove?*

And Ron had to admit in his confusion that it could mean very little. Possibly not a damned thing.

His head began to ache again as he closed the front door of the carriage house. He had no sooner fastened the safety chain when the telephone began to ring. Quickly he snatched the receiver from its cradle.

"Hello?" he said in a half-whisper.

"Ron?"

"Yes. Who's this?"

"It's Dr. Luther."

"Oh. I hardly recognized your voice. Is anything wrong?"

"I'm afraid you'll never believe what happened to me after I left the house. I've been involved in an accident. The cab I was in collided with another car."

"Are you all right?"

"Yes, yes. A nasty bump on the head, but I'll survive. I'm at St. Vincent's down here in the Village. I'm afraid we'll have to cancel tomorrow's session. They want me to stay the weekend. We'll pick it up again on Monday."

"But, shouldn't—"

"I'm sure everything is going to be all right. You get some rest. And take care of our little girl. Okay?"

"Is there anything I can do? Do you need anything?"

"No, I'm fine. We'll go again on Monday. Say around eight o'clock?"

"All right."

"Good night, Ron."

"Good night."

Ron slowly lowered the receiver. Then he put his head in his hand and closed his eyes. Some distant, remote part of his mind was trying to send him a message, trying to communicate something urgent, but his slamming headache was so agonizing that he was unable to concentrate. "What the hell is going on?" he muttered. "What?"

In the silence, there was no answer.

CHAPTER TWENTY-SIX

EARLY SATURDAY MORNING, IT WAS SPRING THAT CAME FULLY alive in New York. The temperature climbed into the mid-sixties and the morning newspapers forecast more of the same over the weekend.

At eight A.M. Ron checked out of the Hilton and came back to the carriage house with baggage, *The New York Times,* a bag of fresh bagels and a spring bouquet of flowers. Chandal put the flowers in water, and they listened to a melodious, soothing radio station that accompanied them as they munched their breakfast in their separate corners, Ron with the *Times* on the sofa, Chandal with her checkbook and a multitude of bills at the dining table.

They were comfortable in their silence and a trustful calm took hold. It was a triumph of sorts as early morning was not their finest hour. Beyond the briefest mention of Luther's accident, Ron did not pursue the topic, but it remained on Chandal's mind in a contemplative way. She wasn't exactly sure why it bothered her so much since apparently Luther was quite all right.

She sighed and glared at her checkbook. There simply was no way to stretch one hundred and twenty-seven dollars to eight hundred and sixty-three, the total amount due on invoices facing her, with several stores still not heard from. God knew how she had landed herself in this predicament on top of everything else. The strange thing was that now she couldn't even remember what she had purchased. Articles of clothing had blended with her old wardrobe, never even to be remembered except when she would suddenly come across a new article such as a pair of silk panties or her new spring coat hanging in the closet still unworn.

The only purchase that seemed to her to have validity was the statue. A slight smile came to her lips as she turned to stare at it, but then almost immediately her attention shifted back again to Dr. Luther's accident. Why did she have this strange feeling about his accident? As though constantly drawn to compare it to Billy Deats' death. She knew they were non-related. She had reaffirmed this fact to herself time after time. Probably it was egocentric to compare them, as if they had fallen victims because both men had had clues to her past.

Irritated, she decided to send Bloomingdale's thirty dollars. She wondered why in the hell they had been so willing to give her credit on the spot (the official charge card had arrived in yesterday's mail) and decided it was probably because of her Master Charge card acquired in California, not to mention American Express and a Gimbel's charge card which had arrived unsolicited through the mail.

Suddenly she felt two arms embrace her.

"Hey," Ron said, leaning over her shoulder. "What do you say we take a walk?"

Puzzled, she turned to look at him squarely. His tousled hair, his clean good looks, the fresh male cologne smell of him, all helped to cut through the maze of her confusion, and she grinned. Swiftly he bent down and kissed her. The kiss was reassuring, comforting.

"Again," she whispered.

His lips closed over hers again in a fuller, longer and more satisfying manner, though non-possessive still. He was being there for her, she realized gratefully, but being careful not to ask for more than she was ready to give.

"Now," Ron smiled, "there's a world out there. What say you?"

"No, I need to get some of these bills paid."

"You could do that later."

"Later, then I wouldn't—"

"You're stalling."

"You're right." She shrugged. "I don't want to go out looking like this!"

"Like what?"

"Twenty-nine, going on fifty."

"You look like no such thing."

Then, abruptly, she laughed. "Of course, I do, and so what? Fifty is a perfectly respectable age. Why, some of my best friends are fifty!"

Actually, Ron noticed, Chandal looked better than she had in days. By some twisted sense of fate—she was even lovelier that day than Ron had ever remembered her. She had come down that morning wearing a pair of jeans, a comfortable pair of shoes and a silk blouse, with the sleeves rolled up.

"Christ, you look like a teenager!" Ron boomed and dragged her up from the chair.

"Yeah," she said, "from across the room. But when you get up close—"

"I am up close."

"I know."

"I like what I see."

Chandal smiled for a moment, then allowed the corners of her mouth to turn down a little. "What will it be—ham, eggs, toast, more coffee . . .?" She turned away.

"You're not running away from me, are you?" he asked, the tone of his voice indicating half-kidding impatience.

She hesitated. "Matter of fact, when you get right down to it, maybe I am."

"Why?"

She shrugged her shoulders. "Maybe part of it's because. . . ."

"You suddenly had an urge that scared you."

"God! There's no keeping any secrets from you!"

"Why would you want to?"

"I wouldn't, I guess."

"Sorry, kid. I've finished my coffee and my bagel. I don't want—what was it—ham, eggs, toast. And you don't want to go out." Ron smiled wickedly. "So . . ."

"So?" Chandal felt wide awake now, with the bright sunlight streaming in from the outside world. She let out a deep breath. "What the hell, why not!"

They laughed a good bit. And touched each other. Ron hesitated a moment longer, looking at her nude body in the sunlight that splashed across the sheets and pillows and then at her smiling face. He kept whispering that she was lovelier than he had ever seen her.

She could not resist, and she forgot everything else now as Ron stroked the soft suppleness of her flesh. She moved her face against his, and pulled him over on top of her. The love they made was tender and warm. And for once, nothing was held back.

The gasp of pleasure Chandal gave as she felt herself explode with passion had to do with a great deal more than sex. It was being able again to touch and be touched by love.

"A blue ribbon experience," Ron laughed and nibbled at her ear.

She tried to hold him closer than she had ever held him before, closer than she had ever held anyone before, then had a strange sensation that she was also trying to hold onto a part of herself she was in danger of losing.

"What's the matter?" Ron asked with some sort of ESP.

She answered him with a kiss which was the only way she could think to put it.

Around two they threw on clothes. "Comfortable, but classy," Ron directed, "just in case we decide to get ourselves a piss-ass elegant dinner."

Today, walking was more like flying, Chandal decided, hand-in-hand with Ron as they entered Central Park at 72nd Street. Just one more carefree couple in hundreds who were out enjoying a brilliant day.

"I want a hot dog," she giggled.

"No, absolutely not. I refuse to have you be a cheap date today," Ron ordered decisively. "You will starve, woman. I want you so hungry that when we saunter into the Plaza in a few hours, you will order without looking at the prices."

"Oh, my God, you'd have to starve me for six months before I could do that," she decided.

"Six months it is!" proclaimed Ron, waving his index finger at her. "And then, by God, when you walk into the Plaza—"

"—crawl into the Plaza," she corrected him, helpless with laughter.

It was ridiculous, she thought, how easy it was to talk then, to tell Ron absolutely everything. Things poured out of her that she had thought impossible to express. About the senseless debts she had run up; about the feeling she sometimes had that she was losing her ability to be a good, caring person; or on the other hand her confused feeling that perhaps this coarsening was a natural part of growing up— becoming less vulnerable, becoming a modern woman free of the need to "do good for one and all except herself." About the experience of being cast in the play and how important playing Rachel had become, how she had horrified herself by her own conduct.

Ron cast a quick puzzled glance at her.

"What's wrong?" she asked instantly, a slight fear leaping out clearly as if she had just realized she might be offending him.

"It's just that you never mentioned to me that you have a job, Del. My God, you already landed yourself a role in a legit play. . . . Do you realize the odds against that?"

She reddened. "Well, I hate to spoil it by mentioning I got fired."

"Oh, Jesus, that's too bad."

"I'm not sure," she said somewhat vaguely. "It might be all for the best."

"Who's the director who was brilliant enough to cast you in a play and then damn fool enough to fire you?"

"His name is Eric Savage."

"See there?" he exclaimed triumphantly. "I knew he had to be a loser. I never heard of him."

"God, you're wonderful."

"You want to talk about how it happened?"

Briefly she told him the story and he whistled. "You poor baby," he sighed and then added matter-of-factly, "so you went too far one time because you were having a rough time of it emotionally. But it happens to the best of us, Del. You'll go on to hundreds of jobs. I'll make sure of that."

She could think of nothing more to say in the face of his calm noncritical acceptance of her failure, and they walked on for some time in silence.

It was Ron who finally spoke. "Del, that envelope I brought you from California. Do you remember?" He could feel her sudden tension by the way her hand drew up in his as if trying to escape.

"Yes," she mumbled.

"Well—" he hesitated, "—did you open it?"

"I hate that sort of thing," she exclaimed softly.

"Yes," he agreed, relieved. "I didn't care for it myself. But, Del—I found it in your apartment in Malibu. . . ."

"My apartment?" she exclaimed blankly. "You went to my apartment?"

"I—I hope you don't mind. I don't know, I was just, I was lonely for you and . . ."

"You found that—that thing in my apartment?"

"Yes."

Thoughtfully she pondered, her eyebrows drawn tight together and concluded, "I never saw it before. Never."

"Well, that's okay, isn't it?" He squeezed her hand. "We stole it then. One of your friends left it or something."

She nodded. "Joyce down the hall. Maybe it's hers. Where was it?"

He avoided the question by pointing out they still had time to duck into a movie before dinner. "Let's see what's on. Come on, run! We're not five blocks from ten theaters."

The frown cleared from her brow as they raced hand in hand down the street. The new Gene Wilder comedy was at Loew's and laughing seemed to be the tonic for the day. Later, they were ravenous, having denied themselves both popcorn and candy, but they were fortunate enough to stumble into a new restaurant specializing in both an excellent French cuisine and an unusually elegant atmosphere.

The day was officially a success, they decided, toasting each other over martinis. Later in the evening at the carriage house, it seemed even better as they crawled into bed together and lay holding each other before Chandal finally succumbed to sleep.

Smiling, Ron thought: from a hotel bed, to a couch, to sleeping beside her. He was definitely working his way up.

The sun was getting high—nearly ten o'clock—and Chandal still hadn't woken up. Ron lay there quietly, softly, beside her. The pleasure from the night before lingered. How long he remained that way, he couldn't tell. He wondered if she was asleep. Then he thought she might be pretending; there was something too shallow in her every breath, as if she were regulating her breathing, anticipating his next move. He decided not to disturb her, whatever the case might be.

After a while, he quietly got out of bed. The stairs creaked under his feet as he dropped into the downstairs hallway. He moved into the bathroom and urinated. Then stood motionless before the bathroom mirror. He breathed deeply, in a steady, unbroken rhythm, and he supposed he was all right. Still, he looked much worse than he had appeared yesterday, or last week, or even the week before that.

Massaging his cheek with his palm, he yawned, and then drew water for a bath. He would have preferred the vigor of a shower, he reflected as he reached for his shaving cream and razor, but then . . . He broke off the thought. While shaving, he nicked his chin. He seized a tissue, dabbed blood. When the flow stopped, he moved to discard the tissue. His eyes shifted to the small trash basket under the sink filled to overflowing. On the top was a round plastic container. Slowly he reached for it. Chandal's birth control pills.

He reflected for a moment. Why would she throw the pills away, he wondered. He fidgeted with the container as his thoughts swirled around. Finally he shrugged. Oh, well— maybe she had decided to use other means.

After his bath he dressed, then ambled into the kitchen, where he set about making a fresh pot of coffee.

From the instant Chandal's daintily muled feet hit the first step of the stairway, Ron, who stood looking up, coffee pot in hand, knew that she had shifted gears again.

"Good morning," he said with guarded enthusiasm.

"Have you touched that statue?" she asked at once, pointing toward the mantel.

"No, I haven't."

"It's been turned around. That's one thing in this house that isn't supposed to be touched. It's irreplaceable."

"Would you like a cup of coffee?"

"No. A glass of milk." Heedlessly she dragged a chair back from the table, scratching the floor.

Ron felt his temper automatically boil up. He restrained himself from comment only with effort, but remained calm enough to rationally decide whether or not to fetch the milk. No, he eventually made up his mind. Being tolerant was one thing. Catering to moodiness was merely a way of encouraging it. Deliberately he strode into the kitchen, poured himself coffee and returned to the table without the milk.

She shot him a brief incredulous look, then decided to fend

for herself—strictly for herself, pouring the milk, making toast and soft-boiled eggs.

Ron gritted his teeth, wondering how much effort would have been involved in dropping an extra egg into the water. Still, he managed to mutter as good-humoredly as possible, "It's another great day. I thought we might surprise Dr. Luther with a visit. See how he is." He waited for her to reply. There was none. His anger began to grow in reluctant degrees. "Maybe he could use some cheering up." Silence. "Maybe we could all use some cheering up!" Silence.

Disgustedly, he dropped his cup into the sink.

"I'll be back," he said stiffly.

Twenty minutes later he had managed to reclaim equanimity of mind over a ham and egg crepe, orange juice and coffee. She's not herself, he thought, and now he could see it very clearly. It was the other personality, possibly even "Elizabeth" who had come down those steps and he had been so wrapped up in his own ego, he had missed it.

"Check," he said briskly to the cone-capped waitress who had come to pour more coffee.

Defeated, he wandered aimlessly around a city that made him extremely anxious. Everywhere—he had the sense of vigilance and distrust; iron-gated stores with quadruple locks, police-trained Doberman pinschers, mace hidden away in handbags and coat pockets, peepholes, latches and everywhere—chains. If it could be moved, no matter what the size, it was securely shackled and chained. All the protection seemed nighmarish in itself.

He walked fitfully, stopping here and there to peer into a store window, until finally he ducked into a corner drugstore for a gift. Cologne or something, he reasoned, unable to think of anything more original, and then stopped short. At the front of the store were tables heaped with Easter baskets of varying sizes and prices.

"It's Easter Sunday," he thought, shocked that he had forgotten such a thing. It came to him in a flood of reality that over the last week he had paid attention to nothing—nothing —save Chandal. Day by day, moment by moment, she had obsessed him completely, even on those first days when she wouldn't see him, wouldn't even talk to him by phone. Everything else in his life had no more substance than a shadow. He remembered the messages from Mimi. He had called her only once at the beginning of the week. For all he knew, decisions might have arisen that only he could make. But even now he couldn't feel that it made all that much difference.

Shaking his head, like a dazed man without much desire for salvation, he picked up the largest, most extravagant Easter basket and made his way to the cash register. Humming a little, he took a cab back to the carriage house.

"What in the world is that?" Chandal demanded, staring at the bright-colored basket, wrapped in green paper and containing chocolate Easter eggs, bunny-shaped candies, jelly beans, gilt-wrapped chocolates and a large chocolate Easter bunny. In the center of it all was a stuffed rabbit, a delightful creation of soft yellow fur, with white cuddly chest and feet and floppy ears. In its paws, a bag of still more eatables.

"It's your Easter basket, silly!" Ron chuckled and kissed her lightly on the cheek. "Come on, enjoy it. Did you know it's Easter Sunday? Everywhere people are giving their little kids Easter baskets. So I bought my little kid one."

Chandal's face was drawn. "Easter Sunday?" she murmured, lifting her hand to her pendant. She seemed to gasp for air as her fingers closed frantically around the stone. Her mouth began to shape silent words, nothing Ron could decipher, except that she appeared to be praying. Both of her hands were now clasped about the bloodstone in a prayerful way; her eyes were cast downward. The basket sat ignored on the coffee table.

The rest of the day passed in anguished silence. For an hour or so Chandal paced restlessly, her lips continuing to move in a ritualistic response to an inaudible ceremony. At least, it was inaudible to Ron, who attempted to console himself with some of the chocolate from the basket. The chocolate tasted cheap and stale and he wondered if it had always tasted like this or had they used to make it better? Maybe it's me—my Easter spirit is low.

In the afternoon Chandal took the statue and went up to her room, locking the door behind her. Ron heard the decisive click and knew that meant he was on the outside for today, although maybe she would still get a hold on herself, change back to the Chandal of yesterday, he hoped wistfully. Hours passed silently. He occupied himself by reading an old book he found on a shelf in the den and by eating more bad Easter candy. Shortly before seven he went to stand at her bedroom door. He thought perhaps he would take her for a bite of dinner. He paused, on the verge of knocking, when he heard her voice, hardly recognizable.

"He has been accursed by his own voice of good."

"Yes, I know." Chandal's normal voice, as if in reply.

"You will receive your instruction in pain and in darkness. Alone."

"Alone," she repeated obediently. And then the chanting began.

Ron listened, instantly realizing where he had heard such chanting before. From the record he had played at Chandal's Malibu apartment. Frowning, he quickly retraced his steps downstairs and settled on coffee, toast and a jar of canned peaches for dinner. A strange flush seemed to scorch his neck, growing hotter as he swallowed the last of his coffee.

Dizzily he placed his hand to his forehead. He knew that he had started to run a high fever. Almost in a daze he went into the bathroom, swallowed aspirin and went through the motions of washing up for bed.

Moments later, he was back in the living room. Stripping to his shorts, he lay prone on the sofa, a comforter over his hot aching body. It seemed like mere seconds before he fell asleep. Even in his sleep, however, he was aware of physical discomfort and something else. Danger.

The clock in his mind moved forward and Easter Sunday came and went, its spirits having risen, leaving a *gestalt* of images mirrored in the everlasting consciousness of man. Now he started to retreat into the darker side of time.

PART THREE

BURIAL

CHAPTER TWENTY-SEVEN

We leave traces of ourselves wherever we go, on whatever we touch. Proof lies in the odd phenomenon that when two stones that have been touched by human hands are struck against one another they emit, faintly, a curious smoky odor. The odor fades when the stones are cleaned, vanishes completely when the stones are heated to oven temperatures, and reappears instantly once they are again touched by human hands and then struck.

At first he thought he had imagined it, imagined that Chandal's hand had actually physically reshaped itself. Bone structure, skin tissue, even her fingernails had seemed to grow longer since the session had begun. Her hand, for a moment, had appeared thinner, older, the flesh flaccid—lifeless.

Blinking away his exhaustion, Dr. Luther glanced at his watch. It was nine P.M. Chandal had been hypnotized for more than an hour, and still no new information had been uncovered.

Deep in a trance, Chandal continued to rock in her chair, softly thumping time with her feet. Her body moved as if she were in a rocking chair. She was chanting a hymn.

But it was not her chanting.

The voice was not her own.

Luther turned toward Ron, who sat silently in the corner. During the past hour Ron had said very little: now and then a question; once an objection; other than that, little else. Luther was worried about him. His lack of proper rest, his incessant smoking, his red-veined eyes. The doctor did not think he could last. Over the weekend Ron's illness had grown worse. Today his temperature had risen to one hundred and two, then one hundred and four, and hovered there. His face was gray, his teeth chattered. Still, he had insisted that Luther go ahead with the session as planned.

Luther cleared his throat softly. "Are you all right?"

"Yes," Ron murmured.

"Perhaps you should go upstairs and lie down for a while."

Ron struggled to straighten himself in his chair. "No. I'm fine, fine."

"Ron, I want you to prepare yourself. I'm going to push ahead now with Chandal. I mean, really push hard. It could get pretty rough."

Ron nodded. "I understand."

Luther waited a moment longer to allow the implication of what he had said to be absorbed.

"Watch her!" Ron hissed suddenly. "The expression on her face. . . ."

Without turning, Luther studied Chandal from the corner of his eye as she began to chuckle, a deep guttural sound that was at once beguiling and cynical. Then she slumped forward in her chair and inhaled deeply. There was a long silence.

It occurred to Luther that perhaps he hadn't imagined it—that in some subtle way Chandal's physical appearance had begun to reshape itself. Schizophrenic personalities tended to do that. As though they longed to adapt their bodies to the different realities of consciousness that were trapped within them.

Luther turned toward Chandal, careful to keep his eyes on her face. He positioned himself in a chair to her left. "Chandal? Chandal, can you hear me?" he said.

"Yes." Her voice was weak.

"Lean back," Luther encouraged. "Be very comfortable. Relax."

Ron felt and heard his own heart pounding rhythmically to Luther's soft commands.

Chandal nodded. Smiled.

"That's it. Just relax. You are relaxed now, so relaxed, and nothing can harm you. You are completely relaxed now and

moving back in time. Back, Chandal . . . back in time.
You're moving back in time to the night of February 19th.
The night the brownstone caught fire. Your memory is sharp
now. I want you to go back to that night. I want you to tell me
all your thoughts, all your feelings, all you can remember.
And you can remember in sharp detail." He paused, then
added, "You and your husband are together. . . ."

"He's gone out."

"Where to?"

"Somewhere . . . I'm not sure."

"And you? Where are you?"

"Locked away."

"Where? And remember, you are—"

Before he had finished speaking, Chandal circled her arms
around her body and began to cuddle herself like an imagi-
nary baby. Tears welled in her eyes. She lowered her head so
Luther wouldn't notice.

"How do you feel?" Luther asked quickly.

"Cold. Very cold."

"Why?"

"I broke the window. No heat. The wind keeps coming in
through the window. I keep stuffing rags between the broken
glass—but the wind, the wind . . ."

"Where are you?"

"Locked away. I am locked in a room."

"Why?"

The color began to leave Chandal's face. Her hands and
legs visibly trembled as she angrily turned from the doctor's
question. Tears ran openly down her cheeks. "They . . . they
want to . . ."

Ron winced inwardly at the sight of Chandal's tears. He
remembered how happy she'd been only two short days ago.
And—just as vivid a memory—how carefree she'd been just
before coming to New York. Perhaps that was the hardest
thing for Ron to bear, his remembrance of Chandal as she
used to be.

"Go on," Luther coaxed gently. "Your memory is sharp.
You're in a room. You've been locked away. What are you
thinking?"

"I'm thinking how dark it is. Funny. But there's a small
pinhole of light."

"You can see this light?"

"Just a pinhole. Shining through the closet wall from the bathroom. It's a way out!" Her eyes lit up with excitement.

"Of where? A way out of where?"

"The spare room next to the kitchen."

"Is that where you are?"

"Yes, but I can get out now. See. The boards are loose. Yes. Oh." She held her hands up to her face as if shielding her eyes from a harsh light. "The light—it's hurting my eyes."

"Where are you now?"

"In the bathroom." Her eyes darted around the room. "How strange," she shrilled with a nervous giggle.

"What is?"

"To be suddenly free. Look, see—I can just walk out the door. I—" She stopped abruptly.

"Where are you now?"

"In the hallway. I was thinking . . . that's funny. . . ."

"What is?"

"Now that I can leave . . ." Chandal's mouth dropped open.

Ron nervously leaned forward in his chair and watched Chandal gasp for air as if someone had suddenly punched her in the stomach.

Her breath came in shallow bursts, inwardly forced. Her expression tightened. ". . . Now that I can leave the brownstone," she whimpered, "I can't leave. I can't leave!" she wailed. Tears sprang again from her eyes.

"Chandal, we'll stop here for a moment. Just relax, be comfortable." Luther's soft voice immediately neutralized the charged atmosphere. "Until you hear me speak, you'll hear no sound. Just relax."

Luther wiped sweat from his brow with a handkerchief. His entire shirt was soaked with perspiration. He removed his glasses and squinted across the room at Ron, his fingers working the handkerchief over each glass set in black frames. He nodded a gesture of encouragement and then, unhurriedly, turned back to Chandal.

Ron could only stare in dumb amazement, anxiety giving way to incredulity. It was impossible, he thought. Chandal couldn't be asleep. She had to be awake. Must be. It's all wrong. Everything was all wrong.

"All right, Chandal—" Luther replaced his glasses, "—you can proceed now."

Chandal's eyes fluttered a moment, then opened wide.

"You're in the hallway."

"Yes."

"What are you thinking?"

"I'm thinking how still the house is. What if Justin should come back?" Chandal's jaw slackened and her pendulous lower lip began to quiver. Her eyes, brimming with terror, darted around the room. "Please, I want to wake up."

"You won't wake up. You're in a deep sleep. This won't trouble you. This won't hurt you. Go on. You'll experience it now."

"I'm afraid. Please. . . ."

"Just a little longer. You'll get through this all right."

She paused to wipe the tears from her eyes. Her expression turned inward, remote. "I should leave the brownstone, you know. I know I should leave now, before it's too late."

"Then why don't you, Chandal? What's stopping you?"

Chandal neither moved nor spoke nor wept. Her body was simply rigid.

Then both men heard the click. It sprang from inside Chandal's skull as if someone had slammed a bolt shut on a door.

Ron stared dumbfounded at the doctor, who kept his eyes locked on Chandal.

"Rat bastard," she muttered, her lips curled around in a tiny chuckle, which then turned into a heinous laugh. "Nothing is *stopping* me!" she spat. "But there is still something I must do."

"You don't seem to be frightened anymore."

"No. I'm going to get them now," she chortled. "They have lost their power over me. They can't harm me anymore. I'll show them. . . ."

"Are you moving?"

"Yes."

"Where?"

"Down to the basement. Yes, the mannequins. I'll pile them all up and watch them burn. The kerosene." She started brushing her dress. "Damn it. I've spilled kerosene all over my dress. I must be very careful not to get too close to the flames. There, now I'm ready. Now I'll watch them burn . . . burn . . . their souls burn. . . ."

"What are you doing now?"

267

"What?"

"What are you doing now?"

"My—" she glanced around the room, "—my mind, it's a blank."

"No, Chandal, you can remember."

"I can't get beyond that moment."

"You can remember because you're there now."

"No, I can't remember. She told me I can't remember."

"Who told you?"

"Elizabeth." She hissed the name.

"She told you not to remember. When?"

"I'm so tired, please. . . ." Chandal's body began to fall limp in the chair.

"Chandal. Don't fall asleep. I want you to stay awake so you can remember. Go on, the mannequins are . . ."

"All lined up on the stairs. They look funny. Kerosene is dripping from their mouths and hands and eyes . . . wet. They're crying kerosene. They're afraid to burn. I don't care. Yet I feel so sorry for them. So sorry. Still—see? I lit the match now. The flames jumped up the stairs so quickly . . . so quickly and I hardly have time to stand back. I must move back—my dress. The smoke is so thick. I can't see. Barely see. Yes, I can see Justin, but he can't see me. He can't see the knife either. He sees nothing now but Magdalen. He loves her. Wants her. He hears nothing but her screams. Good. He can't get up the stairs. He can't help her! He can't save her! She's going to die! Burn up! Fuck her—LET HER BURN!"

"Jesus!" Ron jumped to his feet. "Stop her!"

Chandal's face froze. Her eyes grew in expectancy. "Justin sees me now. Only now does Justin recognize me. Now, after all these days—he sees me!"

"Chandal!" Luther shrilled. "We are moving away now. Moving away in time."

"Justin's coming toward me now. He still doesn't see the knife. Won't he be surprised?"

"Chandal, we are moving back. One . . . two . . ."

Chandal screamed. Her arm shot forward in a sudden thrust. There was another loud click. "It's Valentine's Day! Happy Valentine!" she screamed, sending her fist in a downward thrust through the air. Again and again she stabbed away at the air.

"You will awaken, Chandal!" Luther commanded. "One . . . two . . . three . . ."

"Eeeeeeeeeee!" shrilled the voice from within Chandal's body.

Luther grabbed hold of her. "Four . . . five. Chandal, obey me!"

"Not Chandal, me . . . ME!" She thrust Luther back, catching him off guard and sending him to the floor. Still, Luther persisted.

"One . . . two . . . three . . ."

Chandal jumped to her feet. "Damn you! Damn you all!"

". . . four . . . five! Awaken, Chandal!"

Her eyes turned to stare at Ron. "Come on, lover—you're next. You'll see—you're next. Come just a little closer, you fucker!"

"Chandal, you will obey me!"

Panting, she whirled around and glared at Dr. Luther, who slowly stumbled to his feet. She spoke in a slow, seductive whisper. "Go fuck yourself, Doctor. Go to hell!"

With that she laughed, then screamed until her last breath stuck in her throat, and convulsing, she started to gag.

Luther and Ron rushed forward and took hold of her.

"Chandal," Luther calmed her, "nothing can harm you. You are in a deep sleep. You'll remember nothing. Calm yourself." Chandal drew back involuntarily, her face tense, her eyes riveted on Luther. "That's it. Nothing . . . nothing will harm you. You'll remember nothing. Just relax now. Relax."

Chandal dropped helplessly into the chair. Each man held his breath. Waited. Finally Ron let out a shuddering breath that echoed through the room like a shock wave.

"Oh, my God!" he breathed.

Luther quickly knelt down and checked Chandal's pulse. "She's all right."

"All right!" Ron shrieked. "You call that all right?"

"Calm yourself," Luther demanded.

"How the hell can I calm myself? Did you see her? Did you?"

"I'm going to give her a mild sedative and put her to bed. She needs rest now."

Ron shook off his confusion and turned to Chandal, who

sat huddled in the chair, hands covering her face, deep sobs of grief heaving silently in her chest walls.

Gently, Luther lifted her from the chair and guided her toward the stairs. "I'll awaken her once she is lying down." He paused at the first step. "Don't worry," he said to Ron reassuringly, "she won't remember any of this. Not a thing."

Ron stood motionless and watched them disappear up the stairs.

Some minutes later Luther came down the bedroom steps with an empty glass and a wet towel in his hand. "She's sleeping now," he said. He looked away quickly and moved off into the bathroom.

Ron took a deep breath, turned away wearily and waited for the water to boil. "Jesus," he mumbled and closed his eyes. Feeling a sudden dizziness, he reached out and gripped the counter for support. He felt himself getting sicker by the moment. Also angrier. A heavy, rebellious anger that threatened to explode at any moment. He tried to let it ebb, but it spilled over anyway as he stepped from the kitchen and exclaimed, "I don't believe this! I don't believe what just happened. Damn it! It was as if she were someone else. Her voice, gestures. All someone else's."

With his hands thrust deep in his pockets, Luther moved quickly past Ron with his face averted. "You're over-reacting," he murmured and glanced down at his notes on the dining table. He looked gravely concerned.

"Over-reacting, for God's sake. Did you listen to what she said? She's never used language like that in her life."

"Earthy language and a harridan's voice prove nothing. It's a purging of sorts. Also used to confuse, distract us—draw us away from the issue."

"Which is?"

"Her obsession with Elizabeth Krispin."

A sudden whistle-blast from the kettle on the stove turned Ron with a start. He grimaced.

For a time, Luther watched Ron blunder around the kitchen, opening and closing drawers, scooping coffee into cups, and splashing water into saucers as he attempted to make instant coffee. With an effort he steadied his hand and completed the task.

Without expression, Luther sat down at the dining table, gratefully accepting the cup offered him. "Thanks."

"Got a cigarette?" Ron asked, rifling through his own empty pockets.

Luther looked up at him, slightly incredulous. "I don't smoke," he said.

Ron shook his head. "I don't know, it's all so damn confusing." He began to mop his brow with his handkerchief.

"You're still feverish, aren't you?" Luther observed.

"I'm fine."

"You're burning up. Why don't you let me—"

"I said I'm fine!" Ron cried, the blue veins of his neck standing out in sharp relief to his white tennis shirt. "What do you intend to do about Chandal?"

"I intend to devote the next session to Elizabeth," Luther said unperturbed. "Elizabeth, I believe, is the key to the problem."

Ron's jaw slackened. "You're not serious," he muttered hoarsely. "You can't possibly intend to put her through that again."

"I think if we go about it in the right way, it won't be at all violent and we may—"

"I won't permit it," Ron stated coldly.

Luther leaned forward on the table, an indomitable truth visible in his calm eyes. "Would you rather," he inquired gently, "have her keep all that misery and confusion locked up inside where it's been all this time?"

Ron hesitated, stunned past the feverish haze, the dull headache, even the panic inside. After a long moment, he shook his head.

Luther rose and began to reach for his coat. His mind tried to search for the exact words to put Ron's mind at ease. He found himself immeasurably touched but at the same time frightened at Ron's zeal to help Chandal at any and all cost. Encouraging Ron to get a good night's sleep, he slipped quietly into the night.

But Ron did not sleep.

Not by dawn.

Not by noon.

By nightfall Luther had returned to the carriage house and entered quickly into the session.

Surrounded by deep shadows, the two pale lights seemed to blink like eyes on opposite sides of the bed. The thick vapor of lilac and the pungence of mildew filled the air, and Chandal sat propped immobile on her bed, tapping out the passage of time with a single finger, tapping slowly a death-march cadence on the ornate blue-black quilt of her bed.

The dim illumination sent shadows downward across her face, patterns that mocked her loveliness and distorted her features. A sharp pinpoint of white light set deep within her irises shattered her once calm eyes, now half-shut in trance, and seemed to diminish the pupils to an alarmingly small size. Her face was at once young and old. Timeless.

Chandal turned her head slowly to stare up through the skylight, past the tree branches that resembled bars, to the fifth-floor window of the brownstone. Yes, the old woman was there. Chandal smiled. The old woman smiled back.

There was a long silence as Luther considered the rightness of his decision to conduct this session with Chandal lying in her bed. The depth of his concern did not delight him. How much easier, safer—he could not help but think—to have taken Chandal back to Lakewood where conditions were clinically safer. Still he had no choice. Lakewood did not recognize hypnosis as therapy for its patients. Besides, Chandal was in such a weakened condition that return to Lakewood would most likely cause regression.

Chandal turned her gaze from the skylight and let it rest on Ron's ashen face. She smiled a sad smile. "How long—how many hours do you think we've spent in this room together? Like a blink of the eye—gone, yet it seems like forever. The trouble is, I really don't know the time involved because there is nothing to use as a marker—a sign. Like being on a train, looking out the window into darkness. Seeing . . . only darkness. You don't know if you're really moving or not, where you are, only that you feel yourself in motion. You can't determine the direction even—is it backward, forward?"

She paused for a moment, then sighed.

"I don't like trains. . . ." she breathed. "I never told you that, did I? I suffer from claustrophobia. I'm terrified at the thought of one day being laid to rest in a coffin. Yet I don't want to be cremated either. It's so definite. Final. If I die, Arthur—don't let them bury or cremate me. All right, Arthur? I want to be able to see myself in the hereafter."

Ron buried his face in his hands.

"How are you going to see yourself in the hereafter, Chandal?" Luther slipped in smoothly.

"I suppose I'll have to die first."

"Then?"

Her lips curled into a tight smile. "We'll see."

With a shudder, Ron rose and began to pace. "Are you telling me that's Chandal?" He glared at Luther.

"She is acting out what she had seen the sisters do. Elizabeth had probably told her these things."

"What about the other things? The room she said they locked her away in, the mannequins, the ceremony she spoke of?"

Abruptly, Chandal began to hum. A song of sorts. Unhurried.

"Why are you humming that song, Chandal?" asked Luther.

"Mother's favorite."

"Your mother?"

"Yes."

"She liked to hum it?"

"To me, yes. I was her favorite. She always preferred me to Magdalen."

"Magdalen?"

"My sister."

"Are you Elizabeth?"

Chandal smiled.

"Where is Chandal?" Luther asked.

"I'm here."

"Where is Elizabeth?"

"I'm here."

Luther straightened up. "Chandal, Elizabeth is dead. Can you understand that?"

Chandal tensed. Tiny jerks vibrated at the corners of her eyes. Her hands and face wrinkled up. She moaned.

"Chandal, can you understand that? Elizabeth died in the fire that night. Elizabeth is dead."

Without warning, Chandal began to experience both sides of her personality at once. She watched in horror as the core of her being blew open and separated—blackness on one side, a blinding light on the other. Dead center was a whirlpool of bubbling blood. Opposing forces rushed each other, collided—became an intestinal writhing pain, more chaotic than an electrical current gone berserk. Shrieks and shrills echoed, a terrifying scream rose, bees buzzed, flies hummed. Sound became a mass of contradictions, an outpouring of unspeakable terror that rose and dove-tailed into orgasm and lust.

With the innocence of a newborn child she watched a world of spirits enshrined in glass, shattered suddenly by the Holy Ghost. He laughed and the demon strangled him to death. Black crepe and plumes fanned out and everywhere people danced. Chandal was one of them.

In the next instant Chandal's body went rigid. Her eyes widened.

"Chandal, what do you see?"

"People."

"Who are they?"

"Evil."

"Who are they?"

"The woman."

"Who?"

"Me!"

"You said the woman. Is it Elizabeth?"

"ME! SHE IS ME!"

Suddenly spittle bubbled from Chandal's lips. Her head snapped forward as her back arched; something unseen lifted her out of the bed and smashed her to the floor.

"Chandal!" Ron yelled.

Chandal screamed, her hands flailing the air as if fighting off an attacker.

Ron rushed to her side. Luther reached out and grabbed hold of his arm.

"No, don't!" Luther ordered. "Leave her alone. You don't understand."

Ron pushed him aside, knelt, and grabbed hold of Chandal's hands. "Chandal, wake up. It's Ron. Please—wake up!"

Then a vicious slap as Chandal freed her hand and brought it hard across Ron's face.

"Chandal! Stop it! STOP IT!" he screamed, again taking hold of her hands.

A rapid quivering sensation shot up Chandal's body, through Ron's hands, upward toward her face. Blood began trickling from her nostrils—then flowed. With one last violent jerk, her body lifted from the floor, held for a moment, then dropped into Ron's arms. In the next instant, she passed into unconsciousness.

Later, down in the living room, Luther went over it all again, Ron probing, the doctor answering his questions as simply and non-clinically as possible.

"When a person suffers a shock as Chandal did the night of the fire, fantasies usually follow." Luther sighed. "The evil she speaks of could be hallucinations, illusions. They may even be a dream she once had."

"Dreams or real, she believes it!"

"Chairs and lamps become monsters to a mind racked with despair," Luther continued patiently. "Chandal's amnesia is an attempt to relieve that despair. The cause of her trauma is obvious." He glanced at the metronome he held in his hand and then, with an air of finality, zipped it into its case. "She could not bear to watch Elizabeth Krispin burn to death that night," Luther continued. "So—" He shook his head. "She took the woman inside her own body where it was safe. And since she had lost part of herself in the fire, her husband, there was room for these two personalities to coexist."

"But then . . ." Ron stopped himself.

Luther began to roll down his shirt sleeves. "Chandal is suffering from severe 'ego-breakdown.' The distorted images, cut off, detached—without relationship to one another; the limitless space she speaks of; the feeling that everything is strange and evil—it's all there. And I'm afraid she's now extending the phenomenon of unreality to herself." He stopped for a moment to press his fingers into the bridge of his nose, then added, "It is my opinion that Chandal should be returned to Lakewood as soon as possible. I know it won't be easy. But it will be in Chandal's best interest."

Ron was completely taken aback. Questions immediately sprang to his mind, but he found himself unable to speak. With an emotion bordering on panic, he realized that he was totally unprepared for Luther's sudden about-face.

"I . . . couldn't we . . ." Ron broke off.

After a moment of mutual silence, Luther said, "You don't have to come to a decision tonight. Wait until morning. If Chandal appears receptive, broach the subject. But . . . carefully. Any further excitement could be dangerous."

Ron nodded dumbly.

"Well—" Luther rose wearily from the couch. "Tomorrow is Wednesday. Give it a day. Perhaps on Thursday. . . . But it must be soon."

In the deadening silence which followed this solemn pronouncement, Luther slipped into his coat, after which both men moved into the courtyard. The unanticipated explosion of fresh air left Ron feeling lightheaded.

"And damn it! You get some sleep!" Luther boomed, as though he were trying to breathe new life into Ron's sagging body.

Ron nodded and unexpectedly felt his eyes moisten. "Don't worry about that," he said and forced a smile.

With a brief show of compassion Luther placed his hand on Ron's shoulder. "If you have any trouble tomorrow, call me."

"I might just do that. And thanks."

Luther pushed up his coat collar from habit, then disappeared around the side of the brownstone. His footsteps clicked along the flagstones, faded, then disappeared.

Moments later Ron opened the door to Chandal's bedroom after knocking gently. Chandal lay asleep on top of the quilt. The moonlight caressed her face softly. One arm was crooked under her head, her legs pulled up tight against her chest in a fetal position.

She moaned uneasily, then turned over so that her face became hidden. She was mumbling something, but Ron could not make out what she was saying.

Transfixed, he watched until the restlessness in her body subsided, and her mumbling ceased. He swallowed, decided not to disturb her. He tiptoed to the window, cracked it open slightly, then hesitantly left the room.

He started to undress, but could only manage to kick off his shoes before flopping on the couch where he stretched out. Awkwardly he threw a light blanket over himself. He lay awake for a long time, every passing minute falling upon him like a stone causing ripples through his mind, until finally— things reshaped themselves, and all that remained in his mind was a large black uncertainty.

And then he slept.

CHAPTER TWENTY-EIGHT

THE SPRING NIGHT AIR MADE NO MOVEMENT, AND THE clouds pressed inward like a cloak of death. From the far horizon came a faint flicker of lightning, its momentary glare an evocation of Ahriman's brilliant intelligence, driving light into the cracks and crevices of the room. Objects quickly changed shape, and highlights shimmered on the dark polished headboard of the bed, dresser and small night table.

To Chandal, lying still on her bed, life seemed made up of these sudden flashes of clarity. She stared in her discomfort at the dark shadows of tree branches that contorted on her ceiling. Tiny droplets of perspiration covered her forehead and trickled down across her cheeks, under her armpits, beneath her lacteal and swollen breasts.

The more she thought about it, the more bitter she became. Arthur with sister. The two of them sneaking off together while she lay here alone, always alone and bored. So bored. She blinked, suddenly confused. But all that had happened a long time ago, hadn't it? Hadn't it? Why did the past refuse to relinquish its hold on her, leave her in peace to live in the present, where there was no responsibility, no identity, no history.

A groan rolled from her tightly pursed lips. Arthur with Magdalen. She would never be able to leave that image behind her. Yes, it was time she had it out with Arthur M. Showalter, Jeweler. Then, once and for all, the past would be obliterated.

Chandal rose from her bed, another in charge of her thoughts. The smile she smiled was not her own, but that of someone else. It was much easier for her to feel than think. She allowed the hate to rush freely through her body. She would not grope for causes or reasons—she would just do it.

No longer would she allow Arthur to make her "feel like she was not needed. Not loved." It was deliberate and cruel, Arthur's treatment of her. He did not even sleep with her anymore. He preferred the couch. He was down there now. Lying there, asleep. Satisfied with himself. Yes, he had been with sister again tonight, while she had been left to tend the baby. Always the baby. She clenched her fists.

Marry me, she had pleaded. The answer had always been no. So she had deliberately set out to make Arthur marry her. It had not been difficult. He was always so passionate. So willing. So eager. At first the baby had pleased her. It had been a great triumph. But she soon realized the baby had been conceived while Arthur had been thinking of sister. He had always been thinking of sister.

She hesitated and glanced at the azure light fixture in the stairwell. The light held her eye. A wry, thin smile twisted her mouth. A mocking smile that carried her forward to the edge of the steps. She peered down into the living room. Quiet. She had to remember to be very quiet. Mustn't wake Arthur. No, mustn't wake him.

Slowly, one step at a time, she descended the stairs. Her fists tightened as she viewed his sleeping body stretched out on the couch, a thin blanket covering his wiry frame. He hadn't heard her come down the stairs. He hadn't heard the low cry of the child. Sister's child, not hers. Sister's lover— not hers. He didn't even care that sister was married to another man. Neither of them cared.

She moved softly into the kitchen with a kind of possessive fury and reached for the kitchen knife. Far off, lightning flashed again. A dog began to bark in the next yard. She froze. Waited. Would the dog wake him? No. He was too exhausted. He had been with sister for a long time tonight. Sister had consumed him. He was spent.

Outside, the wind rose. Tree branches scratched at the windows. Brittle fingers that sensed an inward itch. An itch to right a wrong. An itch to see the look on Arthur's face when . . .

She stood over him now.

"Dear, sweet Arthur," she moaned.."Dear, sweet sister." She watched him roll over on his side. A sigh escaped his lips. She leaned forward and placed her knee on the couch. Raising the knife, she allowed herself to feel the weight of his body pressing against her knee. His face wore an expression of anxiety. Yes, sister had woven her magic again tonight, leaving him expectant and vulnerable. So vulnerable.

She tried to imagine them together. Him pouring out his feelings freely, his passion. Magdalen drawing him closer, devouring him completely, as she had devoured all the others. It was always Magdalen's perverse appetites that kept them apart. It was Magdalen's fault. Not hers. She was only doing what had to be done.

She gave a guarded look across the room. The baby's cry had grown louder. Much louder. A disgruntled whine that screeched in her ear. Shut up! Her hand flexed around the knife's handle. She drew the blade up and touched it to the left side of Arthur's jaw, just below the corner of his mouth. For a brief moment she thought about running the blade through his flesh.

"Do it," the voice hissed.

The baby's cry quickened, came in short gasping howls.

"Do it now."

"Please . . . please," Chandal begged. "No more."

"Kill him now!"

Chandal turned suddenly and moved toward the den.

"No. Stay out of there!"

Chandal rocked back on her heels. Why doesn't Arthur wake up? Why doesn't he hear the baby crying? Why doesn't *anyone* hear the baby crying? Can't they hear it? Can't they?

But it wasn't the child crying now, it was Chandal.

She swayed slightly with the knife in her hand. The child raised itself momentarily in the bassinet, hanging on, his two hands clutching the edge of it. The nostrils of his upturned nose glared at her. His mouth glittered in a downcast grimace. Great gushes of blood poured forth from the child's chest, seeped through his nightgown, turning the blanket into a river of red.

With a last gasp, the child let go and toppled over onto his side. And then lay perfectly still.

Chandal screamed. Awoke suddenly to find herself standing in the den. Ron was beside her now, ashen-faced.

"Del? Del! It's all right. It's all right."

Chandal turned. Stared into his eyes, the knife limp in her hand.

The fear was still visible in Ron's eyes when he came into the living room a few minutes later. He quickly handed Chandal a glass of sherry. "Here."

"No, I . . . I can't drink it," she moaned.

"Of course you can. It will help calm you."

"No, please." She pushed Ron's hand aside. "Ron, it happened. You . . . you must believe me. Elizabeth killed her own child in that room."

As she spoke, she rose on the couch to a sitting position and groped blindly for something to wipe the perspiration from her face. Her hand fell upon the blanket Ron had been using a few minutes earlier, and she began to daub her face with it.

"Del, please—lie down. I don't want anything else to happen."

"Nothing will," she said. "I'm feeling much better." She slowly looked around the room until her eyes settled on the door to the den. She rose. Memories suddenly flooded her mind. Dizzily she rocked back, placed her hand on the arm of the couch to restore balance. "Jesus. . . ." She placed the tips of her fingers to her forehead. "I can see it."

"What?" Ron asked anxiously.

"Where they've hidden the baby's things. I know where they are. In the basement of the brownstone." Slowly she began to unravel the details. "After she killed the child . . . they, he was hysterical. She was much calmer. They argued. She won. They had the child cremated. I don't know where or how, but they did. And then they gathered up all the child's belongings and hid them away down in the basement." She turned to stare at Ron. "Mike told me they only stored old furniture in the basement. But when I asked Doreen if I could go down there—she said no. That Mike didn't allow anyone to go down there. I can see the room clearly. And the baby's things are down there."

Ron made an attempt to reestablish himself on a terrain where he would feel a bit less confused. "Del, relax. Drink the sherry. We'll talk about it later."

"Damn it!" she cried. "They've hidden the baby's things down in the basement, I tell you. Why won't you believe me?"

Ron shook his head. "I do. It's just that everything seems to be happening at once. First—"

"Don't you see? Elizabeth used to live here. With Showalter. This used to be his carriage house. And they lived here together. I'm sure of it." She spun around. "Of course! That's why she has brought me back here."

Chandal's words, combined with his own confusion, roused Ron to a peak of frenzy. He grabbed hold of her. "Del! I'm interested in the reasons. What would be accomplished?"

"I don't know!" she said, making a supreme effort to control herself.

Ron waited for her to go on. She didn't. He tried another tack. "Suppose what you say is true. What then?"

Her eyes went up. "What then? Then I know I'm dealing with something real. Oh, Ron—if only I could know that, be sure of that." Her eyes darted suddenly around the room. "Ron, we must get into the basement. I have to know."

Ron shook his head. "I'm afraid—"

"Please. Help me."

"How are we going to get in down there? If Mike didn't let anyone in before, he's certainly not going to let anyone in now."

"We could break in."

"Mike would hear us."

"No, their apartment is in the front of the building. They'd never be able to hear us at the back of the house. Here, I have a hammer. A screwdriver, pliers—anything you need. Please, Ron. I have to see if I'm right."

"Oh, Jesus!" Ron threw up his hands, in a gesture conveying both helplessness and irritation.

Moments later, Ron made his way down the extremely steep stairway with care, knowing that one false step in the darkness could send him toppling to the cement floor below. With Chandal holding onto his shoulder, he reached out for the brick wall which he touched for support as he edged his way downward. The heavy air that assailed his nostrils had an odor of mildew and decay.

Only after Ron had reached the bottom and Chandal had

let the outer wooden door close behind them, did he turn on the flashlight.

"Can we get in?" Chandal whispered.

"Christ, yes. Whoever put the lock on, put the hasp on backwards. All I have to do is turn a few screws. Here, hold the flashlight. That's it."

The first two screws came away without any trouble. The last two refused to budge.

"Damn it!"

"Couldn't we pry them loose with the hammer?"

"It would make too much noise."

"Try again."

"I've been trying. My hand is killing me."

Chandal waited as Ron took a handkerchief from his pocket and wrapped it around the palm of his hand. Pressing down hard on the screwdriver's handle, he twisted. The screw gave way. Ron let out a gasp and smiled. "One more."

With every ounce of strength left in him, he drove the screwdriver in and twisted.

"It's coming," Chandal exclaimed.

He twisted harder. "There!" A few flicks of his wrist and the hasp fell away. Slowly Ron pushed and the door swung open. An odd, cold air fanned outward.

In the dim beam of the flashlight between them, the leaden air scented with ammonia, great gusts of rotted wood varnish and paint suggesting a carpenter's shop, an old wardrobe against the wall—the stuffed birds, the yellowing newspapers, the discarded mattress and springs—Ron was aware of the perverse nature of his actions. For God's sake, what am I doing down here? he asked himself.

He saw Chandal looking at him.

She stopped a foot or so from him.

Ron was shaking his head now as if in doubt or fear, as if he were trying to shake clear some strange idea that was twisted and tangled in his head. "There's nothing down here, Del," he whispered.

There was a moment of silence with Chandal standing frozen in an attitude of deep concentration. Ron could hear her slow, harsh breathing.

"In there," she said.

"What?" Ron flashed the light in the direction she had indicated. There were two small doors in the west wall. One of them was obstructed by furniture. The other was completely hidden from view by a large cement column.

"We'll never be able to move that furniture."

"It's not in there. It's in the other room."

Ron looked at Chandal, her face pale, her eyes half closed, her hands clasped together. Her mouth hung open and her face appeared distorted, as if it had been shaped by some primitive sculptor.

"Del, are you all right?"

"It's all there, Ron," she moaned more than whispered. "The baby's clothes, his bassinet, carriage, it's all in that room."

As if she were bewitched, she moved slowly toward the door. As Ron followed closely behind her, he kept thinking of his own relationship to reality. Obviously he had not escaped the dilemma of doubting Chandal. His doubt intensified as they neared the door. He suddenly felt the wild despair of a person separated from a loved one.

"It's nailed shut," Chandal said. "Hand me the hammer."

"No, you hold the flashlight. I'll do it."

As the flashlight passed hands, Ron caught full sight of Chandal's eyes. She was crying.

"Oh, Jesus, Del. Why are you crying?"

"I'll be all right. Hurry. Open the door."

Suddenly Ron thought he heard something. He snatched the flashlight from Chandal's hand and spun around. "Ssssh."

"What is it?"

"Hold it." The shadows seemed to thicken. There was somebody watching them, Ron was sure of it. He took a step away from the door and flashed the light around in an arc. The narrow beam stopped on a small faucet over an aluminum tub. Small drops of water beat tatoos against metal. In a frenzy of embarrassment he turned back to face Chandal.

"Goddamn, this place gives me the creeps!"

Chandal made no comment.

Hammer in his hand, he began to extract the nails from the door. First the top three, then kneeling on the cold pavement, he removed the bottom two. There was a bad taste in his mouth now, almost medicinal, as though fever and antibiotics had combined to produce bitterness. But he had taken nothing except aspirin. He rose, wiped beads of sweat from off the bridge of his nose and reached for the door handle.

"It's locked," Chandal said.

"What?"

"The door is locked." She spoke softly, her face inclined downward, as if she were talking to herself.

"How do you know?" He glanced at the door handle, then back at her. He broke into a nervous laugh and turned the handle. The door was locked.

"The key is . . . on the top shelf to your right."

He reached up. Stopped. Then slowly withdrew his hand. "Jesus."

"Open it."

Ron hesitated a moment before putting the key into the lock. Once he began the action, his tempo increased, until he felt the door leave his hand as it swung silently into the darkened room.

Carefully he stepped over the doorsill, inched forward, then turned suddenly with a start. He caught sight of his own reflection in a large mirror resting on the floor just inside the threshold. His image emerged as a ghostly stranger, someone doomed within his own startled eyes. He shook his head. There seemed to be no limit to what the imagination could do. Quickly he focused his attention on the room.

Chandal stood center, having passed him in his moment of confusion. Her image wavered like a mirage in the pale light, her beige silk dress appearing almost transparent. She stood white and motionless, with her hands folded and raised to her breast.

Startlingly Ron could feel the air leave his chest. Directly in front of Chandal was a small bassinet. Next to that, a baby's carriage stuffed with clothing, an infant's clothing. Off to the right, two boxes, their lids opened, stuffed with children's books and toys. Everything appeared clouded and was covered with a mantle of dust.

Ron's heart was pounding. In spite of standing in chilled air there was perspiration at his temples. Then from some faroff place he heard the soft patter of music. He glanced at Chandal. She now held an ebony music box in her hands. She began to sing to its soft melody.

"Sleep, little one, and be good,
The birds are all in the wood;

They fly in the wood
From tree to tree . . ."

Ron moved up behind her and touched her lightly on the shoulder. "Del?"

Without turning to face him, she tilted her head to one side as if staring down at a child, using a small piece of clothing as a blanket to cover its body.

> *"And soon they will bring*
> *Sweet sleep to thee.*
> *Sleep, little one, and be good."*

Ron stepped around front and flashed the light on Chandal's face. He caught his breath. Her eyes were mere pinpoints of light. Sparkling-hot. The rest of her face seemed to possess an extraordinary calm. He watched as she moved to one side and sat in a large stuffed chair. She laid her head back and closed her eyes. She was silent and still as if in a mild trance.

Ron wanted to shout, but he controlled the impulse. Instead he whispered, "Del, you were right. It's all here, just—" He broke off abruptly. He had the impression that he was the victim of one of life's droll jokes, or that he was involved in a game of sorts in which he was psychologically being mocked. He really believed that for a moment, until Chandal's eyes shot open and he could see the terror written across her face.

"Elizabeth is in me . . . I know it. *I know it,*" she said. *I know it,* she thought . . . I know it! I know it! I know it! She pressed her fingers against her eyelids, as though the thought and the mounting nausea it brought could be banished in the internal blackness. She cupped her hands now, fists actually, and began beating her chest. "In here. She's in here! In here! In here!"

"Chandal, stop it!" Ron grabbed her hands.

Her eyes flew open again. "Ron, take me out of here. Now!" She tried to rise from her chair.

"No. Wait."

"Let's leave now. . . ."

"Chandal, listen to me. There must have been a reason

why Mike didn't want you down here." He paused, licked the dust from his bottom lip. "We must look around. Maybe we'll turn up something important."

"I can't . . . I can't. . . ."

"Yes, you can. Now just sit here for a minute. It'll only take me a minute. Okay?"

Chandal hesitated. "Please—"

Ron placed his fingertips to her lips. "Only a minute," he said softly.

Nervously, Chandal let her body drop back into the chair.

"There must be something." Ron turned and saw that the room was almost entirely free of furniture except for the chair Chandal was sitting in. Against the back wall was a raised semicircle alcove with platform. A low circular table was draped in dark cloth and bore a pair of candelabra and a white porcelain basin. Next to that was an altar of sorts, with Gothic figures carved along its base. Two robes with symbols embroidered on the backs with red thread hung from hooks.

His eyes wandered from the robes to the shelves of dusty books that reached above his head in three separate places along the wall. Quickly he pushed several aside, sending dust scattering into the air. A large book just above his head dropped to the floor with a loud thud. Ron started and turned to stare at Chandal.

"Please, Ron," she whimpered, "can't we just leave?"

"In a minute," he muttered and turned to shine the light into the corner. His eyes fell upon a large metal chest encrusted with soot. It opened without any problem. It contained several blankets, nothing more.

He stood glancing around, filled with the weird sensation that right this minute someone might be watching them from some concealed place. Tension mounting, he pulled a heavy cardboard carton from behind the carriage. The books inside were mostly accounting ledgers from years of business and reference books: *Jewelry, The Art of Jewelry Making,* etc. They were dog-eared and yellowish from age and use. There were also a number of catalogs and advertisements.

Ron was just about to discontinue his search when his hand closed around a stack of letters—each addressed to Arthur M. Showalter in a small, distinctive hand—the kind of writing that indicated the sensitivity of a woman's touch. Ron lifted the letters from the box.

At that instant he heard the cellar door bang open.

"Who's down there!" boomed Mike's voice.

Ron quickly shoved the letters into his jacket pocket.

"Chandal, let's go." He stepped out of the room first. A small beam of light fell across his face, causing him to squint.

"Mike, it's Chandal. Ron's with me." Chandal stepped into the small beam of light next to Ron.

Heavy footsteps descended the stairs. Mike's face became visible above the light. "What are you doing down here?"

"We were . . ." Ron hesitated.

"You broke in," Mike said calmly and stepped closer.

For the first time, Ron could see that Mike had a rifle held in the crook of his right arm, and that he had it pointing directly at him.

"I could have killed you." Mike's face drew up into a knot.

"Would you mind putting the rifle down."

Mike held the weapon steady. "What were you looking for?"

Chandal inched forward. "I asked Doreen about that small table—if I could have it back."

"At one o'clock in the morning you decide you need a table?"

"I didn't know it would cause this much trouble."

Mike puffed out his jaw. "I don't know what you two are up to, but—"

"We're not up to anything," Ron protested.

"No?" Mike chuckled. "Like I've said, I could have killed you. I would have been in my rights. You broke into my house at one o'clock in the morning." He inched closer and lifted the rifle level with Ron's stomach. "I didn't know who you were, so. . . . This is the last time I'm warning you. I don't know what your game is, but the next time, well . . ." He used the rifle to indicate the door. "I'll expect you to fix that hasp in the morning. Just the way you found it." He paused. "Understand?"

Ron took hold of Chandal. "Come on, Del."

Together they climbed the basement stairs.

Ron let the safety chain on the front door of the carriage house fall into place. He turned and shook his head. "Did you see the look in that bastard's eyes? How would you like to meet him on a battlefield?"

"I'm going to bed."

"Del, wait. . . ."

Chandal turned on him suddenly. "Elizabeth wasn't clutching her shawl the night of the fire. It was a pendant. This pendant! And she wasn't crying out for help. She was laughing!"

Chandal tore the pendant away from her throat and flung it across the room. Without looking back she climbed the stairs and locked herself into her bedroom. The carriage house fell silent.

Ron dropped wearily onto the couch and closed his eyes. It wasn't until later, much later, that he remembered the letters. Carefully he removed the package of letters from his pocket and stared at them. With no apparent sense of urgency he opened the first envelope and began to read.

CHAPTER TWENTY-NINE

THE NIGHT WENT ON FOREVER. TIME HAD NO MEAN-
ing. Ron found himself seated in the den, his legs stretched
out beneath the desk, reading ancient scribblings under the
absurd light that was much too dim for normal use. Yet,
oddly, here he sat, reluctant to leave this niche that wrapped
around him like a skin of dust.

Outside, rain poured in a steady torrent. In the dull light
Ron seemed to share a medieval fear of nature's force with a
faceless line of mankind. He pictured the earth flooded with
water and thought not of the healing nourishment of rain, but
rather of swarms of earthworms washed up from the depths
of the earth, twisting before his eyes like small snakes. He had
seen this phenomenon once before and had never forgotten
it.

Now he leaned closer to the thin paper in his hand, the
words blurring before his tired gaze. Pushing himself to the
point of exhaustion, he dozed off from time to time, but no
sooner had he allowed his eyes to shut, than something
nudged him awake, jolted him into consciousness. He had
read each letter numerous times. They all began "Dear
Arthur," and ended with "Your Elizabeth."

Straightening, he adjusted his spine to a more comfortable
position against the back of the chair, and read:

March 12th: Now I am certain. Magdalen and I have
had a long bedtime chat about my circumstances. She

believes that I should go ahead and have the child. Please understand and do not think that I wish to pressure you in any way. I love you, dearheart. Please try to love me in some way despite my decision to have our child. I want so much to see you. If you've a mind to, please come and see me at the brownstone.

April 1st: When I kissed you goodbye, I wept. It was exhilarating to see you again. Please, dearheart, before it is too late, say you want me. You looked so sad and I want so desperately for you to be happy. I will make you a good wife. A good home. Let me share with you those little regularities by which we measure our lives.

May 9th: I wish I could see you again. I have forgotten what it is like to be alive and whole in your arms. Our child grows fuller within me, while our lives grow emptier. If you do not wish marriage, I understand. But couldn't we live together in the carriage house, just until our baby is born? Please, Arthur, let us erase the past and begin anew.

June 19th: You have asked me what birthday gift I would like from you, and I can give but one reply: your love. Before I met you, my head was filled with so many dreams and aspirations. But they have all fallen away, and in their place has sprung a reality that we have conceived together. I ask only that you share this happiness with me, with or without marriage. People can say what they will, and gossip if they will. I differ from other young women, Arthur. At this early age, I am already an orphan and so have no one whom I must please. No one except Magdalen and she does not care what I do or where I go. So you can see, can't you, that idle tongues have lost their power over me. That is why I can beg you: Let me come to you.

June 28th: Magdalen has become impossible. She claims that I am ruining all our lives. Please, take me away from the brownstone. I fear for our child's life. Plans are being made. You don't know Magdalen as I do. Please, dearheart, if you have any pity left in your heart for me, you will help me.

Ron leaned back and paused for a moment. A continuity of understanding had begun to form inside of him—as though he had developed a new sense—the ability to see reality through Chandal's eyes.

"Elizabeth," he muttered through tight lips and knew that he was reading the words of a very determined woman. A hurt young woman, yes; a devastated young woman. But a young woman whose will would prevail.

Marveling, he realized he could feel very little pity for the younger Elizabeth and knew that he had come to believe that Elizabeth had grown to be evil. And that years later at the brownstone, there had been a conspiracy against Chandal. Something real, not in Chandal's mind. And that in some way, not only Elizabeth had been involved, but her sister Magdalen as well.

Seconds ticked away. Ron reached for another letter. Drops of sweat ran into his eyes and stung like acid. Despite his discomfort, he forced himself to read.

July 27th: My loneliness has become intolerable. Magdalen is not to be trusted. She torments me. And torments me. And torments me! I think now only of death. A quiet death where my body will pass whole to the other side. I shall take our child with me. Please forgive me.

Ron noticed that the dates of the next few letters skipped to what must have been the following year. The penmanship had changed. The script was larger, freer—the writings of a woman who insisted on having things her own way. The stationery had also changed. These letters, unlike the others, bore a business address.

February 2nd: Surprise. A letter from home. I love you. Please, don't pout all the time. I miss you when you are not here. Please, couldn't you spend more time with us, dearheart. We miss you so and we grow lonely.

February 28th: Forgive me for constantly sending letters to your place of business, but it is just my frustrated desire to communicate with you. We don't seem to be able to communicate the other way. If I seem querulous, and severe—such is not the case. But I know what is going on. Where you spend your nights. Please, Arthur, I want it stopped.

March 16th: I cannot go much further. You have not been home in days. Must I remind you that sister is married? My frustration grows deeper. The thoughts within my head grow more horrible with each waking hour. I want it stopped!

April 22nd: I have given it much thought. I cannot go on like this any longer. My sickness grows worse. . . .

Ron stopped suddenly and turned the envelope over. It contained no address, no postmark. Apparently the letter had never been mailed.

He turned quickly to the last letter.

July 7th: J. is dead. We are all dead. Happiness is joyous expectation; it is a sea of hopes; it is, therefore, an illusion without end. Yes, dearheart, it has all been an illusion.

Ron blinked and could feel his eyes closing. He fought against it, became lost in the struggle. His head dropped to his chest and he slept.

The sun rose in the clear sky like a large, luminous coin. Its rays fractured the rooftops and sent people scurrying into the street, each seeking his or her personal destiny, dream, or perhaps just continuing to perform out of a lifelong habit, without a thought in their heads.

Ron's body jerked suddenly and his eyelids shot open. His eyes had a crazy glint in them as he sat for a moment quite stunned with his own confusion, then he mumbled, "Son-of-a-bitch."

With a lurch he stood up and sent the letters fluttering to the floor. He stared down at them with distaste. In a rush of thought he bent to scoop them up. Then he glanced at his watch. It was a few minutes past ten. He opened the desk drawer and was just about to put the letters away when he noticed the crucifix.

He felt weak and faint, yet somehow he was able to control himself, only because he knew giving way to his illness would not help matters any. He lifted the crucifix from the drawer, leaving the letters in its place, and with his hip pushed the drawer closed, never letting his eyes leave the cross.

He lowered his head. Whatever was happening he had to stop it.

Hastily he left the den and searched the living room for the bloodstone pendant. He found the pendant lying near the fireplace where Chandal had thrown it last night before climbing the stairs to her room.

Closing his hand around the bloodstone, he placed it alongside the crucifix on the coffee table. The room had suddenly become stifling. Sitting down on the couch, his eyes focused on the stairway, he thought about what Chandal had said, the implications, the terror if it were true. But he still couldn't understand why.

He analyzed all the information he had gathered, unsure of its meaning and importance. It all fit together in an insane sort of way, and yet it did not. Quickly he moved to the foot of the stairs. He paused momentarily to stare at Chandal's door. He hadn't heard a sound coming from her room all night.

On a sudden impulse, he went to the Manhattan Consumer Directory. He turned the pages rapidly until he found what he was looking for. "World Wide Jewelers, Inc. We'll pay top dollar for Art Deco, Art Nouveau, Antique jewelry. Private offices/Free appraisals."

He dialed for an appointment.

In the bathroom he splashed cold water on his face and then noisily sipped the water he cupped in his palms.

Moments later he scribbled a short note to Chandal, propped it on the dining table and left the carriage house. He did not even stop for his first meal of the day, but took a cab directly to the East Side where he found that World Wide Jewelers was located on the second floor of a professional building. The daylight was growing in intensity when he rang the doorbell. A buzzer sounded and the outer door sprang open.

Now he waited in the small foyer, inhaling smoke from his cigarette. The overhead light flickered on, and the window in the front door opened. Ron saw a tanned, young man looking at him. The man was younger than he would have expected. The male voice asked, "Can I help you?"

"I'm Ron Talon. I called about an hour ago," he said, somewhat afraid that he might never get past the front door.

"Just a sec," the boy said. After a moment he reappeared and said politely, "Yes, you're expected."

The older man behind the counter took a pencil out of his mouth and put the papers he'd been working on into a small desk. He spoke slowly as though he had a lot of time to spare for Ron and the two items Ron had laid on the plush velvet pad: the crucifix and the bloodstone pendant.

He looked at Ron and smiled, then examined the crucifix. "It's very old. In marvelous condition, too."

"How old?"

"I really couldn't say, offhand."

"Ten years? Twenty—fifty?"

"Oh, no, much older than that. I'm sure it's quite valuable."

"Yes," Ron muttered. "I'm sure it is."

"I'll look it up. It will only take a moment."

The man placed a book on the counter and opened it. He turned the pages until he came to a section named "The Cross and the Crucifix." Ron was surprised to see that there were so many variations of the cross, and that the swastika was one of them.

"Yes, here it is. Look for yourself." The man spun the book around to face Ron rightside up. "Notice the cross bottom-left, last in the row. The cross with returned arms. Italian, most definitely. I would say your crucifix is fifth century of the Christian Era."

"How can you be so sure? I see nothing here—"

"It was customary to add symbolic representations of Christ to the cross during that time as, for example, a figure of the sacrificial lamb. . . ." He picked up the crucifix. "In this case, however, it looks more like a goat."

"What?" Ron's eyes widened. "Let me see that."

Ron stared at the crucifix in disbelief. The face on the Christ figure had changed again.

"Wouldn't you say that was a goat's head?"

"Yes," breathed Ron.

"The curious thing," the man said, lifting the pendant, "is that I believe this chain belongs with that crucifix. May I?"

"Sure."

Ron watched as the man removed the chain from the bloodstone and slipped it through the loop at the bottom of the crucifix. "Yes, you see. They are most definitely a match." The man shook his head and mumbled something Ron could not make out.

"I'm sorry?"

"Oh, curious, that's all, why the loop for the chain has been placed at the bottom of the cross. That would make it hang upside down, wouldn't it? If it were worn."

"Yes, it would."

"Well, at any rate . . . I'm interested in purchasing the chain and the crucifix if you've a mind to sell. Naturally, the chain is broken, and—"

"What about the stone?"

"An average stone really, except for its setting. Rather unique, also quite old. Perhaps I can give you one price for all three pieces."

"Ah, about the cross. Have you any idea why the loop is at the bottom?" Ron felt the man hesitate. "I mean, doesn't that lessen its value?"

"Not necessarily."

"Then there's a reason for it?"

"Well, there have been crucifixes used in ceremonies."

Ron tensed. "Oh? I don't understand."

"Devil worship."

Ron blinked. "Are you sure?"

"Well, no one knows for sure, naturally. But it has been talked about."

"I see." Ron scooped up the pendant and the crucifix. "Thanks."

"I'll give you a good price!" the man hollered after him.

"Let me think about it!" Ron hollered back.

Ron was on the street again; a soft noon rain was falling. He ducked into the phone booth and dialed the carriage house. There was no answer. Nervously he reasoned that he should return as soon as possible. Yet something drove him on. He hastened down Third Avenue until he reached Forty-second Street, and then, feeling pursued by an unseen force, turned west.

The sidewalk was crowded with people. How ordinary everything seemed. A policeman directed traffic, people window-shopped, others popped in and out of stores and restaurants, some with umbrellas, others with raincoats, most not really paying much attention to the slight hazy drizzle that fell like mist from a sun-drenched sky. It might have been almost any other ordinary spring day.

Ron smiled when he saw the two stone lions standing sentinel over Fifth Avenue. Briskly he climbed the steps and entered the library. He did not take the time to remove his jacket, but went directly to the catalogue table where he began turning pages of the thick index. Somewhere over his shoulder he heard, for the first time, the sound of a solo violin. It seemed to be coming from a small room down the hall. He looked up. A one-man concert, he imagined.

Keep looking—he scolded himself.

Twisting his hands together, he squinted at the small print on the yellowing pages that appeared to go on forever. He read further, realizing that he was experiencing a small anxiety attack of sorts.

Time. He needed more time.

He shuddered.

It was a little after two when he found the last of the books he'd been looking for and dumped it with the others on the long wooden table in the reference room.

Jesus. He felt so damn lightheaded and knew that if someone so much as whistled, they'd blow him away. Removing his jacket, he sat down, took a deep breath and began to read.

The first book he browsed through was a reference book on Death and Dying. At first he read somewhat carefully, but then he started to skim.

Human beings have been known to survive physical death. . . .

The body and the spirit do not always die together. . . .

The spirit can continue to exist after death at varying levels of awareness.

Ron wiped small beads of sweat from the back of his neck. He turned to a section that covered "Hauntings." He read carefully.

The behavior of some spirits clearly shows that they have been so traumatized by their deaths that they are completely 'fixed' at that point in time, and re-live their deaths over and over again.

Further on down the page:

Spirits of the dead have been known to cling to other living beings in order to attend to unfinished business. Long dead, the disturbed spirits are obviously unaware of the passage of time, and continue to search for something they urgently wanted or needed—before death.

Ron let the cover of the book fall shut.

His right hand remained clutching the book, while his left hand, resting on the table, began to clench into such a tight fist it seemed that he was about to swing it. As soon as he relaxed it, his hand trembled where it lay.

Was it possible, he wondered. Was Chandal correct in her belief that in some way Elizabeth had become part of her? This altogether confounded him. The whole idea of anything outside of what he was actually able to see was beyond his belief, beyond his own limited range of consciousness.

Yet his hands continued to shake as he reached for the next book. And the book after that. And the one after that, until finally his mind started to merge with words sprawled across the pages before him. Through his mind flashed gigantic winged creatures, clouds, wind, thunder and lightning. The hours passed. He was caught in a kind of Black Mass of strange words, grotesque pictures, where demons smiled and mocked the divinity of mankind; where the world was one long continuation of fantasy and imagination; where Satan proclaimed himself supreme ruler of "The Selfhood"; where great Homeric heroes slew each other; where alchemy, magical doctrines, witchcraft and life after death prevailed;

where witches held orgiastic ceremonies at which their god appeared to them, sometimes in human form, sometimes in the form of an animal—frequently a goat.

As time wore on, Ron found it harder to concentrate on what he was reading—it was difficult even to move his eyes—and he kept transposing words, substituting the ones in his mind for the ones on the page, missing entire phrases, and then whole sentences—conscious all the while that his shirt was drenched with sweat and stuck to the back of the chair—and finally, after hours of reading, ended up staring dumbfoundedly at a picture of the Satanic Goat of the witches' sabbath.

Ron blinked and knew instantly where he had seen the image before—Chandal's statue. The one that sat on the mantel. The picture in the book and the statue were identical. The same cloven hooves, the same goat's face, and . . . of course . . . !

Shaking away the haziness from his mind, he quickly removed the crucifix from his pocket and laid it next to the picture. He examined both closely. They, too, were identical.

Exhausted, he leaned back in his chair to watch images loom large and small against the backdrop of his eyelids. Thoughts flooded his mind, strangled each other, faded. There was no criterion to follow, no system of ideas. Such was his conclusion as he left the library, but he knew this was only a postponement of the real and final answer.

The knob turned easily in her hand and the door swung soundlessly open. Chandal hesitated, but someone seemed to guide her forward across the darkened room over to the window. As she walked, a cool mist formed at her feet, and she trembled slightly.

"The Divine Sarah. We must make this our best perform-ance ever," cooed the voice as Chandal hesitated several feet from the window. *"Don't be afraid. You like the view from here. Go on, dear, just a little closer."*

"Yes, it's very pretty," breathed Chandal, bending forward. Feeling lightheaded, she steadied herself by placing both hands on the window sill. Five floors below, the carriage house stood nestled in its rose bushes and vines—a cottage out of a dated fantasy.

Something inside of Chandal yearned for the carriage

house as a home she had wanted very badly one time or the other and she leaned even closer as though reaching down to embrace it. She felt weakened, almost faint. She swayed slightly, her eyes fastened hungrily on the carriage house.

"*Lovely, isn't it?*" the voice observed. "*I was so happy there for a while. A short while. But Arthur never really cared for me. Only for Magdalen. Magdalen had some quality—I'm not sure exactly what—something frail, vulnerable, perhaps that was it. Men found her irresistible. But I'm sure you know that. How silly of me to go on like this.*" The voice stopped for a moment to chuckle, then added like a whimpering child: "*I only loved two men, that's all, just two—Arthur and, of course, the young Dr. Rock, Magdalen's husband. She took them away from me just as she took your husband away from you.*"

"Justin," Chandal sighed softly, her voice mixing with the sound of light raindrops that tapped against the window, running down the glass like tears.

"*It's so right, you see,*" whispered the voice, "*that we should be together. We could have been so happy living together in the carriage house. Perhaps in time, Ahriman would have allowed the child I asked him for. We would have raised him together, you and I. I would have liked that. Mike wanted that too. We all did. We tried.*"

"Child?" murmured Chandal, allowing herself to sit now on the window sill. She could feel herself being pulled forward; she was so tired.

"*Now none of it can be. None of it realized. None, none, none. . . .*" She chuckled like a mischievous child. "*They won't leave us alone. They want to separate us. Take us away. No,*" she whispered, "*I can't allow that, you see. Can't allow that.*"

Chandal's eyes were starting to close. Using the last of her strength, she fought to keep them open. She blinked dazedly. Five stories below, she watched as Ron entered the carriage house.

"*It will be a nice death. Ahriman will be pleased. Very pleased.*" The voice paused, then added, "*Smooth your hair back, dear. We must look our best.*"

Ron shook the rain from his jacket and slung it over the back of the chair. "Del?"

The living room was empty, the kitchen was empty. Turning lights on as he passed through them, he came back to the dining table and paused. The note he had written Chandal this morning sat exactly where he had left it—untouched, or so it seemed.

"Del, I'm back."

He moved down the hallway, slightly off-balance, shuffling his feet as if unable to lift them out of the entanglements he could not see, his legs heavy as if lead were circulating through his veins. Then, feeling a sudden fear—he stopped.

Chandal's bedroom door stood ajar. But the light was out.

"Del?" He hesitated. "Del, are you up there?"

Slowly at first, he climbed the steps until he reached the top, where he leaped into the room. He flicked on the light. The room was empty.

Where could she be? he wondered and did not like the thoughts that now swirled in his head. He glanced at his watch. Seven-thirty P.M. He hadn't realized he'd been at the library that long. It had already grown dark.

He dropped wearily on the bed and sat still for a moment. He felt blankness and dislocation and saw, as he stared up through the skylight, shades of lavender and gold and whiteness, soft and still, imprisoned in the glass of the window on the fifth floor of the brownstone, and found himself engulfed in Chandal's misty-blue and quivering gaze. Chandal lifted her hands to her face and quickly disappeared.

"Oh, my God!" he cried. "Chandal!"

He bolted down the stairs, stumbled, almost tumbled headlong into the living room. Regaining his balance, he lunged for the door.

"Del!" he screamed and took the flagstones three at a time, until he found himself banging on the interior door of the brownstone. He hit the super's bell, then reached for the doorknob and turned. The door was open. Open? He didn't wait to reason why.

His legs struggled to take the stairs faster, even though his knees shook violently, threatening to collapse every second step. Using the banister, he pulled himself upward, swearing to spur himself on, teeth angrily gripping his lower lip. At one point he miscalculated the landings and ran halfway down the hall before discovering he was on the fourth floor, rather than the fifth. An agonized exclamation broke from between his lips as he discovered his mistake. Retracing his steps, he stumbled up the last flight of stairs.

"Chandal!" he yelled, now racing down the hallway.

The door to 5B stood open. Ron's heart beat in great painful thuds as he forced himself to slow his steps, to assume a façade of calmness.

God, don't let me frighten her, he cautioned himself, making his way into the room, and then he lost all control when he saw that she was no longer at the window.

"Del? It's Ron." He inched forward in the silence, the rain tapping against the window the room's only sound, and pushed open the door to his right. The room was empty. "Goddamn it!"

Bewildered, his eyes scanned the outer room again. Its only light source came from the dim light burning in the hallway. Still, he could see there was no place for her to hide. The bathroom, he thought suddenly. That, too, was empty.

He turned swiftly and moved to the front door, glanced around the apartment one last time, then stepped into the hallway.

At the far end of the corridor a door suddenly swung shut. He inched forward. "Del, is that you?" Closer to the door now, he realized that it was a fire exit to the roof.

"Good Christ!" he shrilled.

He dashed up the metal steps, pushed down on the bar and the door shot open.

Stepping quickly onto the roof, he paused to look around. Nothing. He let go of his hold on the door and started to move. After two steps he caught sight of Chandal. She was standing stiffly with outstretched hands at the edge of the roof. The very edge. She did not move when the door behind him slammed shut.

In spite of the darkness and the light drizzling rain, Ron could see the glazed expression on Chandal's face.

He called out, "Chandal?" She remained in the same frozen position. "Del, come away from there." She made no response.

Ron took a slow, careful step. "Del, you're standing too close to the edge. Move away, please." Chandal did not speak, nor did she move. He took a third step and a fourth and now he was close enough to touch her.

He reached out his hand, but so carefully that it scarcely

seemed to move. He managed to get two fingers on the sleeve of her blouse.

Slowly, slowly, he cautioned himself through a haze. Damn it. Another step. He'd have to take one more step. Gathering all the calm he could muster, he paused, then took that step.

In the next instant, he heard an unbelievable animal cry escape Chandal's lips as she tried to fling herself from the roof. Ron grabbed hold and tried to restrain her when, with a violent thrust of her body, she spun around and lunged at him with incredible strength.

It happened so suddenly he was only vaguely aware of what she was doing until he felt her nails sinking into the flesh of his throat. Tearing at his face.

He twisted away in pain.

She was on him now, clawing at his face, screaming, beating her arms wildly about his chest. She drew her hands back—another wild scream rose to her lips. Her face contorted in rage as the last gasp of air left her body.

Silence . . . brief. There was no time to think. Ron was stumbling forward now, as if something had come to sit on his back. From the impact he knew that it was large and heavy. He staggered under its weight, his heart beating wildly, and despite his fear, he reached back his hand.

There was nothing there.

"Chandal!" he screamed.

Chandal leaped for the edge of the roof.

Ron reached out and took hold, grabbed hold, yanked her back so hard that her head snapped back, almost seeming to leave her shoulders.

There was another sound, loud, grating, like metal smashing against metal. A moment later Chandal looked up, dazed, her eyes rapidly changing color, dilating, then all sound and movement ceased until finally she stood rigid and still.

"Del." Ron shuddered. "Are you all right?" He shook her. "For Christ's sake, answer me!"

Chandal's hands dropped to her side. Her head fell to her chest. She stood motionless and limp like a rag doll.

"Del, please answer me. Look at me. Please," Ron pleaded.

Obediently she lifted her face. Her eyes looked at him for a second. Then her gaze swept down as though she was afraid and ashamed of his close scrutiny. He could feel her trembling in his hands. He pulled her into his arms and held her against him.

"Oh, Del," he whispered and felt her arms slip around his neck. She was sobbing softly, the sound that children make when cradled in a parent's arms after a hurt or a fright.

They remained in that position for a long time, the light rain falling around them. Ron asked for no explanations and made no further demands. He forgot everything but the reality of holding her in his arms. Finally he put his hand under her chin and tilted her head upward.

"Are you all right?" he asked anxiously.

She blinked. "What?"

"Are you all right?" he repeated.

Her eyes were a little wary now. "All right. Yes."

"Come on."

The crying and the heartache seemed to leave her as they made their way down the darkened stairwell.

Mike and Doreen Hammer stood motionless in their doorway. Chandal moved past them, her eyes glazed as if she did not see them, as if they were not there.

Ron glared at Mike. "Your front door was left open."

Mike shrugged. "The lock is busted."

"How convenient."

"Come on, Ron." Chandal pulled him forward.

"How fucking convenient!" Ron scowled.

Chandal went directly to her room without saying another word; without allowing Ron to say another word. It seemed that no matter what he had to say—it was too late.

Ron sat on the couch, drink in hand, and drained it, annoyed and worried. It was ridiculous, he mused. One moment she was there, the next, she was not.

Dazed, totally unnerved, it seemed to Ron that, like all the other bizarre happenings of the past week, Chandal, like his common sense, had simply vanished in a cloud of confusion.

CHAPTER THIRTY

AT NINE O'CLOCK THE NEXT MORNING DR. LUTHER arrived at the carriage house. He found Chandal semicomatose and barely able to stand up. He auscultated her chest area. Her heartbeat and lung activity were normal. He checked her pulse—normal. He shone his ophthalmoscope into her eyes; apparently no sign of trouble there either. After conducting some perfunctory tests, such as having Chandal hold up the number of fingers he had suggested, he put her to bed. She had passed into an extraordinarily deep sleep before he left the room.

Convinced that Chandal should return to Lakewood as soon as possible, he rejoined Ron in the living room, where the conversation became a constant and tiring round of conflicting opinions.

Ron was painfully defensive.

He was too frightened to be otherwise. The thought of Chandal returning to Lakewood sent a shudder through his body. Suppose Chandal was right? Suppose everything he had uncovered was true?

"But it's not true," Luther corrected gently, wiping sweat from beneath the rims of his glasses.

"Why Easter Sunday? Saturday, she was fine. Suddenly, the next day, she just turned into another personality."

"You must forgive me for not pandering to your superstitions—"

"Superstitions!"

THE BLOODSTONE

"Yes. Evil spirits. Religious holidays. . . ."

"I saw her. . . ."

"We are not involved with possession here."

"She became another person."

"Of course—yes. Because she is suffering paranoid schizophrenia, with a surfacing and submerging nature. The classic dual personality, compounded by paranoia, the sense of being persecuted. The result is her inability to differentiate between right and wrong—who she is. There is no imagining what she is liable to do next."

"I'm telling you that woman is living out her life through Chandal."

"Ron, we are not creatures to be manipulated. We have minds, wills. We make choices. We choose!"

"But she is not capable of choosing!"

"Exactly."

Ron tensed as he realized what he had just said. What Luther had just said.

Luther shook his head. "Chandal is a person with a disturbed personality. Her actions last night speak for themselves." Luther paused, then added, "She is almost completely shattered now. Her ability to function is becoming more fitful. She has to work too hard now to survive. We must . . . alleviate the pressure."

"But you've seen the letters. They're all right there in front of you." Ron shoved several aside until he found the one he'd been looking for. "Here. 'J. is dead.' Read for yourself. How could she have known a child died in this house?"

"We're not sure that a child has. All the letter states is: 'J. is dead.'"

"Here, look at this one. Dated April 22nd. 'I have given it much thought. I cannot go on like this any longer. My sickness grows worse. . . .' It was never mailed. April 22nd was two nights ago, the exact night Chandal went into the den with a knife and imagined herself killing the child. How can you explain that? Explain how she knew where the child's things were."

"Perhaps Chandal had been in the basement before that night. In her confused state, she'd forgotten. She saw the letters. It could very well have been the thing that triggered her illness all over again. Seeing the letters, she began to fantasize."

305

"And the crucifix, the statue?"

"I'm sorry to keep repeating this," Luther interjected sharply, "but Chandal is suffering from ego-breakdown and nothing more. Guilt. This is her illness. And an abnormal fixation with a woman whom she watched burn to death."

Ron suddenly felt weak, particularly when Luther added in a formal way, "I think you should know that I don't need your permission—nor Chandal's, to recommend that she be institutionalized. Her action last night makes that unnecessary." He stared compassionately into Ron's eyes. "Naturally I would prefer to have you on my side."

"I'm sorry, I can't accept that," Ron burst out. "I won't accept that. To have Chandal—" He stopped, tears filling his eyes. "To have her end up . . ." He couldn't go on.

"It may not be," Luther answered him gently. "I personally believe that the mind, the spirit of man, is indestructible." His voice moved on, even and deep, heavy with conviction. "I'm sure we'll be able to build a more stable life for Chandal, given the proper time and facilities. You must trust that Chandal will someday be lifted by the little we have to offer her."

"Trust in what—Lakewood? In whom, the Board of Examiners? In—"

"No, in Chandal's spirit, in her own power of regeneration."

"Goddamn it!" Ron shouted with sudden vehemence. "It's Elizabeth—she's at the bottom of this. Not Chandal's will to survive."

Luther sighed, almost inaudibly. And then the carriage house fell silent. Every now and then a car passed in the street out front or there was the sound of children playing or someone dragged a garbage can across the pavement to curbside. Otherwise, there was a chasm of silence, of gleaming fermentation, shark-toothed.

The razor was brought forth. Chandal was shaved cleanly. Afterward, the hair from her legs and underarms, as well as her pubic hair, was carefully laid into the fire. She moaned, feeling a union with the heat.

Something lashed hot and wet along her stomach. She opened her eyes and saw the crone standing over her, her body bathed in a red light. Her hands were twisted into balls as if they were full of something.

Chandal felt turned inside out.

"Oh, my God," she whimpered. "What's happening to me?"

"It's a spiritual operation," whispered a voice in her ear. "Don't worry, you won't feel it. Just give up. It's so easy."

"It's so easy," sighed another voice that seemed disembodied, undefined as though the room was breathing the words.

"Elizabeth!" Chandal gasped and suddenly had a clear flash of memory. The little room in the brownstone, the one they had locked her away in. They had tried putting her through this operation before.

"Let go, let go," whispered the crone.

"No!" Chandal screamed. Memory flooded her. Their power had been intense. Justin. Tears ran from her eyes, rained down her cheeks. The crone's fingers tore at Chandal's breasts.

"Let go. Let go. Let the fire burn your spirit."

As the crone's voice grew louder, Chandal felt the knobby fingers kneading at her flesh, twisting, stroking, pulling. Gently, but now and then with fierceness.

"Let go! Let go!" A chorus of voices screamed. She could hear scissors snipping through her hair. Long locks were cut from her head. Ceremonially, the locks were used as a whip to beat her body. Chandal tried to rise and screamed in pain.

Magdalen had taken Justin. Oh, dear God—Justin had become one of them.

Chandal felt a mad laugh explode from between her lips.

"I remember!" she screamed, sitting up.

"A pity," a voice murmured and flung her from the bed to the floor.

Chandal was down now on the floor, prone among the legs, among the roaring figures gathering to encircle her, racing clownlike, kicking her, beating her with sticks, stoning her.

"Yaaaaaaaaaa. . . ."

A sound seemed to be building within the room, some sort of sound, a knocking at the door, or perhaps no sound, Chandal wasn't sure.

"Chandal? Chandal, open the door!" Ron screamed.

Convulsed with fear, Chandal reached out for the doorknob. She was suddenly smashed flat by the heavy thud of a large fist. They lifted her again like a jerking marionette, comical, her nose busted open with blood, held her for a moment and then sent her crashing to the floor.

Chandal screamed, her vision fading into soft red, slushed away like blood down a drain.

When Ron finally splintered open the door, he found Chandal lying naked in the center of the room, unconscious and bloodied. "My God, my God," he murmured, gathering her into his arms. In that moment he wasn't sure if his words were a curse or a prayer.

CHAPTER THIRTY-ONE

"ARE YOU READY, DEL?" RON ASKED AND PAUSED
irresolutely at the bedroom door. He was perplexed by the
aspect of Chandal's body. It seemed thinner than he had
remembered, as if some of the essence had been evenly
extracted from it during the night.

She was dressed conservatively in a beige long-sleeved
traveling suit, its starkness unrelieved by any touch of color
save a brown scarf at the neck. It was noticeably asexual, its
tight lines accentuating her loss of weight. The skirt fell
mid-calf and bordered on an attempt at matronliness. She
wore no makeup and let her hair fall freely over her shoulders.

He found it difficult now to look into Chandal's eyes as she
met his gaze, and turned instead to stare at the sunlight
streaming into the room filled with flowers. During the past
two days, in an effort to keep Chandal's mind occupied, Ron
had arranged for flowers to be delivered to the carriage house
three times a day. It seemed silly now, this gesture. And
senseless. All so goddamn senseless.

"Yes, I'm ready," Chandal said without expression and
closed her suitcase.

Chandal had agreed to return to Lakewood. *I don't want to
go back. I'm afraid to go back. Please, must I?* she had wanted
to plead. It was a plea from her past, she knew that. A past
that reached out to consume her, bury her alive, in the
present.

309

But she did not make this plea.

Instead she had brooded upon herself, as she had done so often in the weeks gone by. She had scanned those weeks in her mind's eye and tried to unravel the hopelessly enmeshed images that crowded her memory, images of her isolation, images of futility and despair.

In doing so, she had become almost convinced that perhaps they were right, that she was essentially insane. Yet there had been some minute part of her mind that resisted and would not accept this judgment.

Ron lifted her bag, then hesitated. "I've talked with Dr. Luther. He's agreed to let me stay on at his place for a while. If all goes well, I'll be able to see you almost every day."

She made no reply, merely looked at him and smiled. His face seemed to have aged so much in such a short time, she noted vaguely. And there was not a trace left of his California tan.

Then turning away, she glanced around the room, and said: "Do you forgive me?"

"For what?"

"For the terrible things I've done."

He paused, groping for a response. "You've done nothing wrong. Nothing in the world can convince me you'd do anything to hurt people."

"Ron, I'm sure people have been hurt. Innocent people."

"No, Del. You haven't done anything," he said and placed the suitcase on the floor.

Instinctively she moved into his arms and rested her head on his shoulder. He suddenly became her protector against torment.

"What are you thinking?" she asked after a moment.

He sighed deeply. "That I'm frightened."

It was the first time he had ever revealed his state of mind to her so simply. So completely. She understood and pressed against him even closer. "Hey, where's that happy-go-lucky businessman I used to know?"

"Is that the way you think of me?" He smiled sadly.

"Only when I want to protect myself."

"From what?"

"From saying—" She paused. "I love you."

"I love you too, Del."

They were silent for a moment.

"Ron?" She looked up at him. "If you don't mind, I'd . . . I'd like to have my pendant back."

Ron felt a hollowness in the pit of his stomach.

"Del, I don't—"

"Don't worry. It can't hurt me now. Please, Ron—I'd like to have it."

He looked at her quizzically. Then he reached into his jacket pocket and handed her the pendant. She looked at it for a moment, its tiny red speckles glittering before her eyes. Then she quickly dropped it into her shoulder bag.

"All set?" Ron breathed, his eyes still riveted on her bag.

"All set."

They descended the stairs in silence. At the front door Chandal discovered that she was unable to move another step without help. She hooked her hand into Ron's arm.

Ron led her outside, closed the front door of the carriage house, then guided her slowly over the flagstone path. Chandal did not look back. From this time on, she would never look back.

A few seconds later the front gate slid open. Dr. Luther was standing curbside waiting for them.

"The car hasn't arrived yet," he said softly.

"Oh?" Ron stared at Chandal.

"Perhaps I should call. See what's keeping them."

"I'll go with you," Ron said, squeezing Chandal's arm. In the back of his mind was a last-ditch argument or plea. Perhaps even now another course of action might be possible. "There's still the small trunk," he said in a curiously controlled tone. "The two of us can easily carry it."

Luther cast an undecided glance at Chandal, who looked very calm sitting on the largest suitcase, her eyes seeming to caress the sky, the clouds, the occasional tree that lined the concrete city block. Perhaps it was her calmness, her obvious need to have one more moment of freedom, that made Luther function on an emotional rather than a clinical level, made him decide to give her that last moment of aloneness and freedom that she was unlikely to have for some time in an institution that would decidedly have her on maximum security suicide-watch.

"We'll be right back," Luther said gently and she turned to meet his eyes with a calm gaze.

"Don't worry. I'll be all right," she said.

Ron felt his control close to the snapping point. He could only kiss her briefly on the forehead and turn swiftly away.

They retraced their steps over the flagstones.

Inside the house, Ron dropped wearily on the arm of the couch and waited for Luther to complete his call. From time to time he glanced at the den. His mind began to wander.

Chandal looked so controlled now, so serene. Impossible to believe that this beautiful young woman he loved was on her way to a state mental institution. His mind frantically turned to the possibility of arranging her transfer to a private hospital in L.A.

He forgot, as even Luther had forgotten for a moment, the danger. Chandal looked so calm, so damn sane and controlled. Just as she must have looked before the Examining Board at Lakewood.

Ron's head suddenly jerked up.

"What's the matter?" Luther asked sharply, dropping the receiver into its cradle, but Ron had already run through the door of the carriage house and was halfway down the flagstone path. Luther caught up with Ron curbside, where both men paused, suddenly past words.

Chandal was nowhere to be found.

It was really amazing, Chandal thought, wandering through yet another room of the Metropolitan Museum, how she had managed to hold onto her self-control for so long. All the time she could feel Elizabeth kicking and screaming within, fighting for the right to be.

Chandal had denied her this right for an hour now as she wandered through the labyrinth that the Metropolitan had become to her. She forced herself to go slowly, to pause in thoughtful contemplation, to spend the hour as a fascinated sightseer. Don't attract attention, she ordered herself firmly. Sit for a moment on that bench. Study the marble fountain god.

God, Chandal knew, was the issue. She had heard Elizabeth whisper so often: "The ultimate sense of powerlessness comes not from any confrontation between man, but from the confrontation with Ahriman." If this was true, Chandal reasoned, then Ahriman's ultimate confrontation had to be with God.

A half hour before closing time Chandal entered the large

room where the Egyptian shrine was displayed—the ruins of the first Christian church on the Nile. It was as she remembered it. Only one guard, a middle-aged black woman, was on duty, her back to the shrine, obviously tired of standing on her feet for hours with no one to talk to in this solitary quiet atmosphere.

Chandal settled on the ledge on the opposite side of the temple. She slipped from her shoes and massaged her feet gingerly as though exhausted from an over-zealous day of sightseeing. The room was almost deserted, but occasionally people walked by.

She hesitated, could not seem to find the right moment. First there was a solitary man with a sketch pad who finally lost interest in his drawing, then a family of five, then a couple, then two girls strolling toward the exit. Please, God, let there be a chance.

Suddenly an instant presented itself. A vacuum of timelessness that seemed to encapsulate her until she was protected, invisible. As she stepped forward in her stocking feet, the guard glanced down at her watch and then moved to the doorway to peer out.

Chandal didn't stop to think, to wonder if she'd made it, just covered the small space soundlessly and fell to her knees, hands clasped, inside the temple. "Help me," she whispered.

And then Elizabeth began screaming inside her.

"She's not here," Doreen Hammer said coldly, her eyes flickering past Luther to Ron. "Did you bring the keys to the carriage house? The owner wants me to get them back."

"Here's your goddamn keys!" Ron snapped and shoved the ornate key ring into her hand.

"Why would Chandal—" began Doreen, then stopped, her eyes widening.

"What's the matter now?" Ron snarled, seeing that her gaze had fixed on his neck. He felt a sudden weakness, felt the perspiration running down his throat. Dimly he reached up to wipe it away and then, looking at his hand, realized that the dampness wasn't sweat. It was blood. And that it was draining from his right ear.

He fell to his knees before he knew on any conscious level that he was passing out. Frowning, he grabbed onto his last thought and clung to it. He believed in Chandal—in everything she had said. Moreover, he believed that there was an even greater danger, something that she herself didn't realize.

"Because I believe you," he murmured hoarsely as Luther grabbed hold of his sagging body.

"Ron!" Luther cried.

Ron's head fell back. "That's why—that's why . . ." The last thing he saw before his eyes shut was the expression on Doreen's face—satisfied but angry and something that suggested that, in a way, in back of all other emotions, she too was a little afraid.

There was no reason to panic yet, Chandal told herself. Still she found herself trembling, her mind focused on her past. She had escaped their power before. She was a survivor. Save yourself. That was the unmistakable voice of her own stubbornness. She knew how to do it. How it could be done.

She leaned forward now, almost totally relaxed, her head touching the ancient brick of the temple that loomed dark around her.

"I know what you're up to," the voice whispered.

Chandal shuddered at the sound.

"Cold, my dear?"

Chandal's hands mechanically loosened the scarf around her neck to ease the tension from her throat.

How strange that the old woman could go on talking to her at a time like this. In a temple of Christian worship.

"Do I make you nervous, dear?" Chandal reached up to wipe sweat away from her forehead, her cheeks. What time was it? Four-thirty P.M. Fifteen minutes till closing time. Where was the guard now? Chandal could only see part of the large outer room. Through a thin crack she watched a young man and his son study the temple. She drew back so as not to be seen.

For one eternal heartbeat Chandal stood immobile. Again she shuddered, hearing the eerie moaning and thumping that had begun in her head. She forced herself not to cringe, fearful she would move, speak out, afraid to . . .

She knew it would take much more than any sort of struggle that could be envisioned through normal human channels of perception, much more. It would mean a struggle that would threaten her on many levels, from her identity in the world right down to her identity in God's eye. If she lost, the cost might be her very soul. But if she didn't struggle, the cost would be the same. The choice was—to be taken as a lion or a lamb. She straightened. She knew that freedom was far away, while the old woman still had her grasping hands on her psyche.

Chandal touched her hair, stroked her head. No! Don't move. Don't even breathe. Turning her head only slightly, she tried to swallow in a dust-dry throat and shifted her attention to the guard who came into view to her right.

Something went click. She heard it distinctly. She opened her eyes and could only see darkness. Yet within the darkness, images.

Click.

Like a camera, her mind began to snap pictures of the past and display them on the screen of her mind. It was similar to watching a slide show at your local pavilion at any state fair.

Click.

Panic seized Chandal. No, I don't want to see! No! Still the pictures came, and her mind began to thaw like a block of ice, flooding her being with a cascade of memories. She glimpsed her own face within the flames.

Click.

Where was Justin?

She recognized the sound now. Justin screaming.

She gripped her hands into fists, took several deep breaths, while the old woman's cracked voice moaned obscenities into her ear. Dust engulfed her. She gasped, choked back a cough. A hand touched her arm and she jerked away in fright. The old woman's voice was an unctuous sneer.

Chandal was frozen now as the frigid air pressed at her face, the acid smell of death and dying and nothing else, nothing to do with the living. This temple had become her tomb and she was sure that she would never get out of it alive.

Hands shaking. Mouth full of saliva. She didn't know in what form the next attack would come. She waited, the sweat running down her face in the cold air of the temple. She could feel the steady acceleration of her heartbeat and the tightening of the nerves through her body.

The movement within her was growing strong, a steady unfolding. Her head was being forced to one side. She could feel a sudden rush of heat as layers of old flesh wrapped itself around her consciousness.

Elizabeth was fully alive now, trying to force herself to the surface of Chandal's skin. Chandal held tight, gasped when she saw that her hand had begun to physically reshape itself. A tremor took hold and sent blue veins rushing to the surface of her skin, forming a network of wrinkles, tumors, and cracks. The tremor took hold of her arm next, her skin writhing in the darkness. Now her whole body was experiencing a chemical nightmare. A boil burst open on her arm, spraying pus on the temple wall.

"God, take me," Chandal whispered. "Please, God—take me, take me. . . ." Over and over again she whispered these words until everything within the temple seemed to stop. She glanced down at her hand. It had returned to normal. "Oh, Jesus. . . ." she gasped.

Her eyes darted left, right—probed the room. She felt hands grasping her, twisting her, and she imagined she heard screams and she wondered if the screams were not her own. She responded in a slow-motion flex of movement. The screams continued and she wondered why no one heard those screams. There was no way to avoid it; she felt the woman's wild strength tearing at her, and fought back the temptation to run.

Slowly she forced herself to relax in the darkness of the stone cube, but her body remained a bundle of unexpected sensations, and once more she caught herself gasping for breath. Caught in a sudden whirlpool of time, she saw a memory image of herself striking a match. Just a glimpse, and then—that twisted face . . . those terrified eyes. Elizabeth burning. Even as she recalled the moment, she imagined the smell of burning flesh.

Did I light the fire? I have to know!

She held her breath and felt someone else's thoughts buzzing through her mind; with the buzzing came dizziness. Each new thought made her feel ancient. She squeezed her fists to rid herself of the sensation.

A violent trembling shook her body.

Abruptly, images began to rush through her mind like a tornado, leveling everything in its path. Bits and pieces at first, an agony here, a face there, screaming that opened into whirling circles of fire, writhing, ceremonies and witches. . . .

But I was not one of them! No! Not one of them! And because she knew this to be true, there was a new strength in her and a sudden clear vision. The little room in the brownstone. Yes, they had locked her away because they had wanted to possess her body. Had always wanted to possess her body, to use it for evil. It had been arranged from the very beginning, and Justin—he had become one of them against her. And with the thought—a thousand images flashed; every hour, minute, second spent in the brownstone became vividly clear in her mind. They were devil worshipers. Magdalen, Elizabeth, Billy Deats—even Justin. All devil worshipers. And she knew now that she had set the fire. And why.

Her mind was functioning clearly now, as though the long years of emptiness and fear had prepared her to defend herself in her moment of need. For an instant she pressed herself parallel to the door of the temple. The lights were dimmer now; at the moment, there appeared to be no one in the area. The museum was now closed and the night guards must be in other parts of the building.

Soundlessly, she slipped down the steps of the shrine, her stockinged feet as sure and stealthy as the paws on a jungle cat. There was a sense of urgency in her motion now. Without conscious decision, she began to maneuver toward the American Wing of the museum. She reminded herself that the cathedral room within the American Wing was the one place where Elizabeth had appeared helpless.

Releasing the door, she stepped cautiously into the hallway.

The dull lights flattened everything before her eyes.

Intensely aware of the crushing silence around her, she glanced down the long corridor. Where were the guards? The dimness of the light was hypnotic. Images wavered before her eyes. She felt the silent wonder of watchfulness—she watching for the guards, Elizabeth watching her, and the guards most likely watching them. She spun around. The corridor door to her left opened and a guard stepped out.

Walking in a slow shuffle, he moved down the hallway and started up the center stairway. Chandal waited until his footsteps disappeared far above her before she stepped into the open. She quickly moved forward.

Midway to the American Wing she hesitated. She could sense a swarm of activity. Nothing on the material plane, nothing that could be perceived by any of the five senses; no, she had picked it up on a special highly tuned antenna as a sixth sense that provided entrance into a dark spirit world.

Now she could actually see the line of worshipers who came marching toward her, their heads in the far recesses of black crepe hoods, their bodies covered in dark capes. She could hear them chanting. Flat music, discordant and yet hypnotic. She started to cover her ears, then dropped her hands. No, she must appear to be one of them. In that way she knew she'd be safe.

The line slowed and parted, making room for her. A figure, a middle-aged woman, plucked at her sleeve, urged her ahead. Nodding briefly, Chandal made eye contact with the woman who wore layers of thick makeup—rings of rouge, red-caked lipstick, black spiky false eyelashes. Chandal froze. Thelma Rose—she recognized with a frightened jolt.

Thelma patted her gently on the shoulder. "It's time to leave now, dear. Move on, mustn't keep the others waiting, you know."

"No," Chandal whispered back, masking her surprise, and moved obediently into place. We musn't keep the others waiting.

The chanting grew fuller, self-satisfied, as the line moved on. Chandal waited a few seconds, marching along in the line, and then, summoning forth her courage, she leaped to the side, spun away and ran toward the cathedral.

Snarling, the line broke. Vicious fingers reached out for her, their long fingernails scraping her flesh, bringing the blood. They were all over her now. They would seize her the moment she believed in their power.

"I believe in the Father . . ." she gasped, her arms covering her head. "The Son . . ." Their tongues licked at her face, their teeth punctured the soft skin of her throat. She ran faster. The cathedral room was just ahead. She fell over legs, crawled forward, almost overcome.

"Ahriman loves you!" cried a voice.

"Ahriman loves no one," Chandal screamed back. "He hates. There is no power in hatred."

Now she was on the cathedral steps. Hooded figures barricaded the doors. Arms held her back, more powerful now in their strength, which meant her will was bending, weakening. . . .

"I believe in the Father, the Son . . ." she screamed,

tearing them from the entrance. Suddenly she was past them. A low hiss reverberated behind her. Tears flowed down her cheeks. They would never come in here, she realized, faltering forward down the aisle on the red carpet that led to the altar. They would never dare enter this room.

Still she could feel their eyes peering at her from the doorway, even looking downward through the stained glass. Frantically she threw herself to her knees on the steps leading to the altar. Even here, amidst the peace of God, panic engulfed her.

"There are so many of them," she whispered and bowed her head. At that point, she felt a great rush of calmness, as though an invisible hand had come to rest on her head in a kind of benediction.

And then it happened. The first shudder within her as Elizabeth began to panic. Chandel sensed new powers being invoked—a harsh pull that tore at her and attempted to drag her away, back out the door. The entire room began to shake.

Chandal held tight and was startled when she thought that several of the sainted statues had turned to face her. All things seemed to move . . . like great waves in a endless ocean.

"GOD!" Chandal screamed, "SAVE ME!" She threw herself at the foot of a large crucifix. She stared into Christ's downthrust face, at the man she knew little about. Christ's expression looked threatening, more threatening than Elizabeth had ever looked. Still, she forced herself to look into his face. A dim illumination seemed to erase Christ's face for an instant as a goat's head sprang forth.

"What do you wish of me?" the goat hissed. Then laughed, saliva dripping from the corners of his mouth. Through piercing glasslike eyes, he peered down at her. From his nostrils poured a cold gas. Chandal held fast, forcing herself not to cringe, aware of the plans he had in mind for her.

"Christ! Come to me! Help me!" she screamed and once more looked up—the goat's eyes, his melting flesh, dissolved into the image of Christ. Christ's face remained threatening.

"Somebody doesn't want us back," Elizabeth howled with laughter, then choked.

A sense of failure engulfed Chandal. The crucifix began to turn, slowly at first, until now it spun out of control, around and around, until finally it stopped.

Chandal gasped as she stared at Christ's face, upside down before her very own. His crown of thorns drew blood that oozed from his wounds.

"*Where have I seen that before?*" Elizabeth said, hysterical with laughter. "*He looks familiar, doesn't he?*"

Chandal felt that her body was beginning to lose power, energy—her whole being went limp with exhaustion, shame, sorrow and fear.

She spoke without thinking, the words pouring from her mouth in rapid succession.

"May God rise up, and may his enemies be dissipated."

"*No!*"

"Let those who hate him flee before him."

"*NO!*"

"Let them be dissipated like smoke!"

"*Ahriman!*"

Chandal's head was wrenched back by a violent tug on her hair.

"Look on the Cross of the Lord," she moaned. "Be defeated!"

Suddenly a snake slithered up from her shoulder bag, its flat head and neck raised, waiting to strike. Chandal could actually feel her heart stop as she lurched back.

Moving its head slowly from one side to the other the snake rose higher until its elastic throat extended fully, longing to devour its prey.

The snake lunged. Chandal stumbled and fell. In the next instant the snake wrapped itself tightly around her neck and began to squeeze. Chandal struggled with both hands to rip the serpent from her throat. She shuddered as her hands grasped scales which swiftly turned ice-cold. The snake's body began to reshape itself as it squeezed tighter, until finally Chandal realized she was being strangled by a chain.

Gagging, she pulled, her fingers connecting with the bloodstone pendant.

"Let your mercy be with me, O Lord!" She could hardly get a breath as the chain choked the life from her. The room began to spin—everywhere blackness started to close in. "Free me, O Lord! Free me!"

The crucifix and the room stopped spinning at one and the same time. Rightside up, Christ stared down at Chandal's limp body.

With a final desperate pull, Chandal tore the bloodstone pendant from her throat. She began to crawl toward the crucifix. "Our Father Who art in Heaven! Hallowed be your name. May your kingdom come. May your will be done on Earth as it is in Heaven."

Reaching the foot of the cross, she touched her finger to Christ's blood, then pressed her finger to her lips and drank. "Give us this day our daily bread."

"Ahriman, hear me!" screamed Elizabeth.

"And forgive us our offenses, as we forgive those who offend against us."

"Father of darkness. Save me!"

"And lead us not into temptation."

"Bring down all things!"

"But deliver us from Evil."

"Blood turn to stone. Stone to fire. Burn!"

"Amen."

Chandal rose unsteadily to her feet. She saw them now, all of them—Thelma Rose, Miss Ramsey, Mrs. Stoner, huddled in a group at the cathedral door with their heads together, looking like a flock of frightened blackbirds. *"Blood turn to stone, stone to fire, burn, burn, burn. . . ."* they hissed.

Staggering forward, Chandal placed the bloodstone pendant on the altar. She stared at the stone for a moment, her face ashen and her eyes enormous. The voices roared through her head, and she could hear them calling her.

"Chandal, Chandal . . . Ahriman loves you, loves you. . . ."

Sparks flew from the stone, but Chandal did not look away. Did not look away, as the tiny red speckles within the stone began to burn. Chandal moved suddenly with the speed of the possessed, dipping her fingers into holy water. She genuflected, then quickly splashed holy water onto the pendant.

"Burn, burn, burn. . . ."

Just as quickly, Chandal lifted a heavy metal crucifix from the altar, lifted it high into the air. She bowed her head, whispered a final prayer, then started to bring the crucifix down.

"Chandal, don't!" shrilled a voice from above her.

Chandal turned and saw Doreen Hammer staring down at her from a small balcony just above the altar.

"Think what you're doing!" Doreen screamed.

Without waiting a moment longer, Chandal brought the crucifix down on the bloodstone.

"Ahriman!" Doreen cried. "Take me!" And then she jumped.

The crucifix smashed dead center of the bloodstone, shattering the stone into a million droplets of blood and fire, as simultaneously Doreen's body crashed upon the altar, her death sudden and complete.

Chandal tried to go to her, but the blaze was now too fierce and she stood with her hands across her face, shouting in her anguish. "Doreen! Doreen!" She could only hear the crackling of the flames, the horrid moan that shook the cathedral to its foundation. Chandal reeled back . . . back . . . into darkness—then, a blinding light.

CHAPTER THIRTY-TWO

"WHAT NOW?" RON ASKED. HIS FACE WAS FLUSHED under a few loose curls of hair on his forehead and his eyes flickered with vagueness as he gave a quick glance around Dr. Luther's hotel room. The room wasn't what he had expected. It was small and airless and a bit of a mess. Luther himself looked pretty exhausted—they both did.

The little travel alarm beside the bed showed six-twenty P.M.

"Well, she remembers now," replied Dr. Luther. "She's recaptured that part of time which was lost. Who knows at what cost of anguish—but in my view, she was prepared to pay it. She had to know. She simply had to know."

"But you still don't believe any of it, do you? The ceremony, the coven . . . Chandal hasn't convinced you."

He shrugged. "I have no doubt that in her mind there was a ceremony of sorts going on. A self-exorcism, if you will. Oh, not of an evil spirit, the way she sees it. But a well of stored-up terror, self-doubt, guilt for surviving the fire when others had not." He drew a deep breath. "I'm sure when she's ready to accept that, she will." Luther watched the blood leave Ron's face, until it was gray and twisted in a grimace of confusion. "How are you feeling?"

"Still a little shaky."

"Well, it's no wonder. You had one hell of an ear infection. Most people would have been laid up for weeks."

Ron made a vague gesture, intending to convey nothing

and everything. "I don't know, it still seems so damn extraordinary to me."

"Extraordinary?"

Ron thought again. "Weird. I mean, don't you think there's a chance—just a chance, that maybe she didn't imagine it? Oh, I know that seems ridiculous, but is it possible—"

"No," said Dr. Luther gently. "It's completely impossible. It's all in Chandal's mind. The possession, the coven, the demon—all imagined. Now that she is better, she will come to see that." Slowly he arose, stepped quietly across the room until he approached the window. "Chandal will be coming home from the hospital tomorrow. She's going to need all the help she can get. Believe me, after enough time has gone by, everything will work itself out. Things will return to normal."

"There's something I need to ask you."

Dr. Luther smiled. "I think I know."

"What would you say?"

"I say for your sake, be very careful. For her sake I say, go to her. Love her. It's what she needs the most."

"Thank you. I suppose you know what I'll do."

"Yes, of course." His eyes crinkled slightly and he nodded. "Sentimentalist that I am, I'm very glad. I hope you'll both be very happy. I think you will."

"Well, thanks again for everything." Ron extended his hand. Luther nodded reassuringly as they clasped hands. Ron turned to leave, lingered at the door for a moment, then straightened and spoke frankly. "There's something I think you should know. I still believe it. I believe everything Chandal said."

Dr. Luther chuckled. "You'll be a wonderful husband!"

"I can't help it. There's just too many damn things that don't add up."

"Like what?"

"Doreen Hammer. What was she doing in the museum that night? And why did she jump—kill herself like that?"

"Evidently she knew that Chandal had gone to the museum. When I took you to the hospital, she followed after her. Hid in the cathedral. I know it's incredible to believe, that two people could penetrate the security system as they did, but nevertheless it happened. We must accept that." He refused to soften under Ron's skeptical gaze. "When she saw

Chandal enter the cathedral, she moved forward, stumbled and fell."

"How do you explain her husband's disappearance? He never even claimed her body."

"The man fought in Viet Nam. He had seen death every day. Perhaps he just couldn't face another one."

"What about—" Ron stopped himself mid-sentence. "You know, something just occurred to me."

"Yes?"

"I'll bet you have a logical explanation for everything, don't you?"

"Ah," the doctor smiled wistfully, "I'm a psychiatrist. Where would I be without logic?"

Ron sighed. "I'll see you."

Luther clapped him heartily on the back and said, "As soon as you're settled. Write. I'd enjoy hearing from you."

"Right." He paused to smile. "And thanks."

Only later when Ron had gone did Dr. Luther stand frowning by his hotel window. It was getting dark. There had been black clouds piled up outside his window for a long time now. He was tiring, though of course he'd never admit that to himself. I'm a scientist, he mused. A man of reason, of sanity. I am the man who knows how much can occur to cloud the human mind, to confuse the brain, to traumatize it into hallucination. The girl had delusions. Her mind was possessed only by advanced trauma. Nothing else. No demon, no other possession of any kind. And yet—he paused and then finally filled in the unspeakable: I believe her too.

Sighing, he sat hesitantly at his desk and began to complete his notes.

CHAPTER THIRTY-THREE

THEY BOARDED AMERICAN AIRLINES FLIGHT 33 OUT of Kennedy. In the plane they sat silent and still in the near-empty first class section. Offered their choice of champagne or orange juice, they chose the champagne while awaiting takeoff.

After a while Chandal carefully placed her half-empty glass on her tray, took out a handkerchief and pressed it to her eyes. Ron turned to her. "Are you all right?" he asked and moved imperceptibly closer.

The words took a long time to reach her. Almost inaudibly she replied, "Yes, fine. . . ."

"You're crying," he said softly. He was, she knew, making an effort to smile.

She gazed at the handkerchief in her hand and saw it was damp. Yes, those were her tears. Her eyes seeing them. Her hands holding the handkerchief. Hers and only hers. And for the first time in three years Chandal knew she had nothing more to fear.

They held hands during takeoff, feeling fearless of being in the sky. The plane banked smoothly and then leveled. It had been climbing for some time, but suddenly they were free of the clouds which rolled beneath them in shimmering whiteness. It was an extraordinary day. The kind of day where anything was possible.

171